The Fire in the Flint

Candace Robb

arrow books

Published by Arrow Books in 2004

1 3 5 7 9 10 8 6 4 2

First published in the United Kingdom in 2003 by William Heinemann

Arrow Books
The Random House Group Limited
20 Vauxhall Bridge Road, London, SW1V 2SA

Random House Australia (Pty) Limited
20 Alfred Street, Milsons Point, Sydney,
New South Wales 2061, Australia

Random House New Zealand Limited
18 Poland Road, Glenfield
Auckland 10, New Zealand

Random House (Pty) Limited
Endulini, 5a Jubilee Road, Parktown, 2193, South Africa

The Random House Group Limited Reg. No. 954009
www.randomhouse.co.uk

A CIP catalogue record for this book is available from the British Library

Papers used by Random House
are natural, recyclable products made from wood grown in
sustainable forests. The manufacturing processes conform to
the environmental regulations of the country of origin

ISBN 0 09 941014 1

Typeset in Caslon 540 by SX Composing DTP, Rayleigh, Essex
Printed and bound in the United Kingdom by
Cox & Wyman, Reading, Berks.

The Fire in the Flint

Candace Robb studied for a Ph.D. in Medieval and Anglo-Saxon Literature and has continued to read and research medieval history and literature ever since. The Owen Archer series grew out of a fascination with the city of York and the tumultuous 14th century; the first in the series, *The Apothecary Rose*, was published in 1994, at which point she began to write full time. In addition to the UK, Australia, New Zealand, South Africa, Canada and America, her novels are published in France, Germany, Spain, Denmark, Italy and Holland, and she is also available in the UK on audiobook and in large print.

She is also the author of the Margaret Kerr Mystery series, set in Scotland at the time of Robert the Bruce. The first, *A Trust Betrayed*, was published in November 2000 to great acclaim. *The Fire in the Flint* is the second in the series.

Acclaim for Candace Robb

'It's . . . the Machiavellian intrigue that makes this such an enjoyable read. When the iron curtain came down people said the spy-thriller genre was dead. They were wrong. This is as full of intrigue as a Deighton or a Le Carré' *Guardian*

'Thirteenth-century Edinburgh comes off the page cold and convincing, from the smoke and noise of the tavern kitchen to Holyrood Abbey under a treacherous abbot. Most enjoyable' *The List*

'Meticulously researched, authentic and gripping' *Yorkshire Post*

'A rich and satisfying novel' *Publishers Weekly*

'Brilliant . . . Robb presents a feisty new heroine who proves to be no fool' *Woman & Home*

'Once again, Robb provides the reader with an evocative and suspenseful whodunit thoroughly bolstered by a wealth of authentic historical detail' *Booklist*

Contents

In loving memory of my mother,
Genevieve Wojtaszek Chestochowski
(19 March 1920–16 July 2003)
whose courageous battle with cancer showed me
what stuff women are made of

ACKNOWLEDGEMENTS

My thanks to Elizabeth Ewan, Kimm Perkins, Nicholas Mayhew, and David Bowler, Derek Hall and Catherine Smith of the Scottish Urban Archaeological Trust, generous scholars who have fielded my questions and kept me honest about medieval Scotland and coinage; Evan Marshall, Joyce Gibb, Elizabeth Ewan, and Kirsty Fowkes who read the manuscript and made thoughtful suggestions; Jan and Chris Wolfe of the Willowburn Hotel on Seil Island who loaned me a book about Argyll, pointing out the magical glen of Kilmartin; and Charlie Robb who photographed locations, sat in on meetings, crafted the maps, and simplified travel and home with tender loving care.

HISTORICAL NOTE

With the death of the Maid of Norway, who was the last member in the direct line of kings of Scotland from Malcolm Canmore, two major claimants of the throne arose – John Balliol and Robert Bruce; eventually ten additional claimants stepped forward. In an effort to prevent civil war, the Scots asked King Edward I of England to act as judge. In hindsight, they were tragically unwise to trust Edward, who had already proved his ruthlessness in Wales. Edward chose John Balliol as king, and then proceeded to make a puppet of him.

Robert Bruce, known as 'the Competitor' to distinguish him from his son Robert and his grandson Robert, still seething under the lost opportunity, handed over his earldom to his son, who was more an Englishman at heart than a

Scotsman. He in turn handed over the earldom to his son, who would eventually become King Robert I. Through the 1290s this younger Bruce, Earl of Carrick, vacillated between supporting and opposing Edward. When he at last resolved to stand against Edward, he was not doing so in support of John Balliol, but was pursuing his own interests.

As for William Wallace, he was in 1297 and thereafter fighting for the return of John Balliol to the throne. He was never a supporter of Robert Bruce.

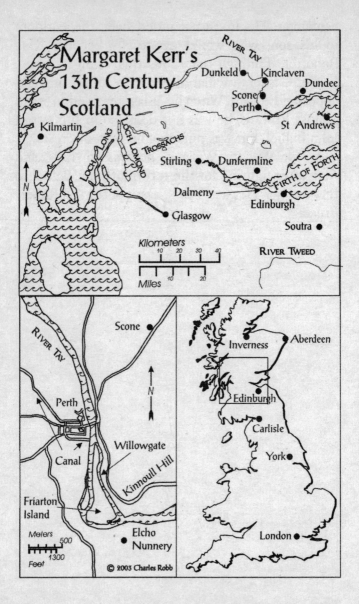

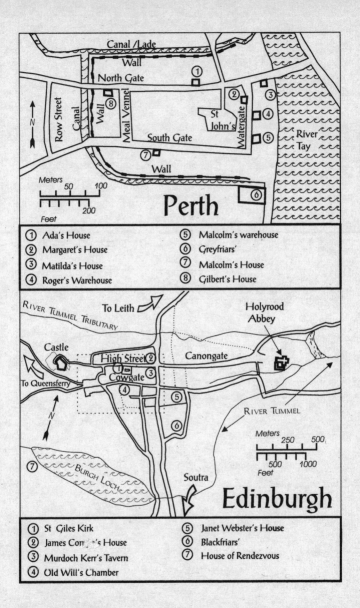

Perth

① Ada's House
② Margaret's House
③ Matilda's House
④ Roger's Warehouse
⑤ Malcolm's warehouse
⑥ Greyfriars'
⑦ Malcolm's House
⑧ Gilbert's House

Edinburgh

① St Giles Kirk
② James Comyn's House
③ Murdoch Kerr's Tavern
④ Old Will's Chamber
⑤ Janet Webster's House
⑥ Blackfriars'
⑦ House of Rendezvous

EPIGRAPHS

'The fire i' the flint/ Shows not till it be struck'
Timon of Athens, Act I, l. 22

'. . . oftentimes, to win us to our harm,
The instruments of darkness tell us truths,
Win us with honest trifles, to betray's
In deepest consequence.'
Macbeth, Act I, scene iii, ll. 123–126.

PROLOGUE

Though it was close to midnight, twilight glimmered on the water meadow between Elcho Nunnery and the River Tay. Night creatures croaked and called in the background, and ahead the waters of the Tay and the Willowgate roiled and splashed as they joined at the bend beneath Friarton Island. Christiana's bare feet cracked the brittle crust of the soil dried by the summer drought. With her next step, her right foot sank to the ankle bone in saturated ground. With a shiver of loathing, she freed herself. For the twenty-three years of her marriage she had lived just upstream in Perth, and in all that time she had remained unreconciled with this marshy land. She had grown up amidst mountains, lochs, and the high banks of the Tay upriver. She missed the sharp, fresh air and the land always solid beneath her feet. Here the fields along the river were unpredictable, some-times more water than land, changing with the weather, as uncanny as her mind.

Terror had awakened her. She had fled her chamber in the nunnery guest house, sensing an intruder, a feeling so strong she had thought she heard his breath, breath which she still felt at the nape of her neck. Fear had squeezed her heart and compelled her to run. Now on the marshy ground she slowed down, though still hardly daring to breathe. She glanced back over her shoulder in dread, but although the July night was light enough that she might have seen any movement, she saw no one. Gradually, as the chill of her wet feet drove away any remnant of sleep, she remembered that her handmaid had not stirred on her cot at the foot of the bed. The intruder had not been a fleshly presence then, but a vision.

Christiana struggled to reconstruct the con-fusing face. It had seemed that as the man turned his features shifted, changing so quickly it was as if his face were drawn in oil and his movement stirred the lines. It was too fluid to know whether any part of it was familiar. Or perhaps he'd worn many faces overlaying one another. She could not recall precisely where in the dim room she had seen him as she woke and rose breathless.

On the river bank she stopped and tried to calm herself by listening to the water and imagining it washing away the residue of fear. But her attention was drawn across the river to the cliff overhanging the opposite bank. In the midnight sun someone standing at the edge would be able to see her. She felt too vulnerable for calm.

Her mind eased a little when she remembered that the sisters would soon awaken to sing the night office; then she might seek sanctuary in the kirk. Turning her back on the disturbing cliff, she was puzzled to see lights multiplying in the priory buildings, flickering as the candle- and lamp-carriers moved in and out of the window openings and doorways. They were moving across the yard, not in the direction of the kirk but the guest house whence she had fled.

Perhaps they had been awakened by the intruder she had foreseen. She must go back, she might be able to help – why else would God have warned her? As she walked towards the nunnery she heard women's cries and the authoritative barks of the prioress. The voices drowned out the river's quiet song. She called out to the lay servant guarding the nunnery gate, and two sisters ran out to her, one with a lantern swinging so wildly beside her that Christiana had to shield her eyes against the dizzying dance of light.

'Dame Christiana! We feared you had been taken!'

'Are you injured?' the other asked.

'Your handmaid cannot be consoled, fearful you're dead,' said the first.

Christiana could not bear the dancing light. 'Steady the lantern, I beg you.'

The sister complied, and Christiana was now able to focus on the two who seemed to speak as one. 'As you see, I am neither dead nor injured, thanks be to God. Is the intruder still in the grounds?'

'You knew about them?'

'Them,' Christiana said. So there had been more than one. She had not the energy to explain. 'Forgive me, but I must see my chamber.' She pushed through milling servants and sisters and into the guest-house garden, which looked trampled in the moonlight. Two voices came from the opened door, one reassuring, one pitched high with emotion. Christiana stepped over the threshold.

Dame Katrina, the elderly hosteleress, sat holding a servant's hands as she said, 'You are not to blame.'

'I should have heard them on the steps!' the servant cried.

Christiana interrupted. 'Did they enter the hall?' she asked.

Both women started. The servant shook her head.

Christiana hurried out and up the steps to her chamber. She found her handmaid Marion weeping in the protective arms of Prioress Agnes.

'Marion, calm yourself,' Christiana said with a sharpness that she had not intended. She inclined her head. 'Prioress Agnes.'

Marion glanced up, her eyes widening in surprise, and cried, 'You are safe! Praise God.' She rubbed her eyes as if to clear her vision and make certain she'd seen aright.

The prioress rose from the bed, hands clasped before her waist, ever dignified. 'Where have you been, Dame Christiana?' Her handsome face twitched with emotion. She disapproved of women withdrawing to nunneries after their children were grown but while their husbands yet lived. She'd made it clear to Christiana that she'd expected trouble and now it had arrived.

'I walked to the river.' Christiana took in the room, the upturned chests, the emptied shelves. 'Did they harm you, Marion?'

The handmaid shook her head, her breath coming in gasps.

'Did you see them?' Prioress Agnes asked.

'I was not here.'

Agnes studied Christiana, then apparently decided to believe her, for she said, 'There were three men. They pulled Marion from bed and shoved her out of the room in her shift, barefoot—' Her gaze travelled down to Christiana's muddied feet. 'Her shrieks woke us all. I see that you, too, are barefoot. You ran out like that without cause? You were not fleeing from the men?'

'I had a vision of what was to come,' said Christiana. 'I confess I fled, thinking I had truly seen them in the flesh. But afterwards I understood that God had sent the vision to me as a warning.'

5

'What were they after?' the prioress asked sharply. 'Did the Lord tell you that?'

Christiana shook her head. 'I have prayed that He take the Sight from me. I am too simple to use it. I have not the wit to ken the meaning.'

'We shall discuss this in the morning,' Agnes said in a tight voice. 'Now see to your maid.'

After Prioress Agnes withdrew, Christiana sank down on the bed and picked up a small wooden box, emptied of its physick powder.

'They have ruined all your medicines,' Marion said. 'And torn one of your veils.' She lifted a square of unbleached silk.

Something in the simple gesture made it real to Christiana. Her home had been invaded, her treasured belongings thrown about, ruined. The medicines were not a serious loss, Dame Eleanor here at the priory was a skilful apothecary and healer with plentiful stores. But the clothing and the furniture held memories that would now be soiled by their handling this night. Most upsetting was the torn veil – it had been a gift from her daughter Margaret, a generous gift that she could ill afford since her husband deserted her.

The anger that arose in the pit of Christiana's stomach was vaguer than the fear that had sent her out into the night, but it settled there throughout what was left of the night and into the next day. Neither food nor prayer dislodged it.

❧ 1 ❧

OLD WILL

In the evenings throughout spring and into the summer of 1297, many of the folk of Edinburgh congregated in Murdoch Kerr's tavern trading rumours of war. The English still held the castle that loomed above, crowning the long, narrow outcrop on which the town crouched, and their soldiers were bored and nervous, ready to take offence and resolve any slight with violence. The Scots townsfolk who had survived the initial siege and the periodic purges of suspected traitors, who had nowhere to escape to or no inclination to leave the town to the enemy, trod the streets and wynds with care. They voiced their complaints behind closed doors, or in the smoky, noisy safety of Murdoch's tavern.

Elsewhere the tide was turning. King Edward Longshanks had considered it unnecessary to stay in Scotland, believing his deputies and troops sufficient to administer the conquered people. He had either overestimated his governors or underestimated how much the Scots valued their freedom. The occupying English were losing ground in the north. Folk spoke of Andrew Murray's skirmishes from Inverness along the north-eastern coast to Aberdeen, and William Wallace's to the west and up into Perthshire and Fife.

Margaret Kerr, niece of Murdoch, the taverner, spent much of her time in the tavern of late, ensuring that customers were well served. She had come to Edinburgh in early spring seeking news of her husband Roger Sinclair. Once she had learned he had joined the struggle to restore Scottish rule she'd resolved to stay in Edinburgh and do her part.

Strangely, her mother, Christiana MacFarlane, gifted with Second Sight, had predicted her daughter's involvement in two visions: 'I saw you standing over a table, studying maps with two men. One was giving you and the other orders, concerning a battle'; 'On another day I saw you holding your baby daughter in your arms, your husband standing by your side, watching the true king of Scots ride into Edinburgh.' For most of her nineteen years Margaret had suffered the stigma and deprivation of being daughter to a woman who walked more often in the spirit world than on solid ground. She'd found no practical value in her mother's visions. But now they had given her the courage to keep her ears pricked in the tavern for information that might be of use to those fighting to restore the rightful king, John Balliol, to the throne of Scotland.

Her uncle's business partner and kinsman of the king, James Comyn, had come to depend on her reports. Not that she was his only source of information – a member of his own Comyn family, who were related to Balliol and Murray, had come to James in late July with the news that Murray had recaptured Urquhart and Inverness castles. Most recently Murray was said to have ousted the English from Aberdeen, then continued on down the eastern coast, intending to join Wallace at Dundee. Margaret knew that although James told her much, he kept more to himself. Every so often she sensed she was telling him things he already knew. The speed with which news travelled through the war-torn countryside amazed her. Sometimes she suspected that those who had chosen to remain in Edinburgh were all there as spies.

She worried about her family, scattered and torn in their loyalties. Her brother Andrew, a priest and canon of Holyrood Abbey, had followed his abbot in supporting Longshanks until his shame provoked him to disobey. For this he had been condemned to the post of confessor to the English army encamped at Soutra Hospital, which was a death sentence – he would know too much to ever be freed. Margaret feared Andrew would take terrible risks, having little to lose. She also worried about her younger brother, Fergus, whom she'd left in charge of both her husband's and their father's businesses in Perth. There was little to the responsibility with the English all but halting trade, but Fergus was an untried seventeen-year-old and had never been so alone. He might very well seek adventure as a soldier. Their mother could not be depended on to advise Fergus for she had retired to Elcho Nunnery several years earlier and even though so near Perth she sought no contact with her family. Margaret's father, too, might now get caught up in the struggle; though he had fled to Bruges to avoid trouble with the English, it was said that King Edward planned to sail soon to the Low Countries. He was assisting the Flemish in containing an uprising to thus secure their support of the English against the French, who had made an alliance with the rebellious Scots. Rebellious against whom, she wondered – they merely wished to return their king to his throne, to repel Longshanks's attempt to annex their country to his.

And though she had tried to harden her heart against her absent husband, whenever his lord Robert Bruce was mentioned she pricked her ears in hope of hearing something of Roger. But none spoke of him. Indeed, Margaret did not even know

10

how he had come to join the company of the Bruce, who many suspected would fight against Longshanks only as long as he thought his own ambitions for the throne of Scotland might be realised. She had never thought Roger a man to betray his own king. Sick at heart at her husband's defection, Margaret tried to forget him by focusing her energy on the tavern and her work for James Comyn.

On this warm summer evening James himself was seated at one of the tables, listening to Angus MacLaren's tales. The storyteller's wild red hair clung damply to his temples and cheeks and his beard was frothy with ale, but his voice was strong, drunk or sober, and he had more tales than any man Margaret had ever encountered, many of them bawdy, but all providing a good laugh, something they all sought these dark days as a respite from the talk of war. Now Angus was sitting back, pressing a tankard against his hot neck for the coolness of the smooth wood.

The talk returned to what was on all their minds.

'They say men are gathering round Wallace in the countryside, at Kinclaven Castle near Dunkeld,' said Sim the server.

'He's doing us no good up there,' Mary Brewster muttered, her head sinking down towards her almost empty cup.

Margaret drew closer. Dunkeld was not so far

from Perth and her brother Fergus. She slipped on to the edge of Mary's bench.

'Have you any news of Perth?' Margaret asked.

'Some say the folk there are welcoming English ships,' said Angus.

'Who else can get through the watches on the coast?' James said with a slow shake of his head. 'But as to their welcoming the English, how can we know what's in their hearts from so far away?'

Margaret glanced at him, wondering if he'd said that to comfort her. He sat with cup in hands, moving it lazily and watching the pattern in the ale. His hands were those of a nobleman, clean, smooth, unscarred. His high forehead and long straight nose were fit for a coin. He raised his eyes and caught her watching him. She realised she had lost the thread of the conversation.

It did not matter, because Old Will had pushed himself up on to his feet and careened drunkenly their way, knocking over a bench and unseating several men whose bowls of ale crashed to the floor. As the men rose, their flushed faces turned ugly and curses flew. Margaret called for Sim to refill their bowls and asked for a volunteer to take the old man home.

'The old boller won't thank you for an escort home,' said Angus. 'He'd rather crawl beneath a table and take his rest than walk out into the night with one of us steadying him. Leave him be, that's what I advise.'

It was true that the refilled bowls had prevented a fight and most folk present had resumed their conversations, but Margaret could not bear the thought of anyone lying down in the rotting straw. The English had confiscated all the new straw she had collected to refresh the floor and what was left had not been changed in months.

'Murdoch doesn't bother to shift him,' James said. 'Why should you?'

'Because if he stays I cannot lock the doors.'

'He won't wake before you in the morning,' James argued.

'He's sure to wake in the night with his bladder full,' Margaret said. 'This place already smells like a midden.'

'Then what's the worry?' Mary Brewster asked, chuckling at her own wit.

'It's no matter now,' Angus said. 'Will's gone.'

James shook his head at Margaret's sigh. 'I'll go after him.'

Angus laughed as his friend walked out into the night. 'Now you'll have two men cursing you, lass. Och but you're a match for your uncle. Blood shows.'

Mary, grunting as she slid along the bench, rose a little unsteadily. 'I'll see to Will.'

Margaret looked at Angus, who grinned but said nothing until Mary had departed.

'She fancies him, so they say.' He nodded as

James stepped back inside. 'I see the Comyn has left the old boller to Mary's care.'

James shook his head. 'I did not find him.'

In the morning Margaret and her maid Celia climbed High Street for Mass at St Giles. The fog that lay over the town was chilly on Margaret's face, but she knew it to be a sign of a warm, sunny afternoon and looked forward to taking her mending out into the sunlight. She wrapped herself with the promise of warmth as she entered the drafty nave.

A priest stepped into her path. 'Father Francis,' she said with a little bow. He should have been in the sacristy preparing for the service. 'Is there no Mass today?'

'I would speak to you first.' He drew her aside into a corner well away from the arriving parishioners. 'You should hear this before the gossips spread the word. Mary Brewster sent for me early this morning after finding Old Will lying in his rooms in a faint, beaten about the head. He reeked of ale and vomit. I thought you might know something of his last evening.'

Margaret hugged her stomach, recalling the state the old man had been in when he left the tavern. 'I sent James Comyn after Will when he left the tavern, but he'd disappeared,' she whispered. 'What was Mary doing in Old Will's chamber?' She had not believed Angus MacLaren's claim that

Mary fancied the old man.

'She says it had been her habit to take him bread and ale after such an evening.' The nave was filling. 'I must be quick,' said the priest. 'He said something to Mary about an open door and crawling inside for warmth, that he'd lusted after other men's women and other men's wealth, particularly Murdoch Kerr's wealth, and swore that he'd meant no harm.'

'Had he stolen something?' Margaret asked.

'I don't know. He said much the same thing to me. Part of it seemed a vague confession of his chief sins. But the open door . . . And he said, "I emptied my belly without and crawled in for the warmth. I saw naught." Murdoch might wish to check his undercroft.'

Margaret nodded. 'I'll tell him. And when Old Will recovers—'

Father Francis shook his head. 'He passed as I was blessing him. At least he died shriven, may he rest in peace.' The priest crossed himself, as did Margaret. 'Now I must leave you.'

Expectations of a sunlit afternoon's work no longer cheered Margaret and in a solemn mood she turned to Celia, who had stood by near enough to overhear.

Tiny Celia shook her head and drew her dark brows even more closely together than usual in a worried frown. 'He named only your uncle?'

'Yes. I pray Mary does not spread that about.'

'But it can't be Master Murdoch who killed him. I won't believe it.'

'I don't think it was my uncle. In faith, I can't think who would commit such an act against Old Will.'

They moved forward to join the others.

'Poor old man,' Margaret said under her breath. 'He harmed only himself with his drink, no others.'

'Sim said Will had angered some at the tavern last night.' Celia did not look up from her paternoster beads as she spoke.

'He upset a bench. They were happy with fresh drinks.'

'Was your uncle there last night?'

'No. God help us, Uncle was always kind to Old Will. He never sent him home until he had slept off some of the ale.'

'I only wondered whether your uncle was there.'

'I'm sure he was with Janet Webster.'

'Master Murdoch's so attentive to Dame Janet of late, do you think they might wed?' Janet Webster had been widowed in the spring.

'Her children would have much to say about that, and none of it good,' Margaret whispered, then bowed her head and said no more, though she could not still her thoughts.

After Mass she went straight to Murdoch's undercroft. There was little light in the alleyway, so she could not make out whether it was her imagination or whether it smelled fouler than usual, as if someone had retched near the door. She found the lock hanging from the latch as it should and almost turned away in frustration, but something made her give it a tug. It opened. She lifted it off and carefully opened the door. She knew at once that this was not as Murdoch had left it, for he was a tidy man and would not leave a barrel lying on its side in the aisle with staves littering the floor, or a casket half closed, the lid crushing a rolled document.

The casket reminded her of her brother Fergus's letter, received a few days earlier.

All summer the English had worked on walling Perth, which irritated merchants because the wall cut off access to their warehouses along the canals. Fergus was not so inconvenienced because the Kerr and Sinclair warehouses were right on the Tay, and in fact he had been the guest of honour at many merchants' tables earlier in the summer in case they needed to make use of his accessible spaces. But the garrison was now away and the merchants grew complacent, neglecting Fergus. With so many his age having disappeared into the countryside to fight or hide, he had little occupation beyond seeing to what little business he had and checking that Jonet, the serving woman who looked after Margaret's and his father's houses, was keeping both in order. He resented his sister Maggie and his brother Andrew for being in the thick of things. Growing lazy, in the heat of the day he took to napping in the shade of the fruit trees behind the family house.

One afternoon he'd awakened, puzzled that his dog was not lying beside him. Thinking he heard Mungo's wheezing whine, he searched the out-buildings. At last he found the poor creature shut into a feed box in the stable. Once free, the dog ran straight for a puddle and lapped up the muddy water. Fergus puzzled over the dog's entrapment because he was certain that Mungo had settled down next to him to nap. He could not have wandered off afterwards and trapped himself in the box, for the lid was too heavy. Someone must have put Mungo in the box. But why? To keep him from waking Fergus? He broke out in a cold sweat thinking how close to him someone had come in order to coax away the dog. It must have been someone from the town for, although Mungo was friendly, he barked at strangers. Had the dog made an enemy of one of his friends, or had he been the victim of a jest that might have gone very wrong if Fergus had not found him quickly?

Fergus checked the kitchen first, thinking of the reported thefts throughout the spring and summer, as the troops on both sides wanted feeding. But he found the kitchen undisturbed. With Mungo padding along beside him, Fergus crossed the yard to the house, entering by the back door. Once inside the dog ran ahead, nose low, following a scent. He was still crossing and recrossing the middle of the hall when Fergus noticed documents littering the floor in front of a cabinet, some of the rolled parchments crumpled so that they lay open, some undisturbed. A cracked leather-backed wax tablet lay against the wall. The dog was content with sniffing the floor round the littered area, so Fergus guessed whoever had searched his father's papers was gone.

While he put the documents back in the cabinet and searched for the lock, he grew concerned about the servant – Jonet should have been seeing to supper by now. It was not market day, such as market day was now that the armies were seizing all that was worth eating.

Securing both doors, Fergus and the dog headed for Margaret's house. A chill breeze stirred from the river. There would be rain tonight.

A stranger approached, a cleric, modestly attired. As he grew close he hailed Fergus by name, albeit with a hesitance, as if making a good guess.

'You seek me?' Fergus asked.

The man bobbed his head. 'I am David, come from Elcho Nunnery, sir. Your mother, Dame Christiana, sent me. I thought I might find you at the house of your goodbrother Roger Sinclair, but I encountered only a maidservant – badly frightened, she was. I think you might wish to see to her.'

'I was on my way there,' said Fergus, not waiting for more conversation. 'Come along if you wish.'

He found Jonet kneeling in the midst of chaos in Margaret's hall. It was much as his father's had been, documents tumbling off the shelves of a large dresser. A crock of lamp oil had also broken and stained several of the parchments. Jonet was picking up the shards of crockery and weeping.

'They took neither food nor blankets – I had them airing in the backland,' she said, when Fergus had coaxed her up and into a chair. 'And the oil lamps on the wall, they were not taken.'

'Did you see the intruder?'

She shook her head. 'I came in from the kitchen and found it like this. The Lord was watching over me. I might have walked in on the thief.' She crossed herself. 'But I should have heard.'

'I am glad you weren't accosted,' Fergus said. 'The hall can be tidied.'

'But the letters and deeds, sir. Some of them are ruined.'

'I'll see to them. I know you are upset, but we have a visitor. We would have some wine.'

When Jonet had left them, both men stood for a moment silently surveying the room.

'I see that I come too late,' said David. 'Dame Christiana sent me to warn you that intruders broke into her room and searched it last night, and she feared they might come here next.'

'Did her chamber look like this?'

'Far worse. It is crowded with clothing and much else. It was all pulled out, turned over, spilled, trodden on. I saw no documents, however.'

'She sent you – she was not harmed?'

'Dame Christiana was frightened but not hurt.'

'God be thanked.'

Fergus said nothing else until Jonet had served them and withdrawn, but he thought the cleric's expression had changed a little, become guarded.

'Did my mother recognise the men?'

'It was her handmaid who saw them. She said there were three. The room was dark when one pulled her from her bed and pushed her to the door, where another pushed her out. A third guarded her. Once they released her, she woke the convent.'

'And my mother?'

David averted his eyes. 'Dame Christiana had gone out to walk along the river, and thus she was saved the encounter.'

Fergus thought he left much out. 'I would hear it all.'

The cleric put aside the cup he'd just lifted. 'Dame Christiana—' He hesitated, glancing at Fergus as if asking for his help.

'She had foreseen this?'

The cleric looked relieved. 'Yes. She knew of the intrusion before it happened, but knew not *when* it would occur. No, that is not quite right. She said she awakened to the terror of their being in the room and fled out of doors. I am afraid that Dame Christiana's explanation has caused much discussion about her wits.'

Fergus could imagine. 'My mother can be difficult to understand.'

David nodded over his cup.

Fergus recounted this event in a letter to Margaret, then debated with himself about sending it, for he could come to no resolution about what to do. He felt he'd been of no use when needed, allowing such a break-in to occur, and he admitted as much to his sister. He might just as well have gone to Aberdeen, where he had been about to become secretary to his uncle, a ship-builder, when his father had decided he was needed at home. At least he might have been of use there.

Margaret had gone over the letter many times since Father Francis had read it to her, picking out the words she had learned to read over the summer. She feared she'd been wrong to remain in Edinburgh, that perhaps she had left Fergus with too much responsibility. He sounded frightened. And with the inn so little used as a hostelry of late, Murdoch could manage without her. Still, the countryside was dangerous, full of men with bloodlust and little to do, so she might not have found an escort to Perth.

She closed the door to the undercroft, secured the lock, and then headed for Janet Webster's house.

2

A VISITOR

Leaving Janet's, Murdoch hurried along beside
Margaret in his smuggler's rolling, ship-born gait,
barking questions to which she had no answers and
would not have responded to in public even if she
did have them. By now all in the town would know
of Old Will's death and they would be eager to
overhear anything concerning it, even Murdoch's
litany of questions. His foolhardiness in speaking so
loudly did more to convince Margaret that his shock
was genuine than did all his protestations that he
had been far more patient with Old Will than
anyone else in town had been, or Janet's assurances
that Murdoch had been with her all night. Janet
often lied for him.

Once in the undercroft, Murdoch slammed the
door, then commanded Margaret to open wide the
shutter on the lantern. That he did not order her to

leave was even more telling.

The light picked out the scar that split Murdoch's thick eyebrows off-centre. 'It was a brave thing you did, Maggie, opening this door.'

She basked for a moment in her uncle's praise but as she surveyed the chaos in the aisled chamber, fear stole her breath. Barrels, caskets, chests, usually stacked in rows, some on trestles, were turned over, spilling their contents on the packed earth floor. Wine pooled nearby. What she had seen earlier in the light from the doorway had been nothing compared with this.

'They spent a good long while here,' Murdoch said, sounding weary. Most of the treasures in the undercroft were booty from his years as a smuggler. 'They took a risk in staying so long, with folk passing down the wynd to the tavern all evening.' He began to pick his way through the overturned barrels and chests.

'Anyone passing by would think it was you they heard in here,' Margaret said.

'That may be, but it was still a risk, and someone thought it worth taking. I doubt they hesitated before cracking Old Will's head open. It's a wonder they let him crawl away.'

Margaret did not want to think about Old Will at the moment. When fear overtook her she was of use to no one, particularly herself. She watched Murdoch crouch to set a casket upright and scoop the spilled contents back in. The ring of the coins and trinkets sounded incongruously cheerful.

'How will you ever tell what they took?' Margaret wondered.

'I can see already that a few costly items small enough to fit in a man's palm are missing. But they left much of value, so it's not trinkets and coins they were after.' He set the refilled casket aside and waded further into the room. 'Follow me with the lantern.'

Margaret tucked one end of her skirt into her girdle so that she could step over the tumbled items with the lantern in hand. Murdoch had paused to wait for her. When she began to move, he continued. He swung his head back and forth surveying the damage, but stopped for nothing, heading steadily towards the furthest corner.

Margaret knew what he kept back there. 'You are thinking they were after the casket Da left in your care.' Malcolm Kerr had left the casket of documents with his brother when he departed for Bruges the previous year.

Murdoch set a barrel upright to clear a path. 'Or your husband's. Or both.' Roger had also entrusted to Murdoch the small document casket that he usually carried behind his saddle when he travelled on business.

'Have you been expecting this sort of trouble?'

'I'd be a fool if I hadn't, lass. It's no secret that your husband Roger is the Bruce's man, or that my brother found it too easy to sail for Bruges, perhaps the result of some bargain with the devil himself. I've feared someone would tell the English or our own folk that they might find much of interest in here. Not to mention my smuggling spoil.'

'Da bargaining with Longshanks? You've not said that before.' Such a betrayal would be worse than Roger's.

'You didn't ask and I've been gey glad for that. You're learning that questions are dangerous.'

'I think it more dangerous not to be aware that both my husband and my father are known to be caught up in all this.'

Murdoch grunted as he crouched by the small chests belonging to the family. Margaret's father's casket was closed, but when Murdoch touched the lock it sprang open. 'Forced open. It's of no use now.'

Margaret set the lantern on a ledge and joined him as he lifted the lid. Documents had been jammed in with no care.

'They put these back in haste,' she said, trying to steady her voice.

'I agree. My brother Malcolm is tidy; it's his only virtue. They also searched your husband's casket.' Murdoch turned it round to show her how the lid had been forced down on a parchment roll and the lock left unfastened.

Their eyes met. 'They did not bother tucking anything else back,' Margaret said.

'You are right about that, lass. I regret my own

honesty. Now I cannot tell whether anything's missing from either casket. And I don't like not knowing.'

'Who do you think was here?'

Murdoch rose and shook out his legs. 'My partner James comes to mind. He kens I have them here, and he might be spying for his kinsman.'

'That is toom headed. He's known all along you've chosen no side yet he's never searched before.'

'You've grown too fond of him, Maggie. I warned you.'

Murdoch did not know about Margaret's pact with James, but they made no secret of being friends.

'He would not force locks, toss goods about, spill wine.'

Murdoch grunted. 'And why not?'

'Why would he leave signs of a search? As your partner he knows whether you're about the place and can explore as he pleases in your absence. He has no need for such haste.'

'You said yourself that he followed Old Will out of the tavern,' Murdoch reminded her.

'I have you there,' said Margaret, triumphant. 'James was in the tavern at the time you suspect him of having searched the undercroft.'

'He has many to do his bidding,' Murdoch said with a little laugh.

Margaret realised her folly. 'You aren't serious.'

Murdoch shrugged. 'You were so eager to defend him.'

'I merely sought to prevent you from accusing an innocent man.'

'Innocent is not a word I would use to describe Comyn,' said Murdoch. 'But this is not the place to discuss him. My real fear is that the English have been here.'

So he knew he was not invincible. But it seemed to Margaret that her uncle acknowledged it too late. 'You have perhaps been careless to hide all your goods in one place and let so many know of it.'

'What I've been a fool about is what I stored here.' Murdoch sighed. 'Come, let us go out into the sunlight and warm ourselves.' He handed her father's casket to her and then took up both the lantern and Roger's casket. 'I have a better place for these.'

A while later they sat outside Murdoch's kitchen drinking ale with Hal, the sandy-haired groom on whom Margaret depended for much of the news gleaned in places where she would be conspicuous. He had little to do of late in the stable with so few coming to stay.

'They say English soldiers have searched Old Will's rooms,' Hal said, his face averted as was his custom when speaking.

'Searched *his* rooms?' Murdoch looked bemused. 'Couldn't they see the rags he wore?'

'He wore a good pair of shoes when I last saw him,' Hal said.

'When was that?' Margaret asked.

'A few days past.' Hal looked up, and Margaret saw that he was pleased to have interested her. 'The shoes fitted him.'

So unless God had guided Old Will to the shoes it was unlikely that he had stolen them. Coin for ale, for shoes. 'Where did he find the siller?' Margaret wondered, shading her eyes as she turned into the sun to see her uncle's face. 'When were you last in the undercroft?'

Murdoch studied her from beneath his bushy brows for a moment. 'You're thinking that it was Old Will hunting for coins in there? And who attacked him? Someone defending my goods out of charity?'

'He'd been in there before, taken some, and then returned at an unfortunate time?' Hal suggested, his young face alight with interest.

Murdoch shook his head. 'I cannot recall at present when I was last in there, but Old Will was no lock picker. Had he been he would have drunk himself to death long ago.'

Margaret reluctantly agreed.

'I haven't the head for such things,' said Hal, rising. 'I should groom the MacLaren's horse. He'll be wanting her soon.'

Margaret took the tankards into the kitchen.

Murdoch followed. 'I don't like how keen you are to solve my problems, lass.'

'It would be unnatural for me not to want answers. My parents, my husband – what is someone looking for, and who is looking for it?'

'I meant Old Will's sudden wealth.'

'He was attacked in your undercroft.'

'You'd do better to wonder what your father's doing in Bruges.'

'Da has never confided in me. I might wonder all I like and never ken the truth of him.'

'You're curious enough about others, but not your family?'

'Are you about to confide in me?'

'No.'

But he was right, she should concentrate on what her family might possess that someone might want. 'I should go to Perth,' she said.

'What?' cried Murdoch.

'I'm no use to you here, we've had few people staying of late and there's little for me to do in the tavern,' she reasoned.

'Fickle woman,' Murdoch growled. 'In spring you cursed me for saying you should bide at home.'

'I did, though it was my husband I should have cursed. You were but the messenger. Fergus's letter has me worried, even more so after seeing the state of the undercroft. I should be with him.'

'I don't like it, Maggie. The English will be

certain we had a hand in Will's death if you suddenly run off.'

'You're never at a loss to find ways to ease their worries, Uncle.' His was the only tavern still open in Edinburgh and she knew he traded something with the English in order to prevent their closing such a place where Scots gathered.

'They grow greedier by the day,' said Murdoch. 'I doubt I'll hold them off much longer.'

Margaret saw that he was serious.

James Comyn sat near the window in the hall of his house on High Street considering the conversation he'd just had with a messenger from William Wallace. He was not at all confident that the young man had understood James's response. Once before he'd had this feeling, and indeed Wallace had taken offence in his reply and a long, inconvenient silence had ensued. Perhaps it was time James met with Wallace again. The messenger had said Wallace was headed for Kinclaven Castle, east of Dunkeld, to keep watch on the English garrison there.

As James stared out of the window, debating whether to risk such a journey, he watched Margaret Kerr striding up the hill. She wore her everyday gown, which hung from her strong bones of late – life in Edinburgh was more difficult than it had been at her home in Perth or with her goodmother in Dunfermline, and her curly red hair was caught up in a simple white cap. The clothes were not elegant but she carried herself with regal ease. A handsome woman, he thought, by any standards. She was talking to herself, apparently deep in argument. He wondered who was winning. Shortly after she passed out of sight at the front of the house, there came a knock at the door. Waving away the servant who'd rushed in to answer, James opened it himself, inviting Margaret in. He guessed what she wished to discuss – he'd heard about the old boiler's death – but she surprised him by handing him a letter.

'Father Francis helped me read it,' she said, explaining the lack of seal. 'It's from my brother Fergus. I hoped you might advise me on it. Would you read it?'

'You trust me with such a personal letter?'

She glanced behind her. 'Am I not alone? Who else might have placed it in your hand?'

Sometimes James did not know what to make of Margaret's apparent trust in him. Had someone treated him as he had treated her when she first came to Edinburgh, he would have kept far away. He had bullied her and threatened her for discovering his part in a woman's terrible death, then made a weak atonement by helping her meet with her brother Andrew on the morning he left for Soutra, where the English troops occupied the great Hospital of the Trinity. James had gone to some bother to arrange the meeting but it hardly made up for his earlier behaviour. On the other hand, he was her uncle's business partner, and kin to the man she believed the rightful king. Margaret had changed so since the spring, becoming brusquer, more comfortable with him and many of the townsfolk. He liked her new manner, but he wondered how stable it was.

'I merely thought to give you the opportunity to think again about the contents, embarrassing family secrets—'

'I'm no fool,' she said. 'I'd not make the mistake of showing you such a letter. I pray you, read it and save me the breath.' She stationed herself a little away from him, hands clasped behind her.

His curiosity roused, James settled back to read. In short order he saw the possible connection to recent events.

As soon as James put down the letter, Margaret said, 'I've no doubt you are fully informed about Old Will, and my family's caskets being searched in my uncle's undercroft.'

'Yes. I take it you think that last night's search was a continuation of those in Perth.'

'I cannot help but think so,' she said with emotion, for a moment allowing him to see her fear.

'You won't find me disagreeing. What would you have me do?'

She placed her hands on the table at which he sat and leaned close. 'My uncle swears he knew nothing of the contents of the caskets, so he cannot tell whether anything was taken. I would go to Perth, talk to Fergus and Mother. By now they might be aware of some missing items.'

James met her frank, almost eager gaze, but did not speak for a moment, wildly wondering whether she could have overheard his conversation with the messenger, for Perth was on the way to Kinclaven.

His silence made Margaret uneasy. She blushed and straightened, moving a little away from him. 'I should not have left Fergus alone. He is too young.'

James sensed no artifice in Margaret. 'Of course you are concerned. But such a journey is difficult in the best of times. Now it is difficult and foolhardy, particularly for a woman. The soldiers tire of their camp followers.'

Margaret blushed. 'I do not suggest this lightly. My family — we must know whence comes this danger.'

'There is a difference between possible danger and certain danger, Margaret. No one was hurt by the intruders.'

'Old Will?' she challenged, her eyes bold.

'Of course, but none of your kin.'

She sighed with impatience but dropped her gaze. 'I'd hoped you might escort me, or know of someone who might.'

James wondered whether the messenger had

been fool enough to stop at the tavern. He hesitated.

'I ask too much,' she said. 'I have nothing with which to repay you for the risk of such a journey, or the time away from more important matters regarding King John. I pray you, forget my request.' She began to turn away.

'Stay,' said James. 'What you propose is dangerous, but I understand why you wish to go.' He did not want to part so uncomfortably. 'I might find a way to do what you ask.'

Now she blushed for pleasure. Hope lit her eyes and turned up the corners of her mouth. He found himself wanting to agree right now even though he knew he should consider it with care. More than his own life was at stake.

'God bless you, James. I shall be grateful for any help in this – advice, someone who might be travelling that way, anything.'

'I'll do what I can.'

She left him standing in the middle of the room feeling burdened by his duty as the deposed king's kin.

By the following afternoon Margaret regretted having told her uncle of her wish to return to Perth. He had snarled and glared at her, told her blood-chilling tales of women attacked by English soldiers, ordered her about until she had shouted back at him, and then he had announced he was going to Janet's and knew not when he might return. She was in charge and she had better not allow anything to happen that would bring the English to investigate.

'As if I'd murdered Old Will,' she'd muttered at the last.

'You'll be the death of me, and I've said that before.'

He had indeed, more than once, and she had begun to think it was her uncle's perverse way of expressing affection, for most of the time they worked together in concord, each understanding their own limits and the other's strengths. Perhaps she had been right, but it could be that her talk of leaving had hurt him. The thought cooled her anger, although she still resented her uncle's announcing his departure in Sim's hearing. When the tavern servant knew Murdoch was away he slowed so much in his work that Margaret lost her temper, which was exactly what he wanted. Sim would express righteous indignation and storm out, leaving her alone to do all the work. Margaret had complained to her uncle, but he had his own reason for keeping Sim at the tavern. He distrusted him and preferred to have his enemy in sight. Margaret comforted herself with the thought that with Angus MacLaren off to the Trossachs the tavern would empty early.

In late afternoon a tall man in travel-stained clothes came into the yard leading two sweating horses. Hal leapt into action, ever solicitous of animals. The man thanked him courteously and then enquired about a room for himself and his master – Margaret, overhearing, introduced herself.

'Dame Margaret,' he said, bowing. A fleeting expression on his moon-round face made her wonder what he had heard about her. 'I am Aylmer,' he said. 'My master will pay you fairly for your best room.'

She could tell that by the quality of this servant's clothing. Servant – no, she did not believe it. He did not bear himself as a servant. Unless his master was of a class that she never saw in the tavern. And she guessed he was English, for 'Aylmer' was not a name she'd heard before. 'Whom do you serve?'

'He will be here anon.'

'You do not wish to answer my question?'

'He would rather do that himself, I am certain.'

She detected a smirk, barely suppressed. 'You may wait for him in the tavern. When I have met him, I shall decide where you might be most comfortable.' She motioned towards the rear door of the tavern.

She left him then, moving stiffly away, her irritation tightening every muscle so that each step took effort to execute without a jerk. In the stable Hal was humming as he brushed down the finest of the two horses.

'What can you tell me about him?' Margaret asked.

Without pausing in the long, smooth strokes, Hal said, 'In Edinburgh, only the Comyn's horse is so fine. They are well cared for, though they have been ridden hard of late. The riders should be praying that the English have not noticed them.'

'They came far?'

Hal nodded.

'What of the rider?' Margaret asked.

'Aylmer speaks with a fineness. His master must be very grand to have such a servant.'

'Is he lying?'

Hal shrugged. 'I have not the gift to judge, Dame Margaret.'

'Might he be English?'

Hal met her eyes for a heartbeat. 'I pray he is not.'

'I pray so, too. I am grateful for your observations, Hal.'

'Shall I stable these beasts?'

'Of course. They need care.' She left him, deep in thought about what might bring noblemen to Edinburgh, and to this inn. Such people usually sought the hospitality of Holyrood Abbey. What worried her was their timing, just after a murder and a search, or burglary. And the possibility that they were English, come to spy on the tavern.

The rooms that shared the upper storey of the

inn with her room were the most comfortable, but she would wait to meet the other man before committing to that. She might not turn them away – indeed, if they were from south of the Tweed she would not dare – but she did not need them near if she liked the master as little as she did the servant. She paused at the foot of the steps leading up to her chamber, deciding instead to check the rooms above the undercroft in case she chose to put the men there. She had one foot on the steps up to that when Celia came hurrying across the yard towards her.

'Mistress, you have a visitor.' Celia looked close to tears and her voice trembled.

'What is wrong, Celia?'

'He's up above, Mistress. He insisted I let him wait for you in your chamber.'

'God's blood, who does he think he is.' Margaret lifted her skirts and turned to follow Celia. 'This is a customer I *will* turn away.'

'You don't understand, Mistress. It's the master – your husband.'

Margaret stopped in mid-stride. 'Roger?' She turned back. 'Are you certain?'

'I was his mother's maid for many a year. It is he.'

'Dear Heaven.' Margaret pressed her arms to her stomach, feeling as if she had been hit squarely and lost all her breath.

'What can I do?' Celia asked.

Margaret shook her head. 'How goes he? Is he well?'

'He looks weary, but much the same otherwise.'

'Does he come in friendship?' Margaret heard herself ask the question and wished she could suck it back inside.

'He was sharp with me.'

Hence the tearful face, the trembling voice.

'I must attend him. He is my husband.' With a deep breath to steady herself, Margaret headed towards the tavern. But seeing the man Aylmer, she returned to Celia. 'We have guests tonight. The man by the tavern door is the servant, Aylmer, and I have yet to meet the master, but I think he must be a nobleman, perhaps English, for so fine a servant. With Roger here—' Her mind went blank.

'Were you seeing to a room for the strangers?' Celia suggested.

'Yes. Hal is stabling their horses.' When Margaret turned again, Aylmer was gone. She was relieved. She needed no audience as she climbed to confront her long-absent husband.

❧ 3 ❧

A GOOD HUSBAND

Celia had noticed the stranger watching Margaret
and her as they spoke and had felt an urge to shoo
him away. He must have sensed that he was
unwelcome for he was gone now, and Celia alone
witnessed Margaret pausing at the foot of the
steps, squaring her shoulders and continuing up.

Often in the past months Celia had wondered
how Margaret would behave when or if Roger
returned. To have left his wife of only two years
for such a long while during such frightening times
had been reprehensible. But he'd compounded
the offence as if he never considered Margaret's
feelings: in the sole letter he'd written to Margaret
he'd promised to return at Yuletide but then did
not appear, and sent neither an explanation nor an
apology; when at last Margaret had caught sight of
him in Edinburgh he had run from her; shortly

thereafter he had sent word ordering her home to Perth but provided no escort; and perhaps the most humiliating discovery for her mistress was that he had spent the time arranging safe passage to Carlisle for a wealthy Englishwoman who had stayed in the very room Margaret now occupied and he'd been a frequent visitor in the room. Although Murdoch had denied they were lovers, Margaret's brother had assumed they were and so must most of the townsfolk.

All this being so, as time passed Celia had imagined Roger less and less welcome. She herself had never wed, nor even bedded – her former mistress having run a strict household – so she could only guess at the emotion of such a reunion as was now commencing. But having heard her mistress weeping many a night, watched her search crowds for a sign of her long-absent husband, and noted her listening for his name when the Bruce was mentioned, Celia had grown to hate her former mistress's son and presumed Margaret felt much the same.

Dame Katherine had impetuously loaned Celia to her gooddaughter Margaret for the journey to Edinburgh to seek the murderer of Jack Sinclair, Roger's factor, and to trace Roger's own whereabouts. He had by then been gone months longer than he had originally planned. Oblivious to the danger of travel and the tension in English-occupied Edinburgh, Celia, eager to please the mistress who was training her to be a lady's maid, had gone without protest. She had not understood the sacrifice she had unwittingly undertaken until they arrived at Murdoch Kerr's tavern. The rawness and the filth had first frightened, then disgusted her. She knew that Margaret had regretted bringing her along, considering her desire to be a lady's maid ludicrous in the midst of war. But that very war had forced them to abide together long enough that they came to appreciate each other's virtues. Margaret had begun to confide in Celia, who did everything she could to help her new mistress's cause. Even now only Celia and Hal knew of Margaret's spying work for James Comyn, and Celia had grown accustomed to evading questions about her mistress's whereabouts.

But since the murder of Old Will, Celia had wondered whether their subterfuge was as successful as she had thought. She feared that someone else had learned of Margaret's work for Comyn and had searched the undercroft for information.

'If you've naught better to do, you might help me in the tavern,' Sim barked, badly startling Celia.

She wondered how the weasel had managed to creep up behind her. 'I've rooms to ready,' she snapped, thinking Sim her prime suspect.

'Where's the mistress?'

'Busy.' Celia picked up her skirts and hurried up the stairs before he could ask any more.

Margaret's feet felt weighted down and her heart pounded so hard she feared she might faint before she reached the landing. So many times she had imagined this moment, but nothing had prepared her for the jolt of hearing it had finally come. At the top of the stairs she found herself irritated by the need to deal with her estranged husband on the night that a nobleman was to lodge here. The mundane practicality steadied her. This was all part of her life, her own familiar life. Roger was her husband after all, not a stranger. She smoothed her apron as she crossed the landing to her chamber door. Reaching for the latch, she wondered whether Roger would be pacing or sitting. Upon opening the door she was startled to find him standing just within, blocking what little light came through the shutters.

'Maggie,' he said softly, reaching out to her.

She backed away. She did not doubt it was him, but she was not ready to walk into his arms. 'First I would see you, Roger. I must see with my own eyes that you are truly here.' She felt for the lantern just inside the door and opened the shutter, marvelling at how steady her hands were when she felt so breathless.

Roger tucked his thumbs in his belt and watched her as she studied him. His clothes were unfamiliar. They were well made, but they hung loosely on him. She had never seen him so thin. His face – she had known to expect the four long scars on his cheek, wounds that she had seen in spring, but not the tidy beard that partially hid them. Nor had his hair been so cropped then and sprinkled with grey – he was fifteen years older than she, but he had not looked it before. Strangest of all were his eyes. They had been his least attractive feature, unflinching and, perhaps because they were such a pale blue, icy. She knew they could not have darkened, but they seemed so, darkened with sorrow, pain, suffering, she thought. The changes in him frightened her more than anything had since his cousin Jack's death.

'Am I much changed?' he asked.

She was glad to find his voice familiar, deep and warm.

'I had not thought what you might have suffered,' she said. 'I knew of the wounds on your face, but I had not seen how thin you had become.'

'I am stronger than I was.'

She could think of nothing else to say. It was as if she had convinced herself that their factor's murder, Edinburgh's transformation into a town scarred by fires and bloodshed with the townsfolk terrified by Longshanks's soldiers who watched every move, her uncle's dangerous missions, the unexplained disappearances, the corpses, the dread rumours of battles – all the horror of the past months had been but a waking dream and Roger's changed appearance now proved it real. There was no going back. Her old life no longer existed.

Roger touched her face. 'You are as bonny as ever.'

The tender gesture closed her throat and brought tears. 'Roger,' she sobbed, and stepped into his embrace. He smelled of sweat, wood smoke, horses and leather. His body was harder, his grip tighter than before, and she knew that though he was her husband in name he was yet a stranger. He murmured tenderly how he loved her, had missed her, had worried about her. Although she feared his words false, all the old hopes for their marriage stirred within her. Roger pressed himself against her and she grew warm with desire, her body betraying her.

He lifted her and carried her to the great curtained bed, laid her gently on it. 'It has been too long, my Maggie.'

She found her resolve and rolled away from him, into the curtained darkness. 'I cannot erase the months so quickly,' she said, 'no matter what you have suffered. When we met for a moment on that cold, rainy day in spring you did not reach out to me, you ran. Why?'

Roger said nothing as he finished pulling off his boots, dropping them on the floor one by one. Then, with his back to her, he said in a quiet, patient voice, 'I thought I could protect you,

Maggie. Some of the English know of my work for the Bruce, and if they had witnessed our meeting they would have followed you, found some reason to question you.' He unlaced the sides of his tunic, pulled it off, then sat cross-legged on the bed facing her.

She wanted to wrap her arms around him and sink back on to the pillows clutching him tightly. But she was frightened to lose herself in him, to fall into the role of wife as blindly as she had before. 'And afterwards, when Janet Webster told you why I'd come here, could you not see that you couldn't protect me in such wise?'

'I thought you'd gone mad. My young wife, safe in Dunfermline, had suddenly decided to abandon all sense and come here, walking among the English. Don't you remember that soldier in Perth?'

She knew of whom he spoke, one in Longshanks's army who had grabbed her as she walked to the kirk. 'I do, Roger. I remember how you ran from the house to defend me. I count it as one of my best memories of you – I thought at that moment that you loved me, that you had not married me simply for the show of having a young wife.'

'What? How could you not know how much I love you, Maggie?' Roger reached for her. 'Come here.'

Margaret moved beyond his reach. 'What of

Edwina of Carlisle, your comrade in spying? Did you sit here on this bed with her?'

He lay back with a groan. 'She was also working for the Bruce. You have been told that, and that she is dead.'

'Did you share her bed?'

'I am your husband. I have kept my vows to you.'

'A simple yes or no would suffice.'

Roger propped himself up on an elbow. 'No.'

'Then why did you not tell me about her?'

He sat up. 'God's blood, for the same reason I didn't embrace you on the street in spring, wife, for fear of endangering you.'

'Am I such a simple little thing I cannot be trusted? A lap dog rather than a woman?'

Roger grabbed her shoulders. 'Listen to me,' he said, giving her a shake. 'I love you, Maggie. I have thought over and over of you on High Street, calling out to me. You cannot know what that did to me, seeing you, hearing your voice. You must have seen that I moved towards you, not thinking how I might endanger you. But my companions were sharp and they drew me away, brought me to my senses.' He pulled her to him and kissed her.

It was a passionate kiss. She wanted so to believe him, wanted to feel safe here in his arms. He was her husband. He was kissing her forehead, her temples, her neck. It was God's will that they be here in this bed, that they comfort one another.

He was so warm, stronger, rougher than she remembered, insistent, his hands everywhere, helping her undress. She shut out her anger and hurt and took pleasure in him, kissing his eyes, his cheeks, his lips. She pulled off his shirt and kissed the hollow of his neck. When he was freed from his leggings she pressed her head to his warm, flat stomach.

Roughly he pulled her up on top of him. His lips closed over her mouth with a new fierceness that felt more like anger than passion. He pressed her lower back against him with such strength she thought her spine would snap, and then rolled so that he was now pressing her down into the bedding. She could barely breathe. Her passion turned to fear. He slipped down to mouth her breasts, kissed her stomach, and then with a groan rolled away and pushed her aside.

Her body ached with desire. Her fear dissolved into an overwhelming sense of bereavement. He could not follow through with the pretence of loving her. She moved away from him, clutching a pillow as if it were someone come to comfort her, and wept.

She did not know how long she lay there, mourning something intangible, before Roger moved close to her, and lying on his side, his head on her pillow, stroked her hair.

'I have dreamed of you. Your wild locks, so bright, rivalling the sun.'

'You need not lie to me,' she whispered.

'I love you, Maggie.'

She heard a slight catch in his voice and wondered if it could be true. How she had yearned for him. She had hoped for a husband who sought her counsel, shared his thoughts, listened to her; who showed her in simple ways that he cherished her; who knew that she would worry and would find a way to tell her he was safe. Who would not lie to her.

'I don't think I understand what you mean by love.' Her voice, trembling and high, made her words sound peevish. She pushed herself up, clutching the covers to hide her nakedness from the stranger lying beside her.

Roger lay on his back. He ran his hand along her shoulder with a gentle, caressing touch. 'What happened just now – I have ridden a long way, and I wanted you too much. The heat of my passion – they say it can unman one. But we'll have many nights, Maggie.' There seemed a yearning in his voice.

'You mean to stay?'

'I mean to be a good husband to you. Teach me how.'

She was searching her memory for other nights with him, trying to recall whether he had ever said such words, and it came to her, their wedding night, after he had spent himself so quickly that he rolled away from her just as she was warming to his lovemaking. He had said, 'I shall be a good husband to you, Maggie.'

'You are tired,' she said now. 'Sleep.'

'I cannot until you tell me how to be a good husband to you.'

Her mind was in turmoil and she did not trust what she might say. 'Not now.' She lay down with her back to him and tried to quiet her storm-tossed thoughts with Hail Marys.

She'd managed only a few before Roger put his arm around her and leaned close to kiss her neck.

Margaret tucked the covers up higher.

'Maggie, we must talk.'

'On the morrow.'

He tugged at her, trying to turn her around to face him.

'Let me be,' she cried, resisting him even as she searched the chatter in her mind for an excuse that would buy her some peace. She must think how to cope with his return without either dissolving in tears or shouting at him. Rolling on to her back she said, 'I've not slept well since Fergus sent troubling news.'

'So you are not angry with me, just weary?' Roger stroked her forehead.

Oh, angry I am, Roger, but we must not yet speak of that. 'He wrote of intruders searching our house and Da's, and Ma's room at Elcho as well.'

'What?' Roger lifted the cruisie that still burned

beside the bed and brought it close to Margaret's face. 'In Perth?'

She nodded, turning a little from the lamp, the light startling her.

'What did they take? Was anyone injured?'

'No one was injured. Not there. Fergus cannot tell what is missing, but it appeared to him, as in the undercroft here, that they were after documents.'

'Here, too?'

'You didn't know? I thought that was why you've come, to see what they took. They searched the caskets you and Da left in Uncle's keeping. And Old Will was murdered in the wynd that night.'

Roger crossed himself. 'How did he come to cross their paths?'

She explained how drunk the old man had been when he left the tavern, and how he'd disappeared. 'I think he found the door ajar and slipped in to sleep off the drink.'

'And you believe the intruders killed him?'

'Yes. So, you see, I've had much on my mind and I yearn for sleep.'

'I am not surprised to hear of such searches,' Roger said, apparently not yet willing to let her sleep. 'The English respect no Scotsman's property. Nor do English abbots.'

Margaret had begun to turn away, but she sat up instead, putting a finger to Roger's lips. 'Do not condemn my brother until you know the truth.'

'He raided all the kirks for the royal treasures, and now he's confessor to the English garrison on Soutra Hill. What else can I think but that Andrew is cut from the same cloth as his abbot?'

'You know nothing. He despises himself for obeying Abbot Adam. And as for his post to Soutra, it is a death sentence, his penance for defying Adam and going to Sir Walter Huntercombe at the castle asking for news of you. He did it for me.'

'Is this true?'

'Do you have cause to call me a liar? That is how I learned of Edwina's death. Sir Walter believed the corpse found with hers was yours. But I'd seen you—' A sob rose in Margaret's throat, silencing her.

Roger set down the cruisie and gathered her in his arms. 'Oh, Maggie.'

Too agitated to rest in his arms, Margaret pushed away. 'You might explain yourself, why you lied about going to Dundee seeking a new port, why you abandoned me to help an English-woman.'

'Let's not talk of that now.'

Margaret let out a mirthless laugh. 'How brief-lived was your resolve to learn to be a good husband to me.'

'I meant from this day forward, Maggie. I know full well I failed you in the past.'

'I'm to have no explanation? Will you command me to forget? Oh, but of course, you've always thought me naught but a child. What was I thinking to ask why you lied to me, why you lay with another woman, a false wife who—'

The slap shocked Margaret into silence. In that moment she hated Roger.

'Don't speak so of the dead,' he said sharply. 'Edwina was a brave, noble woman who died carrying messages to the Bruce.'

'She was not returning to her husband? To England?'

'No.' Roger swung his legs off the bed and bowed his head. 'God help me, I wake at night wondering how I might have prevented her death and that of her escort.'

Margaret crossed herself. 'Forgive me,' she whispered, hearing the pain in his voice, reaching for one of his hands and holding it to her heart. 'But if you had trusted me with the truth of your activities . . .'

He jerked his hand from her grasp and rose, facing her with a murderous expression. 'I have explained my silence.'

'What happened on the way to Dundee?' she asked, knowing they would never heal this rift without more of an explanation.

Roger dropped his gaze. 'I'd prefer to talk of other things.'

'I need to know. Tell me and be done with it.'

He sat down on the bed with a sigh. 'This is a sorry homecoming.'

'What happened?' she asked more gently, touching his shoulder. 'It would help me to understand your long absence.'

Roger groaned. 'It is painful to talk of it.'

'I beg you.'

He gave a resigned nod and looked down at his hands, but said nothing for a moment. 'It was what I saw at the house of my old friend George Brankston,' he began in a quiet voice. 'It was my custom to stay the night there on my journeys to Dundee. I was treated as kin, not a guest, and though they were seldom forewarned of my coming I was always made to feel welcome. But this time . . .' He covered his eyes for a moment.

When he looked up, Margaret saw tears. It was unsettling to see his emotion over a family he'd never spoken of to her.

'The northern army of Edward Longshanks had ridden through George's property in the summer on its march from Dundee,' Roger continued. 'They'd stolen the horses, the falcons, all the livestock.' He took a breath. 'They raped his daughter Emma, and so injured Isabel his wife that she lost the child she carried and the use of one leg.'

'My God,' Margaret said. 'Why did you not tell me of this before?'

'Where was John Balliol in all this?' Roger demanded loudly. 'He should have made a last great attack, caught the army on the road. He made no effort to help.'

'I believe our king was in England by then, along with many of the Comyns, under close guard,' Margaret said quietly. 'And Robert Bruce was in Carlisle helping his father protect that English city from our people.'

'Our king.' It sounded like a curse from Roger's lips.

'You can't blame him for Longshanks's brutality.'

Roger swung his head from side to side slowly, as if trying to stretch out a pain. 'You asked what happened to change my heart on the road to Dundee. It had nothing to do with Robert Bruce at first. To find the family I had loved as my own so broken, so . . . The light was gone from their eyes, Maggie. I thought of the soldier who had grabbed you for a kiss and I knew how much worse it might have been.'

'If you were worried for me, why did you not come home?'

'Edwina of Carlisle was the sister of George's wife, Maggie. Isobel feared that what had happened to her and Emma might happen to her sister. I wanted to do something. George's family needed him there, so it was up to me. It was a beginning.'

Margaret took a deep breath. It did change things.

'I did not go south with the intention of binding myself to Bruce. I wanted only to bring some relief to Isobel, who had always been so gracious to me.'

'You'd promised to return by Yuletide.'

'I am sorry, Maggie. I thought I would yet be home by then.'

'In all that time, I received only one letter from you.'

'I still hoped, Maggie. It would have been dangerous, perhaps impossible, to communicate with you. Dangerous for both of us. I'd left you safe in Perth, with Jack to look after you and my trade.'

'You emptied the coffer and entrusted me to a man who was planning to take his leave to be with his lover.'

'I left you sufficient funds to survive for a good while.' There was a whisper of indignation in Roger's tone. 'I did whenever I left, ever praying but never certain I would return.'

'There was money sufficient for but a month, and little trade to compensate.' Margaret managed to keep her voice steady. 'And what about before you left?' she persisted. 'I thought you were seeking another port for shipping.'

'At first I was!' he shouted, rounding on her. 'My confiding in you would not have prevented anything that happened.'

'I envy you such certainty.'

His gaunt, angular face was rigid with anger. She

had not set out to make him so angry.

'You refuse to believe my good intentions in all that I have done.' His voice was as cold as his eyes. 'You are behaving like a pampered child annoyed to discover that life is difficult.'

Margaret opened her mouth to retort, but she stopped herself, thinking that there might be a little truth in what he said. But others had been as condemning of Roger's behaviour as she was, especially Murdoch. 'I do not claim to be better than I am, Roger. Nor am I so simple as to believe that now you're here all is well. I don't think you have any idea how I worried for you, thinking you might be injured, dying somewhere—'

'You should not have left the safety of my mother's house.' He'd risen and taken the cruisie to a small table by the window, settling down and pouring himself some wine.

'You refuse to see. Jack had been murdered, Roger, and it had happened while he was searching for news of you. I feared someone wanted to keep him from discovering where you were. I feared you had been killed, or captured. No one else was going to search for you, everyone was caught up in the troubles. It had to be me or no one. Can't you see that? I could not bear to sit day after day watching the door, wondering whether the clatter on the street was someone bringing you home shrouded, as was Jack.'

Roger began to speak, then stopped himself. He

poured himself more wine, then shifted on the stool to gaze out of the dark window.

Margaret turned away from the light and, pulling the covers over her head, resumed her Hail Marys. She wished he'd stayed away.

Celia slept fitfully in a strange room, waking now and then in confusion. She could not seem to shake off the edginess of the evening.

After she had prepared a chamber for the strangers, she had thought of readying one beside Margaret's for herself, but was uncertain whether the reunited couple would wish for more privacy. Or whether Roger would spend the night – after all that she had suffered, Margaret might not wish him to share her bed. The sun was low in the sky and the evening cool. Celia's stomach rumbled and her mouth was dry. But if she went into the tavern someone might ask after Margaret, and Celia had not yet settled on what to say. She has a guest? She is on an errand? Visiting . . . who? At the kirk, perhaps. She slipped inside the little maid's hut between the two kitchens, Murdoch's and the tavern's, and settled on a bench by the window where she could watch for Margaret on the steps.

Dusk came and there was still no sign of Margaret. At last, starving, parched and cold, Celia went into the tavern. It was almost empty.

'Folk fear the English are watching us to see if more corpses crawl out of the wynd,' Sim said.

As if his unpleasant conversation were not penance enough, Celia glanced up to find James Comyn walking towards her with his tankard in hand. He slipped on to the bench opposite her.

'Though the day was warm there is a chill in the air this even,' he said. 'Where will you bide while your mistress is entertaining her husband?'

Celia should not have been surprised that he already knew of Roger's presence, but there was something about James Comyn that made her stubborn. 'I don't know what you're talking about. My mistress is asleep, and I was still hungry.' She forced herself to wait for her food and drink, and then gave it her full attention. When she must look elsewhere she gazed around the room. She noticed the servant Aylmer. He sat away from the others. She noted that he was simply but tastefully dressed – she had made it her business to notice such things.

'Has his master arrived?' she asked James.

He followed her gaze. 'Him? He arrived with the man I'd mistaken for Roger Sinclair. I did not think your mistress would entertain any other man in her chamber.'

Celia did not like Comyn's smirk. She thought him like many well-born folk, seeing servants as simpletons, people to be teased and ridiculed when he wasn't ordering them about. She made no attempt to retort. He would only smirk more. She was also dumbstruck by the news that Aylmer was Roger Sinclair's servant.

Fortunately Comyn soon wearied of her silence and returned to his former spot by the fire. In a little while, full and now almost too warm, Celia withdrew, thinking to retire early. But as she drew near the maid's cottage she heard voices from within. Thoughts of Old Will's murder made her heart pound. But stubborn curiosity made her creep closer, until she could make out the quiet murmur of a man's voice and a woman's sigh and giggle. She could guess who the lovers were, Roy, the tavern cook, and Belle, a former chambermaid who had been forbidden on the premises. Celia went to the tavern kitchen where she found Geordie, the cook's helper, sullenly cleaning.

'So it's Roy and Belle next door?' she asked him.

'Aye. It will be bad for them both if Master Murdoch finds out.'

Belle had left Roy for another, then returned heavily pregnant with the cook's child, or so she said. Murdoch had not banned her because of her morals, but rather because he could ill afford Roy's destructive tantrums whenever Belle crossed him. Foodstuffs were too difficult to replenish.

'Well I'll not be the one to betray them,' Celia said. 'Could you give me a warm stone?'

Geordie drew one out of the fire.

She carried it across to the stairs, her eyes searching the dark corners, then hurried up. All was quiet in her mistress's chamber, and no light shone beneath the door. She chose the smaller room on the right and put the hot stone beneath the covers, then returned to the kitchen for another for Aylmer's room. He, too, would be sleeping alone tonight.

Throughout the night she woke, thinking she heard her mistress call, but she was loath to knock on the door. She hoped Margaret was resting more easily than she was.

~§ 4 ?~

HER COMFORTABLE SANCTUARY

Fergus applied himself to the task of tidying the documents in both his father's and his sister's homes. None seemed of much importance, most merely recording business contacts and deals made, or proposing future arrangements. He knew there must be more. He was experienced enough to know that Roger and his father, Malcolm, must have records regarding the less respectable dealings necessary to evade a tax or buy a councilman or a courtier. He conducted a second, more thorough search of both the houses and the warehouses, not holding out much hope for finding indiscretions, but thinking he might find inventories that would allow him to determine what items, if any, were missing. But he found no such lists in either house, or indeed any lists of the property stored in them or in the warehouses.

His frustration fuelled what had been a slow-growing anger directed at his family. They had trusted him with little while they were in residence, no matter how much he had begged for inclusion in the business, if not assisting in the purchase and sale of wine, leather items, cloth and various other goods then at least keeping the shipping records. Bored with Perth, he had rejoiced when his uncle Thomas Kerr had sent word that he needed a secretary in his shipyard and had hoped Fergus might come to Aberdeen. But before Fergus could depart his mother had withdrawn to the convent, his father had decided to sail for Bruges, and suddenly Fergus was needed in Perth to run what remained of his father's business. Even his hope to accompany his father to Bruges as his apprentice factor had been killed. At first Malcolm had encouraged him in his expectations, but when the time came for Fergus to be outfitted, his father had inexplicably bowed to his wife's advice for perhaps the first time in his marriage and had agreed that Fergus must remain in Perth to assist Maggie and watch over the family's warehouses. Fergus had been furious; his mother had chosen a fine time to notice her youngest child. If she was so concerned about Maggie she could come out of her comfortable sanctuary and see to her herself. But his father would not be moved, and Fergus had nursed a bruised face for his insolence.

He had once adored his mother. She had ever been distant – he could not recall a single instance of her gathering him in her arms and comforting him. Her preoccupation with her visions had seemed to prevent such intimacy. But he had held her in his heart as a boy does his mother. He had judged all women against his mother's beauty and found them wanting, against her religious devotion and found them worldly. Maggie had often teased him about his mother worship, pointing out the problems they had that other families did not, such as how impossible it seemed for Christiana to recall where she had put things, how frequently she lay abed for days, even weeks, after a vision, and how some of her predictions caused chaos in the town. But despite Christiana's failings as a mother, Fergus had steadfastly maintained his devotion to her. It was only when she withdrew to Elcho saying little more to him than 'Pray for me, and respect your father', that his love had finally turned to resentment.

So when the shock of the intruders eased, he had wondered at his mother's effort to warn him by sending the cleric David. A day later he had rowed downriver to see her and enquire whether she had any idea what had motivated the search.

The hosteleress sent a servant to inform his mother of her visitor.

'Was anyone injured the other evening?' Fergus asked.

The nun had drawn paternoster beads out of her sleeve and begun to mouth prayers. She did not answer at once, but completed a decade before lifting her gaze to him. 'Dame Christiana's maid-servant has a bruised arm, but that was the worst of it, God be praised. Many things were spilled or torn, that is all.' She intoned 'things' as if of the opinion that his mother had too many possessions. 'And what of your intruders?'

David apparently had not confined his report of the incident to Fergus's mother.

'No one saw them, but they left a jumble of deeds and correspondence.'

The door opened. Marion, his mother's maid, bobbed her head to him. 'Dame Christiana says she is too ill to see anyone, but assures you that the messenger told you all she knows. The vision took all her strength. I am sorry.'

The hosteleress straightened up, looking non-plussed. 'But her son has come all the way from Perth.'

Marion hung her head and shrugged.

Overcome with embarrassment and anger, Fergus had not trusted himself to speak. With a stiff bow to the hosteleress, he had departed. He was halfway home, struggling against the currents, before his mind cleared and he realised he'd behaved like a disappointed child. He might have treated Marion more courteously, for it was not her fault that his mother snubbed him.

For a day he had moped, having Jonet purchase twice the customary amount of ale for the two of them and proceeding to drink through his anger and humiliation. In the morning, covering his head with a pillow in a futile attempt to stop the hammering, he cursed himself for yet again behaving like a fool. The following day he had decided to set his mind on what had happened and what he ought to do about it, and wrote the letter to Margaret. He did not whine, but tried to impress upon her the importance of finding out why intruders were interested in Kerr and Sinclair property and what they were looking for. Then he had begun his second search of the houses and warehouses, occasionally overcome with the memory of his behaviour at Elcho. He considered writing to his mother expressing all his resentment, and had already put pen to parchment when he remembered that she could not read and would therefore rely on one of the sisters, the cleric David, or perhaps the chaplain to read the letter to her. That took all the joy out of attacking her.

When he told the sad tale to his sweetheart, Matilda grew quite excited and suggested that he ask his father's and Roger's former clerks, if any were still about, whether there were caches of money or record books that might be of interest to thieves. 'Although I'll warrant it's treason against King Edward one of them is about,' she said excitedly, obviously savouring the potential drama. 'And no clerk would be trusted with such documents.' She'd been favouring Fergus with smiles and flirtation for lack of a better suitor now that so many were off to war. It was Fergus's only consolation.

Celia had not fooled James about the identity of Margaret's visitor. He had received word from more than one reliable source that Roger Sinclair had arrived with his man, Aylmer, and headed straight for Murdoch's inn. James thought it unlikely that Roger's appearance so soon after someone had been searching his belongings was an accident. Robert Bruce would have as many spies as the Comyns, if not more so. James's family had held sway over the country for so long they had become overconfident. The Bruces had never yet had the opportunity to rest on their accomplishments.

James had met Roger Sinclair occasionally in the past, before he'd had much interest in the man. Before Longshanks had stepped in to choose the Scots' ruler for them, James had enjoyed a comfortable life as the itinerant negotiator of marriages, trade transactions and occasional ransoms for his wealthier Comyn and Balliol kin. He had been seldom in Edinburgh, and his interest in the tavern had been limited to an occasional drink with someone passing through until Longshanks's invasion, when it had become useful for spying.

Roger, an older, moderately successful merchant trading in Berwick and Perth, had been of no concern to him.

The timing of Roger's return could not be more inconvenient for James. In considering the route that would allow him to accommodate Margaret he had become reacquainted with the location of Elcho Nunnery, not a great distance south of Perth along the Tay. Dame Christiana MacFarlane, Margaret's mother, now lived there, the seeress who had been blessed with a vision of Margaret's future that included a glimpse of the rightful king of Scotland riding into Edinburgh. William Wallace put much weight in prophecies, particularly those of Highland women. Wallace would like very much to know the identity of that king. Margaret need only provide her mother's description of the king in the vision to compensate James for his trouble. He had therefore decided that escorting her to Perth would benefit both of them.

But with Roger Sinclair's return, James would not likely be escorting Margaret anywhere. Curse the man and his belated attention to his wife.

It was not merely the timing that bothered James. Margaret had been of much help to him in gathering information, anything from overheard conversations between English soldiers to the names of women from the town who visited the castle garrison. He worried that Roger might persuade her to change sides, abandoning Balliol for the Bruce, and if she did, she might share information with him. James wanted to believe that her sense of honour would prevent her from betraying him, but love often pushed people beyond moral behaviour.

It all put James in a foul mood and, though it was the middle of the night, he woke his servant to fetch him wine and a cold repast.

Voices raised in anger woke Margaret. They were so loud that her heart raced as she peered out of the bed curtain. The room was empty, the argument now more clearly down in the yard. One of the voices was Murdoch's. Someone had arrived yesterday – the English servant. And what of his master? She realised with a start that she had neither met him nor resolved whether to let them stay. The light streaming in through the slatted shutters alarmed her. She could not think why Celia had not roused her much earlier.

But a hat on one of the hooks and a leather travelling pack on the chest jogged her memory. Roger was here. Had she not seen his things in the room she would have thought his return a dream. Yesterday afternoon had been like any other. She'd had no premonition that her wait of almost a year was about to end, not even a fleeting thought that Roger might appear. In fact, of late she had ceased to pray for either his safety or his return, an omission born of resentment. She was not even twenty and condemned to the chaste life of a nun while her husband yet lived. Though he might never venture near her, she was condemned to await his pleasure while he might change his name and marry or bed as many women as he pleased – or so she had come to think over the past year, usually in wakeful hours before dawn.

And now he'd arrived, pledging his love, teasing her with passionate play, promising . . . what? No more than he had promised on their wedding night, to be a good husband. She had told him she did not understand what he meant by 'love' but she might have added 'husband'.

About one thing she was adamant – she would not let his return erase the strength she had gained in his absence. Nor would she withdraw her support from John Balliol. With that resolve she forced herself to rise and begin her day. Her eyes burned and her face was tender from Roger's scratchy beard. Worst of all, she had been left unsatisfied and abandoned, as if he'd opened his eyes this morning and realised she was the wrong woman.

Celia knocked – her timing was uncanny. After pulling her crumpled shift over her head, Margaret called out for the maid to enter. As the door swung open the arguing voices grew louder.

'With whom is my uncle debating so long and loudly?'

'English soldiers,' said Celia. 'They are carrying

out orders to board up the High Street door to the tavern and guard the yard entrance.' She glanced at Margaret, then quickly averted her eyes. 'The tavern is shut.' She shook out Margaret's dress.

Margaret turned her back to Celia to receive the gown overhead. 'Shut?' This was disturbing news. 'Uncle feared this would happen. Does it have something to do with that stranger who arrived yesterday?'

Celia looked confused. 'Stranger?' She shook her head as if she didn't know whom Margaret meant. 'The soldiers say it's because of Old Will.'

'Old Will,' Margaret whispered. 'They searched his rooms and now they close the tavern.' She turned back to Celia. 'Why has death stirred them like no other among us? Who do they think he was that they find him so important in death?'

Celia stole another glance. Her pained expression was like a mirror held to Margaret – she must look as ragged as she felt.

'Whatever their reasoning,' Celia said, 'they are eager. While your uncle argues with one, the other soldiers make haste with the carpentry. But I don't believe their mission surprised him. Your uncle and Hal were up before me, loading a cart in the dark.'

So her uncle had another hiding place. Margaret should have guessed. As she stretched out her arms for the sleeves she asked, 'Where did you sleep?'

'The east chamber up here – I thought I should be near.' Celia worked at the laces, her fingers cold. 'But I woke at every sound.'

'Where did you put Aylmer, the English servant? And what of his master?'

'Oh! Master Roger did not tell you the man is his servant?'

Margaret could not believe it. Even in her father's house they'd never had such a well-spoken, well-dressed servant. 'No, he said nothing of him.'

'I put him in the other house. He and Master Roger were up early, out in the town.' Finished with the sleeves, Celia looked Margaret in the eye. 'Are you well, Mistress?'

Margaret wondered just how bad she looked. 'I am tired, that is all.'

When dressed, she went out, avoiding her uncle and the soldiers while she looked for Hal. She could not help but notice when passing them that the English soldiers had begun to look shabby, and in fact one wore a tunic so large for him that he'd tucked the hem into a wide belt so it didn't drag in the mud. They'd not looked so when they'd marched into Perth the previous summer. It gave her a little hope, or at least the satisfaction that they, too, suffered deprivation. She found Hal in the stable, combing Murdoch's sable-coated cat.

'Agrippa wanted to hide from the soldiers,' Hal said to the ground.

Heavy-lidded green eyes watched Margaret approach, then closed as she gently touched Agrippa's round, silky head. 'He is calm now,' she noted.

Hal nodded. 'The master's voice, though it be angry, reassures him.'

'What do you know about my uncle's movements with the cart?'

'Celia must have told you.' Hal nodded. 'I saw her watching from above.'

'I wonder who else saw you.'

Hal shrugged. 'The master wanted the cart brought round to the close after curfew, when I'd seen no one about for a good while, but long before dawn.' Hal raised his head and she saw by the slackness of his young face how weary he was. 'I helped him load barrels and trunks, and then he led Bonny away down the backland. I was to watch a good while to see whether someone might think it safe to run off and report him. I saw no one.'

Margaret's petting inspired a loud purr from Agrippa.

'What is to happen to us, Dame Margaret?' Hal asked. 'With the tavern shut, Master Murdoch will have no need of me.'

The cat jumped away.

'I don't know, Hal. Have you any kin?'

He shook his head.

Margaret had begun to reach for his hand, but thought better of it, and glad she was, for at that moment Roger and Aylmer appeared, leading their horses. Hal stepped forward to relieve them of the beasts.

Handing Hal the reins, Roger swept off his cap and bowed low to Margaret. 'How goes my lady this fine day?'

'With the soldiers about it is hardly fine,' she said, noting once more the change in his appearance, the hollows in his cheeks, the grey-flecked hair. 'You cannot have missed them.'

'I am only surprised they left it so long.'

Margaret was unsettled by the warmth in his eyes as he looked at her. 'They seem to allow you much freedom at the gates,' she said.

'We came through Blackfriars' to Potter Row and then down the backlands. Unfortunately, one of the soldiers saw us. He said nothing, but he will to his superiors. It is best that we leave soon.'

So already he planned his escape from her.

'Would you not rather bide at home in Perth?' he asked. 'You said you've lost sleep for worrying about Fergus. And you are right, he is too young and lacks the experience to deal with such problems.'

'I had no choice but to leave him there alone,' Margaret said, suddenly feeling defensive. So Roger meant to send her off to Perth. Damnable man, meddling with her plans.

Aylmer joined them.

'This is my manservant, Aylmer,' Roger said.

Aylmer bowed. 'Dame Margaret and I have met.'

'Of course,' said Roger.

Aylmer was a little taller than Roger and of a muscular build, but his moon-shaped face was unscarred, so Margaret did not take him for a soldier, or thought he had not been one for long. His speech was more like James's than Roger's. She guessed him to be part of Robert Bruce's household, particularly with such an English name.

'Well, what do you think of riding to Perth, Maggie?' Roger asked. 'Murdoch has his Janet, and no tavern. He'll have little need of you.'

'Who would escort me?'

Roger gave a surprised laugh. 'We would ride together, Maggie. I do not mean to leave you here among the English.'

Margaret glanced over at Hal, saw his arm pause over one of the horses. 'I must consider,' she said.

'Consider?' Roger cried. 'It is decided, Wife.'

She would be damned if she would be ordered about. But she checked her impulse to take issue with his declaration when she noted Aylmer's sly smile. They would discuss this in private.

Fergus learned that only two of his father's former clerks were presently near Perth. John Smyth, who had been dismissed under suspicion of theft, lived a few miles out in the countryside. Fergus did not think it wise to prime a thief's memory of his da's business with questions about records. The other clerk was now employed by Elcho Nunnery.

Elcho – Fergus's face burned with the memory of his humiliation there. He cursed his mother for sending a messenger warning him on one day, then refusing to see him the next. Considering that she had been well enough to walk along the river the night of the intruders, he guessed her sudden illness was either from the damp or from the lethargy that came over her after a vision, and far more likely the latter. Often as a child he had crept in to see what horrible spots or sweats she suffered in one of her frequent illnesses and never had he witnessed anything more frightening than her sleeping with her eyes opened.

But he had a right to hear what she knew, no matter how exhausted she was. It was her interference that had trapped him in Perth. He resolved that he would return to the nunnery and refuse to leave until he had spoken to her. He had his rights. And while he was there he would talk to his father's former clerk.

Dame Katrina, the hosteleress, received him, tactfully making no mention of his previous abrupt departure. He explained his double errand, impressing on the elderly nun that he would stay as long as he must to speak with his mother. She sent a servant to inform Dame Christiana of his presence and to fetch the clerk.

Even she did not believe his ma would agree to see him at once.

The clerk was an elderly man who had worked for his father when Fergus was a child. He described a leather-bound casket, the type often strapped behind a saddle, in which Malcolm had kept his private papers.

'Oft times he sailed with it,' the clerk said, 'but I recall a time when he left it in the keeping of Father Stephen, late of St John's in Perth.'

Fergus recalled the small chest of which he spoke and was almost certain his father had carried it with him when he'd departed. Perhaps there was nothing of substance to be found at home or in the warehouse.

After the clerk had returned to his work, Dame Katrina brought Fergus a plain but filling midday meal, with a mead so sweet he was still sipping it with pleasure in mid-afternoon, when his mother at last appeared. She bowed slightly to him, and Marion, close behind, said that he should join his mother out in the garden. One of the guest-house servants already held open the door.

Fergus gulped the last of the mead and followed.

His mother settled on a bench in the sun. Though her gown was a simple cut it was of fine wool, a blue-grey to match her eyes. Her veil and wimple were white and completely hid her red-gold hair. Fergus was sorry for that, but he supposed she felt more a part of the community so clothed. Even so, she was beautiful.

She proffered a hand and smiled a little at Fergus's greeting, then patted the bench beside her.

'Come, my son. Sit beside me and tell me how you bide upriver.'

'You know how, Ma. The houses were searched before your messenger arrived to warn me. Who is searching, Ma, and for what?'

'Fergus, Fergus, you have ever been hasty in speech and too quick to anger. Calm yourself. Speak first of the little things. Give people ease before you attack them.'

He knew his approach was clumsy, but she made it necessary. Years of being diverted by her had forced him into blunt tactics. She had made him tenacious. Gathering his mental armour about him, he sat down beside her and took her hand. Here her age had begun to work, enlarging the joints, raising the veins. He was sorry for that too.

'How goes the household?' his mother asked, easing her hand from his and angling herself so she might see his face.

'Jonet and I are managing, though we have not enjoyed meat in some time.'

'You were never one for the hunt.'

'Ma, there are soldiers in the wood – ours and theirs.'

'Ours and theirs? You mean the Scots and the English?'

'You know that I do. Do you have any idea what documents someone is after?'

'Do we know they are after documents?'

'That is what they searched through in both houses,' Fergus said, relieved that she had at last addressed the matter, though her eyes looked vague. 'Did they not search for them here?'

'It was impossible to ken what they hoped to find, or what they took. But they have not returned, praise God.'

'You might better praise the prioress,' Fergus said, 'engaging her kinsmen in standing watch over Elcho's gates.'

His mother reached out, touched his knee. 'What? She has set guards at the gates?'

'She did not tell the community?'

'Perhaps the others, but not me.' His mother covered her face with her ageing hands for a moment, then pressed her palms together and bowed her head, murmuring a prayer.

'You had not thought there might be further danger?' Fergus asked. He should not be surprised by his mother's lack of comprehension, but he had thought that seeing her belongings tossed about, and considering the state of the kingdom, she might have understood that she was in danger.

'Dame Agnes believes that my visions are personal,' she said, 'that they do not apply to others and so I am wrong to share them. Yet she seemed angry that I had not gone to her at once when I woke with a vision of intruders.'

'Were you frightened?'

'Yes. So frightened that I ran out of the postern gate down to the river. I feared that they were at my heels, ready to— But when at last I stopped I realised that it could not be real, because Marion had not awakened. Do you see? I had no cause to rush to Dame Agnes.'

For once, he agreed with her. 'What is Da doing in Bruges?'

'Avoiding the English, I thought. Hoping to avoid all the unpleasantness and protect some of his wealth.'

'You know of nothing in his possession that might be evidence against him, from either side? Or that might reveal secrets of either side?'

'Why are there sides? Why must men always take sides?'

Fergus closed his eyes, took a deep breath, and asked her again. And again. The conversation meandered on for a long while, but the only thing that he learned was that his mother lacked any curiosity about his father's activities. He left her meditating on mankind's failure to heed Christ's message of love, which would render war unnecessary. He thought her a strange one to speak of love.

❦ 5 ❧

Vows

Margaret had made excuses to Roger and climbed High Street to St Giles Kirk, where she might have some peace in which to think. Her warring feelings confused her too much to make sense of anything at the moment.

In different circumstances she might have been unconditionally delighted by Roger's suggestion that they set out for Perth together. Only yesterday she had sought an escort for a homeward journey – but she had perhaps already found one, and there was the rub. She should be glad to have a commitment from him – James had said only that he would consider it. Even more, she should prefer travelling with her husband to their home. It was what she had come to Edinburgh to do, to find him, to coax him home. Not that she had expected to succeed in drawing him back to Perth, but that had been the end for which she had prayed most fervently. Clearly she had lost the habit of counting on Roger. Indeed she was working against him in the matter of the king; she did not even trust him with the truth of her allegiance. She felt prickly and unable to think clearly.

Lifting her head, she found herself already past the quiet market place and in the shadow of St Giles. Slipping into the nave, she had a moment of panic such as she had never experienced before in God's house. The high arching ceilings, the empty vastness that the candles and windows illuminated in such a way as to make the unlit spaces seem darker than the night-time streets, the chill of the stones not kissed by sunlight since placed there, all conspired to disorient her as to season, time of day, even whether she were still on earth or had stepped off its face into another, dark and sinister world. She bowed her head and prayed for the terror to pass, for God to forgive her for whatever trespass had earned her such fear in His house.

A man and woman brushed past her, moving towards a chapel in the north aisle, arguing in hushed voices that were louder than their normal voices. 'I did not call you a liar, it's your brother who tells the tales.'

The touch of humanity broke the terrifying spell. Was that her sin, the tension between her and Roger? Margaret crossed herself and sought Mary's altar, kneeling before it with pathetic relief. Feeling like a child who looked to an adult to make everything better, she prayed to the Virgin Mary for peace and joy in her marriage, then amended her prayer to a request for guidance in restoring her marriage. Even as she whispered the words Margaret knew her duty was to go with her husband, to make an effort to heal their rift. Roger's temporary desertion did not free her from her vows. Her promise to assist James had not been made in the sanctity of a sacrament, but her marriage vows had been. The clarity with which she now saw her duty must be the Blessed Mother's inspiration, and she was ashamed by the resentment in her heart. She pulled her paternoster beads from the embroidered scrip at her waist and began a rosary for her soul, praying that she might find the strength to follow the Blessed Mother's advice. Gradually, with the repetition of prayers, her eyes grew heavy and her mind numbed. She must have dozed, for she started with a sudden awareness of James kneeling beside her on the wide prie-dieu. His nearness – they almost touched elbows – was disturbing and yet comforting.

'It is strange to find you here,' she whispered.

'I wondered whether you are still in need of an escort to Perth,' said James, 'or whether your husband's presence has changed your plans.'

How quickly he'd learned of Roger's return. 'Is there anything you don't know?'

'What you've done to inspire such loyalty in your maid.' His voice teased.

'She refused to answer prying questions?'

'Not only that, she lied about the identity of Aylmer's master.'

Margaret smiled down at her folded hands. Celia was a trustworthy friend.

'None of my servants would do so much for me,' James added.

'Roger has suggested we go home to Perth,' Margaret said, answering his original query.

'Ah.' James nodded. 'Do you ken his purpose in coming to Edinburgh? Is it for the Bruce?'

'He says he missed me.' Margaret shoved her beads into her scrip.

'I did not mean to doubt that he has missed you.'

Margaret felt herself blush. 'I did not take it so.'

'I am glad of that.' He sounded sincere. 'You are a brave and honourable woman, and I am sure that only the demands of his lord have kept your husband away so long.'

Margaret did not wish to discuss her marital situation with James. 'I'll find a way to help our king regain the throne, no matter where I am. He is the rightful king, no matter what Robert Bruce thinks.'

James turned slightly towards her with a puzzled expression. 'I am glad of that, though I did not mean to suggest you would not be true. I am concerned about your being near the king's troops in the company of the Bruce's men. I assume that Aylmer shares your husband's loyalties.'

'I know nothing of him. I'm glad I'll have Celia to attend me.'

'Have you spoken to Roger of your allegiance to the king?'

'No. Nor do I plan to.'

James cocked his head. 'So that is how it is to be.'

'Yes.' She peered upwards, fearing the return of the terror to warn her against even this rift in her marriage, but the nave appeared as usual.

'Then I am glad Celia will be with you,' James was saying. 'It is good to have someone you trust watching your back. God keep you.' He rose, genuflected, and withdrew.

With his departure, Margaret felt small and alone in the cavernous nave, though the feeling was nothing like her earlier terror. Footsteps behind her made her turn in their direction with dread, but she was relieved to see a tall, gaunt, black-gowned figure emerge from the shadow of a pillar.

'*Benedicite*, Margaret,' Father Francis said, making the sign of the cross in the air before her. 'Our supplicants are fewer with each new horror. I rejoice to see you seeking grace to fortify your soul against the darkness.'

Rising to meet him, she greeted him a little breathlessly.

'I expected you last evening for your reading lesson,' Francis said.

She had forgotten. 'Forgive me. My husband – Roger returned last night.'

Francis pressed his hands to his heart. 'What good news! Oh, my child, I rejoice for you.'

'Yes, yes of course it is good news.'

The priest tilted his head to one side. 'What is wrong?'

She needed practice in hiding her emotions. 'It is difficult to believe that Roger is back. I had given up hope.' Not wishing to explain more, she hurried on with the news of the sheriff's order closing the tavern.

'It seems to me Sir Walter Huntercombe is making much of an old man's death,' said Francis. 'What is one violent death among so many? I would not have expected him to notice.' He studied the floor for a moment. 'It is said that when Sir Walter was told that Mary Brewster had found the old man, he ordered her brought to the castle for a long questioning.'

'Poor Mary.'

'It did not happen. Her screams and foul language dissuaded the soldiers from following orders. An instance of a vile trait protecting the wicked from greater evil.'

'I am glad she saved herself. Why do you call her wicked?'

'I cannot say. Forgive me,' said Francis. 'I did

not mean to trouble you, not when you have such glad tidings. How goes your husband?'

She must put aside her doubts. 'He says he is well, though he has lost much flesh. He speaks of returning to Perth.'

Francis sighed. 'Soon only the English and the clergy will remain in Edinburgh. You will be missed, Margaret. But Perth may be a safer place for you.'

She wondered whether that was true, and whether Roger would stay there with her. He might merely wish her away from Edinburgh. Perhaps he knew of some trouble from which he wished to remove her. Or despite her efforts to conceal her loyalty, guessed it and meant to interfere.

'Margaret?'

She pulled herself from her thoughts.

Father Francis looked concerned. 'How stands it between you and your husband?'

She could not find it in herself to lie to her confessor. 'Awkward. I pray that will pass.'

'Of course it must be difficult.'

Difficult? That was the best she could say of it. 'I am ashamed of myself, Father,' she burst out. 'My husband has returned – it is what I prayed for – and yet all I notice are his faults.' But that was not true. She had wanted him last night. 'I do love him.'

'He has given you much pain. You cannot

expect to forgive him completely as soon as he reappears. Be patient, Margaret. God's grace is more easily gained in times of peace.'

'Do you not have that backwards?'

'Troublous times test one's vows.'

She wondered whether that last part referred to James, how closely they had knelt together on the prie-dieu. But if she denied being James's lover, Father Francis might think she protested out of guilt.

'Roger is your husband before God,' Francis continued. 'You must forgive his past transgressions and pray that he forgives yours.' He blessed her again. 'God go with you, my child.' He continued down the nave.

Margaret felt cheated out of an absolution that she had not realised she wished for. Platitudes, that is all the priest had offered her. Yet it was true that she and Roger had taken their marriage vows before God.

By the time she reached the tavern it was early afternoon. Weary of searching her soul, she sought out her uncle. She was stiff-kneed with tension as the English guard watched her crossing and recrossing the yard. She found her uncle kneading dough in his kitchen while he watched the soldier through a knothole in one of the boards that blocked an unused window. Margaret had not noticed the hole before and wondered whether it was as natural as it looked. In fact it was precisely at the level of her uncle's eyes when he bent over the table to his work, sprinkling some water on the dough. She doubted nature had been so cooperative. On noticing her presence, he straightened.

'God is not smiling on me this day,' he said, his voice gravelly.

'The damp night has gone to your chest,' said Margaret.

'It's shouting at that devil's spawn of a captain all morning that has stolen my voice.' Murdoch bent his knees to peer out of the hole at the guard by the tavern. 'I've a mind to go to the castle and shout some more, but I must needs wait until my pipes are healed.' He straightened and nodded for her to sit down. 'Ale?'

She nodded. 'Are you going to tell me about moving your treasures last night?'

He poured and handed her the tankard. 'No need – I ken you've already been told. Your man Hal, was it?'

'Celia saw you.'

Murdoch frowned down at his hands. 'By St Vigean, I grow too old for this life if I've become so careless.'

'Where did you move them?'

'I'll not tell you. It's best that way.'

'Have the English searched the undercroft?'

'Not yet. But they'll do it soon, I'll warrant.' He returned to the bread dough. 'So Roger has come for you?' he asked, not looking at her.

'He is here, yes, Uncle.'

'And he means to remove you to Perth, eh?' Still he did not make eye contact, but instead picked up the dough, turned it upside down and slapped it back on the table.

'He has mentioned it, and with the tavern closed—'

'Och, it's better that you leave now.' He punched the dough. 'You've no work here and you're better off away from the soldiers.' His thick fingers sank into the sticky mound. 'But Perth, Maggie – if Wallace is there, you'd be safer with James.'

'You and James have marked that. But Roger is my husband.'

'When it suits him.'

She did not know what to say. To admit that she trusted James more than she did her husband seemed tantamount to breaking her vows. 'I have made no decision.'

'Humph. You were looking for an escort just the other day. Women. Never ken their own minds.' He kneaded energetically. 'I've asked Roy to help me with a welcoming supper for Roger. And that servant of his. Celia could use a good meal, too.'

'How long do you think the inn will be closed?'

'For ever, if they win.' He almost choked on the words.

She had feared that. 'What will become of Roy and Geordie now?'

'They have homes to go to. Sim, too. I've no use for them. Hal can manage anything that arises.'

'The close will be so quiet,' Margaret said.

Her uncle straightened and looked at her with a mournful expression. 'It's a great loss to me, the tavern. Angus's tales, the fiddling, the gossip, and of course the trade.' He sighed and punched the dough half-heartedly. 'Damn Longshanks to hell.'

When they had retired to Margaret's bedchamber that evening, Roger brought up the journey to Perth again.

'Are you keen to be home?' she asked, keeping her head averted as if more interested in folding the linen than in the conversation.

'It is you I am thinking about,' said Roger.

'It *would* ease my mind to go to my brother. But are you not just as concerned, hearing that your belongings were searched?' She plunged ahead. 'Or do you know what someone is looking for?'

'By now many know I'm the Bruce's man. Balliol's men, the English, any of them might want to find something to use against me. Or perhaps it's just a common thief, hoping I left something of value.'

'You left precious little of value.'

'I did not mean to cause you pain, Maggie.'

She caught her breath, feeling unprepared for this conversation. 'A common thief would not move on from Perth to Edinburgh to scarch your belongings. Nor would he have passed over the goods stored in the same room as your casket was here.'

Roger crossed over, took the linen from her and set it aside, then drew her into his arms. She kept her own stiffly down by her sides.

'Maggie, Maggie,' Roger whispered, kissing her neck, her ear.

'You did not think of the pain you would cause me,' she whispered. 'You had little thought for me.'

He straightened, looked at her from arm's length, and she cursed herself for pushing him away. His kisses had been sweet. But she could not push away the questions that plagued her, such as the fact that the Brankston story did not explain Roger's connection with Edwina of Carlisle. She knew from others that Roger had brought the woman to Murdoch's tavern before returning to Perth the previous summer, *before* he knew of the Brankston tragedy. But she did not yet know how to broach it.

'Why are you here, Roger? How is it that after all this time you appear a day after someone has gone through the documents stored here, both yours and Da's?'

She stopped, shaking with fear, as if expecting him to hit her again, though last night's slap was the first time he'd ever struck her. But there was something so changed in him, she saw it in the sudden tightening of his face, and the equally quick change of expression to one of wounded affection.

'Oh Maggie, I did not wish to frighten you. Of course I'm concerned about someone searching here, and in Perth. That is why I'm keen to go home. Come now.' He opened his arms once more, and she stepped into them. 'You are shivering. Let's go to bed.'

Shivering. Yes, she was. And his embrace did nothing to quiet her fears, for it was plain to her she knew him less than ever.

6

SO MUCH SADNESS

For a little while, preparing for the celebratory supper, Celia had forgotten about the soldiers in the yard, the crumbling of the life she had begun to enjoy in Edinburgh. Geordie and Hal had set up a trestle table in the largest of the guest rooms in the house beside the tavern and Celia had spent the afternoon cleaning the room, arranging cruisies and candles, and helping Geordie set up. She had been included in the party, as well as Janet Webster and Hal. The seven ate and drank well. Murdoch had conjured three salmon and a large hare for two of the courses. It was more fish and meat than Celia had eaten in any one week, let alone a day, since she'd left Dunfermline. Enjoying herself, she perhaps drank the claret too quickly.

For as the meal wore on she noticed an almost visible, certainly palpable screen of tension around

Roger and Margaret, distancing them from the others at the table. They spoke when others addressed them, and ate, laughed and drank, but they seemed truly aware only of one another, reaching for their shared cup at the same time, then awkwardly apologising, trying to spear the same slice of hare and barely missing the other. No one but Celia seemed to mark it.

When the diners rose from the table, Margaret and Roger moved as one to the door. Celia hurried after, offering to help Margaret. Her mistress blushed a little – or was it a flush from the food and wine? – and said it was not necessary, though Celia might leave a tray with wine and cups outside the chamber door. Celia wished she knew whether or not Margaret was happy about Roger's return, whether she should be reading more into what was said, whether she should be hearing cues to do more than Margaret requested aloud. Certainly the ravages of the previous night visible on her mistress's face this morning had not boded well. But Celia reminded herself that she was ignorant of the marriage bed, of any bedding with a man.

She felt discarded. Hal and Geordie seemed to sense her mood, for they quietly assisted her in the clean-up. When she could find no more to fuss over, she sought out Murdoch in his kitchen. Janet sat by the door that looked out on the maid's cottage.

'Is that where you arc biding?' she asked Celia.

'No, I thought my mistress might need me, so I'm in a room near hers.'

'Someone has been spending time in there.'

Not wishing to anger Murdoch by saying in his presence that the cook and the former chambermaid were meeting there, Celia merely requested the wine for Margaret and Roger.

'What?' Murdoch said, feigning disbelief. 'Had they not enough to warm themselves?'

'Celia has worked long and hard today, Murdoch,' said Janet, 'give her what she needs so she might rest.'

'Humph. You lasses stick together,' Murdoch complained. But he filled a pitcher and set it on a tray with two wooden cups. 'I suppose you'll go with your mistress to Perth.'

'If she wishes me to,' said Celia. So it was settled enough that Murdoch knew of the plan.

'Och, she wishes you to be with her, I'm certain of that,' said Murdoch. 'If I allowed it she'd have Hal with her, too.'

Celia would as lief stay in Edinburgh, but not without Margaret. It cheered her a little to know she was not to be cast aside.

Roger had gone out to relieve himself. Margaret sat on the bed, hugging her chest to still the shivering. But she was conscious of a deep sadness. She had swallowed it all these months, drop by drop of poison, swallowed it all the months of her marriage. She had hidden away so much sadness, hidden it from prying eyes, even from herself. *Blessed Mother, why was I so misled?* She had loved Roger, wanted him, trusted him, and trusted those who had encouraged her with him. But once the wedding was over, they had all withdrawn, leaving her to discover how to exist in a suitable but empty marriage. Even Roger had departed as soon as he could.

The depth of her pain frightened her, as did the knowledge that she had carried this grief unconsciously, convincing herself that she was content, or at least managing to find some contentment in her role. She did not know whether she had ever actually loved him. She was not so innocent as not to know that many women merely tolerated their husbands, but surely she cared for Roger, for she had worried about him all the while he was gone. She must not give in to despair.

Perhaps her benumbed state had been a blessing, a divine gift to help her perform her duties. But then there must be cause for her sudden awakening.

She dropped her hands and took great gulps of air, sucking it deep within, steadying herself. Roger returned with wine and cups.

'Bless Celia,' she whispered.

'She was only doing your bidding,' Roger said. He handed her a cup and sat cross-legged at the foot of the bed. 'Wasn't she my mother's servant?'

'Yes. I've borrowed her over-long. But I've grown to depend on her.'

'Well, we've no need for another servant, nor can we afford one.'

Margaret had not considered parting with Celia. 'I'll discuss it with her.'

'You don't really believe she'll work merely for food and a roof over her head when she might be paid?'

'Your mother paid her until Martinmas. It is only August, so we need not worry until November. And she has gained more by my uncle's pay.'

'We can escort her to Dunfermline on our way north.'

'That would be out of our way. The English control the ferry across the Forth.'

'Celia is not yours to command.'

Margaret tried to bite her tongue, but the thought of losing her one friend compelled her to speak. 'Celia is a great aid and comfort to me. Jonet is caring for both our house and Da's, and she'll need help once we're all there.'

'Celia returns to my mother, Maggie. That is how it must be.' Roger's expression made it clear that he considered the case closed.

His tone angered her. What did this matter to him? He had not been there when Dame Katherine suggested that Celia accompany Margaret. He was using this to avoid more unpleasant subjects.

100

'Listen to us,' she said, controlling her anger, 'arguing about a servant so that we might avoid mention of more painful things. What is to become of us?'

Roger said nothing for a moment, and then rubbed his eyes and dropped his hands to his sides as if weary. 'Is it possible to begin again?'

'I don't know.' Her face suddenly hot with emotion, Margaret fought tears. 'I have understood these past months how far outside my ken you have been and it frightened me.'

'Can man and woman ever understand one another?'

'God help us if we can't. Why would He have made us so?'

Roger stared at the floor, saying nothing. His expression was difficult to read in the flickering light. After a long silence, he asked, 'Why did you remain here after finding Jack's murderer?'

Margaret had hoped for some words of conciliation. 'Because this is where you'd seen me last,' she said, a half truth, though of late not true at all.

'Why else?'

She must not tell him about her work for James. 'Until Fergus's recent letter I dreaded the idea of returning to Perth without you. At least here I was occupied, helping my uncle. The countryside is dangerous as well.'

'You've changed, Maggie.'

'And you.'

He came to sit on the edge of the bed beside her and took her hand. 'Will you go home with me to Perth?'

'Have I not said so?'

'I am asking you anew. Without expectation.'

She feared that her acceptance would end all conversation. That is how it had worked in the past. 'Your mission south from George Brankston's house must have brought you past Perth. Why did you not stop to tell me what had happened? I would have known about Edwina.'

Roger rose up with a muttered curse. 'Will we always be divided by that brave, unfortunate woman?' There was a harsh edge to his voice, and he faced the window, not Margaret.

It was time to confront him. 'You brought her here before you came home to Perth last summer. Uncle Murdoch said you'd brought her here before you returned to me. You're still lying to me, Roger. I don't know which of your stories to believe – looking for another port from which to ship goods, going to Dundee – you might be lying about those, too. And I've never heard you mention the Brankstons.'

'God's blood, woman, what must I do?' he shouted, kicking aside a stool in temper. 'You said we must listen to each other. Then listen!'

'I am listening. But I catch you in lies, I sense you holding things back, and I fear that.' Though

God knew she kept much from him, and lied a little.

'You have nothing to fear from me, I am your husband. If I tell a half truth or hold something back it is for your protection.'

'I believe that ignorance is dangerous in times such as these. What you call protection does not work now.'

He began to speak, then paused, and dropped his head for a moment. Nodding, he looked up, opening his arms in surrender. 'I have made mistakes.'

It was a concession, such as he had never made to her before. She feared pushing him further. 'Then yes, Roger, I shall go home with you.'

They undressed shyly this time, and once in bed merely held one another.

Margaret woke in the night and thought Roger had gone. She sighed and rolled over, then noticed a soft light beyond the bed curtains. Peering through, she found Roger sitting partially clothed, with his head bowed, his elbows resting on his knees, his hands clasped. A lamp flickered beside him on the bench. His posture saddened her, seeming one of defeat.

'Sleep will not come?' she whispered.

He jerked up, startled. 'My candle woke you?'

'No,' she said, sitting up, pulling the cover round her. 'What woke you?'

'The devil torments me at night with thoughts

of what might have been had the Maid of Norway lived, or had Longshanks been honest.'

'Celia could mix you a sleep draught.'

'Perhaps tomorrow.'

'Tell me about where you have been.'

He gave a dispirited laugh. 'On horseback, on foot, in leaking boats, sleeping on uneven, damp ground beneath shedding trees. This room is far more comfortable than anywhere I have slept in a long while. Perhaps that is why I'm wakeful.'

'What of Robert Bruce's household?'

'I am not of his household, so I cannot say. When I have met with him he has looked a landed man, but not grand.'

'Did you see battle?'

'In Ayr it was unavoidable. Percy and Clifford came through in such force that my lords Stewart and Douglas approached them about surrender. Only the Bruce stood firmly against the English. None were great battles. I've yet to see thousands of troops marching towards me.'

Margaret crossed herself at the image he conjured. 'You were willing to die for him?'

'For us, Maggie. It is all for us,' he said wearily as he shrugged off his shirt, blew out the candle, and climbed back on to the bed.

Margaret kissed him on the forehead and opened the blanket to pull him into the warmth. It was a beginning.

*

The next few days were filled with chores that cheered Celia. There was much Margaret wished to set to rights before they left. As Celia helped Margaret plan how to accomplish the work, she watched for changes in her mistress's behaviour, seeking a clue as to whether or not she and Roger were reconciled. Each morning Margaret looked a little more rested, but it was a gradual change. Often Celia heard the murmur of voices when she woke in the night.

After sending a quantity of bedding to the laundress, they began a systematic cleaning and emptying of the guest rooms, Margaret deciding what items should be moved to the undercroft, such as mattresses that would moulder if the rooms were unoccupied for long. The undercroft, lined in stone, was drier.

A few mornings after Roger's arrival they were working in the room across from the one Celia was occupying.

'I am sorry you have been displaced,' said Margaret.

'Truth to tell, the chamber up here is nicer than the maid's cottage where I had thought to stay.'

'Perhaps we can make it even more comfortable.'

'But we're leaving.'

'Surely not for a week or so. There's much to do to prepare.' Margaret stepped across to Celia's room, then returned. 'Another cruisie, I think. Or several.'

When they were finished upstairs, Margaret suggested that they move on to the maid's cottage. 'Janet mentioned that it seems to be in use, that there's bedding and lamps within. Did you ready it and then change your mind?'

Celia knew her mistress's tenacity in unravelling mysteries, so she told her of Roy's meetings with Belle.

Margaret looked embarrassed. 'I had not guessed. Uncle would be furious to hear that they've been meeting in the cottage.'

Celia knew. 'They've been foolish to risk it, but they'll not continue for long . . . Roy started quite a row the other day, telling Belle that with the tavern boarded up he has no occupation, and therefore no choice but to choose a side and arm himself.'

It was sadly true, Margaret thought as they went down the steps. There seemed no occupation but the war at present. Longshanks was not only stealing their country but their livelihoods, their lives. She wondered whether she and Roger might have been happier in better times.

They stood now in the cottage doorway, taking in the rumpled bedding, the chairs and a small table with two cups and a flagon.

Margaret cursed beneath her breath. 'They've been bold enough,' she said. 'I can't think how Murdoch has missed them. Why didn't you tell me of their trespass before?'

'I thought you had worries enough,' Celia said. 'When did you discover it?'

'The night Master Roger arrived.'

Margaret walked in and picked up the cups and flagon. 'Strip the mattress,' she said, 'and remove the lamps. I'll speak to Roy.'

'Do you think they might have heard something the night of Old Will's death?' Celia asked.

'I wish I'd known of their meetings.'

'What is the harm of allowing them what little time together they might yet have?' Celia asked.

'Roy might wish to work here again one day, Celia. Have you thought of that?'

Celia shook her head. She thought it unlikely that Roy would return. She could not imagine a man, once he'd tasted soldiering, wishing to cook again.

Margaret considered sitting out in the yard for a while to enjoy the late-afternoon sun. Since Roger had arrived she'd filled every waking hour with work. But she would just fret about speaking to Roy if she tried to relax before resolving the issue. So she set her shoulders and carried the flagon and cups into the kitchen. She was disappointed to find Geordie alone, looking glum.

'It didn't feel right to leave without tidying the kitchen,' he said.

'Murdoch has told you to go?'

Geordie nodded, his features pulled down by

the weight of his unhappiness with the circumstances.

'What will you do?'

He shrugged. 'Ma says I'm not to get myself killed.'

'Where is Roy?'

'He's meeting with someone about going north to join Wallace's company. He thinks to win Belle's loyalty by taking up the fight. But he's a fool. She won't think of him once he's out of sight. The English soldiers will suit her just as well as he did.'

'So he's gone?'

'We're all gone – Sim hasn't been about since they closed the tavern.'

Margaret would not miss him, but Geordie and Roy had become part of her family.

'I'll miss you.'

Geordie nodded, suddenly shy.

'Geordie, when did Belle and Roy begin meeting in the maid's cottage?'

He shrugged. 'I saw them the night Master Roger arrived.'

'How long had Roy been leaving you alone in the kitchen?'

'Early summer – not so long after their babe was born. But I thought he was seeing Belle at her ma's.'

'If you see Roy, tell him I wish to speak with him.'

Geordie nodded. 'God speed, Dame Margaret. I pray that we meet again in this life.'

Such a chilling prayer. 'God speed, Geordie.' Margaret walked out into the sunshine and lifted her face to the warmth, trying not to think of how final these farewells might be. It was time she had a quiet moment in the warm and fresh air. She sat on the bench outside the kitchen and leaned back against the wall. She wished she'd seen Roy before he left. She doubted Belle would tell her anything. The woman was slippery as an eel.

A TRAP?

Margaret grew drowsy in the sunlight and began to nod, but was roused by the sound of James and her uncle taking leave of one another. James appeared in the yard between her uncle's kitchen and the tavern and headed straight for the archway between the two inn buildings, not bothering to look around. It was then that Margaret noticed there was no English soldier behind the tavern. Thinking perhaps he had withdrawn to a shady spot, she searched the close, but saw no sign of a soldier.

She found her uncle sitting, seemingly napping, near his kitchen fire despite the heat of the day, his bare feet propped on a bench. But as she approached him he said, 'You've tidied all the rooms now, eh?'

'I thought you were asleep.' She glanced

around, thinking the guard might be in here, but her uncle was alone. 'The soldier is gone.'

Murdoch chuckled as he sat up. 'You'll not find him in here.'

'He's not in the yard,' Margaret said.

'He is not.' Murdoch's grin stretched ear to ear.

'What have you done?'

'Made him welcome.'

'If he's not really gone, but he's not in here . . .' Puzzling over her uncle's self-satisfied grin, she settled down beside Agrippa, who was curled into a ball. It did not take long for her to venture, 'You've fed him a barrel of ale?'

Murdoch waggled his head side to side. 'Not quite a barrel. He's lying in the straw on the tavern floor, sleeping it off.' It was evident he was proud of the prank.

Margaret thought him foolhardy. 'You trust that he won't report what you've done?'

'Och, Maggie, it's worth the risk to be free of prying eyes for an afternoon.' He swung his feet down to the floor and stretched his arms overhead.

'I saw James leave. Surely the English already know he is your partner.'

'I've no doubt of that.' Murdoch's voice lilted with delight.

Margaret still did not understand why he thought it worth the risk. 'Why did you need the guard drunk this afternoon?'

'He was to make a list of all the items in the

undercroft. A rare thing, a soldier who can write. I sat down with him to explain the order of things. One drink led to another, and he lay down to rest.'

'You needed time to remove something.'

'James did.' Murdoch's grin soured into a scowl. 'In another day you'll be gone, Maggie. What I do no longer concerns you.'

Margaret shook her head. 'Another day? But there is still so much to do.' Her hands were suddenly cold. 'Has Roger said we leave tomorrow?'

Murdoch nodded solemnly. 'He told Hal to have the horses ready after dark on the morrow.'

'I'd heard nothing of this,' Margaret cried, feeling a confusion of anger and panic. 'I must speak with him. Where is he?'

'He tells me naught, lass.' Murdoch reached out, squeezed her shoulder. 'To delay will not make it easier.'

He used to squeeze her shoulders thus when she had taken a tumble as a child, or been scolded. *Courage, Maggie*, he used to say. She wanted to stay here with him.

'But the laundress has the bedding for washing,' Margaret muttered to herself. 'And we've not discovered who searched the undercroft.' Her pulse pounded in her ears.

'We may never find the intruder. As for the laundry, no one bides here now.' Murdoch's voice sounded as if it came across a great distance.

'*You* bide here,' Margaret said. '*You* need clean bedding.'

'I sleep at Janet's more than I do here. You need not worry about me, lass, or the bedding. It will be delivered whether you're here or no.'

Margaret said nothing, almost choked by bile rising up from her roiling gut.

'Och, Maggie.' Murdoch's hand was suddenly beneath her elbow. 'Sit down, lass.' He led her to a bench. 'You've gone all pale. You can't be with child already – Roger's been here only a few days.'

'No,' she said softly. 'I'm not with child.' *And if I were, what would we do?* She struggled to think clearly. 'Roger said nothing about departing in such haste. I can't—' Could not what? She could not grasp hold of her thoughts. 'It's happening too quickly.'

'You're no stranger to hasty departures, to hear your brother Andrew tell it. According to him, you decided between Jack's funeral Mass and his burial that you would accompany Andrew from Dunfermline to Edinburgh, even knowing he meant to leave as soon as possible.' Murdoch handed her a cup of watered wine. 'Drink that down.'

He was right about her hasty decision to come here. 'But that was different.' Though she could not collect her thoughts sufficiently to explain how. The wine had soothed her stomach but had done nothing for the pounding in her head. 'Why didn't Roger tell me?'

'I'd say he and his man learned today that it must be tomorrow night.' Murdoch took the cup and refilled it.

Margaret refused it. 'My mind's scattered as it is.'

'If I'm right, he'll not change the plan, Maggie. Perhaps he knows that the most careless guards are on duty tomorrow evening.'

'Why must our departure be so planned? Others depart Edinburgh without such thought.'

'Horses don't. Had you not noticed? The English are not keen for us to have mounts, and if Roger is carrying money and documents he'll not wish to draw attention.'

Margaret had not thought of that. 'I should make it clear to Celia how much we risk.'

'You've escorts who ken the perils, Maggie.'

Pressing her cold hands to cheeks that were on fire, Margaret nodded. She was grateful that her uncle had warned her, albeit inadvertently, about her imminent departure before she made a fuss with Roger. They were in a tentative truce, Roger having conceded that Celia would perforce remain with Margaret rather than risk lengthening the journey in order to pass through Dunfermline. She wished to do nothing to change his mind.

'You'll not drink this?' Murdoch asked, still holding the cup of wine.

'No.'

He tipped back his head and emptied the cup in a gulp. 'I'm no happier about this than you are, lass. In a short time I'll be without all that has tempted me out of bed of a morning – the gossip of the tavern, the siller folks pay to bide here, you and all your fussing. I've no purpose of a sudden.'

He looked so sad she searched for something to cheer him. 'You have skills from your smuggling days that our people need, Uncle. You'll still be called upon to board and plunder the English ships anchored off Leith.'

He shrugged, nodded half-heartedly. 'Not often enough to occupy me.'

'And you have Janet.'

'Aye. She's a treasure.' He forced a smile.

Margaret did not trust herself to say much more. 'I must find Celia, ready our packs.' She opened her arms to embrace her uncle. 'I'll miss you more than I can say.'

'And I you, lass.' He gathered her up and kissed her on the cheek.

She almost wept at the familiar scent of him – sea, smoke, sweat, ale, and stable. 'God bless you for all you've done, Uncle.'

'God will bless me for some things, condemn me for others. We'll none of us ken till Judgement Day where we stand with Him.' He stepped back, releasing her. 'Now go, see to Celia. And to James.

He wouldn't take it well to hear you'd gone without a farewell.'

Margaret had forgotten about James. How she wished she were riding to Perth with him. She understood him – he wanted to restore his kinsman to the throne of Scotland. But Roger was a puzzle to her, his allegiance to the Bruce vague and his insistence on a quick departure frightening. Though it had been her idea to return to Perth, now she felt as if she were being wrest away from all she held dear. What had been her journey had become Roger's, and she no longer knew the goal.

Ashen-faced, Celia gazed down at the clothes spread on the bed. 'That one has a stain on the bodice. And there's a tear on the hem of the gown you're wearing.'

Margaret heard the echo of her own confusion in Celia's voice. 'As travellers we'll not be expected to be tidy. Rest a while, and I'll help you later.'

Celia regarded Margaret, her eyes dark beneath the heavy brows. 'I see by your expression this haste is not your doing.'

Margaret told her of her uncle's theory. 'So it is for our own good.'

With an expressive sigh, Celia folded a corner of a gown and sank down on to the space so cleared, her small hands on her knees, studying the plank floor. 'Tell me again what your house is like.'

Celia had never been to Perth. Margaret

recalled how uneasy she had felt as a child travelling to Dunkeld to see her mother's parents. Her keenest memory was how the alien smell of everything made her lose her appetite for a few days. Celia had not been interested in food when they'd first arrived in Edinburgh last spring, and though tiny the maid usually had a healthy appetite.

'Are you certain you wish to come with us?' Margaret asked. 'I've just told you of the danger.'

Celia's thick, dark, almost joined brows bunched beneath her broad, pale forehead. 'I am in danger whenever I encounter a soldier in this town. I think nowhere is safe at present. Tell me about the house. It will give me something pleasant to think about.'

'It's larger and tidier than this, you can be sure,' Margaret said, forcing a smile. 'It is the second house from the market cross, near the river, but not too near. There is a large kitchen in the backland, and two small chambers over the far side of the hall. We have few furnishings, but it is solidly built to withstand the fiercest winds and the hall sits over an undercroft to protect us from the floods.'

'Floods?'

'Sometimes the mountain snows melt so quickly the Tay runs over its banks,' Margaret said. 'But the canals on three sides of the town catch most of the flood to turn the mill wheels and carry barges,' she hastened to add, noting Celia's apprehension. 'And there are water meadows around the town, full of birds.'

'You never want for water, then,' Celia said, with an uncertain laugh.

Margaret thought it better not to speak of how floods might contaminate wells. 'You'll like my friend Ada. She is my mother's age, but nothing like her – she's practical and clever – in faith, she's educated. She was the mistress of a great, generous lord. He bought her the home in which she lives on Northgate and the costliest silks.' She was glad to see Celia's eyes light up at that. 'I have missed her good counsel.'

But the day would soon fade. 'I must see James and Father Francis.' She regretted deserting Celia when the maid needed reassurance, but there was so little time.

James guessed Margaret's errand by her boldness in coming to his home, something she had not risked since Roger's appearance. He was not surprised by her news, understanding the need to depart when the time was right. More interesting was Margaret's distress. She looked ready to burst into tears, or to scream, neither of which he cared to witness.

'It is what you wanted,' he reasoned, offering her a chair.

Margaret ignored his offer, choosing to pace

between the hearth and James, cupping one fist with the other, then reversing, as if warming her hands, though the room was actually stuffy. 'Is it what I wanted, or have I walked into a trap?' As soon as she said it, she pressed a hand to her mouth and shook her head as if arguing with herself. 'I did not mean that.'

'You did, I believe,' said James. 'What has happened?'

She turned away and bowed her head. 'I caught Roger in a lie.'

'I'm sorry.'

'I asked what had happened between here and Dundee last summer.'

James heard with interest Sinclair's tale of the Brankstons, how it was because of them that he'd gone to the aid of Edwina of Carlisle.

'But he'd brought her to Edinburgh before he returned to Perth,' Margaret said. 'Before he knew of the Brankstons' tragedy.'

'Ah. She did come in summer. Did you point that out?'

'He said he tells me "half truths" for my protection.'

James merely nodded. 'I should be able to learn more of the Brankstons for you.'

'You are a good friend. I wish . . .' She stopped. 'I'm making little sense. I decided to leave Edinburgh without thinking how I would miss my uncle. I might never see him again.'

James found it an odd shift in subject, but Margaret was overwrought. 'If it is any comfort, I'll shortly be travelling north. I've been summoned by Wallace. He's meeting me near Perth. I'll find a way to get word to you about how you might find me if you need to.'

James had expected Margaret to look relieved, but she disappointed him. She groaned as she halted a few paces from him and her eyes were dark with tears.

'I counted on you to watch after Uncle Murdoch.' The last word caught in her throat.

'Your uncle is his own man,' James reminded her. 'I have no influence over him. And you'd get little thanks from him for assigning me as his caretaker. You should not worry about him.'

'But of course I'll worry about him.' Her voice was almost shrill. 'He's not a young man.'

'Calm yourself, Margaret.' James set the chair behind her, put his hands on her shoulders, and pressed her down on to it. He felt the heat of her agitation through the thin cloth of her summer gown.

Margaret folded into herself, wrapping her arms about her middle. 'God help me, my mind is full of such noise I cannot hear my thoughts.'

'You must take some ease.' Calling his servant, James ordered watered wine. He often forgot these days how young Margaret was, not yet twenty, and as the daughter of a merchant brought up to marry a merchant her background had ill-prepared her for her role in this contest of kings. As a Comyn he'd been born with a taste and a stomach for intrigue. His sister Eleanor could outwit the craftiest courtier. It was in their blood, and feuds between families had been their bedtime stories.

The servant delivered the wine and was dismissed. Crouching before Margaret, James offered her the cup. 'You have a long journey ahead of you, exhausting enough without the added torment of worries and regrets about those you've left behind. Our king needs you to hear what he cannot be there to hear himself. He needs you alert and calm to observe all that happens in Perth.'

Her eyes were barely focused. He repeated some of his little speech and added that Wallace and Murray were pleased with their success in forcing the English from the north and once pushed south-east from Dundee they would make a more manageable target. Gradually she breathed more evenly and her eyes cleared. He admired how she fought to regain her composure.

'Forgive my outburst.' She took the cup in both hands.

James moved over to the fire and fussed with it, giving her some solitude. He congratulated himself on insinuating himself into her life in Perth by calling on her duty to John Balliol, though in truth he doubted that the townsfolk would confide in her. They would be wary of Roger, whose business and whereabouts must have been the subject of much gossip the past year, and of Margaret, too. But he intended to see her once they were up north in order to plant the suggestion that she discover for Balliol whether he was the rightful king in Dame Christiana's vision.

With a rustle of her skirts, Margaret joined him at the fire.

'What do you think Uncle Murdoch will do now?' she asked, her voice not quite down to its customary timbre.

'I know not his mind,' James said. 'Rest a while longer, Margaret. You are not yet at ease.'

'There will be little ease for me until I am settled in Perth. And even then, what peace might we enjoy?' She surprised him by slipping a long-fingered hand in his and looking him in the eyes. 'We shall win back our land, James. God is on our side.'

'May He watch over you on your journey, Margaret.' He lifted her hand to his lips, kissed it. He could not read her expression as she looked on him for a brief moment, but he saw her blush before she withdrew her hand and turned away. He should not have been so bold. But it was she who offered her hand.

'I'm able to hear my thoughts now,' she said, with a weak laugh. 'God speed, James.' She hurried out as if devil dogs were snapping at her heels.

James thought it would be interesting to meet with Margaret in Perth and see how she fared. He suspected she would be as much a puzzle to her husband as she was to him.

Margaret found Father Francis sitting outside St Giles, watching children taking turns riding a toy wagon down the steep wynd that led to Cowgate.

'It's good to see them playing,' said the priest, 'yet I watch and worry that some soldier will find fault with their game and beat them.' He shook his head and turned to her.

'Have the soldiers done such a thing?' she asked.

'Forgive me – I see you are already troubled, and I am adding to your anguish. What is it, Margaret?'

She watched a cloud's shadow move slowly across the twin peaks of Arthur's Seat south-east of Holyrood Abbey as she told Francis of her imminent departure. 'I am anxious, and a little afraid.'

'A journey is a perilous undertaking in these times, but you are on the right path, returning to your home in the protection of your husband.'

Margaret thought of the fear that had gripped her in the kirk.

'Perhaps someone in Perth will help you with your reading and writing,' Francis said. 'Is Roger impressed with your letters?'

'There has been no time to boast,' she said. 'In truth, I may keep it a secret for the time being. We may be husband and wife, but I do not share his allegiance.' Although her reading ability was meagre, a few words from a letter carelessly left out might prove useful. Her stomach fluttered to think of spying on Roger, but she must.

Father Francis nodded solemnly. 'I had almost forgotten that your husband is Robert Bruce's man.' He paused, shaking his head. 'It seems a long while since that morning months ago when I escorted you to the abbey to bid your brother farewell – it disheartened me. I brooded on Father Andrew's plight for a long while. Too long. It ate into my soul that an abbot should so use one of his own. It left me hollow, despairing.' The late-afternoon sun gave his bony, hawk-nosed face a rose glow and coloured the shadows beneath his eyes and in the hollows of his cheeks a bruised purple. 'At least Roger is fighting for our people, not for the English tyrant.'

They talked a little more as the afternoon shadows grew long. She spoke of her fears for Andrew, and Father Francis assured her that if he heard anything regarding him he would get word to her. The children had quit their game by the time Margaret bade him farewell and headed down High Street to the tavern.

As she passed beneath the archway connecting the inn's two buildings she heard unfamiliar voices coming from the house to the right, seemingly from Murdoch's undercroft. Roger sat across the way, at the foot of the steps to their chamber, apparently asleep, but as soon as he heard her footstep in the yard he rose and, taking her firmly by the arm and pressing a finger to her lips, hurried her up the stairs saying nothing until he had drawn the bolt on the door.

'The English are searching the undercroft.' He crossed the room, closed the shutters, lit a lamp.

Murdoch's respite had been brief.

Roger stood tensed, as if ready to spring at an intruder. It frightened Margaret.

'Where is Uncle?'

'He's down there assisting the English in their search.'

'Perhaps I should go to him.'

Taking her by the shoulder, Roger bent close. 'We shall suffer this in silence, give them no reason to notice us.'

'Why are they here now?' Margaret whispered, imagining an ear pressed to the door. 'Could they know about our departure?'

'I pray God they don't.' Roger let her go, sat down beside the lamp.

Margaret put some space between them, settling on the edge of the bed.

'Your uncle plays dangerous games,' Roger said in a more normal voice. 'He did not wake the guard in time for his relief. So now there will be more guards.'

'What are we to do?'

'As long as the English leave by the curfew, we can still depart without bloodshed.'

Margaret gasped. 'You would fight our way out of the town?'

'If necessary.'

'Perhaps if we delay they will grow weary of watching an empty tavern.'

Roger seemed a stranger, sitting back, looking at her with an expression she could not decipher. 'We risk our own people if our plans miscarry now, Maggie.'

'There are others leaving with us?'

'Meeting us. To assist us on the way.'

She nodded and studied her hands, embarrassed to have thought they were going quietly, peacefully to leave town with no one the wiser. 'How long have the English been with Uncle?'

'Not long.'

'Where is Celia?' It was unusual for her not to have checked by now whether Margaret needed anything.

'In your uncle's kitchen. What do you know of the night the old man died in the alley?'

'Why are you asking about that now? What is Celia doing there?'

'She kindly offered to take Murdoch's place

preparing a meal. I'm curious why the English are so bothered by the old man's death.'

'I have wondered that too, but I can't think why they are.'

Noises from the yard brought them both to their feet.

'I believe it's Bonny and the wagon,' Margaret said. 'They wouldn't take Murdoch's donkey, would they?'

'They might do whatever they please,' Roger said. 'Slip out on to the landing, see whether it's as you say.'

Pulling back the bolt, she stole out, through the suddenly menacing entryway. She began to crouch down to look over the railing, but if someone were to look up she would attract far more attention in such a posture than merely leaning out, innocently curious about what was happening. There were several armed men in the yard, surrounding a wagon. Roger's horse was harnessed in front, and Aylmer's was tethered behind. Several men appeared in the undercroft doorway, carrying barrels. They had obviously found items that they considered suspicious or too good for a Scot. Margaret hurried back to the room, fearful what Roger would do and yet knowing how precious the horses were.

'They have your horses, not Bonny. You must do something.'

Roger stretched out his legs. 'They would like

that. We'll do nothing, or rather play cowards.' He smiled at her disbelief. 'Games, Maggie. We must know which ones to avoid.'

'We'll find no horses to replace them. Nor donkeys.'

'That is what they believe.'

'Where do you think to find some?'

He rose and came to her, pulled her into his arms. 'All is going according to plan, Maggie. You must believe me. Now tell me all you know about the night Old Will was murdered.'

❧ 8 ❧

A MAN OF QUESTIONS

After the evening meal Margaret slipped away to
the stable. Bonny whinnied softly, as if wary of
enemy ears, and pressed her muzzle to Margaret's
apron until she found the summer apple in the
fold. Hal sat up in his sleeping loft picking at his
meal, with Agrippa stretched out beside him, chin
near the trencher, awaiting his turn.

Margaret hoisted her skirts and climbed up to
join them. One of the things she appreciated about
Hal was that he knew the value of quiet companionship, of speaking only when necessary.

'I need to think,' she said.

Hal nodded and resumed picking at the food.

There would be no solitude once the party set
out, and to wander away from the others would be
reckless. Yet the journey itself being dangerous,
perhaps she would risk it now and then – if Roger

let down his vigilance. He had tonight, so perhaps she should not worry.

His interrogation this afternoon had her wondering what his real purpose was in reuniting with her, and why he was in such haste to take her to Perth. He had framed question after question, leading her to repeat every which way all she remembered of the night of Old Will's murder.

'Why are you so keen to know every thought I had that evening?' she'd demanded towards the end, her head aching from being dragged through her memories of that evening over and over again. Her guilt about the condition in which Old Will had departed the tavern was already a canker in her stomach, she did not need such a reminder. 'Why does this trouble you so much?'

'The person who killed him searched my casket, my store of personal documents.'

That she was trying his patience he left unsaid, but she heard it in his voice, saw it in his eyes. As if he could be unaware of how he was trying hers.

'I wish I had noticed more,' Margaret said. 'Indeed I wish it had never happened. But I've told you everything I know, several times.'

'Why did your uncle allow the old man to drink even when he had no way to pay?'

'He didn't always allow it, but some nights he would say Old Will had suffered enough and deserved some Christian charity.'

'What had he suffered?'

130

'I've told you, I'm sure of it.'

'One more time, Maggie, I pray you.'

'He and his wife had been atop Arthur's Seat, watching a great ship being guided into Leith port. Though the sky had been blue while they climbed, it had begun to rain. They slipped while climbing down, she to her death, he to a long sleep, from which he woke into a life of bitter mourning.'

'How long ago?'

'About seven years.'

'What did he gain by her death?'

It was the second time Roger had asked that.

'I've told you, nothing. All was given to the kin who took in the children.'

Now the question haunted her.

'Do you remember Old Will's wife?' she asked Hal.

He tore a piece off the trencher and set it before Agrippa. The cat rose, pressed back in a stretch, and then sniffed. Intrigued, he settled down to eat.

'I never spoke to Dame Bess, but I saw her in the kirk, and at the market sometimes.'

'What was the first thing you'd notice?'

'Her smile. She lit up. Her eyes, too.'

'Pretty, then?'

Hal shrugged, considered the plank on which he sat. 'I liked to see her. She could sing, too, her voice carrying far. I think she must have been bonny.'

'When she died, what was the gossip?'

'I didn't pay much heed. Except people said that when Will woke he discovered he'd lost everything.'

'You mean his wife.'

'It seemed like everything. When kin came for his children they took what was left to support them. They'd expected more and accused the townsfolk of helping themselves to his goods. They were greedy. But even so stripped of property, even to the stock in his shop, Will wouldn't go with his children.'

'Did anyone ever prove that property had been stolen?'

'If they did, I never heard of it.'

Margaret was saddened that she'd never bothered to learn just how much Will had suffered. 'All because he'd lost his wits.'

'And made sure they'd not return, drinking like he did.'

'That began at once?'

Hal nodded as he peered up at her through the straight lock of pale hair that fell over his eyes. 'You were never so curious about him before.'

'No. But Roger is.'

Hal nodded again. 'He's a man of questions.'

'He's questioned you?'

'He went away thinking I'm simple.' A corner of his mouth twitched.

'He hasn't looked into your eyes.'

'No.' Hal broke off another piece for Agrippa. 'You'll be gey glad to see your home.'

'Yes, but so much might happen between here and home.' At the risk of embarrassing Hal, she said, 'I did ask Uncle to give you leave to come with me. He refused.'

Hal did not respond at once, keeping his gaze on Agrippa.

Margaret was about to apologise for bringing it up.

'Then he must have need of me,' Hal said quietly. He glanced up at her, his young face solemn. 'I'll miss you.'

'And I you.' Margaret touched his hand, and both smiled a little.

Her uncle had responded to the confiscation of goods with a calm that Margaret interpreted as his having manipulated the soldiers or the situation in some way. She wished she could find Janet alone before she left. Margaret would believe her if she said that her uncle would be fine. It would be good to know that.

She did not notice Aylmer standing below until Agrippa growled and moved deeper into the loft.

'Boy! Have you seen Dame Margaret?' the moon-faced servant asked, though Margaret had noticed how he boldly looked from one to the other.

'Did your previous master accept discourtesy?' she asked.

'Forgive me – I do not see so well in the dark.'

Hal grunted. Margaret touched his hand.

'Nevertheless, turn round while I lift my skirts to climb down.' To Hal she whispered, 'I'll leave you in peace.'

Once on the ground, she ignored Aylmer and went straight to her chamber. He followed, but stopped at the bottom of the stairs. She felt him watching her.

Roger was dozing on the bed.

'What was of such importance?' she demanded.

Waking, he joined her at the small table in their chamber, where she had already helped herself from a flagon of wine. He swore he had not sent for her, and filled his own cup with an impatience that sent wine splashing on his shirt.

'We've no time to launder that,' Margaret warned.

'It doesn't matter, Maggie. What does matter is that I did not send Aylmer to fetch you. How dare he insinuate . . . I knew where you were, I know of your friendship with the groom. I'll speak with him in the morning. Christ, I should have found my own man.'

'You could hardly have refused such a gift from your lord,' Margaret noted.

Roger nodded absently. 'He's not to my liking, and I sensed it from the first.' He leaned over and tucked a stray hair into her veil, his hand lingering on her cheek. 'I pray you, forgive me for this afternoon. I kept hoping that you would recall something more.'

'Perhaps you've been too long away from gentle companions, ones who mean you no harm.' Roger's fury at Aylmer had cooled Margaret's own anger. She touched his cheek in turn. 'Let us leave Longshanks and the troubles outside the door tonight.'

Roger caught her hand and kissed the palm.

Recalling James's earlier kiss, Margaret blushed, thinking how much like this kiss it had seemed. And both times it was she who had proffered her hand.

Roger pushed away from the table and rose to bolt the door. 'The English and all the world but you and I are locked out, I swear.' He leaned down and scooped her up in his arms. 'I love you, Maggie Kerr. I pray you never doubt me again.'

She felt light-headed as he carried her to the bed. Tonight he was all gentleness and consideration. Margaret felt deliciously wanton, and luxuriated in the role. Much later she fell asleep satisfied.

James was puzzled. It was noon of the day Roger Sinclair meant to depart and he had not come to James about replacements for his horses. Surely Murdoch would have mentioned that James kept a well-guarded stable in the countryside. He'd expected Sinclair and his manservant to come to him about a trade, and when James sent them away that they would resort to thieving. But they had not come. It made James uneasy to be so wrong about Sinclair's behaviour. If the Bruce were supplying reinforcements, if Sinclair had access to horses gathered for the cause, then this was no personal journey on which he was embarking. James recalled Margaret's concern that it was a trap.

What did Sinclair want? He was rushing Margaret to Perth. That meant he was not hoping to spy on her work for Balliol, because he would best do that here. He might know Wallace was at Kinclaven, but Margaret could not ride there alone, and she would never be such a fool as to accept Sinclair or his man as an escort. It was possible that James was quite wrong about Sinclair's motives; the man might be dipping his hand into his lord's purse to mend his marriage.

But that was the behaviour of a desperate man, and Sinclair did not seem desperate.

Perhaps his goal was the same as James's – to speak to Christiana MacFarlane, the seer. If James told Margaret he suspected this, she might confront Sinclair. Such a confrontation might prove interesting, even entertaining, but James saw no potential for gain in it. In any case, as a cohort he should share his thoughts with Margaret. Though they might make her feel newly betrayed she should be warned. He sent his man with a message

136

for her, if he could deliver it discreetly, that his master had something important to tell her, and to come if she could, or send word where he might find her.

Margaret and Roger walked along a cow path that wound through the countryside south of the town. For a while now she had felt a constriction in her chest that made breathing difficult, slowing her. The early afternoon sun beat down on them, and the crag along which Edinburgh stretched was blocking the breezes from the firth. Margaret's obsession was that in packing she had forgotten something of great importance, something that might make the difference between life and death on the journey. She tried to recall all that she and Celia had planned.

Roger had paused to look back at her. 'Why such a frown?' Sunlight picked out the grey strands in his hair as he took off his cap and used it to blot the sweat from the back of his neck. 'Is it the heat? We'll soon have the wind off the loch to cool us.'

'You gave me little chance to say a proper farewell to Janet and forced me to abandon Celia on such a busy day. Shame on you, Roger Sinclair. You've reverted to the tyrant I believed you'd left behind.' She turned away from him, hiding tears.

'I did it for you, Maggie. I could see how you were dreading tonight, and so I schemed to steal away with you so that we might enjoy the day, just the two of us, before we join the others.'

'There was yet much to do.'

'Celia seems able, as is Aylmer. My condemnation of his behaviour last evening has made him have more care with me. They are our servants, Maggie.'

'I cannot help my worry.'

Margaret had gone to Janet Webster's house, at her request, to say farewell but mostly hoping to be reassured that her uncle would be left in loving hands.

'What a woebegone countenance I see,' Janet had said. 'Aren't you happy to have Roger by your side? You came here all those many months ago searching for him, fearing he might be in a grave you'd never see.'

'God has smiled down on me, Janet, and I am grateful. My grief is in leaving all of you. You've been a good friend to me. Uncle, Hal, Father Francis, Roy and Geordie . . .'

'And the Comyn?' Janet had turned away from her loom and quirked an eyebrow at Margaret.

'Yes, I don't deny it. But not for the reason you're suggesting.'

Janet waggled her head and picked up the shuttle. 'You're young, Maggie, and you have a taste for the company of men, and they you. It is nothing to blush about.'

Margaret changed the subject. 'Roger has asked

over and over about how Old Will's Bess died. He's disappointed that I have only the barest details of the accident.'

'You're fishing for gossip?' Janet continued to work the shuttle across the cloth. 'For shame, Maggie!' A dimple in her cheek reassured Margaret that her friend was teasing.

'I'm not proud of it, but he is so curious.'

'Why?'

'He says he's looking for anything that might explain what happened the night Old Will died.'

'He *says*. What do you think?'

'It's no secret that I have much to learn about my husband. But he has me wanting to hear more about what happened to Bess.' Margaret laughed self-consciously, though it was true. She told Janet what she knew of the tragedy.

'There's little more to know, it being only the two of them on Arthur's Seat. What folk suspected was more interesting. Bess was much younger than Will was, so there was talk of his pushing her in a jealous fit. Most of us could not believe he'd do that, so in love with her as he was. And she with him, if you ask me. He was a vigorous man with a heavenly voice, no matter his age. When they sang together . . .' Janet shook her head. 'It was a blessed thing to hear.'

'So it was an accident.'

'I say so. Unless they were not as they seemed.' Janet used the weaving sword to pat down the weft along the warp. 'I often wonder about the children. They were lovely bairns. It was fortunate that kin came at once, took them in, but to lose both parents so.' She sighed. 'It must have changed them.'

'The kin came at once? Before Old Will woke?'

Janet shook a teasing finger at Margaret. 'You'll find no guilt with them. His sister sat with him throughout his faint, and tried to arrange things so he might have the children with him. But he dived into a bowl of ale and went into rages whenever someone poured him out.' She wiped her hands, set the shuttle in the wool. 'Would you like to see Tess's wean?' She was very attached to her first grandchild. 'They're in the kitchen.'

It was while they'd been playing with the baby that Roger came for Margaret.

'I'll take good care of your uncle,' Janet had said as she hugged Margaret. 'And I'll pray for you.'

At least Margaret need not worry about Uncle Murdoch. In fact Roger's explanation of why he'd interrupted her preparations to bring her out at midday had cheered her enough that she'd begun to look about her. It *was* good to be out in the countryside in such fine weather, alone with the husband she had yearned for.

'Here we join the loch path,' Roger said, sounding gay and relaxed. The path forked, one following along the north and one the south side of Burgh Loch. Roger led them south.

Margaret lifted her chin and smiled. 'A blessed

breeze.' A welcome coolness kissed her hot forehead.

Roger glanced back. 'Do you forgive me?'

'I think I must.' Margaret caught up with Roger
and slipped her hand in his. 'I cannot fault your
intention.'

She led him to a warm rock on which they sat
arm in arm. In time they turned to one another and
kissed long and passionately, and then, agreeing
that they were too exposed in a countryside full of
spies, they retreated from the sun-baked rock to
make love in its shadow. They whiled away the
afternoon talking and lovemaking.

'Tell me of the west country where you fought
for the Bruce,' Margaret said.

'Much of it is very like the countryside around
Perth, with good pasture as well as bogs – it is
rainier than here, and a braw wind blows all the
day. The coast is rocky and treacherous though the
bays are inviting.'

'What of the Bruce? Does he look like a king?'

Roger shrugged. 'He looks a noble, with high
forehead and long, narrow nose, sharp-boned of
cheek and chin. He has a pleasant voice and a
ready laugh.'

Margaret spoke of Dunfermline and the altar
cloth she'd worked on with his mother, trying to
speak of pleasant activities and not **her constant**
worry. They lingered there until Margaret
remembered the long walk back to the town.

'I'd thought of that,' said Roger. 'I told Aylmer to meet us out here this even.'

Margaret felt a twinge of alarm. 'You said nothing of this. I never would have agreed. I must help Celia.'

'No. We'll call attention to ourselves. It is enough that our servants must sneak past guards tonight. You must understand, Maggie.'

She could, but she didn't like it. 'You might have explained that back in town.'

'You cannot mean that you haven't enjoyed our afternoon together, eh?' He reached over, gently stroking her cheek. 'My bonny Maggie.' His eyes were soft with love.

'I've had much joy in you here,' Margaret admitted. Yet she was uneasy. 'Why did you not tell me we were not returning to town?'

'I feared you would refuse me,' said Roger.

She felt queasy to have been tricked and changed the subject to lighter things.

James's servant returned with the news of Margaret and Roger's early departure.

'Their servants will follow tonight, like pack horses,' he said.

'Who told you this?'

'Celia, Dame Margaret's maid. She is troubled about her mistress going on ahead. She distrusts the master, I think.'

James, too, was troubled. 'Was she given any reason for the change of plan?'

'An opportunity for husband and wife to spend a day alone.' The servant waggled his thick eyebrows.

'What of the loss of horses?'

'She's been reassured she won't need to carry the packs all the journey, but knows not what it means.'

James was certain now that Sinclair was manipulating Margaret. But he could only conjecture why.

Celia was uneasy. Proud of her abilities as a lady's maid, she had little fear she would forget anything that she and her mistress would need. What she disliked was Roger's power over Margaret, or his use of it. A husband was the master of his household, but a good one sought his wife's willing cooperation. It did not bode well. And she dreaded breaking the news of Margaret's early departure to Hal. She dreaded no less beginning the journey alone with Aylmer.

To distract herself, she took some time to visit Mary Brewster, knowing that Margaret had hoped to learn more about Old Will's tragedy. If there was anyone in Edinburgh who knew Old Will, it was Mary.

The elderly woman stood defensively in her doorway, as if expecting Celia to force her aside

143

and enter the house. 'I've had naught but trouble about Will since I found him lying in his own blood,' Mary said. 'I'll speak no more of him.'

Her daughter Belle reached past Mary and closed the door firmly in Celia's face.

Cursing her, Celia headed towards St Giles, thinking Father Francis might tell her more. But it occurred to her that there was scant point in any of this as they were about to depart Edinburgh and, conscious of her responsibility, Celia returned to the inn to complete the preparations. She expected Aylmer to complain about the three packs she had him carry down from Margaret's bedchamber, but he had already engaged Geordie and Hal to help them as far as the horses which would await them somewhere to the south of town. At least she had been spared the task of telling Hal about the change in plans. It was small consolation.

As evening settled over the valley and the fading sun no longer warmed her, Margaret asked where they were to wait for the others.

'In a house nearby.' Roger rose, then offered her a hand to help her up. 'We'll find food there. I made sure of it.'

He embraced her and gave her a lingering kiss. 'I love you, Maggie. Never doubt it.'

Margaret hated to let go of him, fearing that the moment they resumed their journey the magic of the afternoon would dissipate and only her misgivings would remain.

'Come,' he said. 'We don't want to linger so long we'll not be able to see the path.'

He led Margaret around the loch to the south end, and off the main path on to one less travelled. They had not gone far when a noise in the brush behind them made both stop. Roger pressed down on her shoulder and she crouched. He stepped between her and the sound, shielding her, watching the brush. At last a raven hopped out of the underbrush, cocking an eye at them.

Margaret crossed herself and rose, grateful for Roger's protective stance, and for the outcome. And yet a raven cocking an eye at them seemed a dark omen. The peace of the past hours had been shattered and she walked now in wariness, reminded that she accompanied a man who had hidden from her in Edinburgh last spring so she would not be troubled by the English.

'How is it you were able to come to me openly now, when you couldn't in spring?' she asked.

'The beard, and sufficient time and trouble between then and now. Others have become greater threats than me.'

'Does your side consider the supporters of King John your enemies?'

'You mean Wallace's and Murray's men?' Roger took a few more steps before going on, seeming to search the trees at the edge of the wooded area they were approaching. 'We might brawl after too much drink. The worst we might do is steal their supplies and horse.' He put an arm round her. 'So many questions, Maggie. When did you become so curious?'

'I was ever so.' She left it at that. She was hungry, tired, and discouraged to think they would journey through the night.

Still he searched the tree line.

'What is it?' she asked.

'I don't see the escort who was to await us.'

A rustle in the bracken reminded her of the raven, and she crouched before Roger told her to.

Quietly he said, 'Who goes there?'

A lad rose from the scrub three strides from them, holding up a rabbit. ''Tis only me, sir, come to lead you. And this beast happened to join me in my hiding place.' He was a dirty, skinny boy no more than twelve, Margaret guessed, barefoot and dressed in tatters.

'Then lead on, Daniel.'

As they followed the boy, Margaret commented to Roger, 'He wears rags. Do you pay your guides nothing?'

'This is his disguise. If you had come upon him accidentally, would you not have believed he was just a starving lad hunting?'

'I would,' Margaret said, comforted and yet perversely uneasy about Roger's thorough planning.

They wound their way in amongst the trees,

over decaying stumps and thick, twisted roots, Roger always there with a supporting hand or arm whenever Margaret felt unsteady. Although he'd required an escort, he seemed to have far less trouble following in the lad's footsteps than did Margaret. In the midst of the tangled wood a tiny house appeared. It seemed almost an illusion it blended so with the trees, built of logs with a roof spread with the mulch of leaves and moss. Within, a small hearth fire burned and a meal was already spread for more than two.

'Where are the horses?' Roger asked the lad.

'Just beyond, in the shed,' said Daniel.

'And the others?'

'Seeing to the beasts, fetching water. They had trouble and came late.'

'What sort of trouble?'

'An ambitious soldier thought to gain horses for the castle sheriff.'

'What happened?'

'He fell down a terrible steep embankment, I'm told.'

The indifference with which the boy told the tale chilled Margaret. 'How old are you?' she asked.

The lad shrugged. 'Old enough to hate the English.' He grinned, showing black teeth.

She wondered why Roger took the risk of trusting such a lad.

*

Murdoch, Aylmer, Geordie, Hal and Celia said little as they sat around a table in the tavern eating the evening meal. Murdoch had requested the guards' permission to take their meal in the tavern, hoping that they would ascribe any suspicious activities later in the evening to drunkenness.

Celia tried to eat, knowing she needed nourishment for the journey, but her stomach was taut with fear and anxiety. Earlier, after thrice reviewing her preparations, she'd taken out her paternoster beads and said several rosaries but she seemed beyond divine help.

Hal and Geordie discussed various strategies for carrying the packs, Aylmer listening to them with an amused detachment that Celia found irritating. Who did he think he was, to be so condescending towards fellow servants? And yet she had been much like that when she'd first come to Edinburgh, determined to be a lady's maid, trying to avoid work that would toughen the fine, smooth hands she had pampered in Dame Katherine's employ so that she might handle the most delicate silks.

Murdoch was solemn when towards midnight they gathered in the stable. 'I'd come along, but someone must be here to divert any unexpected attention.' Fortunately, suspecting nothing, the guards had departed at curfew.

'I know my master would wish me to thank you for all you've done,' said Aylmer. 'We'll have a scout escort Hal and Geordie home once we've transferred the packs.'

Celia held out a hand to Murdoch, but he stepped forward and embraced her.

'You're a brave lass and a good friend to go with Maggie,' he whispered. 'God watch over you.'

She clung to him and fought tears. 'God go with you in all your work,' she said.

Hal and Geordie had arranged packs on Bonny and hoisted others. In a surprising last-minute gesture, Murdoch had loaned her to the travellers so that more food might be taken.

'You'll see your men and your beast before dawn,' Aylmer assured him one last time.

Four men had joined Margaret and Roger for the evening meal. They were introduced as another of the Bruce's men and a merchant who had done business in Ayr, both with their servants, all heading east and glad of more company. Unlike Aylmer, their servants seemed of humbler stations than their masters. Roger did not know the Bruce's man, Macrath, but the merchant Alan was an old acquaintance. The latter was tall, grey of hair and slender to such a degree that he seemed ill, yet he was of good cheer and had an excellent appetite. He was also the most gregarious at the table, with tales of the challenges of trading in the present conditions. He reminded Margaret of Angus MacLaren, another embellisher of tales. Macrath was a short, muscular man with thick dark hair and a beard. He watched and listened, occasionally laughing with the others, but speaking only in monosyllables when he could not maintain his silence.

Watching and listening herself, Margaret compared Roger's behaviour in this rough hut to the few times she'd witnessed his meetings with merchants in Perth. He'd become easier in his posture, muted in his speech; sure of himself yet wary, even in this company. Perhaps she was tired and overwrought, but he seemed even more of a stranger than the day he'd come to her in Edinburgh.

9

A DEATH OF SOUL

By the time the packs had been unloaded it was long after midnight. Margaret had been surprised that Aylmer and Celia were accompanied by Hal, Geordie, and particularly her uncle's beloved Bonny. The loan of the ass touched her as a gesture of affection, though it was painful to bid farewell to the beast and Hal once more. She stroked Bonny while she fed her an apple.

Hal avoided eye contact until Daniel announced he was ready to lead the three back to Edinburgh. He glanced up then and met her eyes. Margaret took his hand and pressed it. He nodded once, wished her God speed, and then ducked out through the door of the small house into the night. Geordie bobbed his head to her and wished her a safe journey. She said the same to him.

Celia shaded her eyes. 'It was so dark without,

I thought we could not make our way, but after a time I came to see more clearly. Now the light in here seems too bright.' She forced a little laugh.

'At least you'll be riding for a good part of the night with your horse following the leader,' Roger said. 'It will not be as difficult.'

Remembering Celia's inexperience with a horse, Margaret imagined her discomfort and invited her to sit beside her. The maid's first and only experience on a horse had been the crossing to Edinburgh. Although she'd sat her steed with grim fortitude, she had been in agony for days afterwards.

Margaret did not like the plan. 'Is that safe, riding at night? Should we not lead the horses?'

'They are accustomed to night riding,' said Roger.

Macrath offered Celia a cup of warm ale. 'You'll be chilly from the walk in the damp.'

'I am. God bless you.' Celia glanced at Margaret as if wondering at such behaviour towards a servant.

Though Margaret was a decade younger than her maid she was responsible for her well-being. She had noticed Macrath studying Celia from the moment she arrived. Perhaps he thought them kin, with their similarly pale complexions, thick dark brows and short builds. His offering her the ale was a small gesture, but Margaret would watch Macrath for signs of designs on Celia.

Eventually the men went out to ready the horses, giving the two women some time alone.

'We will need to ride slowly,' Margaret said, 'so it should be less uncomfortable than your last journey, when my brother Andrew was in such haste.'

Celia arranged her skirt. 'I regret only that I took no opportunity to ride in Edinburgh.'

Margaret smiled at Celia's stubborn dignity – there had been no opportunity for her to ride in Edinburgh, except on Bonny, who rode quite differently from a horse. 'You managed so well before, you'll find it quite familiar, I'm sure.'

Celia's dark brows knitted together as she solemnly nodded. 'Let us speak of something other than my coming humiliation. Had you time with Dame Janet?'

'Yes, but I learned nothing useful from her,' Margaret said. 'Old Will and Bess were by her account a loving couple.'

'I approached Mary Brewster for you today, but she said she's had naught but trouble since finding Old Will, and then Belle slammed the door on me.'

'How unlike Mary,' Margaret said.

'I found it so,' said Celia. 'Not even the town gossip wants to be of interest to the English. I wish I came with better news.'

'You were good to attempt it.' Margaret cursed Roger for all the questions that had opened up this new avenue of possibilities, only

153

to have him rush her away. 'How did you leave my uncle?'

'Unhappy. You'll be missed, have no doubt of that.'

'It's not only myself he'll miss, but the companionship of his customers. He'll have only Janet now. And Hal.' They grew quiet, and in a little while Margaret felt herself begin to nod. 'I need occupation. Shall we review what we've brought?'

The party departed in the dark of the summer night, a slow procession of riders following Macrath's lead. Margaret was glad of the great beast beneath her, both for his warmth and the physical contact with something real, solid, alive; the countryside at night seemed an echoing emptiness, a void into which she expected the riders ahead to disappear. The watery meadows were alive with sounds, some of them familiar from the bogs around Perth, but they were midnight sounds associated with the terror of being abroad too late, hastening back to the town. The pebbly paths among boulders magnified the sounds of their passing. The woods seemed treacherous, low branches ready to catch the unwary rider and hang her. Margaret pressed down over her horse's back.

As dawn grew in the east behind them, the procession moved further inland to the woodlands and marshes, seeking a thick morning fog to keep them safely out of sight until they reached the first day's shelter. Margaret was relieved when just after dawn, as the fog swirled around her, word passed down the line that they were at their resting place.

It was a modest farmhouse, the inhabitants unobtrusive in their hospitality. Margaret drank a little ale and then crawled into the box bed she would share with Roger, shivering with cold and exhaustion, her limbs stiff and clumsy. Some time during the day she woke to Roger's snoring and cuddled up to him, though the house was warming in the daylight that she glimpsed through the open door. It bothered her that they were exposed until she noticed the woman seated just without, churning butter. Closing her eyes, Margaret fell back into a deep sleep in which she dreamt of ghostly landscapes. It seemed but a moment later that Roger was coaxing her awake. Beyond the door she glimpsed the muted colours of twilight.

The sound of Celia moaning brought her fully awake.

The farmer's wife was kneading Celia's thighs. ''Tis naught to be shamed of,' the woman was saying. 'Warming them up stops the cramping.'

'She'd never sat a horse until she rode with me to Edinburgh,' Margaret told Roger.

'Then she's a brave woman and quick to learn,'

he said, turning to Margaret and searching her face. His own looked haggard. 'How are you faring?'

'Better than you, I think. Did you not sleep well?'

'I stayed up till midday with Macrath and Alan, planning. I'll not do that tomorrow.'

The second night's journey began in the late evening twilight. Against the stars Margaret became aware of the great crag on which stood Stirling Castle. In the pre-dawn mists she could see neither the top of the crag nor the marshy ground beneath her. Although her mount knew to follow the others as closely as possible, step for step, she was so disoriented by the subtly rippling mists that changes in his gait unbalanced her.

A sudden loud splash and cry ahead brought her head up to see whether to pause and dismount, but Macrath did not pause. Only Celia glanced round. Even the horses seemed unconcerned when another cry followed, fainter than the first. Reminding herself not to clutch the reins or dig in her heels in panic, Margaret thought she might calm herself by reciting a decade of Hail Marys. She did not want to fuss with the search for her paternoster beads, so she used her fingers to keep track of the prayers. It seemed a good distraction until she missed Alan's servant, who'd ridden behind Macrath and his servant, and then noticed that Aylmer, who'd been fourth in line, was also gone. Neither man rode behind her, only Roger and Alan.

A shift in her mount's gait brought her gaze forward again. The mist was now thicker, but she heard sluggish water, and then the sound of Macrath's horse on timber. This must be Stirling Bridge. Margaret said a prayer of thanks, for it meant that they were soon to be at the new day's lodging. Celia's horse neighed softly as it reached the bridge. Margaret held her breath in fear that if it balked her maid would fall. But Celia leaned a little forward and the horse continued calmly.

Margaret felt the chill of the water beneath that flowed down from the mountains as she crossed. For the length of the crossing the mist was icy on her face, warming again as she reached the far bank. There she saw that Aylmer and Alan's servant had rejoined the company. Both were wet. Had they been in the river? When Roger reached the bank he brought his horse near hers. Margaret asked him what had happened.

'The English had guards on the bridge – this is where tracks cross north-south, east-west. We knew of this. If God is watching over us, the bodies of Longshanks's soldiers will float out into the firth.'

'Holy Mary, Mother of God, pray for us sinners,' Margaret whispered, crossing herself. She had not thought to be part of the killing. Though she hated Longshanks, the guards had only obeyed orders.

'We have passed through what is likely to be the greatest danger on this journey,' Roger said.

The company fell into line and moved forward into the thinning mist. Margaret could see the highlands rising in the distance, which cheered her a little.

When they arrived at the day's lodging, she was just as weary as she had been the morning before but too agitated to go to sleep at once. She ate a little and drank more of the farmer's ale than was her custom, fighting a compulsion to watch Aylmer's eyes as he sat across the fire from her. They were dead eyes, expressing neither remorse nor satisfaction. She began to ask him how he had learned such dispassion, but she held her tongue. He would think her lacking gratitude for his protection. She knew she must become accustomed to such violent encounters. But still she wondered how Aylmer had trained himself to be so calm afterwards. Perhaps she misread his eyes, and the emptiness was a death of soul.

Roger joined her. 'Had you the opportunity to visit your mother at Elcho before going south at Easter?'

'No. I last saw her at Yuletide.' Margaret was glad to return to the ordinary, although she thought she had already told him of her last meeting with her mother.

'Is Dame Christiana attracting pilgrims to the priory, come to seek her advice?'

'If she is, she said nothing of it.'

With a grunt, Aylmer rose, bid them a good day, and withdrew to the pallet he was to share with one of the other men.

Margaret had relaxed enough to feel the night's ride in all her muscles. 'We should retire as well.'

But Roger continued. 'Was it at Yuletide she foresaw the end of our troubles, saw us standing together, our daughter in your arms, watching the true king of the Scots enter Edinburgh?' He sat back with a sigh of contentment. 'It is a happy scene.'

'Happy, yes, it is,' Margaret said, wishing she felt so. But this was nothing she had shared with him. 'How did you hear of the prophecy?'

'Murdoch, I think. Yes. I recall we were at Janet's house.'

As Margaret was when Roger had come for her. She began to think that had been no accident.

'And you going over maps,' said Roger, 'receiving instructions . . . perhaps we shall work together, eh?' His tone was light, but now Margaret wondered if it did not sound a little forced.

'You know I do not live by Ma's predictions,' she said.

'So you have not changed in that.'

'No.' Margaret rose and shook out her skirts. 'I should step without before I sleep.'

'I'll come with you,' Roger said, rising with a

groan. 'By St Fillan, I grow too old for all this riding.'

It bothered her that her uncle would have told Roger of the prophecy, angry as he had been with Roger's treatment of Margaret. It was a good reminder that she must trust no one.

A scout informed James the following evening that Margaret's company had crossed Stirling Bridge, first dispatching the English guards.

'Spies, all of the men, is that how it seems to you?' James asked.

The man nodded. 'Their mounts are too steady through it all for merchants' horses.'

'Not mounts they could have bought along the way.'

'Not such horses, sir.'

No, not such horses. 'We'll set out after the curfew – you've little time to eat and rest.'

'I'm accustomed to that,' the scout said. He bowed and moved on to the kitchen.

James left the house, wanting a few last words with Hal.

Hal was brushing Bonny, but when James entered the stable the groom dropped his hands and, fixing his gaze on James's boots, shook his head. 'I cannot do it.'

James had expected argument for he had discovered to his surprise that Hal was a stubborn young man. 'Murdoch has no need for you now that the inn is closed.'

Hal shook his fair hair from his eyes and looked directly at James for a change. 'I don't agree on the master's choice of king, but the Bruce is far better than Longshanks.'

James was irritated by Hal's echo of Murdoch's reasoning. He burst out, 'How can Robert Bruce be king with his father still alive?' He checked himself, reminding himself to focus on his goal. 'That is no cause to stay,' he said more rationally.

'Who would watch over Bonny and Agrippa when the master's at Dame Janet's?' Hal asked.

'If the town burns Murdoch would come for them, you cannot doubt that,' James countered.

'No. But if the soldiers come for Bonny while the master is away, she would be gone before he knew.'

They might continue in this vein for ever. 'I don't believe that is your only reason,' James said, closing the argument.

Hal gave a little shrug and resumed his grooming.

The young man was impossible. 'You'd meet William Wallace,' said James. 'Fight with him.'

It was enough to make Hal pause. He stared at James's feet, his hair hiding his face, but his hands, clenching and unclenching, expressed his uncertainty. After a while, he met James's gaze.

'It was not for the fighting I wanted to go to Perth, sir,' he said, and quickly looked away.

161

So that was it. James had wondered whether it was truly only for Margaret that Hal had been willing to go north. Poor fellow. He must have been heartsick at the return of her husband.

'We need men like you who know animals,' James said. 'Dame Margaret would be proud to hear you had joined the fight to put King John back on the throne.'

Hal had fallen into a rhythm again with the combing and did not reply.

James was now even less willing to give up on him. They did need grooms, and young men dedicated to the cause without wife and children, or any ties that would tempt them away home when most needed. Hal was ideal. But it was knowing the cause of this stubbornness that now motivated James. He knew the pain of loving someone who could never be his – his love was a beauty of wit and surpassing grace. It was his own skilled negotiations that had joined her to his cousin. All these long years James had cursed himself. And still he dreamt of her.

'You're wrong about the master favouring the Bruce,' Hal said, stepping away from the ass, his head tilted to keep his hair from his eyes. 'He helped Master Roger only because he was Dame Margaret's husband.'

'Maybe.' James gestured towards Hal's hair. 'For soldiering you'd need to slick that hair back, or cut it away from your face.' He got the grin he'd hoped for. 'You won't have another chance like this, to be so close to Wallace. How will you keep yourself busy? You can't groom the ass all the day. You know Murdoch can manage.'

Hal shifted feet, then dropped to a crouch, tracing something in the dirt. 'I could not leave without telling Master Murdoch.'

'I did not think you would. Come to my house as soon as you can.'

Still on his haunches, head down, Hal gave a nod.

James left him to his farewells, satisfied in having liberated a worthy young man.

When word of a scouting party delayed the departure of the company, Margaret and Roger took the opportunity for some time alone, finding a bench behind one of the outbuildings. The evening was soft with summer and yet held a hint of cooler air from the highlands above them. Delicate high clouds streaked the twilight sky. Margaret watched them passing as she rested her head on Roger's shoulder. He kept an arm around her as they talked idly. They wondered whether Murdoch and Janet would wed, marvelled at Roy's loyalty to Belle after she'd gone off for a time with another man, explored what might have happened to Old Will and Bess on Arthur's Seat, then drifted into talk of Perth, how it had changed with the English in the country.

'We are strong people,' Roger said, 'and I doubt the English will hold sway in Perth for long.'

'It is good to be going home,' Margaret said. 'I have missed it more than I knew.'

'You've missed Fergus most of all, I suspect.'

'Yes. He'll be so surprised.' Margaret struggled straighter to kiss Roger's cheek, a difficulty with the beard. 'I'm grateful for this journey.'

They grew quiet watching the sky.

'Do you hear anything of Andrew?' Roger asked after a time.

'I've had no word of my brother,' Margaret said, feeling a wave of sadness.

'I am sorry I doubted him,' Roger said. 'I grieve to think of him at Soutra with the soldiers. By blindly obeying Abbot Adam he hurt his kith, but he does not deserve such a grievous penance.'

'They'll not let him go, the English.' Margaret felt a band of sorrow tightening around her chest. 'I pray for Andrew every day.'

'I have as well, since I understood it was a punishment.' Roger withdrew his arm, took her hand, turning a little so that he might kiss her forehead. 'Does your mother know of his plight?'

She studied Roger's face, saw no dissimulation, just affection and concern. 'No.'

'Then we must see her, find out if she can offer us any hope.'

'You've changed your opinion about the Sight?' Margaret asked, for he'd been a non-believer.

He shrugged. 'It seems a comfort to believe in it at such times.'

'She'll know nothing of his future,' Margaret said, although her mother had once foreseen that Andrew would go through fire.

'And the sisters can pray for him,' Roger added.

'The sisters' prayers – I had not thought of that. Yes, I should go to her.'

'And soon, I think. We'll stop at the priory as we near Perth.'

It was too neatly tied up for Margaret's comfort. 'Why the haste? I'd rather see Fergus as soon as possible.'

'It will make little difference in time, Maggie.'

'Aye, that is my point.' She wondered a little at her stubbornness. It would not matter a great deal. But she felt he'd manipulated her into agreeing with the plan.

'You'll not wish to come away once you're home,' he said, smiling down on her with a touch of insulting bemusement, it seemed to Margaret.

'Have a care, Roger Sinclair. You may not know me as well as you think.'

He kissed her hand and rose, offering his arm to her. 'It grows dark and chilly. Let's go within.'

Margaret would have something new to ponder as she rode – an encounter with her mother, never a happy experience.

❧ 10 ❧

It Will Bring You Only Grief

A sudden summer storm delayed the company, now riding cautiously in daylight. A thrown shoe on another day forced them to stop. It was four days before they reached Elcho, long days and nights in which Margaret fretted about the coming meeting and her growing suspicion that Roger was manipulating her towards his own ends. When she questioned the genesis of his plan he insisted that a stop at the priory had not occurred to him until the evening he had suggested it.

'I've not forgotten your feelings about your mother, Maggie, but we must think of Andrew.'

Was she being selfish? She was partially to blame for Andrew's trouble, having urged him to do the very thing that his abbot had forbidden, going to Edinburgh Castle to ask for news of Roger.

The conversation left her in a familiar state of self-loathing. Roger had a knack for turning Margaret against herself. During his absence she had gradually shed the habit and resented its return.

She was grateful when her flux began and cooled his ardour. A few days earlier she would have been saddened that she was not with child, but at the moment she welcomed neither Roger's attentions nor a stronger bond with him. She prayed God to forgive her for such antipathy towards her husband. *But he gives me cause, my Lord*.

Her anxiety over the reunion with her mother was a lesser matter, but when one worry ebbed, the other flowed. Her mother's indifference to her family always unsettled Margaret. She felt diminished by her. If her mother did not love her, who else would? And her mother's lack of compassion made Margaret question the source of her visions – Christ had preached love. It was the devil who was dispassionate. It was this aspect of her mother's character that made her leery of her prophecies. At present Margaret was even less easy about seeing her mother than usual because if her fears about Roger's purpose in taking her there were founded on fact, then her mother's most recent prophecies regarding Margaret were central to her husband's fresh betrayal.

Arguing that she was most anxious about Fergus, she tried several times to convince Roger to ride on to Perth first, but he stood firm. It strengthened her belief that this was no charitable visit.

On an afternoon of gentle breezes and golden sunlight, the company reached the Tay and continued east towards the nunnery, its tower visible ahead. The familiar countryside and the weather cheered Margaret until a shout up ahead brought the riders to a standstill. Four men, two of them archers with bows drawn, rose up from behind a stone wall.

'God help us,' Celia whimpered.

Margaret's heart pounded. They rode high above the brush in the meadow with nothing to shield them, easy targets. She caught a glimpse of Roger's grim expression as he rode forward to consult with Macrath.

'English?' she heard Macrath ask.

'Unless they've taken the nunnery, no,' said Roger. 'The prioress is a Scotswoman of no great family. They would not bother to protect her.'

The two dismounted, handed the reins to the servants, and walked out to meet the four. Margaret crossed herself and prayed. As Roger drew near the four challengers, he called out the name de Arroch, which was the prioress's family name. Margaret told the others they must be Dame Agnes's kinsmen.

'I'm glad to hear it,' said Alan. 'I've not yet killed a man in the presence of ladies.'

'Perhaps they are guarding the priory from the English,' Celia said in a shaky voice.

'I've little doubt that is what Roger will discover,' said Margaret. But she said another prayer for good measure as Roger returned.

For once her prayers were answered, and Roger, Margaret, and their company were escorted to the priory.

When at last Margaret dismounted in the yard she submitted to Celia's usual fussing with the grace of one too nervous to argue. Anything was worthwhile that might avert her mother's frequent criticism. As the maid dabbed at dusty smears on her face, brushed off and tugged at her skirts, and adjusted her veil, Margaret wondered in what mood her mother would receive them. She glanced up at the guest-house windows but caught no one observing them.

On Margaret's earlier visits to the nunnery the yard had been full of life, chickens strutting about, labourers coming and going, the high voices of the lay staff's children at play competing with the rush of the river. But today the yard was deserted, despite the fair weather. Not even the chickens were about.

Dame Katrina, the elderly hosteleress, greeted them with wonder. 'Dame Margaret! We understood you to be in Edinburgh. So said your brother Fergus.'

'I was, Dame Katrina, and now I've come home. This is my husband, Roger Sinclair.'

'Oh.' The elderly nun looked aside, as if searching for a memory. 'There was something . . .' She shook her head. 'Well, it must have been of little importance.' Her smile took in all the company. 'You are welcome, come away in, I shall arrange for some refreshments and send word up to Dame Christiana that you are here.'

The hall was of moderate size, chilly after the warmth of the sun.

'We must light the fire,' the hosteleress said to a servant. 'The damp has spread out from the corners.' Turning to Margaret, she explained, 'Dame Christiana rarely uses the hall.'

Margaret murmured something reassuring, her mind on the coming reunion. She must not hope for any particular outcome, for her mother was too unpredictable.

The company settled on benches or stood stretching and shaking out their legs.

The plan was that only Margaret and Roger would speak with Dame Christiana. The others would stay in the hall enjoying the hospitality. It was not long before her mother's servant joined them.

Marion was a rather simple woman of thirty or so, Celia's age, who had long been her mother's choice of servant to keep by her. She was devoted to Christiana but had been despondent at th thought of retiring to a nunnery. Margaret was glad to see that Marion had not abandoned her mistress.

The handmaid greeted Margaret and Roger with happy affection. But as both began to follow her out to the steps she halted and, humbly averting her eyes, said, 'Forgive me, Master Roger, but the mistress said only her daughter and her maid were to come.'

Dame Katrina made a disapproving sound, her hands fluttering ineffectually.

'Why my maid?' Margaret asked. 'My husband wishes to see his goodmother, as I expected she would wish to see him. They have not met in many a day.'

Marion bowed her head. 'I pray you, Dame Christiana was very clear. You are welcome, and you might bring your maid if you care to choose some items from her trunk to brighten your house.'

Glancing at Celia as she considered this suggestion, Margaret saw the maid's obvious curiosity. And why not use some of the trappings her mother was hoarding?

'Come, Celia, we shall accept Ma's invitation with gratitude.'

'Am I discarded so lightly?' Roger protested.

Margaret squeezed his arm, feeling his muscles tensed, and gave him an encouraging smile. 'You know Ma,' she said. 'If we press this, she might

171

banish us all. As you so wisely said, we must think of Andrew.'

Coldly withdrawing his arm from her grasp, Roger bowed his acquiescence, though anger still darkened his countenance. Margaret was too agitated about the coming meeting to have the patience to soothe his feelings. Besides, Christiana had foiled whatever had been his plan, and Margaret regarded that as a favour.

Margaret and Celia followed Marion out into the quiet yard and up the covered steps to the first floor. Her mother's chamber was down the covered gallery facing away from the yard, looking east. Marion knocked, then opened the door and bowed Celia and Margaret in. A confusion of furnishings alive with coloured patterns crowded the room, distracting Margaret's attention as if the trappings of her mother's life shouted at her. As her mother rose, Margaret noted the costly wool of her simple gown, the impeccably white wimple.

'My child,' Christiana said, offering her hand. It was that of a lady, soft and white, as Celia had wanted hers to be. As Margaret bent to kiss it, her mother said, 'I'd had news you were in Edinburgh, Maggie.'

Straightening, Margaret nodded. 'I've come home. With Roger.'

'Oh yes. I could not see your husband today.' Hand at her throat, Christiana gazed down at

Margaret's hem. 'Your gown is travel-worn. Surely the journey from Perth is not so muddy?'

'I've come from Edinburgh, Ma. We have stopped here before continuing on towards home.'

Christiana searched Margaret's face. 'What is wrong that you come to me in such haste?'

'I bring news of Andrew.'

'Sweet heaven.' Christiana raised her voice. 'Marion, refreshments.' Then she noticed Celia, who stood behind Margaret. 'Where is your family?' she asked Celia in Gaelic.

'I do not understand, Dame Christiana,' said Celia.

'She does not speak the tongue, Ma. Celia is Dame Katherine's maid. She accompanied me to Edinburgh, as was proper, and will now help me reorder my household.'

'She looks like one of my clan, a MacFarlane with her dark hair, joined brow, and pale skin.'

Marion had arranged a table and two chairs, one cushioned, near a small brazier. Wine and oat cakes and a bowl of berries were set out for them. Margaret's mother settled in the cushioned chair and motioned Margaret to the other.

'A maid should not be so tiny,' said Christiana. 'How can the MacFarlane carry your things?'

'Mistress, I am not—' Celia began.

Margaret interrupted her. 'Celia has proved her worth over and over, in a most difficult and dangerous time.' She was angry to be caught up in one of her mother's tortuous arguments. 'Do you not wish to hear about Andrew?'

'He told me what he'd done, Maggie.' Christiana nodded to Celia. 'Do you see that trunk in the far corner? Take a lamp and look at the gowns, sleeves, shifts, gloves, veils. See if there is anything that would be of use to your mistress. I have no need of such finery among the sisters.'

Celia bobbed her head and withdrew. She would be content for a long while, handling Christiana's fine clothes.

'Your offer is generous, Ma. I thank you,' said Margaret.

'See whether you might be of help to my daughter's maid,' Christiana said to Marion, then trained her eyes on Margaret with a formidable stare. 'I am aware that Roger has not provided you with much. He is a disappointment. But you need not suffer.'

Margaret blushed and busied herself pouring wine for both of them. 'You know what Andrew did for his abbot, but do you know how his abbot rewarded him?' She handed a cup to her mother.

Christiana took it, but set it down with a clatter and leaned back in her chair.

Margaret saw that her mother's eyes were unfocused.

'He will go through fire.' The vein in Christiana's left temple pulsed.

'Andrew has been sent as confessor to the

English at Soutra Hill,' said Margaret.

With a sigh, her mother pressed her throbbing temple, closed her eyes, head tilted, as if listening.

'As confessor, Andrew is privy to their secrets,' Margaret continued. 'The English will fear what he might tell his fellow Scots. They'll not let him go, Ma. When they return to England . . .' She stopped, reluctant to say the words.

'They'll either take him with them, or execute him here,' Christiana finished in a fluting voice quite unlike her normal speaking voice.

Margaret was uncomfortable with her mother in this state. Silence sometimes quieted the spell, so Margaret turned her attention to the room, let her gaze wander over the small caskets, footstools, silk-wrapped cushions. But a flutter of fabric and a clatter of beads drew her attention back to her mother. Christiana was fingering paternoster beads, flying through the decades. Margaret covered her mother's hands to still them and then slipped the beads from them. Christiana lunged for the beads, but Margaret held them out of her reach.

'You don't understand, Maggie. I must say my penance.'

'For what?'

'My visions are not to be shared.' Her mother spoke sharply, almost angrily. 'God gives the visions to *me*. No one else.'

'What are you talking about?' Margaret had

been taught that the Sight was never used for oneself.

'The prioress says I am wrong to share my visions. It is sinful.' Christiana spoke in a rush of words, her colour high. 'God tests me with them.' She hesitated. 'No, Dame Agnes did not say that, but it must be so or they would have ceased long ago. I revealed so many, too many. God have mercy on me, a sinner, and forgive my error.' She crossed herself.

Margaret was familiar with her mother's agitated state. It often sent her to her bed for days. Margaret tried to draw her mother out of her thoughts.

'Will you ask the sisters to pray for Andrew's deliverance?'

Eyes wide, Christiana gave a strangled laugh. 'What are you thinking? Pray for Andrew? They curse him, Maggie.'

They curse him. It had not occurred to Margaret that the sisters might know of how Andrew had assisted the English in stripping the kirks of Scottish royal documents.

'He was observing his vow of obedience, Ma. But later he saw how wrong it had been to obey Abbot Adam, and it is because he disobeyed – to help me – that he is in mortal danger.'

'As are we all with the English in our midst,' said Christiana, calmer now. 'But I shall ask them to pray for him if you wish it.'

She should wish it. 'He is a good man,' said Margaret, 'and a brave one. I do wish it.'

Her mother pressed her temples, shook her head. 'If you say so. But you know he should have been a merchant. Malcolm was so disappointed. First sons do not enter the Kirk.' She was like any mother now, fussing about how her children came up short of her expectations.

It was useless to argue with her, and besides, while she was calm Margaret wished to learn what detail she could about the visions regarding herself. Whether or not she would share them with Roger she would decide after she heard them, though she doubted she would.

'At Yuletide you told me about two visions of my future. Do you remember?' Margaret recounted them, knowing her mother's absent-mindedness.

Christiana had resumed her prayers, despite her lack of beads, using her fingers to count out a decade.

'Who are the men in the visions?' Margaret asked.

'I should never have told you of the visions.' Her mother stilled her hands for a moment and looked at Margaret, a deep, long look, that seemed to bore into her soul. 'You've told others, haven't you? Fie, daughter. You should not have done so. It will bring you only grief.'

Margaret trembled in her mother's gaze. The

telling had caused her grief, that was true. 'Who is the king of the Scots in the vision?'

Christiana pinched her lips and shook her head. 'You'll draw me out no more, Maggie, I'll not sin for you.'

The prioress had turned her mother against using the Sight for Margaret's enlightenment. 'Damn your prioress. She blathers on about things beyond her ken. You know that the Sight is to share with the people. It is not a gift for the selfish.'

'You will burn in hell for cursing the good prioress, Maggie. I should not have let you grow so close to your Uncle Murdoch, I see it now, too late. He taught you the devil's ways.'

'He saved us many a day when you were abed and Da away, Ma.'

Christiana waved away the comment and turned her attention to the maids. 'Well, Celia,' she called, 'have you found anything to your taste?'

Bright with their explorations, Celia and Marion joined them holding several gowns and surcoats.

Examining them, Margaret shook her head. 'I have little occasion to wear such fine things.' She said it rather sharply, irritated by her mother's changing the subject.

'But where will you get the wool to make anything else?' Celia asked, her face pinched beneath the dark brows. Apparently she was not enjoying herself as Margaret had thought she would.

Weary of arguing, Margaret said, 'We'll accept whatever you feel appropriate, Celia.' She could always put them away somewhere.

'And now the tapestries,' said Christiana. 'Marion, show Celia those.' She turned to Margaret. 'I approve of your little MacFarlane. Your goodmother has made up for the neglect of her son by gifting you with such a clever lady's maid. I hope you are duly grateful.'

'I am. Ma, the visions. You've already told me of them, so it cannot be a sin to fill in the parts you left out before.'

Her mother rose and wandered over to the maids, pulling out two of the tapestries that Celia had set aside. 'These will keep out the drafts and cheer the hall. And that small one for the bed-chamber. Now gather all this and put it together so that the horses might carry the pack. No doubt Maggie and her husband are eager to reach home.'

'Send it upriver on a boat, Ma, to our ware-house.' Margaret was trying to keep her head out of the mists of prophecy by focusing on the figure her mother cut, graceful in her straight carriage, though showing her age in a greater girth round her middle that was not quite hidden by the soft folds of the fabric. She was an ageing woman afraid of dying in sin.

'So be it,' sighed Christiana. 'By boat. But you'll shiver tonight without the tapestry over your chamber doorway,' she warned Margaret.

'We'll stay here tonight, I think.'

Christiana frowned as she gazed around her crowded room. 'Here?'

'In the guest house, but not this room.'

'Oh yes, you should all be comfortable here, Dame Katrina has borrowed many of my furnishings to improve it.'

'Why could you not see Roger today?' Margaret asked.

'I felt I should not. I felt it keenly.'

'You were keen to see us wed.'

'Malcolm assured me that Roger Sinclair was a good match for you.'

Margaret did not doubt her father instigated the match. 'You will say no more about the visions?'

Christiana shook her head. 'You must go now, Maggie. I have not the strength for long visits.'

Christiana wished the children would leave her in peace, but she suspected that these visits were not of their doing, but that God sent them to her. Not so long ago He'd tested her when Fergus twice appealed to her for help, and now she must embrace her daughter's problems. It was frustrating to have tasted contentment, peace, and now have the turmoil of her maternal unhappiness intrude.

She was selfish, that is what God wanted her to face. All three of her children had good cause to seek the solace of their mother's love. They had a right to expect her to be a fount of comfort and wisdom. But she had not the strength to be the mother they deserved. No one had ever understood her frailty.

She yearned for the quiet of devotion, to repeat the prayers until a white light enfolded her in absolute serenity, withdrawing all pain, physical and spiritual. She knew that this was possible, for she had long watched Dame Bethag, whom all in the convent knew to be a most blessed mystic, at her devotions in Elcho chapel. Christiana had witnessed Bethag's uplifted face illumined by God's grace. At other times she had witnessed the nun weeping while from her throat rose a song expressing ineffable joy. Bethag moved about her day with such serenity that all loved to be near her. Even many of the other sisters experienced benedictions, though more modest than Bethag's. But not once had Christiana's prayer lifted her into the presence of the divine. Were the nuns of Elcho so much worthier than she?

Maggie's visit had ripped open the veil of peace Christiana had managed to draw around her. Her daughter was disappointed in her husband, and with cause. Roger had been wrong to worry her so, and to leave her so little money on which to live while away, but he had returned and Maggie must abide with him. Her journey to Edinburgh and her sojourn there with her uncle had been dangerous and unwarranted, and Murdoch's influence could be seen in her new bold stubbornness. Yet Christiana knew she was also to blame. It was probably her vision of Maggie with soldiers that had filled her daughter's head with ideas like running off to Edinburgh. That she had no control over her Sight was an agony none comprehended. She must say no more. Prioress Agnes had made that clear.

And yet how satisfying it would be to share what knowledge she had with her daughter. How like herself at that age Maggie looked. It was a pity she had not been given the Sight – she had the courage for it.

The weary travellers ate well, drinking temperately as had been their custom all along the way, and spent some time relaxing around the hall fire before bed. It was a luxuriously large fire and, though it was summer, all seemed drawn to its bright warmth.

Margaret watched Roger talking quietly with the other men. Gone was the proud swagger and calculated elegance of the ambitious merchant. He had hardened and withdrawn to some inner core of which she had been unaware. He watched others closely as they spoke and gestured. He seemed complete in himself, needing no one, not even her.

She turned her attention to Celia, beginning to plan the airing of the house in Perth.

*

Celia climbed wearily to the chamber she was to share with Margaret. After the warmth of the hall, the covered steps and gallery felt cold. It was a pity that the men would have all the benefit of the fire, while she and Margaret had to make do with a tiny brazier. But the chamber above was properly private. Celia feared her mistress's mood tonight. Margaret surely could not be happy about her mother's reception.

Nothing Celia had heard about Dame Christiana MacFarlane had prepared her for the depletion of strength in both body and soul that resulted from being in her presence. Margaret's mother reminded Celia of a holy man she had once seen preaching near her family's kirk, thundering about the day of judgement with a fervour that was more curse than sermon, staring into the faces of those listening with such intensity that he caused them to shrink into themselves with the horror of their damnation. That such a beautiful woman, with such grace, could cause a similarly frightening despair simply by being in the same room appalled her. She had thought Margaret a complaining daughter, resentful of the things that her mother withheld, as so many daughters were. But now she thought Margaret was to be admired for her strength.

Judging the chamber ready, Celia heated some spiced wine to soothe Margaret to sleep. Soon Margaret appeared and began nervously plucking at the laces at waist and shoulders. Celia put down the cup and hurried to assist her.

'Marion came down after you left the hall,' said Margaret. 'Mother wishes to see me tomorrow morning before we depart.'

'To apologise for her pathetic welcome?' Celia muttered, working at the knots that Margaret had tightened with her impatient tugging.

'What you witnessed was her customary behaviour,' said Margaret. 'But perhaps she has relented, and means to explain the visions. I could see Roger hopes so.'

That bitch holed up in luxury and safety in this nunnery while her children are abroad in the world without kin to protect them. Celia bit her tongue and put some valerian from her travel supplies in Margaret's spiced wine. She seemed to need it.

As James's small party approached Kinclaven Castle, the long-shadowed evening wood was so quiet that he thought they had come too late, that Wallace and his company had already moved on. When he halted, Angus MacLaren rode up beside him.

'They've gone,' said James.

MacLaren grunted. 'And left their fires burning, their horses feeding? You're too much in the towns, Jamie, your ears and nose are numb.'

Angus moved to the head of the party and led them slowly across a stream, over a small rise, and into a circle of wary-eyed guards with daggers and bows drawn. The encampment was not yet visible, but James now detected the smoke that MacLaren had smelled much further away.

One of the men recognised James. 'It is James Comyn, kinsman of our king,' he told the others, 'and friend of the Wallace.'

When the weapons were lowered, James and the rest of the party dismounted and followed one of the men over another hill and round a bend, where the size of the encampment brought a cry of surprise from Hal.

James fell back to reassure him. 'You'll find few of high birth here, my friend. It is the men who work the land and tend the herds who fight for our land under the Wallace.'

'So many.'

'Christ, we'd hoped for twice as many – several hundred. But come, we're all the more critical to our king's welfare when we count for so goodly a portion.'

James, his servant, Angus MacLaren, Hal, and Will, the messenger, were greeted with good cheer and welcomed at one of the fires. But soon James was called to the fireside of William Wallace.

'Come along with me, Hal. I promised you would meet the Wallace, and it shall be so.' Regarding the young man as he rose, James nodded with satisfaction at the fair hair trimmed to reveal the strong-boned features, only slightly hidden by a pale, dusty beard that bespoke their haste in travel. 'Remember to look the Wallace and all his men in the eyes,' James said. 'In this place a man watches his feet only when he has something to hide.'

Hal lifted his chin and then his gaze to James's. 'What do I say to such a man?'

'What you might say to any of your brave comrades. William Wallace expects no more.'

They were guided through the trees to a fire circle like all the others. William Wallace came forward to welcome James. Tall and muscular, he always made James feel like a lad. But James never doubted that the Wallace had need of him. James was the shrewd one with strong ties to the Comyns and Balliols, and other great families of the land. And he had met Longshanks when he was yet a young squire to an English lord.

Wallace nodded towards Hal. 'Who is this fine young man?'

'Hal of Edinburgh, a groom at Murdoch Kerr's inn whom I've known a long while. He has a way with horses and asses, keeps his head in dangerous encounters, and can hold a secret closer to himself than his own skin.'

Hal stepped forward. 'I am yours to command, my lord.'

Wallace grasped Hal's arm. 'I'm no lord, Hal. Just a loyal subject of King John who means to return him to the throne. You are welcome, sir.

I have need of you.'

Hal bowed his head, and when he raised his eyes they shone with emotion.

James himself was not unaffected. He cleared his throat and suggested that Hal return to his companions. 'I must tell our commander all the news. You need not hear it again – what you need is rest.'

Hal nodded and withdrew, the guide joining him to take him back to the others.

❧ 11 ❧

TREACHEROUS SANDS

Wallace motioned James to a log spread with a skin, then eased down on a similar seat at an angle.

'You have not brought the woman of whom you spoke – Margaret Kerr?' Wallace asked.

'I could not.' James explained the unfortunate timing of her wayward husband's return.

Elbows on knees, Wallace opened his hands, studying his dirt-encrusted palms. Someone added a log to the fire and the light flared, revealing new lines on Wallace's face.

'Unfortunate or canny, I wonder.' He looked enquiringly at James.

That was the question. 'Either is possible,' said James. '*She* does not believe her husband knows that her allegiance lies not with Robert Bruce, but it is clear that she is poorly acquainted with Roger Sinclair.' James spoke slowly, choosing his words with care, keenly aware of his own ambivalent relationship with Margaret. Though some ineffable quality in her convinced him that she was solidly loyal to Balliol, her marital situation gave him pause. Yet he had recommended her to Wallace as a spy.

'Let us put her aside for now,' Wallace said. His face had angles James did not remember from previous meetings, but he had grown brown in the summer sun, so it was difficult to judge. 'Longshanks's mission to Flanders is much on my mind. What is he up to?'

'I can but guess,' James said. 'King Philip of France convinced Edward that he would honour a secret agreement between them, then publicly revealed the agreement as Edward's treachery. Longshanks has lost what he gave up in the feigned agreement and gained not a whit, nothing that he'd been led to expect. The worst of it is the public humiliation. Edward of England will not rest until his reputation is restored, until all fear him once more. I pity the Flemish.'

'Damn the Flemish with their duke who is so easily bought,' Wallace growled. 'Pity *us* if Longshanks arrives in Flanders to find the rebellion over.' He ran his hands through his thick red hair and stretched out his legs with a groan. 'We must strike before Edward comes west to Scotland again. Murray and I are agreed in that.'

'I've heard something of your plan. A sudden

rush southwards to recapture Stirling Bridge.'

Wallace tossed a stick into the fire with wrist-snapping energy. 'God's blood, can no Scot keep a secret?' he shouted, hauling in his legs and rising. 'We've no chance if we cannot stand together.'

Men at the far end of the fire looked their way, one rising and drawing his dagger.

James hastened to reassure Wallace. 'My cousin had it from you, my friend, he knew he could trust me with the information.'

Wallace grunted and turned to those on alert. 'It is nothing,' he said to them. 'Rest easy.'

The dagger disappeared, but the men were more attentive now.

Wallace had dropped his head and now sat very still. He seemed able to withdraw in company, turn inward and study his thoughts in quiet. James believed it was this ability even more than his fierce energy in battle that made Wallace a consummate warrior. Any ploughman might fight with wild abandon for a cause he believed in. But when necessary Wallace could shut out the clamour of men in order to consider his moves. James did not always agree with Wallace's conclusions, but he was confident they were well considered.

In a while, Wallace raised his head. 'We traverse treacherous sands, James. They blind us and threaten to swallow us. But temper must be saved for the battle. Tell me the rest of your news.'

'Some of our wealthier merchants living in

Bruges are back among us, anxious to avoid Longshanks. They talk of growing discontent amongst the townspeople, a rebellion brewing against the Duke of Flanders.'

'We must move before Longshanks returns.'

'You know about the discontent among his nobles.'

'And here as well. All this works for us, but only if we can convince the arrogant that our only hope is union.'

'Tell that to the Bruce.'

'He's the worst of them,' said Wallace. He flung another twig at the fire.

In the morning Margaret attended Mass in Elcho's chapel before returning to her mother's chamber. Kneeling on a cushion borrowed from Dame Katrina, she said countless rounds on her beads, praying for her mother's cooperation and for guidance in her feelings about Roger. About the latter, she was increasingly confused. When love-making, and when talking of their lives, truly anything that did not touch on the Bruce, King John, or Longshanks, she believed herself still in love with him. And yet when the issues concerning the kingship were in play, she distanced herself from him. Last night, Marion's appearance in the hall had excited her, affording a chance to speak with the maid about the intruders who had come upon her in Christiana's chamber. But

191

before Margaret had a chance to ask the maid anything, Roger had joined them. Margaret had swallowed the questions and merely listened to Marion's message and assured her that she would attend her mother in the morning. Afterwards, she felt shaken, as if Roger had almost caught her in the act of something forbidden. Was she afraid of him, or did she distrust him, or both? Until recently one of her dearest hopes had been to bear Roger's children. She still wished for them, but it frightened her to think how much more dependent on Roger she would be as a mother. She had hoped to gain some insight into her doubts through prayer; but God was silent on the matter this day. Margaret hoped He would at least encourage her mother to help her. If He spoke to her through her mother, Margaret would willingly embrace her mother's visions.

Celia had accompanied Margaret to the kirk, and afterwards offered to accompany her to her mother's chamber.

'Today I'll go alone,' Margaret said. 'Perhaps she will be more open if I am alone.'

She could see from the maid's raised eyebrow that she doubted it would make a difference, but Celia said only, 'I'll make certain that all is ready for our day's ride.'

The morning was bright and already warm, and as Margaret crossed the dusty yard she was cheered by the prospect of the brief ride north, and then stabling the horses in Perth and biding at home for a good long while. She was even hopeful that with her mother's gifts and Celia's help she might succeed in making her house in Perth feel like a home.

A manservant bent over the roses in the guest-house garden, snipping the spent blossoms as he hummed off-key. A cat was stretched beneath a sapling, a paw shielding its eyes. This morning the priory seemed a friendlier place than it had yesterday.

Marion leaned over the gallery railing outside Christiana's door, face up to the sun. Margaret put a finger to her lips when the maid noticed her, and beckoned to her to come away down the gallery. It was a chance to talk a moment in peace. Marion's long, homely face was tense as she reached Margaret.

'What is it, Dame Margaret?'

'I beg a small favour. I know you were accosted when my mother's chamber was searched, and I hoped you might tell me about it.'

Marion glanced back nervously, though her mistress would not be able to see them from her window. 'Your mother does not like me to speak of it.'

'Yes, it is her way, but it would be helpful to me to hear what you remember.'

'It all happened so quickly.' Marion shook her head.

'Any little detail might be helpful. I might ken from it whether or not we are still in danger.' She reminded the maid of the related occurrences.

Marion's face relaxed. 'I see. Yes, I do see.' She tilted her head and squeezed shut her eyes. 'I woke as they kicked in the door. I opened the shutter on the lantern and one of them rushed over and closed it. He pulled me out of bed and told me I must go without. Rough he was, but I managed to pull a blanket round me before he pushed me away from the bed.'

'In that moment of light, what did you see of him?'

'Dark hair, dark clothes, not shabby. His speech was like an Englishman, a southerner.'

Many a Scot sounded so, from the lowlands – clerics, the high born, some merchants. Not the usual thief. 'How many were there?'

'Three. One stood by the door and warned me not to run for help. His speech was more like Master Roger's. I saw him only by moonlight, and I cannot say much, but that he stank like a man who had been long on the road. The third kept me by him without. He said nothing to me and wore a head covering that hid his face and his hair. The blade of his knife kept me silent until they departed.' Only now did Marion open her eyes, blinking against the sun.

'Could you tell whether they left with anything?'

Marion looked apologetic. 'I confess I did not look for fear they'd kill me.'

'I ken that feeling. You must have been very frightened.'

'I admit to that, I do.'

'Anything else?'

'I had this thought, later, that the one outside might have been a woman. That one was smaller. A lad, more likely.' She shook her head as if still trying to understand. 'But I keep thinking a woman.'

'What of the guest-house servants? Or Dame Katrina? Did they hear nothing?'

Marion shook her head. 'I was the one who woke them.'

'God bless you for this,' Margaret said. 'And I'll say nothing to my mother of this talk.'

'It might be of help?'

Margaret nodded.

Marion smiled and led the way into the crowded chamber. Hidden behind an ornately carved screen, Margaret's mother lounged on a bed piled high with cushions. There were dark crescents beneath her eyes, and her colour was uneven, ruddy and pale alternating.

'Are you unwell?' Margaret asked, leaning to kiss her mother's forehead, which felt clammy.

Christiana took one of Margaret's hands and pressed the back against a cheek, then kissed the palm.

Margaret was deeply moved by the affectionate gesture. 'I hope I was not the cause of a sleepless night.'

Gently shaking her head, Christiana said, 'I grow old, Maggie. The old sleep fitfully. It is God's way of making us desire the long rest in His house.'

This was but the latest of her mother's theories about her nocturnal restlessness. When they were children Fergus had once suggested that their mother was a cat under a spell, and that she longed to hunt at night. But she did look pale.

'Marion said you wished to see me before I left,' said Margaret.

Christiana closed her eyes and nodded. 'I did. I must warn you, Maggie. Come, bring the stool closer.' She gestured impatiently.

Margaret did as she requested, her heart racing, thinking God had answered her prayers. 'Warn me of what?'

Opening her eyes, Christiana studied Margaret for a moment.

'Ma?'

'You must not believe anyone who claims to want to help you, Maggie. Everyone has selfish motivations now.'

'Are you speaking of my husband?'

'Anyone.' Christiana sighed back into her pillows.

A silence ensued in which Margaret heard

Marion's small movements as she shifted the gown she was mending, the gardener's humming, and her own heart pounding.

'Is that it?' Margaret asked when she could no longer keep still. 'Such a vague warning? Is this all that you wished to tell me?'

Christiana looked sympathetic. 'You expect too much of my visions, Maggie. I saw you bending over a map, men at arms treating you as one of them. I don't know the men. Nor do I know the man riding into Edinburgh.'

'What of the man with me as I hold my daughter?'

'But of course it was Roger Sinclair. I said it was your husband.'

'Did you see his face?'

Her mother seemed to be losing interest, then abruptly shook her head. 'It was a presence with no face. Like the men who— but no, the prioress says these visions are for my eyes only. I must say no more.'

Margaret tried to keep her voice calm. 'But you called him my husband.'

'He bent over both of you as a husband would.' Christiana rolled her head from side to side. 'You are destroying my peace with your insistence on hearing more.' Her voice broke.

'But you sent for me,' Margaret said.

Christiana closed her eyes.

Swallowing her frustration, Margaret changed

the direction of her questions. 'Fergus wrote to me about the men who broke in here and in the houses in Perth. Have you any idea what they sought?'

'Oh, Maggie, you would have wept to see it. They spilled my medicines and some of the costly oils your father brought from France and Italy, they tore veils with their rough hands, stepped on my gowns with their filthy boots.' Christiana sat up suddenly, upsetting several of the cushions as she leaned towards Margaret. 'Trust no one.' She dropped her eyes and seemed to withdraw, whispering something unintelligible.

Margaret wondered at the spilling of medicines and oils. 'Where were your medicines and oils, Ma?'

Christiana glanced at Margaret as if surprised she was still there. 'Where? In the lovely casket Malcolm brought from Italy.'

Margaret knew the one – it looked much like the one her father had left with Murdoch.

'There is one you might trust,' Christiana said, 'your brother Andrew.'

Margaret knew that. 'Yesterday you thought little of him.'

'I have reconsidered.' Christiana noticed a loose thread on a cushion and bit it off.

There was much else in the room that could use her attention, but it was like her to be drawn to the insignificant, Margaret thought. At least she had managed to restore Andrew in their mother's eyes.

'Would you like to see Roger before we depart?' Margaret asked.

Christiana was fussing with the cushions that supported her arms. 'Are you two reconciled?'

'We are trying,' said Margaret.

She moved a few cushions to assist her mother, but Christiana pushed her away.

'I know how they must go,' she said, shifting things again. At last she rested against them, arms well supported. But she was not still for long as she grasped Margaret's hand, drawing her near. 'I do love you, Maggie, though at times that might not seem so.' She searched Margaret's eyes.

Margaret kissed her mother's hand.

Christiana gently touched Margaret's cheek. 'And I am sorry if my silence caused you an unhappy marriage.'

Margaret let go her mother's hand. 'You did not approve of Roger?'

Christiana wrinkled her nose, lifted a shoulder in a slight shrug. 'He seemed . . . oh, he was not like your father riding up to Dunkeld to plead for my hand, swearing he could not live without me. I admit that of late I'd come to think it a lie, or that time had dulled Malcolm's ardour.'

'I don't mean to press you to see Roger. But I did wonder why you wished to avoid him.'

'It is not a matter of avoidance. I'm not good company at present. I wish him well. Tell him that I am glad he has returned with life and limb.'

'I'll tell him.' Margaret rose to take her leave.

But Christiana caught her hand. 'There is another matter. Your father has returned from Bruges.' Her face was now truly flushed.

Margaret sank back down, thinking of the searches. She felt ill. 'You've seen him?'

'I have.'

'Why didn't you tell me at once?'

'Malcolm wishes none in Perth to know that he is in the country – not even Fergus. I think it foolish – he should stay in the comfort of his own house.'

'And you'd only now decided to confide in me?' Margaret shook her head, wishing she could quiet the clamour in it. 'Why is Da hiding?'

'Some trouble,' said Christiana, with a wave of her hands. 'He's come back because King Edward of England is in Flanders. There is an uprising.' She shook her head. 'I ken little of such matters. He thought to collect more of his wealth and do some careful business while English eyes were elsewhere. He was not prepared for things as they are here. But there is more, Maggie.' Christiana paused and fiddled with one of her sleeves.

Margaret held her breath.

'He wants me to leave the convent and return with him to Flanders.'

The held breath escaped as incredulous laughter. 'Even after he agreed tha. you might retire here, that he would not demand his rights as a husband?'

'Do not hate him. He did agree, but he now regrets it.'

He had seemed only too glad to be free of her mother. Margaret wondered whether her father intended never to return to his country. 'What changed?'

Christiana had sat up at the edge of the bed and was hugging a cushion. 'He swears he has no joy without me.'

'Will you go?' Margaret asked.

Christiana looked abashed. 'No. I refused him. I have taken a vow of chastity, and dedicated myself to prayer.'

'I doubt the vow is binding.'

'The chaplain supports my refusal.'

'How long ago did Da return?'

'A week ago? No, he's been here longer, I think.'

'Poor Da,' Margaret whispered absently, her mind on the coincidence of his return and the searches.

'Poor me.' Christiana's tone was flat, as if talking to herself. 'Malcolm swears he will prevail.'

'An empty boast,' said Margaret. 'He cannot prevail against the Kirk.'

'It would have been better had he stayed away,' Christiana whispered. 'He has unsettled me.'

Margaret and Malcolm were a pair, then. 'Do

you know where Da landed? Has he been to Edinburgh?' One of her mother's intruders might have been her own husband thinking to search for something without being discovered. But her mother's servant Marion would have recognised his voice. Still, he might have accomplices.

Christiana shrugged. 'I was not so curious as to ask.'

He'd been gone almost two years now and yet her mother seemed unmoved by his return except as it threatened her comfortable peace. Margaret was not so indifferent; she was furious with him for deserting his family. When Longshanks ordered all land that Scots held in England seized her father took it as a warning and fled to Bruges leaving Fergus and Margaret to fend for themselves. She'd been but four months married with a husband often away. She had felt so alone. And now he returned trailing trouble in his wake, or so it seemed. Her parents were worse than useless.

Roger paced in the guest-house garden, eager to hear of the meeting. Margaret slowed as she drew near, considering what she would divulge.

'Well? Was she more forthcoming this morning?'

She could see how anxious he was, as if half fearing what she would say.

'Yes and no. She swears that the faces in her vision were not clear to her, that she knew it was you from the way you bent towards me and the child.'

'And the king?'

Margaret shook her head. 'She saw no faces.'

'She saw yours.'

'I wish I had something to tell you, Roger. I'm sorry.'

'She's mad.'

'You would not be the first to think so.'

He shook his head, incredulous. 'Of what value is a gift that only teases?'

Margaret shrugged. 'I have always found it a tangle.'

'So why had she sent for you this morning?'

Margaret caught her breath, offered her rehearsed response. 'To explain why she would not see you. But I could see the choler strong in her. She is unwell. She told me to say that she is glad you have returned with life and limb.'

'She might have saved her breath.' The veins on Roger's temples had risen with his anger. 'She said naught else? Had she nothing of use to tell you?'

'That I should trust no one.'

'I might have told you that.'

'I stayed longer than I wished, hoping she might recall something, but I wasted the time.'

Margaret was relieved that the others awaited them to complete the journey. Today they would part ways with Alan and Macrath, who were riding on to Dundee. Or so they said. Margaret still did not believe Alan was merely a merchant, and she wondered what business Macrath pursued for the Bruce in Dundee.

As Roger helped her mount, Margaret glanced towards Celia, wondering who would assist her.

'You need not worry,' Roger said. 'Macrath is seeing to her.'

Indeed, Celia had mounted and looked at ease in the saddle as Macrath checked all the straps. Now she leaned towards him with her ear cocked, her eyes shining. Margaret heard a snatch of merry song and was glad for Celia. She deserved some cheer. Macrath might be no worse than Roger, a good man seduced by Robert Bruce.

'Are you eager to see Perth, Maggie?' Roger asked as he took his reins from Aylmer.

'I am. I can't wait to see Fergus's surprise.' She laughed to think of it.

'I haven't seen you so happy in a long while.' Roger leaned from his saddle to kiss her. 'And I fear I'll now darken your mood, but I trust you'd prefer to have no unpleasant surprises. There's been more of an English presence in the town since you left in spring, the result of the uprisings here and there. They've blocked access to the canal in places where they're shoring up the town walls. They come and go. They're gone at present, which is why we are safe to enter. But we might need to depart quickly if things go badly. Do you see?'

She had not expected Perth to be untouched,

but it was alarming that the English were shoring up the town's defences. They were turning her beloved town into a prison like Edinburgh. Feeling faint, she struggled to breathe deeply and nodded. 'I do see.' She tried to think more pragmatically. 'They think to use Perth as a base from which to secure Scone?' It was where the Scots crowned their kings.

'I think they do,' said Roger.

Perhaps that was why Angus MacLaren had said the folk of Perth welcomed the English. Her joy in coming home was considerably dampened by all this.

Still, the beauty of the water meadows reflecting the blue sky, the flowering brush languid in the warmth, and the smells and sounds of home lifted her spirits once more as they neared the town. Her heart quickened as she caught sight of the Greyfriars' Monk Tower. Roger recommended they dismount and enter the town on foot, stabling the horses at the friary. Their own stable was too small.

Celia looked anxiously at the tower, the new bits of wall. Margaret told her what Roger had said.

'I pray we are not trapped here,' said Celia, 'walled within.'

'We'll not be so shortsighted,' Margaret assured her.

Watergate looked much as it had when Margaret had gone, modest wattle and daub houses gradually giving way to finer homes nearer the

Northgate crossing, a few with stone foundations. Their house stood proudly one short of the crossing. Margaret approached it with mixed feelings, happy to be returning with Roger, anxious that they not fall back into their old, separate ways.

And yet she already kept so much from him. She began to see that she was as much to blame for their being strangers as he was.

As they walked down Watergate, Margaret saw a neighbour hurry down the alley between houses, to share the news of their arrival with someone on Kirkgate, she guessed. Folk watched from their doorways, a few calling out to them, welcoming them home.

'It is a fine town,' said Celia, her eyes busily soaking in the houses, the ships on the river, the size of St John's on the next street.

'There is our house,' Margaret said, pointing to their left. 'And Fergus in the doorway!' She picked up her skirts and ran to him.

'St Columba, it's Maggie!' Fergus cried, his face alight, his long arms pulling her in for a crushing embrace. 'And Roger? You found your man?' He stepped back, shaking his head at her. 'Christ, I sometimes feared I'd not see you again. Where'd you find him?'

'He appeared in my bed chamber when I'd given up all expectations,' Margaret said.

'Come in, Maggie, Celia!' Fergus cried, stepping aside to let them precede him into the house.

Roger bowed to Fergus. 'By the Rood, it's good to be home.'

Margaret glanced back to watch the meeting of her husband and her brother.

'Roger, my goodbrother, I am more glad to see you than you can know,' Fergus said.

'I feel the same,' said Roger. He casually put a hand on Fergus's shoulder and stepped aside, nodding towards the man behind him. 'This is Aylmer, my manservant.'

'You are welcome,' said Fergus hurriedly, eager to join Margaret.

She looked around the hall in wonder. A tapestry hung on one wall, a cupboard held some fine pottery.

'What do you think?' Fergus asked.

'Who did you rob? I own none of these pieces.' She lifted a carved stool.

'Da's warehouse, things that none were taking. I was looking for records and found hoards of little treasures. I say use them.'

Bribes for their mother's affections, Margaret imagined, glancing over at Roger as if he could hear her thoughts. 'You've made a warmer home for us, Fergus. I cannot thank you enough.'

Roger's expression was unreadable to Margaret.

Fergus noted Maggie's furtive glance and cursed Roger for making her even think to look to him for approval. Left her to an empty house, he had, the swine. Fergus took the first opportunity to wrest his sister away from the others. 'Come see the kitchen, Maggie. I found some things for that, too.'

In the yard, between the buildings, he turned to her. 'So? What's his story for all his time away?'

'You must keep this close to you,' she whispered.

Christ, but she looked tired and drawn. She'd lost much flesh since Jack's funeral. He was glad Jonet had called in a lad to help her with the cooking today.

'Do you swear to silence?' Maggie had levelled her eyes at him.

'I do. And I can guess – marching right down Watergate for all eyes to see – he's gone to the English, hasn't he?'

She looked a little surprised. 'Only the supporters of the English walk boldly here?'

'It seems so when they are here.'

'He's Robert Bruce's man. He says the Bruce will save our people from Longshanks.'

Fergus had heard of the Bruce's growing following. 'So you wed a fool, Maggie. What are you to do now?'

'We might find it possible to ignore such matters.'

She turned towards the kitchen, but he'd seen her troubled look, and the resignation in her voice saddened him.

'How is Jonet?' she asked.

He ignored her attempt to change the subject. 'The town is loyal to the English for the most part, Maggie. I doubt the matter of the king can be ignored for long.'

'I suppose not,' she said, not turning her head. 'We'll talk more of this later, Fergus. For now, let me rejoice in my home, let me rest.'

'Will Celia lord it over Jonet?' Fergus asked. He had come to rely on the maid. He did not want her pushed around by the bossy Celia.

'She has changed, Fergus. You'll find her a most agreeable woman, and so will Jonet.'

He doubted it. But certainly Maggie seemed changed. He felt she'd leapt ahead in years compared with him. That was a benefit of travel.

That reminded him of the travel-worn visitor he'd had. He'd wondered about him all day, and because of him Fergus had not been entirely surprised by Maggie's arrival, as she would see when she stepped into the kitchen and saw the preparations for a welcoming meal. 'A black friar came early today, with a message for you, to come to St John's Kirk as soon as you might. He awaits you there.'

Maggie stiffened and Fergus watched her confusion give way to unease. 'A black friar? How would he know of our passage?'

'Perhaps travellers brought news to Elcho and Ma is sending word to you?' he suggested.

She shook her head. 'We've just come from there. Did he say anything else?'

'No. He would not even say how he knew of your coming, or with whom you travelled.'

She was studying the ground now, then turned to the kitchen, back to him. Her eyes were lit with purpose. 'Perhaps I should go now, before I am missed. Stay a little in the kitchen, Fergus, and if anyone asks, say I went to the kirk to thank the Lord for our safe arrival.'

'You're not feared Roger will come for you?'

'He'd see but a black friar. It should not alarm him as long as he knows nothing more. Do you understand, Brother?'

He nodded. Whatever she was about, it was nothing innocent. He decided to follow her.

❧ 12 ❧

A Crook-backed Friar

Spying on his sister was nothing admirable. Fergus hesitated, watching Maggie disappear down Watergate. She was fussing with her veil. What did she care how she appeared to a friar? But women often behaved so, dressing up to return a neighbour's plate or to go to the flesher's shop.

She had treated him as did all the family, ordering him to make excuses for her while she went running about, to stand in the kitchen and let time go by so that she would not be followed too soon. It was time she learned that he was not a child. He took the gravel path into the backlands as she turned left on Northgate.

Across from St John's Kirk he paused. Maggie stood before the door speaking with a white-haired woman – Dame Ada, one of Maggie's friends. This might be a long interruption.

Fergus ducked behind the house that faced the kirk, grateful that no one was about because he was feeling childish, sneaking after his sister. He might simply ask her on her return what the friar had to say. She seldom kept things from him. He peeked around the house and cursed. Dame Ada was well away from the kirk and Maggie had disappeared. Should he return to the house or cross to the kirk and slip into the darkness, hoping not to be seen? He decided to return to the kitchen to resume preparations for the meal. He told Jonet how many were biding at the house, and helped her carry trays of wine, bread, meat and cheese across the yard.

The three travellers watched them set out the food with interest.

It was Fergus's first chance to have a good look at Roger, and he wondered at the change. Roger had always looked like a man fond of long meals and good drink, well padded and with a slightly puffy face, a mien implying a weak nature. Now he looked weathered and hardened, a man who could act decisively.

His servant must cost him a goodly amount, and that seemed at odds with Roger's appearance. Fergus wondered how his goodbrother had raised the money for Aylmer. As Roger's acting factor, Fergus knew that the money had not come from his trade in Perth, and yet such a self-important servant would not come cheaply.

It was Celia who asked for Maggie as Roger and Aylmer took up cups of wine. Fergus had expected her to be trouble, but not so quickly.

'She's gone to the kirk to say thanks for your safe arrival,' he said, almost believing it himself.

He noticed how Roger exchanged looks with Aylmer, then tossed down his wine and handed Jonet the cup. 'I'll join my wife.'

Celia frowned after him. Aylmer offered her a cup of wine. She took it in a trembling hand.

Fergus wondered at the servants' differing behaviour towards one another.

Margaret guessed that it was James who had summoned her to the kirk – he had used the disguise of a black friar before – and he'd said he would likely arrive before her because he would travel lightly and take risks. But she had not expected to hear from him so soon. He might have given her a chance to rest after the long ride, to reacquaint herself with Perth. Her legs ached from riding, her feelings were tangled, she was doubting the wisdom of slipping away from Roger without more forethought, and sorry she had not taken the time to confide in Fergus. He had looked angry, and she couldn't blame him.

Turning on to Northgate, Margaret regretted having rushed out without consulting Celia on her appearance. The street was bustling with acquaintances.

'Dame Margaret!' a woman called out.

Moving through the people, she explained she was off to the kirk to give thanks for her safe return. The familiar voices against the background of river sounds were at once reassuring and disorienting. She was relieved to escape into Kirkgate. In such familiar surroundings she felt a stranger to the new self who was unfolding. The young woman she had been would have been troubled to think she would one day agree to spy on these people, no matter how noble the cause. She prayed God that her transformation was not her undoing.

As she crossed Kirkgate, someone hailed her from the kirk porch. It had not occurred to her that she might see an acquaintance at the kirk in mid-afternoon. The complication was unwelcome. But Margaret relaxed as she recognised Dame Ada, a friend who had long provided her with a sanctuary whenever needed, never asking questions unless invited to. Margaret admired Ada's plainspoken ways and wide-ranging knowledge. She cut a fine figure in her simple gown of costly wool that she kept fashionable with her skilful needlework. Her posture was regal, her face unlined despite the pure white hair braided and netted beneath a veil of shimmering silk.

'Maggie!' The tall woman held out her arms. 'Oh, my dear Maggie.' Ada embraced her. 'When Fergus told me you'd gone with Andrew to Edinburgh I feared I might never see you again.'

The woman's strong, rose-scented embrace brought tears of joy to Margaret. 'I've missed you so,' she said, pulling back a little to wipe her eyes and look at her good friend.

Ada, too, brushed at tears. 'How long have you been home?'

'Long enough to leave my scrip in the house and hurry here to say a prayer of thanks for my safe return.'

Ada gave a curt nod. Her eyes smiled. 'Good. Then I shan't waste time brooding over your neglecting me. Come tomorrow, when you can. My niece and her child are biding with me. I have spoken of you so much it will be a treat for my niece to meet you.'

'I promise.'

'Then I shall leave you to your prayers, my dear Maggie.' With another quick hug, Ada resumed her walk.

Calmed by the happy encounter, Margaret slipped into the kirk. Its thick walls had absorbed some of the sun's warmth, but the dim nave was still cooler than without, a coolness welcome to Margaret, whose hands and back were damp with the tension of sneaking about. Eavesdropping at the tavern had not filled her with such anxiety as this. Margaret walked slowly down the nave towards the screen and knelt in a circle of light shining down from a clerestory window. She wished she had her beads.

'*Benedicite*, Dame Margaret,' a man whispered.

She regarded a crook-backed friar. It was not James after all. '*Benedicite*,' she said. 'You sent for me, sir?'

He bowed. 'I did.'

'How did you recognise me?'

'Might we walk out into the kirk yard? I have missed too much of this glorious day.' He shaped his words with softened sounds as had a Welshman her father had once hired.

'Yes.' She preferred to be in the daylight with a stranger.

'Bless you, my child.'

She rose and followed him out of the side door, matching her pace to his halting gait. He chose a bench, half shaded by a yew, half in the sun.

'I pray you, forgive my leaving you the chilly side,' he said as he settled on the sunny half. 'Old bones need warmth.'

'I am happy with the shade,' Margaret assured him. 'Who sent you to me?'

'No one.'

She turned to him. He lifted his face to the light. The cleft in his chin was unmistakable. ·'James!'

He wore a self-satisfied smirk. 'You truly did not know me at first.'

'No. I did not know you were a player.'

Even now he kept the posture of the aged friar, and the Welsh accent. 'Had my kin less need of my diplomatic skills I might have found joy in a troop of players.' He grew serious. 'Will you be missed?'

'I shall, and soon.' She could not think how she would manage to tell him all without the risk that Roger might grow impatient and come seeking her.

'Then I'll be quick. How goes your mother?'

'My—' Margaret felt her face grow hot despite the shade. 'You, too? Is *all* the world awaiting a sign from my mother?' Her anger surprised her.

James coolly absorbed her outburst, not even straightening his back. 'She was difficult?'

'Did you follow us?'

His brows came together in puzzlement. 'We have eyes everywhere. You are well aware that yours are not the only pair assisting us.'

Of course she knew that. He had chosen not to answer her question. But his reluctance betrayed him. 'Have a care, you're sounding more English than Welsh,' she noted, glad to prick him in return.

'Roger wanted her to explain her visions of you, didn't he?'

Naked to the world, that is how she felt, her situation exposed. 'He did. But he came away unsatisfied.'

'She would not see him?'

She detected pleasure in James's eyes.

'No. Nor would she enlighten me. Damnable woman, what good has she ever done me? All my life, her—' She stopped herself, embarrassed by the outburst.

'Forgive me for pressing you, my friend,' James said, his Welsh accent returned. He cocked his head, then stiffly rose. 'I must go, but I'll come again. Look out for me.'

She heard approaching footsteps and bowed her head in prayer. James disappeared around the kirk, as quickly as an elderly friar could manage, and was almost out of sight when Roger stepped out of the kirk, hesitated, then approached her.

Margaret lifted her head.

'Maggie. I grew worried, not finding you within.' Roger held out his hands to her. His eyes searched her face.

She accepted his help in rising. 'I wanted some air.'

'I did not know the journey so distressed you – to rush to the kirk at once as you did.'

'The truth of it is that I give thanks for your return, not so much for the safe journey, although I am grateful that it passed without injury to any of us.'

Roger pulled her into his arms. 'I, too, have given thanks for our reunion.'

Despite everything, she felt safe in his arms, so safe. Why, then, did she doubt him?

They left the kirk yard arm in arm, walking slowly. But by the time they arrived at the house they were arguing about Fergus's improvements.

'He did us no good deed with such fussing,' Roger said. 'The English will take it all when they return.'

'Now it's the English. Before, our house was bare because you needed the coin to build up your trade, or you wanted to wait until you found just the right items abroad. It was a cold house, Roger, a house with no heart.'

'You never said so.'

'I did. You did not wish to hear.'

Roger paused at the door. 'We must not invite the interest of the English.'

'What cause would they have to enter our home?'

Roger shook his head, as if baffled by Margaret's resistance. 'We'll not argue in front of the others.' His voice was cold.

'Of course not,' Margaret said, angry that he had said it first, that they had fallen back into the old pattern, he ordering, she obeying. And yet she had stood her ground.

They shared no tenderness that night.

It had been a strained trio at the dinner table, Roger, Margaret, and Fergus. Aylmer and Celia had eaten earlier so that the three might enjoy a private reunion. It proved to be no favour. In the morning, Margaret could bear Fergus's round-shouldered petulance no longer and invited him to walk with her along the river, hoping to make amends with him.

'I'm sorry I rushed away with no explanation yesterday,' she began as they turned on to Northgate.

'You're shoving me aside like the rest of them.'

'No, Fergus, never. I won't do that to you. There was just no time to explain.'

He brightened at that, and pointed to Matilda's father's leather shop. 'I'm often invited to sup with the family,' he said, his smile wide and smug.

Ah, Matilda, the beauty of Perth, raven hair and blue eyes. Margaret could well imagine how grand Fergus must feel.

'So what's the truth of your black friar, eh?' he asked. 'He's not your leman, is he?'

Margaret gave a startled laugh. 'I was wondering where to begin, but you've decided for me. You must swear that you'll keep whatever I say to yourself.'

He glanced at her with a conspiratorial grin.

'For the good of our people,' she added.

He grew serious. 'I swear, Maggie. I can be trusted.'

She told him of James Comyn, and her vow to do what she could to help their king return.

Fergus had paused as they reached the river and put his hands on her shoulders. 'God's blood, Maggie, you're the brave one!'

He was a head taller than she, and when they

stood so she found it difficult to remember that she was his elder.

'Do you think so?' she asked, not certain herself. 'Many are doing what they can.'

Fergus glanced around and then leaned closer. 'If you plan to help King John Balliol in Perth, you tread a dangerous path, Maggie. The folk are allied to the English, at least outwardly. There was much nasty talk when the kin of Dame Agnes of Elcho went to guard the nunnery, no matter that it was because of the men who assaulted Marion and searched Ma's chamber.'

Margaret recalled what Marion had said of one of the intruders' accents. 'Perhaps they know something of the event.' She told Fergus what Marion had said about one with a southern accent.

'Marion told me none of that!' he exclaimed.

'Did you ask her?'

He sighed. 'No. Fool that I am, I asked only Ma.'

'Don't blame yourself. We are ever hopeful that Ma will care to help us, though she's never given us cause to expect it.'

'She told you naught?'

Margaret began to shake her head, then checked herself. 'Nothing of that night, but something that might pertain to it. Da is in Perth. Hiding. Doing some secret trading, she thinks.'

'No!'

'And he means to take Ma back to Bruges when he sails.'

Fergus snorted. 'And what's she say to that?'

'It won't happen, so she says. And the priory's confessor supports her refusal.'

'But Da *wanted* her locked away. He said he'd had enough of her Sight.'

'His passion has betrayed his wit?'

They both laughed, and turning south along the river bank, arm in arm, they talked about past summers for a while. Margaret felt comforted by the familiarity of the waterfront, the warehouses, the tarry scents, the children playing along the bank. Giving Fergus only half her attention, she was not disappointed when he grew silent. She pointed out the changes she noticed.

Suddenly Fergus blurted, 'Da didn't even trust me enough to let me know he was here. Or was it Da who went through the houses, searching for something, never mind the bother he caused not telling me? Is someone looking for him, do you think?'

It came out such a jumble that Margaret realised she had almost missed how much their father's secrecy hurt Fergus. 'Ma thought he might be hiding from an unhappy rival in trade. You know he thinks as little about us as she does.'

Fergus was silent for a few steps. 'What news of our brother?'

This was the most difficult to tell Fergus, that

Andrew was confessor to the English at Soutra. She explained his danger.

'St Columba watch over him,' Fergus said in an unsteady voice as he crossed himself.

They had turned at the shipyard and were walking back up the bank when Dame Ada drew near.

'She's on your tail everywhere you go,' Fergus muttered.

Margaret had not told him of her meeting with Ada the previous day. She stopped. 'What do you mean? Did you follow me to the kirk yesterday?'

The blush that dulled his freckles was his confession.

'Why?'

'You none of you tell me anything.'

'Fergus.'

He hung his head. 'I was feeling sorry for myself. Now I'm sorry I believed you'd tell me naught.'

'We must trust one another,' Margaret said, 'you and Andrew and me. We've no other Kerrs to trust.'

'Uncle Murdoch?'

'Oh, there's much to tell you about him. But Dame Ada is upon us.' Margaret lifted her head. 'So you could not stay within on such a day either?'

Dame Ada glanced from Fergus to Margaret. 'I can see I'm interrupting confidences. You've much to say to one another.'

'And much time to say it in,' said Margaret.

'Sinclair will be wanting to go over the accounts,' said Fergus. 'I'll take my leave of you, Sister. God speed, Dame Ada.' He strode off up the bank.

In too much haste, Margaret thought, wondering whether Ada sensed Fergus's aversion to her.

'Is this a good day to meet your niece?' Margaret asked.

Ada beamed. 'It is, Maggie. Come along. Do not mind your brother.'

But of course she knew how Fergus felt – he'd been jealous of their close friendship ever since the brief time in her childhood that Margaret entertained the fantasy that Ada was her true mother and that she was the daughter of a great lord.

Being in Ada's home was a balm to Margaret's bruised and conflicted heart. She left Ada's in mid-afternoon, relaxed and in good spirits. Ada's niece and child were a happy, self-contained pair, and Margaret had heard much of the news of the town from her friend.

She heard raised voices as she returned home – Roger's deep voice, Fergus's slightly higher one, both angry. She found them standing just out of reach of one another, Roger attacking, Fergus defending. Aylmer sat on a bench behind Roger, watching Fergus intently. The voices echoed in the almost unfurnished hall.

'They can hear you on Northgate,' Margaret said loudly. The exaggeration silenced them long enough for her to ask what was the matter.

Roger shook his head and turned away from her, then back. 'Stay out of this.'

'He says I didn't lock the warehouse last night,' said Fergus. 'But I did. I'm sure of it.' He clenched his hands as if ready to defend his honour with a good punch.

When Roger resumed his accusations, Fergus withdrew into his hundredth review of his departure from his father's warehouse the previous day. He remembered checking twice that he'd blown out any lamps, not knowing how soon he would return, with Maggie apparently arriving any moment according to the friar. While securing the door he had thought of his sister's skill in picking locks and wondered whether Uncle Murdoch had taught her anything new. But as sure as he was that he had locked the warehouse, there was no denying the body he'd seen lying in it a little while ago.

When Fergus had parted from Margaret and returned to the house he'd found Aylmer waiting for him. 'Master Roger sent me to fetch you to the Kerr warehouse.' His grim expression had chilled Fergus.

'What's amiss?'

'You'll see soon enough.'

Fergus was pulled from his recollection of the summons by Maggie's voice asking what they'd found in the warehouse.

'John Smyth,' Fergus said.

Maggie frowned and shook her head. 'Should I know that name?'

'He was Da's clerk. When Da fired him for thieving Smyth swore he'd avenge his honour.' Fergus nodded at Maggie's nod. 'I see you remember now.'

She had gone pale. 'Tell me what you saw, Fergus. Everything.'

Roger stepped between them. 'Maggie, this is not your concern.'

She stepped around him. 'Fergus.'

'It looked as if he'd been climbing atop barrels stacked on their sides and they rolled out beneath him and over him. Heavy barrels. His neck was broken.'

Maggie crossed herself. 'Holy Mary Mother of God.'

'If Fergus had locked the door—' Roger began.

'Be quiet!' Maggie shouted.

Fergus was much surprised. His sister was livid.

'What is it?' Roger said in a quieter, but nastier tone. 'You can't believe your brother is so irresponsible? That such an accident could happen when he was in charge?'

Fergus jumped in. 'How am I to ensure that no accidents happen in the warehouses?'

226

'By locking the doors,' Roger shouted.

'I did.'

Roger was nodding. 'Perhaps you did. Where do you keep the keys?'

At that, Margaret withdrew to her chamber and flung herself on the bed, muttering prayers for her father's soul. She believed Fergus, and she would have stayed to defend him but for the trembling that had begun when Fergus had reminded her of the dead man's connection with their father.

'Shall I fetch you some wine?' Celia asked quietly.

Margaret rolled on to her side and contemplated the slight figure with the strong chin and level brows. 'I'm so frightened, Celia,' she said, feeling the need to tell someone her suspicions.

Celia perched on the edge of the bed. 'Is it what they're shouting about down below? The man with the broken neck?'

Margaret sat up. 'He hated my da for calling him a thief. I fear . . . oh, dear Lord forgive him.' She was unable to form the accusing words.

'Even if he's an unrepentant thief, the Lord will forgive him.'

'I meant my father. I don't believe Smyth was just thieving.' Margaret breathed deeply. With enough breath she might get it out. 'I think he was spying on my father, hoping to learn something in the warehouse.'

Celia sighed, smoothed the coverlet. 'With all respect, you are not thinking clearly, Dame Margaret. It does not matter what he was intending, he's dead. Struck down by his own trespass. So what can you possibly have to fear from him?'

'My father is in Perth, Celia. Hiding. Ma has seen him.'

'Oh.' The small word, not a word at all really, expressed far more concern than Celia allowed in her expression.

'I very much fear that he might also have been in Edinburgh, that he caught Old Will in the undercroft, or Will caught him.'

Celia sniffed. 'Well, you've decided all this in a very short time, Mistress. You must need a glass of wine to refresh yourself after so much thinking.' She rose and withdrew.

Margaret sank back down on to her stomach and tried to convince herself that Celia was right, that she was making too much out of a coincidence. But she could not quiet her mind.

And how would it come to pass that Master Malcolm was in Edinburgh the very night that Old Will searched his trunk? Celia might have asked, but she'd kept her peace, thinking Margaret was already too interested. As she descended to the hall she happened on Jonet standing over the bundles brought upriver from Elcho. Jonet swung round as Celia cleared her throat.

'Och, but you gave me a fright,' said Jonet, pressing her chest. She was slightly younger than Celia, sturdily built. Her fluttery behaviour did not fit her appearance.

Celia explained what was in the bundles.

'That will bring Dame Margaret some cheer. She's been so sad in this house.'

'Servants should not gossip about their employers,' Celia snapped.

Jonet pressed her lips together. 'I wish the mistress well, she knows that I do.'

'I'll help you with those in a little while,' Celia said. 'Where is Master Roger?'

'He and his servant went off to the warehouse with Master Fergus,' Jonet said, crossing herself.

So she probably knew about the body. Celia thanked her and hurried out towards the kitchen, distressed that in such a family as this a servant like Jonet might not have the sense to keep her own counsel. Celia had imagined Margaret had come from a comfortable family of a wealthy merchant. But the truth was not so lovely. Madwomen and murderers. She sighed to herself, pouring a cup of wine for Margaret.

'I've no need of that,' Margaret said, startling Celia so she almost dropped the cup. She had not noticed Margaret entering the kitchen. 'I'm going to walk out into the fields. I need air.'

'I'll go with you then,' Celia insisted, not liking the nervousness in her mistress's carriage. She was like a cat with its ears back, looking for an escape.

Margaret suddenly dropped on to a bench. 'Where is Roger?'

'He and your brother went to the warehouse.'

Margaret sighed and sat for a moment, head in hands. Just as Celia was handing her the cup, Margaret sprang up and stepped out into the yard.

Celia stood with cup in hand, watching Margaret's restless gait, wondering whether she should follow. What must she be feeling, to return to this house with such hope only to have everything turn so ugly? As Celia pondered this she noticed a man emerging from the shadows by the stable.

She stepped outside. 'Mistress, do you know that man?' she hissed, pointing to him. As he approached he seemed familiar to her.

Margaret gave a little cry. The man hurried forward, shaking his head, a finger to his lips.

Of course, Celia thought, he reminded her of his brother Murdoch Kerr.

Margaret took him by the elbow. 'Come away in, Da.'

Celia frowned at the affection in her mistress's voice. She'd heard nothing of Malcolm Kerr to think he'd earned that.

❦ 13 ❧

THIS PURGATORY

Malcolm retreated from Margaret's grasp. 'It would be unwise for me to go within, Maggie.'

He looked well. As ever, his long nose, dark eyes, and bushy brows gave him the air of a predator. She noticed that as they'd aged, her father and his brother Murdoch had grown more alike in appearance, their red hair thinning and growing pale, their fair complexions spotted, their girths settling in their middles. But her father had neither her uncle's rolling gait nor his scars. He had lived more comfortably and moderately. At the moment he was glancing nervously towards the street.

'There are only the two servants and me,' she said. 'You'll be safer within.' News of the death in his warehouse would soon spread through the town, and whatever his reason for hiding had been, he might risk his life if he were seen now.

'Two servants – that's bad enough.'

'Anyone passing along Watergate can see you here,' she said. 'Come within, into the kitchen.'

'No. In there we cannot hear whether someone enters the house.'

'Do you ken what happened to John Smyth?' She tried to keep her tone even. Now that she was face to face with him she could not believe her father a murderer.

But Malcolm searched her eyes and saddened. 'Even you, lass. How are those without our tie to believe in my innocence if you don't?'

'I did not accuse you. Come into the hall, do.' She moved towards it, heard him following.

He stopped just inside the door that opened out towards the kitchen, where it was shielded from the hall by a tall wooden screen. 'This is far enough.'

Margaret pulled out a bench and they sat straddling it, facing each other. He smelled of spices.

'Why are you here, Da?'

Again he looked taken aback. 'How can you ask that, Maggie? I worried when I arrived and heard of Roger's abandonment.'

'I mean back in the country.'

He shook his head in sympathy. 'You are hardened by all your troubles, I understand.' He paused, as if expecting her to protest, but shrugged when she did not shift her level look.

'I am here because King Edward is in the Low Countries. It seemed an opportunity to retrieve more of my goods. I'd not heard that so many troops were biding here, and that Wallace and Murray had stirred up the people so. I'd not have come had I kenned the mood of the land.'

Margaret relaxed a little, believing he told the truth – as far as he cared to. 'I did not see your ship on the river.'

'No, and I'll not tell you where it is.'

'I was not about to ask.'

Her father grunted and drummed his fingers on the bench for a few moments, staring out at the yard. 'Edward of England has arrived too late in Flanders. They've no need of him. His ambition outruns his wit. I did not wish to be there when he needed a dog to kick, eh, lass?'

Margaret did not feel obliged to offer sympathy. 'Where are you biding, Da?'

'Best you ken nothing of my activities.'

'You sound like Uncle Murdoch and Roger. But Fergus and I have a right to know, having the care of your warehouse. He will surely be questioned.'

'And neither of you will have aught to say.'

'The English won't believe that.'

'They are not here at present,' her father reminded her.

She would not be so easily dismissed. 'Why was John Smyth in your warehouse?'

Pressing a hand to the back of his seamed neck,

her father tilted his head back and sighed. 'That man has been my bane since . . . What was I thinking when I gave him work? Och, Maggie, the mistakes we make in the name of charity.' He pressed his temples as if just thinking of John Smyth made his head ache. 'What did Roger see in the warehouse? Can he tell what befell the thieving sneak?'

Margaret could not assess whether or not her father was faking innocence. 'I've not been to the warehouse. Fergus is there now. You might learn more from him.'

Her father sighed with impatience. 'I cannot risk being seen there, Maggie.' He grew quiet.

'Was it a difficult crossing?' she asked, finding herself reluctant to part with him, though her feelings for him were a confusing mix of suspicion and love.

'We had good weather, God be thanked, but we were twice boarded by the English.'

'You did not lose your ship?'

'No, no. They were satisfied that we were a merchant ship, nothing more.'

She guessed by his guarded expression that there was more to the tale than he wished to tell her.

'You mentioned my brother,' he said suddenly. 'So it is true that you've been to Edinburgh seeking news of your husband, that you thought Roger had deserted you?'

'You are well informed. He was away for a long while, and things being as they are, and having no word of him . . .' She trailed off, tired of making excuses for Roger. 'Yes, Da. I thought he had.'

'Pray God he intends to do his duty by you. I'd begun to regret your marrying him.'

The words stung her. What was his regret in comparison to hers?

'I never thought he would prove so intractable,' Malcolm continued. 'I am much grieved by his behaviour. And Jack's murder –' he palmed his eyes, then dropped his hands, a wounded look on his face – 'I cannot think why God so punishes us.'

His professed grief did not move Margaret. 'You chose him, Da.'

She was about to say more, but Jonet and Celia's conversation in the hall about the placement of the tapestries was interrupted by Celia's loud comment, 'Here come the men. They can assist us.'

Her father swung his leg over the bench, and with a nod to Margaret, slipped away, crossing the yard behind the kitchen. Pushing the bench back against the wall, Margaret smoothed her skirts, took a deep breath, and stepped out from behind the screen just as Roger entered.

'I wish to go to Da's warehouse,' she said.

Roger glanced at the maids and, taking Margaret's arm, led her back to where she had just sat with her father.

'I want to scc thc body,' she continued.

'You're not to pry into matters that are not your concern, Maggie, not here in Perth. You have your name to uphold.'

'*Your* name, you mean.' She had a wild thought that she did not voice, frightened by both the appeal of it and the finality. Roger might annul their marriage – they had no children, it was done all the time – and then be free of the Kerrs, whom he found so inconvenient. And she would be free. But an annulment was costly, and unless he had hidden money from her, which would be no surprise, he could not afford one.

Furious at Roger's treatment and embarrassed by how ill he'd felt in the presence of the corpse, Fergus did not return to the hall but found occupation in the stable. While cleaning a saddle, he began to plan his departure for Aberdeen. Now that Roger and Maggie were back he would be free to go. It was a good season for travel, and he would have time to learn some of the workings of the shipyard before it was idled by winter storms.

'You're looking gladsome, Son.'

He turned towards his father's voice with surprise. 'I hope I've no cause to be otherwise. When did you return?'

Malcolm settled down on a grooming stool with a sigh. 'You have done a man's work here since I left.'

236

'That should be no cause for wonder, considering I *am* a man.'

Malcolm dropped his head and nodded. 'So you are. So you are.'

Fergus crossed his arms and studied his father, deciding that he looked well but uncomfortable, perhaps worried.

Malcolm squinted at Fergus as if trying to read his mind. 'Maggie tells me you've seen the body in my warehouse.'

Fergus nodded. 'That is why you've come, I'll warrant.'

'So? What did you see?'

Fergus told him.

Malcolm listened impatiently. 'Anything else? Was there anything in his hands? Anything near him that looked out of place?'

'Not that I noticed. Why?'

Malcolm scratched his forehead. 'No matter.'

It was hardly no matter, the way he had asked it.

'I see your goodbrother is here,' Malcolm said. 'What's Sinclair doing in Perth?'

'Coming home with his wife – what else would he be doing here?' Fergus noted the use of Roger's surname, which was not how his father had been wont to refer to him.

'Who's the man with him?'

'His servant. Aylmer.'

'Indeed?' Malcolm worked his neck as if it were stiff. 'So fine a servant, Sinclair must have managed to increase his wealth while away. What has he been doing?'

Fergus had thought his father curious about Roger's loyalties. He was disappointed that he cared only about how Roger had afforded Aylmer. 'Why ask me? I care nothing for costly servants, and Roger has offered no explanation. We have never been confidants.'

Roger and Margaret stood silently brooding on each other's shoes.

'You are my wife,' Roger said, breaking the silence in a full voice that snapped Margaret back from her fantasy of freedom. 'What you do reflects on me.' He looked like the angry prophet from the Old Testament she had once seen on a wall mural.

'If you're so concerned about your name,' she said, 'perhaps we should carry on this discussion in our bedchamber rather than before an audience. When you raise your voice you can be heard beyond the screen.'

Without waiting for his response, she went to tell Celia and Jonet that she needed nothing, and then climbed the steps to the solar. Roger followed, pausing to say something under his breath to Aylmer, and then continuing up the steps behind her. The grim set of his face caused Margaret a confusing pang of regret that she had alienated him. And yet she had just thought how good it might be to be free of him. She was unravelling.

Roger propped one foot up on a stool and rested an elbow on the bent leg. 'Much of your behaviour has displeased me of late: leaving the safety of my mother's house for Edinburgh, serving in your uncle's tavern, taking it upon yourself to find my cousin's murderer.' He looked disgusted.

It was as if he'd heard nothing she'd said to him. 'Can't you understand how I feared for you? Are you made of stone?' She turned away, afraid to say more.

'You were safe at home,' he said. 'Or in Dunfermline with my mother.'

'Oh Roger, Roger, we've already argued about this.'

'You cannot go to the warehouse. You must behave as befits a wife.'

She rounded on him. 'I believe you forfeited any expectation of that when you abandoned me.'

'What? I cannot believe my ears. Is this Maggie speaking, or some devil taken up her body? I forfeited nothing for I did not desert you. I'm here now, wife, and I expect you to obey. And what's more, the laws of both God and man are on my side.'

'How fortunate for you.' She almost spat out the words. 'But by God's law you were to love and protect me.'

'I do—'

'What was I to think when you ran from me in Edinburgh, Roger? What would you have thought had I run from you? Was it to protect me that you fought for Robert Bruce? And now, now you order me about with steel in your eyes and ice in your heart. I sometimes think Jack loved me more than you do.'

Roger's anger seemed to cool and he looked round as if searching for something.

Margaret held her breath, fearing she had gone too far, that she had unwittingly followed on from her thought of annulment.

'I should not have said such things, Maggie.'

Roger's sudden apology confused Margaret.

'Nor I,' she whispered.

Roger sat down heavily and stared at the floor for a long while.

Margaret did not know whether to join him on the bench or leave him to his thoughts. Her heart still pounded. Her fear at the thought of losing Roger was a revelation to her.

Suddenly Roger rose and, stretching, grasped the beam above, then dropped his arms to his sides as if they were dead weights. 'What suffering Longshanks has wrought.' He took Margaret's hands in his. 'All I meant was that we must avoid calling attention to ourselves. And as it is not your custom to go to Malcolm's warehouse, people might make note of your doing so. Do you see?'

Margaret sighed. 'I do, Roger. I do see.'

'It is such a small request,' said Malcolm. 'Engage

Sinclair in talk of the English presence in Perth. See how he responds. Ask what he thinks of all this.'

At least his father's mind was now on the fighting, but Fergus felt the heat rising in him. He was once again being treated as the family toady. 'Come within and ask him yourself. Be a man, not a sneaking coward.'

'You little—' Malcolm slapped him on the cheek.

Fergus grabbed his father by the collar and was about to punch him, but reason stayed his hand. He was not only an elderly man but, more significantly, Fergus's father, and to strike him might create a permanent rift. Fergus's pride was not worth the risk.

Malcolm stepped back to adjust his tunic, forcing a chuckle. 'Well, you've learned a great deal about fighting since I left.'

'I saw a need for it.' Fergus was breathing hard and trembling with the audacity of what he'd almost done. It was no triumph. Twice since Maggie's return he'd behaved in a way he'd afterwards regretted. 'I don't understand why you don't talk to Roger yourself. You liked him well enough when you wed him to Maggie.'

His father did not answer at once, examining an imperfection in the saddle Fergus had been oiling, tinkering with a buckle that had a crooked tongue. 'It was a good match for her, or so I thought.'

'You might have done better to let her choose,' said Fergus.

Malcolm laughed. 'You might have learned to fight, but you've still much to learn of life, son. I'll come again. Surely you can glean something of Sinclair's mind without betraying your high moral code – or me. I don't want him to know I'm here. It's as simple as that.' He peered out of the stable, then slipped away.

Fergus had no intention of biding in Perth long enough to learn anything for his father.

James walked through the camp, observing archery practice, sword drills, wrestling. Wallace's men ranged in age from a little younger than Hal to greybeards. Some proudly carried battle scars, others were skilled in one or another of the martial arts but as yet untried, and many were learning the arts for the first time. What was characteristic of the great majority of them was their common status. As James wandered among them he wondered where his fine kin were hiding while these simpler men fought for them.

A young man caught up to him by a stream. 'The Wallace has sent me to fetch you, sir.'

James followed him to the crest of a hill on which several others were gathered. Wallace was talking to a sweaty, dusty messenger, but sent him off for food and drink when James joined them.

Wallace shaded his eyes from the sun. 'I must

talk to the Kerr woman,' he said, as if he were concluding an argument and would not entertain further debate.

'I have explained the difficulty—' James began.

Wallace waved him quiet. 'You ken not the danger she is in, James. Her father, her husband – they are both sought by the English – her father because of his return from Bruges, her husband because he is known to be escorting people and money back and forth across the border for Robert Bruce. And with a company of English soldiers approaching Perth . . .'

So attempting to get Edwina across the border had not been an unusual mission for Roger. And this was news about Margaret's father. 'Malcolm Kerr has returned?'

Wallace nodded. 'He is in Perth.'

'Why would he return now?'

'I share with the English a keen wish to know that very thing.'

'Are Sinclair and Kerr the reasons the English are headed for Perth?'

'We don't know. But there is rumour of a death in Malcolm Kerr's warehouse. The English will surely hear of it from the traitors in the town. I want to meet Dame Margaret before fear silences her.'

James wondered whether it was too late already. He was glad he had told Margaret nothing of import regarding their dealings in the north. She was still too untried to trust completely. But he must see to her safety.

Christiana knelt beside Dame Bethag in the small nunnery kirk, seeking serenity. The ever smiling, ever calm nun had suggested that Prioress Agnes would be a more appropriate tutor, but Christiana found nothing she wished to emulate in the beauty with the chilly voice and pinched expression who sighed impatiently throughout Mass. She wished to learn to quiet the chaos in her mind, and Bethag seemed the ideal model to emulate.

Sunlight fell on the statue of the Blessed Virgin, and Mary's face glowed. Christiana caught her breath and crossed herself, staring unblinkingly at the illuminated face, expecting a vision.

'Close your eyes,' Dame Bethag said quietly. The nun knelt with rosewood beads encircling hands pressed together in prayer.

'Look at the Mother of God,' Christiana whispered.

The nun raised her eyes and smiled. 'A moment of grace. Come. Close your eyes, empty your mind, and receive the Virgin's gift of grace.'

'But what if she is sending me a vision?' Christiana asked.

Bethag straightened, her expression one of wonder. 'Are you receiving a vision?'

Christiana shook her head. 'No, or perhaps – look at the heavenly light!'

The nun's expression was sympathetic. 'It is but the sun lighting her face as it does every day at this time. There is no mystery to it. Now come. You asked for my instruction.'

Blushing, Christiana bowed her head and closed her eyes. Thoughts surfaced from the roiling pool of her mind, like salmon leaping upriver, flashing silver in the sunlight. She had behaved like a fool. Perhaps she had never experienced a real vision. She was a married woman – what was she doing biding in a convent? On and on. She fought the thoughts and tried to think of nothingness, but it was impossible.

'How can I empty my thoughts when my thoughts do not come from within?' she asked.

And how was this dear nun so patient, still encouraging Christiana with her peaceful smile? Surely Bethag had never had such an inept student.

'But your thoughts do come from within. Even when the devil tempts you, he does so from within, and you are responsible for what thoughts you accept. God holds us responsible, you know that. Now close your eyes, breathe deeply, and feel the Blessed Mother's love bathe you in heavenly light.'

'I don't deserve heavenly light.'

'It is not for you to judge,' said Bethag.

Once more Christiana closed her eyes. This time she tried imagining a white light emanating from the statue of the Blessed Mother before which she knelt. The light flowed around her, enveloping her, filling her with grace. A sweet smell accompanied the light, and the sound of tiny bells. Her sandalled feet grew warm, her heart lifted. Was this a vision? But Dame Bethag had led her to it. And with that thought, the beautiful moment dissolved. Christiana tried to recall it, tried to will the sensations, but her thoughts flitted all about with no order.

'I felt it for a moment,' she whispered.

'What happened?' asked Bethag.

Christiana described what she had seen and felt. 'I began to wonder if it was a vision, and that is when it faded.'

'The Virgin has blessed you,' said Bethag with a radiant smile. She began to rise.

Christiana touched her arm. 'Could we not try again?'

Bethag patted her hand. 'You have no more need of me, Christiana. You asked how you might cultivate a quiet spirit. I showed you the way, and you were able to follow. Now it is a matter of practice.'

'But I lost it.'

'Grace must be earned, Dame Christiana. We must still our minds in order to receive it. And ever the world rushes in to shatter the stillness. And so we begin again. Moment after moment, day after day, year after year. Until we attain the everlasting

246

grace that is the kingdom of heaven.'

Rising, Christiana bowed to Dame Bethag and whispered, 'I asked for the key to your serenity, Dame Bethag, and your clear-headedness.'

'And I have given it to you, Dame Christiana. Rest in the grace of the Blessed Virgin. Have faith that she is ever there to break your fall, to nudge you away from a mistake. Quiet your mind and accept her grace. That is all you need to do.' Bethag bowed and seemed to glide out into the sunlit yard.

Kneeling again, Christiana closed her eyes and tried hard to resurrect the heavenly light. Years ago she had struggled to calm her mind under Aunt Euphemia's tutelage. *A busy mind dims the Sight*, Euphemia had said over and over again, but Christiana could not still the thoughts. She should not have wasted Bethag's time.

'Dame Christiana,' a voice called timidly.

Christiana turned towards the servant.

The woman bowed. 'Dame Katrina bids you come to the hostelry.'

Christiana rose and followed her. An elderly, bearded man in the simple clothing of a labourer sat in the hall of the hostelry with Dame Katrina.

'Your friend has returned,' the hosteleress said. 'I knew you would wish to see him at once.' Dame Katrina bowed to both of them and left the room.

Before taking a seat, Christiana checked the doors for loiterers. A disguise might fool the sisters, but their conversation would give him away. When she was certain that no one could overhear, she sat down across from Malcolm, irritated by his interruption.

'Why are you here?' she demanded. 'We've said all we need to say to each other.'

Malcolm pressed his hands together, pleading. 'Christiana, my love, I have come to beg you to reconsider. Leave this place and return with me to Bruges.'

It seemed a suspicious change of heart. 'Why should I reconsider?'

'I don't know whether I'll ever dare return to Perth.'

Christiana tried to quiet her mind as Bethag had instructed and focus on her husband's face. She did detect fear in his eyes, and a weariness in the way he sat with his usually proud shoulders rounded. 'Why would you not dare return?' she asked in a gentler tone.

'I have taken too many risks.'

Risks. She knew something of his risks. He was not so different from his brother Murdoch. What distinguished them was that Malcolm made his piracy seem like honest trading, whereas Murdoch did not bother. But Christiana felt the same about most of his fellow merchants. It was their wives, their work in the community, that made them appear respectable.

She wondered whether that was the source of

his dissatisfaction with her. 'I am not the wife you need, Malcolm. I haven't the skill to assist you.'

'You are the wife I love,' he cried and, taking her hand, he kissed it and then looked deep into her eyes. 'I am nothing without you. You are my anchor.'

Christiana could feel his need and the force of it frightened her. 'I was your burden.'

From his scrip he drew a necklace of gold, a thick, solid bar bent into a graceful semi-circle with intricately decorated knobs at the two ends.

'Your wedding gift to me,' she whispered.

He had given it to her on their wedding night. *It is an old piece, as old as the gift you carry from your kin, as old as the mountains whence they came*, he had said, and she had wept with joy that he understood and respected her Sight.

'You said I forfeited this when I entered Elcho.'

Malcolm bowed his head. 'I said many ugly things.'

She leaned forward, confused by this change in him, and tried to see his expression. 'You agreed to my withdrawal from the world. In truth, you seemed glad of it then.'

He lifted his head and she saw that his cheeks were wet. 'I no longer remember why I encouraged this, Christiana. I beg you to come away with me.' His voice broke.

This was no clever play-acting. And yet she had seen such moods in him in the past, when he feared he had overstepped the bounds he set for himself. Such moods always passed.

'I cannot be the wife you want.'

His face reddened. 'How can you forsake me? We lay together as man and wife so many years. You bore my children. I held you when you wept over those you lost.'

A lump rose in her throat. But the memories he wished to conjure were of long ago. 'Perhaps this is your purgatory to bear,' Christiana said. 'But I promise you it will pass.'

Malcolm rose with clenched fists. 'I am begging you. Are you not satisfied?'

'You are breaking my heart,' she said. 'You promised that you would not do this to me once it was settled.'

'Did you never love me?'

She hesitated, frightened by the rapidity of her heartbeat, the upwelling of tears. 'Do not ask me in that way. You accuse me of having no heart when you ask it so. I did love you. Faith, I do still. But it is not a carnal love. You have my heart always. You are the father of my children. I do remember how you held me. I do.' She pressed her cold hands to tears on her hot cheeks.

'God help me, I did not mean to make you cry,' Malcolm said, his voice catching.

Both must bear this purgatory. They were unhappy apart, unhappy together. What would she do if he deserted her in Bruges? She breathed deeply and prayed until she calmed. By then Malcolm was pacing.

Christiana reached out to him. 'Come, sit beside me for a moment. Tell me of your troubles.'

He shook his head. 'I told you I cannot.'

'And I cannot go with you to Bruges. I seek peace here, Malcolm. You have no idea how I have suffered with such a cruel gift as the Sight.'

'You'll have all the peace you wish in the grave.'

'And with the English king killing our people – I cannot desert our children, Malcolm.'

Malcolm gave a cold laugh. 'You have never thought of them before.' He made for the door. 'So be it, Christiana. Farewell.' He was out of the door before she could respond.

Her hands were cold. She did not know how she felt. She had not lied to him, it was no excuse. The thought had come to her as if whispered in her ear. She must remain in the land to help her children.

Margaret had Jonet bring wine to the bedchamber and told her that they would dine as usual. She and Roger sipped wine and quietly talked about John Smyth's death.

'If the English learn of it, we are in danger,' said Roger.

Margaret thought of Old Will's death and the trouble that had brought to her uncle. 'I know,' she said. 'Have you a plan?'

Roger shook his head. 'Fergus says John Smyth

had been long absent from Perth, and that he has no kin here. My thought is to take his body without the town and bury him.'

'Not in sacred ground?'

'Maggie, Maggie,' Roger said, shaking his head. 'Do you really think we might find a village full of strangers who would vow to keep our secret?'

Of course he was right, and she felt childish, behaving just as he expected her to.

'There is a rumour of Malcolm's presence in Perth,' Roger said. 'Have you heard it?'

Margaret rose and pretended to wipe up spilled wine, keeping her face averted. 'How odd. But perhaps not. If word of John Smyth's death in Da's warehouse is common knowledge, such a rumour is not surprising.'

Roger nodded. 'What if it were true, that he is here – would he want Smyth dead?'

'I can think of no cause,' she said truthfully. 'I doubt Da has given the man much thought since he turned him out.' Perhaps that was not quite true.

So she had begun again to deceive Roger. It did not bode well for their marriage.

His skiff hidden in the water meadow near the nunnery landing, James stepped out, stretched his legs, and considered Malcolm Kerr's careful disguise, his nervous glances at the shore and behind him as he'd rowed downriver. James parted the grasses and took a few steps towards Kerr's boat, but quickly withdrew as a man rowed past, his eyes on the very boat James was watching. The man seemed familiar, although he was moving away too quickly for James to see his features clearly with the sunlight on the river reflecting on his face. But James thought him one of Wallace's men. He was disturbed that Wallace had not told him he was watching Malcolm. He must not trust James to keep it from Margaret.

WHO IS THE LAW?

A shout woke Christiana.

Marion was already up, pressing an ear to the door. 'They sound far away, not inside the priory walls,' she said. 'Dame Agnes's kin are protecting us, praise God.'

Christiana knelt before her altar to the Virgin Mary and tried to quiet her mind to receive grace. *Is it Malcolm without?* Her heart raced. *Holy Mary, Mother of God, pray for my husband, a sinner, and guide him to the light of God.*

'Shall I go to the cloister to find out what the others know?' Marion asked, sounding close to tears.

Christiana did not respond, intent on reaching out for the calm she had found under Bethag's instruction. But her mind filled with the memory of Malcolm's hands. They had been so warm, strong, and full of life. Prioress Agnes had told her that abstinence from the pleasures of her marriage bed would awaken Christiana's connection with the divine. But she was still so weak that Malcolm had awakened her desire with but a touch. She had lied to him when she said she no longer loved him in a carnal way. It seemed more than a lie, for that was the only sense in which she had ever truly loved him. It was an impossible love if she was to live with the Sight, and that she must do if her life was to be of any consequence. Her parents had once taken her to St Andrews to seek guidance about her gift and when her flux had begun while there, they had interpreted it as a sign she was to abandon her visions for ever for motherhood. This morning Christiana thought that it had meant she was to set aside this gift while a mother, yet now in these mutinous times she must perforce take it up again in order to protect her children, and perhaps her people.

If this was so, and she strongly felt that it was, she must not see Malcolm again, for he weakened her. She would tell Dame Katrina that she could no longer accept visits from the old gardener. It was a sad and frightening resolve.

She rose to tell Marion not to bother going to the cloister, but her maid had already departed.

When she retired for the night Margaret paused by her mother's tapestry, pleased by how it livened the bedchamber. 'Is it not lovely?' she asked Roger, who stood in the middle of the room.

He lifted his hands as if conceding an argument, a soft smile on his lips. 'The colours do improve the room, Maggie. And now I think the bed needs curtains that add to the warmth. One small tapestry cannot do all the work.'

'Do you mean it?'

He stepped closer and gently smoothed her unbound hair. 'I do,' he said, his voice softening as his eyes and hands caressed her hair, her shoulders. 'I could not see it before. Is Celia skilled in such things?'

'Oh yes,' said Margaret, fighting the desire to lift her mouth up towards his. She felt wanton desiring him despite all her doubts. 'She and I might do much, and quickly, with some cloth.'

'Tomorrow morning I'll go to the warehouse and see what we have that might suit, eh?' Roger ended on a soft sigh, lifting her chin, his mouth so close she felt his breath on her eyelashes.

'Yes,' she whispered, kissing him, wrapping her arms around him. Perhaps he truly meant to work on their marriage.

He carried her to the bed, the cold, uncurtained bed.

After their lovemaking Roger fell asleep, with one arm wrapped around Margaret's waist. His breath stirred her hair, his body warmed her down the length of her back and legs. Life seemed so simple here, in this bed, their bodies pressed together in quiet comfort. When they desired one another the past was erased. Now was all that mattered. Would that were enough.

Marion returned to Christiana quite late, apologising for staying to pray with the sisters in the kirk. 'It was a small party of English soldiers, riding ahead of a larger force.'

Christiana noticed that Marion crossed herself despite all the prayers she must have already said.

'The prioress's kinsmen refused the soldiers' request to stay here the night,' Marion continued. 'Trouble will come of this.'

Marion's news was nothing to Christiana at first. She had fallen into a most comforting state of calm, returning in spirit to a great glen with burial chambers, a stone circle, and whispering shadows that her Aunt Euphemia had told her was one of the oldest sacred places in the land. Once again she had heard the sea birds aloft, the sighing winds, the music – rattles, drums, flutes, horns – and then the great voice in the cave. It was said that St Patrick had preached in such a voice. She had no idea where the glen lay. It had taken several days to journey there from Loch Long, where she had been biding with her aunt while learning about the Sight, for it was Aunt Euphemia and not her mother who had carried the gift. Tonight had been a joyous return to the glen for Christiana, the first time her spirit had journeyed there since before her marriage. The memory had lain forgotten in her cluttered mind, buried by marriage, childbirth, and her endless failed efforts at mothering her three children and her husband.

Now she tried to rise, but having knelt a long while she needed Marion's assistance. She asked for warmed wine and a heated stone for her bed.

As she grew warmer and the spell of the glen receded, she grew anxious about the news. 'Are the English headed for Perth?'

Marion, who had settled on to her cot at the foot of Christiana's bed, rose on her elbow. 'They are, and more follow.'

'My children, have a care,' Christiana whispered.

'What, Mistress?'

'Nothing, Marion. I'll sleep now.' Christiana blew out the lamp beside her bed and sat in the dark, holding the wine to warm her hands as in her mind's eye she followed the sacred glen to the sea, seeking wisdom. She might help her daughter if she could trust her visions, and the glen was where they had grown clear to her.

Margaret woke early and slipped from the bed before Roger woke. Sun blessed the morning and she lingered on her way to the privy in the backland, smiling as she passed the kitchen where

Jonet hummed as she ground oats on the quern stone. For this moment Margaret pretended that she and Roger could settle into a comfortable life, bairns would come, and the house would fill with love. This morning such a future did not seem impossible.

As she stepped out of the privy she noticed Fergus's dog in the yard and then Fergus himself in the doorway of the stable. He looked surprised to see her – unhappily surprised, she thought, as she drew closer.

'You are up early,' he remarked.

'It is a warm morning for boots,' she said, nodding at his.

'I'm riding out to see to some matters regarding the business. Da might be back, but he's not seeing to things.'

'You've seen him?'

'Aye.'

'Are you going out to search for him?'

Fergus muttered an oath. 'I don't care to find him, no. There's naught to admire in him. All he's worried about is whether John Smyth had anything about him that would connect Da to the man's death.'

'He said that?'

Fergus repeated their father's quite specific question.

If Smyth were a thief he might indeed have items about him that he'd stolen from her father. It would seem to Margaret to prove his motive, and thus should not worry her father. It is so little, Margaret thought. It might mean nothing. But it suggested to her a guilty conscience. 'Perhaps you put too much weight in what he said,' she suggested, as if she might convince herself.

'Whether or not I'm right is no matter.'

She sensed there was something more significant on her brother's mind. 'You'll laugh to hear it,' she said, 'but despite my recent journey I would enjoy riding out with you on such a day as this. Especially if your route is to the north.'

Fergus shook his head. 'Go break your fast and enjoy your home while you may. There is a rumour on the river that the English are returning.'

And they would hear of the body in the warehouse. She sensed great tension in her brother and imagined he feared likewise. 'I worry what will happen when the English hear of John Smyth's death,' she said.

'Aye, it will go badly for us.'

Margaret knew her brother well and did not think by his response that she had touched on the primary cause of his anxiety. She moved past him into the stable, unsurprised when he grabbed her elbow and prevented her from going further. 'So what is it, Fergus?' She noticed a pack near one of the stalls and a clean saddle atop it. Looking into her brother's eyes, she saw a jumble of emotions. 'Are you leaving?'

He let go her arm and withdrew into the shadows.

She dreaded losing her best friend and ally in Perth, and so quickly. 'Where are you going? Were you not going to tell me?' He said nothing, and she could not see whether he had nodded or shrugged. 'Fergus, would you leave without a farewell for me?' Her voice broke on the last words.

'Oh, Maggie.' He came to her and put a hand on her shoulder. 'I was afraid, and so would you be if you were me.' His young face was so earnest, so solemn. She realised how much he had changed while she was away, how seldom he laughed, how infrequent were his silly tales. 'The family wants me here so that no one else need stay,' he said. 'My life is not my own.'

'You're but seventeen, Fergus.'

'Eighteen by Christmas.'

'I'm older than you and my life isn't my own.'

'You're a woman, Maggie. But even you've had an adventure.'

'Och, I have, and you would have been welcome to it.'

He put an arm around her. 'I know you've suffered, Maggie. I did not mean you hadn't.'

'You must have hated it here all alone.'

He rested his chin on her head with a sigh. 'I'm going to Aberdeen to take up my work as Uncle Thomas's secretary.'

Her head against his chest, Margaret both felt

and heard his words, and how his heart raced to say them. She stepped back and saw the resolution in his eyes. 'But I need you here,' she moaned. 'What if Roger leaves me again?'

'You see? I'm to stop my life so that you or your husband may come and go as you please. No, Maggie, I'm for Aberdeen. I'll not stay here another day, not among townsfolk eager to sell their neighbours in exchange for the protection of Edward Longshanks's army.'

Margaret wished she had considered her objection more carefully. 'I shamed myself to speak so to you. Of course you should go to Aberdeen. We'll devise a plan – you'll need to find others travelling north.'

'I'll go alone.'

Now she was frightened. 'Fergus, there are armed men in the countryside, not only the English and the Scots who are fighting for them, but our own men quick to take offence and practise their fighting skills, and the outlaws are bolder now that there is no rule in the land. You cannot make such a long journey alone.'

'When Longshanks's men hear of Smyth's death they will watch us so closely I'll never get out, Maggie. And how am I to find someone riding to Aberdeen before the English arrive in the town?'

She thought of James. 'I might be able to find someone. Please, let me try.'

'The longer I delay the more likely someone will find a way to prevent my leaving.'

'I won't let them, I promise.' Margaret did not like the way he avoided her eyes. 'You will not leave without saying farewell?'

Fergus put his arms around her and kissed her forehead. 'You know I love you, and I'm grateful for your being both mother and sister to me. If I might have a companion for the journey, that would ease both our minds.'

Margaret sensed that his words were meant solely to appease her. She must act in haste.

In the stable, Fergus removed his boots and his travelling clothes and packed them, then hid his pack and saddle. Maggie's plea was not the cause of his delay – he expected her efforts to come to nothing. He had been invited to dine with Matilda and her family this afternoon and would not miss the opportunity to see her. Though he could not bid her farewell without revealing his plan, he could feast his eyes on her one more time. Meanwhile, he planned to rummage through his father's house for anything that might be useful for the journey or in his new post.

It was the least his parents could do for him, selfish couple that they were. He did not think they would give his disappearance a second thought, considering how neither seemed concerned about Andrew's terrible exile to Soutra

Hospital or Maggie's troubled marriage. He might as well lighten them of something, particularly coin. His father must have some hidden in the house.

Roger was attentive as he and Margaret broke their fast together early in the morning. In a secretive tone he said, 'Aylmer and I buried Smyth.'

Margaret was puzzled. 'You cannot have known Aylmer for long, yet you have great trust in him.' It was something she found contrary to his subtler behaviour with the man.

'We have perforce trusted one another with our lives.' Roger caught her hand as she reached for the pitcher of ale. 'You need not worry about Smyth.'

'It was not Smyth who worried me. I fear what might happen when the town gossips tell the English about his death in Da's warehouse.'

'The gossips are a concern,' Roger admitted. 'You have had much troubling you this past year, and you rightly fault me for that. I lay awake last night wondering how you had managed the household. I'm glad you went to my mother. I have been a glaikit husband to you, Maggie.'

She did not protest, for he had indeed been thoughtless. 'Dame Katherine is a kind, loving goodmother to me.'

'What do you know of Old Will's life?' he asked, leaning towards her with a disarming earnestness.

'I can think of nothing new to tell you,' she said with a little laugh. 'What do you hope to learn about him?'

Roger looked puzzled that she needed to ask about his motivation. 'Are you not bothered by the English reaction to his murder – searching his rooms, closing the tavern, taking Murdoch's goods?'

She had been, of course, and said so. 'But you ken all that I do about the man now. I've no more to reveal. Except that Mary Brewster would not speak of it afterwards. Such a gossip as Mary. That seemed strange to me.'

'It would have been of more use if we knew why,' said Roger.

Margaret shrugged. 'Are you not off to the warehouse today?'

'I've tired you.' Roger looked towards the window. 'And it grows late.' He took one of her hands in his, kissed it, then leaned over and pecked her on the cheek. 'You've great courage, Maggie.'

She touched her cheek after he left the hall and was startled by the iciness of her hands. Roger's affectionate behaviour did not warm her.

A cramp in his side forced James to ease out of his elderly stoop while warming himself in St John's kirk yard. He had spent several hours in the kirk, most of the time bent into his elderly friar posture, for the worshippers had appeared in a steady stream this morning. From their murmurings, he ascertained that most prayed for protection from the English. Even their cooperation with Longshanks's men did not make them feel safe. They were more aware of the treachery of the English than they seemed.

Back in camp James had learned that the boatman he had noticed near Elcho yesterday had also been focused on the English. Wallace had set him to track Malcolm Kerr and prevent any contact between Margaret's father and the approaching troop. James still did not know why Wallace was so concerned about Malcolm's activities, though he was beginning to see how alike the Kerr brothers were. Slippery opportunists.

When an elderly stranger entered the yard from the kirk, James curled into character and hobbled back into the cool darkness within. Standing far enough from the door that no light might fall on him at its opening, James resumed his watch. As his eyes adjusted he discovered Margaret kneeling quite near him. She nodded to him and crossed herself, as she might behave with a friar.

James gestured for her to join him. 'We must talk here. There is someone in the yard,' he whispered.

'I saw him. We need not concern ourselves with him. He has been deaf for years,' said Margaret. She led the way into the yard.

The elderly man sat on a far bench, his head lifted to receive the sun's warmth.

Margaret settled on the bench she had shared with James a few days ago.

He noted a freshness in her face that had been lacking, yet she plucked at a sleeve as if worried. 'What is wrong?'

'Fergus means to ride to his uncle in Aberdeen,' she began.

He listened to her concern with sympathy both for her and for Fergus, a young man itching to fight. 'He's for King John?'

Margaret smiled as she nodded. 'My brothers are of good heart.'

'You're right to worry about his travelling alone.' He would not give her false assurances. But he thought of a way to help. 'There's a good chance a messenger is headed north-east, though perhaps not at once. Would he wait?'

'I'll do my best to convince him that it is worthwhile,' Margaret said, but she frowned and chewed at the inside of her lip.

It was a little gesture, but it served as a reminder to James of Margaret's relative youth. He would do well to remember that.

'I have horses just outwith the town,' he said. 'Would you care to ride out with me? It is a day for the country.'

Her face brightened and she seemed about to agree, but then she shook her head. 'I dare not risk it, not in the daylight. Nor should you be seen too much with me.'

'I had not intended for us to walk together in the town. As for daylight, I proposed it because I did not think it would be easy for you to slip away from Roger at night.'

Margaret blushed. So that is how things went with the couple. James was furious. He was wasting precious time preparing her to spy if she was with child.

'Why are you so keen for me to ride out with you?' she asked, looking closely at him.

His temper must be showing. And suddenly he feared that it was not anger but jealousy that heated him. 'There are people I think it important for you to meet.'

'What people?'

'You will learn their names when I introduce you.' He must be on his guard with her. He must not let his heart distract him, fickle thing that it suddenly was.

She sought his eyes. 'Do I no longer have your trust?'

He grew too careless in her company. 'I did not mean to imply that,' he lied. 'To speak a man's name is to expose him to the treasonous air. You know that the English are returning to the town?'

Margaret nodded.

'How does your family intend to dispose of John Smyth's corpse before they arrive?'

She nervously played with her sleeve as she had earlier. 'I wondered whether you knew of it.'

'I also know that your father is about. We have eyes and ears—'

'I thought I was to be your spy in Perth.' Her eyes accused him.

'That you are, and I hand over the task with thanks. Which is why I am asking about the body.'

He saw that she was torn in her loyalty and he was about to impart some information that would increase her doubts about Roger, but she surprised him by quickly resolving her hesitation.

'Roger and Aylmer have buried it,' she said.

James nodded. 'That was wise.'

'Why? I fear the whole town knows already.'

'If they don't yet, they soon will. But if they see no body, no funeral, they cannot be certain. Sinclair can do little else. He cannot undo the murder.'

'The silence is frightening,' said Margaret.

'It is.' He paused, and when she said no more he continued on to the news about her husband. 'I have enquired about the Brankston family.'

Margaret turned her face away from him and clutched the side of her skirt with one hand as if to keep herself still. 'And?'

'It is true that a family by that name was so abused.'

'God help them,' she said.

'But they have no connection with Edwina of Carlisle.'

He heard Margaret catch her breath and started to reach out to her, but caught himself.

'How do you know this?' she asked softly.

'George Brankston came to our attention when he viciously murdered an English messenger.'

'You would have punished him for avenging his wife and his daughter?' The eyes she turned on James were so filled with pain he looked away.

'No. We worried that he might treat our messengers likewise. But knowing his story . . .' He trailed off, realising it sounded petty.

'In such times, who is the law?' Margaret asked softly.

'The most powerful, or the most ruthless,' said James. 'But we'll do our best to protect you.'

'That is more than most can hope for.' She was quiet a while. 'From whom did you hear about my father's return?'

'One of our messengers. He'd been in Perth on other business. What is your father's present standing with your mother?'

'She wants nothing to do with him.'

'He has pressed her?'

'Why do you ask?'

She had proven herself. He must trust her. He told her of Malcolm's cautious journey to Elcho, the disguise.

'He goes about in disguise as you do?' she asked

with a surprised laugh. 'Oh dear. He must have hoped to convince Ma to return with him to Bruges. She has already refused him once.'

'So he regrets the dissolution of their marriage?'

'So it seems.' She had turned away from him again and he could neither see her expression nor detect her feelings from her soft response.

'Do you think she has said anything to him of her visions regarding you?'

Margaret pressed a hand to her eyes.

'It might be important,' he added.

She shifted away from him a little. 'Her visions are what drove them apart. I don't believe Mother would talk to him about them.' Rubbing her elbows as if cold, she complained, 'I came here to ask a favour and suffer an interrogation.'

James did not respond, silently cursing Malcolm and Christiana for complicating Margaret's situation, indeed perhaps compromising it, and forcing him to pry. Perhaps he should have been subtler, but there was little time with the English near and Wallace liable to give the order to move on at any moment.

The elderly man who shared the yard with them had fallen asleep, his chin on his chest, and was snoring so loudly that a prowling cat gave him wide berth. That would be the ideal spy, a cat.

Margaret must have followed James's gaze.

'His snoring will attract attention,' she said uneasily. 'I should leave. You will let me know tomorrow if Fergus might join another traveller?'

'Why not come with me to the camp this afternoon? You might have news for him by evening.'

'I'll not risk it now, with Fergus so anxious that something might happen to prevent his leaving. And with the English close – how close, James?'

'A day's ride, perhaps a little more.'

She crossed herself.

He had one more question that could not wait. 'Why has your father returned from Bruges at this particular moment?'

'What? Oh. With Edward Longshanks in the Low Countries he thought it safe to return to collect more of his property.' She paused. 'I wonder how he will know when it's safe to cross back to the continent. The timing must be perfect if he is to avoid meeting Longshanks's navy on the way, or still in port.'

'In the end Longshanks took few ships with him. But you pose a good question.'

'Why do you think Da's here, James?'

He shook his head. 'I find your father as difficult to know as his brother. You are thinking he might be a spy?'

'I don't know,' she said. 'I pray he isn't.' Her eyes followed someone on Kirkgate. 'Go now, please. See about Aberdeen for my brother.' She bowed her head for his blessing.

She might not be in disguise, but she remembered her part. Her quietly devout demeanour as she returned to the kirk impressed him. In a little while, he, too, returned to the kirk. Before departing he knelt and said a prayer for Margaret. She had much to fear from the English because of her husband's and her father's activities. He selfishly added a prayer that she was not with child.

❧ 15 ❦

AWAKENING

When Margaret returned to the house the afternoon stretched endlessly before her and she regretted not having gone with James. Risky it might have been, and wise to refuse, but at least she would have been certain that something was being done to assist Fergus.

Pacing back and forth in her bedchamber, she could work up neither the enthusiasm nor the concentration to choose fabric and plan other furnishings. Instead she fell to brooding about her earlier conversation with Roger.

All in all, it had been an uncomfortable interrogation, and as a result she'd been beset with memories of the old drunkard's death and its consequences as she'd walked to the kirk and back. But what still troubled her most was Roger's having arrived in Edinburgh on the heels of the tragedy.

She dropped to her knees by the casket Roger had stored in her uncle's undercroft and another with which he'd arrived in Edinburgh. She ran her hands over them, wondering what they might divulge. There was but one thing to do – search through them. She stepped out to the landing to check that the house was quiet, and considered setting something easily knocked over outside the door so that she might be warned of anyone's approach. But she discarded the idea on realising that either Jonet or Celia would clear it away, and it might simply call more attention to the door.

From their hiding place, she took the lock-picking tools that her uncle had given her long ago and settled down in front of Roger's caskets. She felt a twinge of guilt, followed by a far stronger frisson of fear. Despair might be her reward. She might find proof of an affair, a murder, or some other disturbing secret.

May God grant me the strength to go forward with what I must do, she prayed. *I would know my husband's heart. I would know why he cannot tell me the truth about Edwina.*

Working slowly and as quietly as possible, she opened the casket that had sat for months in her uncle's undercroft. A fine pair of gloves lay on top, and a linen shirt that she had made for Roger shortly after their wedding. Beneath the items was a layer of rolled documents, some of the seals broken, some whole. After memorising their order she set them aside. Beneath them was a leather wallet almost the length and width of the casket. Coins jingled as she lifted the wallet, but the soft leather was taut around something. Removing the cord binding the wallet, she found more documents. Suddenly keenly aware that her activity might have masked noise from the landing, she paused and listened, but heard only sounds from the river.

One by one she took the rolled documents from the wallet to check for broken seals, but she found none. The coins were sterlings, enough to keep her household in comfort for a year. Margaret resisted the temptation to pocket them and inconvenience Roger in his work for Robert Bruce. It was not worth the fuss. Returning the wallet to the casket, she sat back on her heels and listened again. The sounds drifting in from the street and the backlands were comfortingly familiar, and for a moment she forgot her task.

Here she had knelt when first married, hesitantly shaking out Roger's clothes for her first laundry day. The memory was little more than two years old, but she felt she had lived a lifetime since then. She rose and fetched a polished metal mirror to see how much she had aged for her nineteen years. Her skin was still unlined, her hair held no silver strands, but her eyes were different. More alive, she thought, or perhaps more cunning. She smiled at herself and the pain of the past year was forgotten as she considered her courage and maturity.

But shortly she remembered her mission and set aside the mirror. She pressed her ear to the door and then, hearing nothing unusual, returned to the caskets, opening the second one. A pair of daggers lay atop Roger's old boots. The weapons reminded her of the danger in which she placed herself, spying on her husband. Inside each boot were several documents, all with broken seals. Beneath the boots she found a dark scarf folded as if it had been wrapped around Roger's head to keep sweat from his eyes, and a long length of rope.

One by one she opened the unsealed documents that had been in the boots, looking for recognisable names. Roger's name was atop one letter, and the word 'Rex', but the Latin hand was too difficult otherwise. Another letter was in a language completely unfamiliar. After the third document she was about to give up, accepting that her rudimentary reading skills were not enough for such a task. But on the fourth she picked out her father's name, which was curious as the letter was addressed to Roger and held part of what her father had once told her was a royal seal of England. She set that document and the one with Roger's name and 'Rex' aside before she repacked the second casket. Returning to the first, she quickly searched the documents with broken seals, but all were in a foreign tongue. As she began to repack the casket she froze at the sound of footsteps on the stairs, then hurriedly finished and stuffed the documents she'd set aside beneath the mattress.

She was fastening the locks when a knock on the door made her jump. Glancing around and seeing nothing obviously amiss, she called, 'Come in,' letting out her breath with relief as Celia stepped into the room.

'I thought you might wish to know that your father is in the stable.'

Though tempted to ignore it, Margaret wondered what her father wanted. Her feet took her to the yard, where she paused with a sudden memory of Hal in her uncle's stable sharing his meal with Agrippa. She missed Hal's quiet companionship. She wondered what he was doing, how Bonny had fared on her night journey back to the town.

'Mistress?' Celia said behind her. 'Are you unwell?'

Margaret started and realised she was hugging herself so tightly it was difficult to breathe. 'No, just thinking,' she said quietly over her shoulder as she consciously relaxed. 'Thank you for coming for me. Now leave us.' She continued to the stable, stepping in hesitantly.

Her father spoke from one of the stalls. 'Your handmaiden told you I was about, eh?' Margaret's horse whinnied as her father stepped out of its stall into the light. Straw stuck to his clothes, as if he'd been rolling about in it. Without waiting for Margaret's response to his first question, he said,

'You're wise to bring your horses in from without the walls, though they are crowded. The English would have found them.'

Margaret nodded and asked, 'Are you still in hiding?' as she eyed his straw-covered clothing.

He looked down, brushed straw from a sleeve. 'And a good thing I am,' he said. 'Have you told Roger I'm here?'

'No,' said Margaret with an inadvertent glance back over her shoulder. The yard was empty. 'Why do you ask?'

'Are you certain?' Malcolm thrust his jaw forward, challenging her.

'Of course I'm certain. Do you think I talk in my sleep?'

Her father shrugged. 'Or said something of it to your nosy handmaiden in his hearing.'

'You might make such mistakes, but I don't.' His low esteem for her was nothing new to her, but it still stung. 'Do you have cause to think Roger knows?'

'I'm being followed.' Her father took a step towards her, looking past her to the yard. 'Closely.'

'You've been in hiding since you returned. Surely you expected to be sought?'

He shook out his gown. 'I'm going away. It's not safe for me in Perth.'

'Nor is it anywhere in this land, for any of us.'

He sniffed a sleeve. 'Pah! When did you last clean the straw?'

She imagined clean straw was as dear here as it had been in Edinburgh. 'What trouble are you in, Da? Is it John Smyth's death?'

'I touched him not, Maggie. That is all I can tell you. Fergus can manage my business.'

That might be a problem, she thought, but she would not betray her brother. 'Are you leaving Fergus to face your enemies?'

Malcolm sniffed. 'It's no sacrifice, he'll inherit all I manage to keep.'

'Are we in danger, Da?'

'Your brother is quite able to defend himself.'

'What if he doesn't care to fight your battles?'

'Who said aught about battles?' Her father patted her arm. 'Don't fret, lass. Fergus won't desert the business. He'll have nothing if he does.'

'Nor will you.'

'Nor any of us, I sometimes fear.' He dropped his head. When he lifted it, there were tears in his eyes.

Margaret put her arms around him and he clutched her so tightly she thought he might be weeping. But when he pulled away he was only flushed.

'God watch over you, Maggie.' His voice was ragged. Nodding once, he strode past her and out into the yard.

'Da, wait!' she called as loudly as she dared, but he did not turn. She rushed after him, then hesitated. There was little more she could say without revealing Fergus's plans, certainly nothing that would move her father to change his plan. *Dear Lord, watch over my da*.

A change was in the air, heralded by a subtle shift in Christiana's senses, an increased clarity, as if a portion of her that had slumbered was awakening. Marion had remarked about how quickly her mistress had risen upon waking, particularly as the dawn was cool and misty, a morning for lying abed. Though Christiana had made light of her unusual energy she was uneasy, for she'd awakened with a keen sense of urgency. But Marion knew of no appointment.

Christiana was dressing when a servant came with a summons from the prioress.

Wrapping a soft mantle around her veiled head and shoulders, Christiana walked through the damp yard, holding her skirts from the ground and keeping her footfall tentative so she might hear the birdsong and the rush of the Tay. The mist refreshed her after the pervasive dust of the past few days and, pausing before stepping into the cloister, she lifted her face to receive the moisture. The beads that clung to her lashes made rainbows in the early morning dullness of the cloister.

In the prioress's parlour, the commanding Agnes de Arroch sat enthroned, confident in her status, although her usually smooth, high forehead bore lines of worry this morning. She gestured

Christiana to an elegantly carved but uncomfortably straight-backed chair and offered her some honeyed almond milk. She seemed offended when Christiana declined the delicacy.

'It coats my throat and hampers speech,' Christiana explained. The air in the chilly room crackled with tension. She glanced at the bowl the prioress had proffered, a delicately carved mazer. It was such a beautiful piece that she felt compelled to hold it. Perhaps a sip would appease her hostess. 'I find I thirst for the milk after all.'

The prioress nodded to the maid to pour.

Cupping the mazer in both hands, feeling the warmth of the wood, Christiana bowed her head to the prioress and took a drink. The sweetness delighted her heightened senses.

The maid retreated to a corner. The matter to be discussed must not be too confidential for her ears. Yet the tension in the parlour was undiminished.

'We must speak of a matter involving my kinsmen as well as this community, Dame Christiana,' Agnes began.

'The shouts in the night?' Christiana guessed.

The prioress, pursing her lips, paused before continuing. 'Would you object to the inclusion of my cousin Thomas in this discussion?'

'Is he one of the men guarding us?' Christiana asked, and without awaiting a response added, 'It would be discourteous of me to object, Dame Agnes.'

Gesturing to the servant, Agnes sat back to await the arrival of Thomas.

Christiana let her eyes roam the room as she sipped the honeyed milk. On shelves lining one wall the prioress displayed her collection of jugs from Scarborough in Yorkshire. Christiana recognised them by their elaborate decoration – human figures, masks, stylised animals – and especially the lustrous green glaze. It was a costly collection of which the prioress was obviously proud.

In a short while the door opened and a large, pale-haired man entered. He bowed first to the prioress and then to Christiana, who found him familiar. But of course, the kin who guarded Elcho were from Perth. She thought he might be a merchant, someone she had met through Malcolm's guild, although at present his dress was rough and dirty.

He sat in a third chair, one that Christiana knew to be more comfortable than hers, and accepted a mazer of wine. His cup was plainer and larger than the one she had been offered. While he drank, the prioress explained to Christiana what she already knew, that on the previous night the guards had refused hospitality to English soldiers.

'And this matter requires my counsel?' Christiana asked.

'More than that,' said Thomas, closing his

mouth at a slight sound from his kinswoman. Even this most substantial man was controlled by Agnes de Arroch.

'Our discourtesy will be reported to their captain,' said Dame Agnes, 'we may be sure of that.'

Christiana sipped the almond milk as the prioress and her kinsman gradually came to the reason for her presence. In a day or two they expected more English, made suspicious by Elcho's inhospitality, and it would be helpful if Christiana had a plausible 'vision' to proclaim on their arrival, a warning of danger, something that would drive them away to seek shelter within the walls of Perth. Christiana listened with growing incredulity. The Sight was a divine gift and as such should not be used in vain.

'Dame Agnes, you have counselled me that my visions are meant by God for me alone.'

Thomas looked to his kinswoman with a pained expression.

But the prioress coolly nodded. 'Yes, a true vision is God's gift to you. But this would be a vision we prepare in order to protect us. We ask simply that you speak it as you would a true vision.'

Not at all certain that she would oblige them, Christiana stalled by asking what they wished her to say.

Thomas leaned forward, his face more relaxed,

apparently assuming she meant to cooperate. 'William Wallace and Andrew Murray have the English looking over their shoulders, fearing ambushes. All they need to hear is that we found signs of someone lying in wait this morning, and that you sense they're near, and perhaps that the one in charge has recently come to Perth—'

'No,' Christiana interrupted. Thomas stopped with his mouth open. 'Nothing of Perth.' She saw Maggie being questioned, Fergus struggling with someone.

Thomas closed his mouth and slowly nodded. 'Yes. I see. We want them seeking shelter in Perth, not avoiding it. Have you a suggestion?'

Now Christiana knew why she had woken with such urgency. She sensed that she must cooperate in order to keep her children safe. 'I pray you, allow me some time to consider this.'

Thomas glanced at the prioress, who nodded.

'Let us reconvene at Nones,' said Agnes.

Although Margaret did not rise as quickly as she had the previous day, finding her own clean, comfortable bed too irresistible on a cool, damp morning, she found Roger patiently awaiting her in the hall so that they might break their fasts together. His attentiveness made her momentarily regret the previous afternoon's search, until she remembered his lie about Edwina and the Brankstons. Still, she was more at ease with him for not having found additional lies among his belongings.

Their conversation was easy until Roger asked, 'Is Fergus sharing your father's house with someone?'

Margaret kept her eyes on her pottage of oatmeal. 'Jonet sleeps there. Does that seem inappropriate? I thought as Celia is here Fergus might continue to have her there.'

'I meant a man,' Roger said with a touch of irritation. 'I went there to see Fergus yesterday and heard his voice and another man's as Jonet answered the door, but when she showed me in Fergus was alone.'

'Are you certain you heard two different voices?' Margaret asked in a teasing tone.

'Do you mean Fergus was talking to himself?' Roger suddenly grinned. 'He *has* been much alone.'

'Perhaps too much,' Margaret said with a little laugh.

But Roger's amusement had already faded. 'Why do I sense secrets behind that smile?'

Margaret reached for his hand. 'It is the times, my love. We all grow secretive by habit.' She prayed her father had escaped safely.

The meal ended without incident. After loitering until Roger was out of the house, Margaret walked slowly to St John's. This time she found James sitting on a bench in a rear corner of the nave.

Joining him, she asked, 'Have you found my brother a travelling companion?'

James nodded. 'He will depart in two days.'

'Two days? Can he not leave sooner?'

'No.' James shifted a little on the bench. 'Fergus is in such a hurry?'

Perhaps she was panicking. She could not in truth predict Fergus's reaction. She prayed Matilda was kind to him today so that he might choose to linger. 'He's angry, but he may calm. Who would this companion be?'

'One of Murray's messengers. A trustworthy young man and someone with whom your brother might feel comfortable.'

'I'll tell him. When can we talk again?'

'Ride out into the country with me after Nones. Surely that gives you time enough to discuss this with Fergus. Then you can meet the man.'

'I've told you—'

'You have. But it is Wallace himself who wishes to meet with you.'

William Wallace. She had seen him once at Inverkeithing, awaiting the ferry across the Firth of Forth. At that time she had thought him a common thief and wondered at the quiet deference of the men who acknowledged him. 'I have nothing of use to tell him.'

'He would warn you. He says you are in danger. I believe he has information about your husband's or your father's activities.'

Warn her or question her, she wondered. 'I fear for my father,' she said. 'Someone is following him. Is it Wallace's men?'

'Among others.'

'What others?'

'I'm uncertain – but it seems the English are interested.'

'Then I am glad he is wise enough to leave Perth.' She feared he was more like his brother Murdoch than she had known, that perhaps John Smyth was just one of his troubles, and the rest had to do with smuggling.

'I pray he manages that safely, but he might be wiser to stay now that he is here.'

'There was the death in his warehouse.'

'A thief. Even the English understand thieves.'

'I think he is very frightened.'

'I'll watch his house.'

'So you'll be in town?'

'For a while. But first I would take you to Wallace.'

'Not today, James. What of Roger? Are Wallace's men watching him?'

'I am, through you. Why not today? You are concerned about both your father and your husband. I thought Roger and his man were spending their days going through the warehouses and checking the accounts.'

'They are. I can't explain. I don't feel ready. I know too little. I don't even know my own heart.'

She was momentarily upset with herself for having said that, but it was the closest she could come to an explanation. It seemed enough for James. He agreed to meet her the following morning.

Fergus was relieved when Jonet departed for Maggie's house – she was upset about the mess he was making of the hall and his father's bed-chamber in his search, and he had spent part of the morning undoing the neat stacks of papers that she had made the past evening without regard to the organisation he had devised when the tenor of his search had changed late the previous afternoon.

A well-dressed stranger had come looking for his father, having heard a rumour of his return to Perth. He claimed Malcolm owed him a bag of coins, which he now needed. Fergus had convinced the man that he knew nothing of the coins. Once the man had gone on his way, Fergus had resumed his search in more earnest, determined to find out where his father was storing money. But searching through the evening and part of the morning he had unearthed nothing of substance – a few coins and a necklace that might be worth a goodly amount if there were anyone in the market for jewels at present.

Fergus had considered making Matilda a gift of the necklace, but decided against buying her affections. Yet he kept returning to the small casket in which he'd found the jewellery, looking

289

at the delicate jet and silver strands and imagining them encircling Matilda's neck. He was lost in one of his daydreams when there came a loud knock on the street door. Whoever it was rapped again even more loudly and called out to Fergus's father.

Expecting the caller of the previous day, Fergus opened the door muttering about patience, but lost his train of thought as he faced yet another well-dressed stranger. This one was larger and appeared angrier than the earlier visitor.

'Where's Malcolm Kerr?' the man demanded, trying to peer beyond Fergus into the hall.

'In Bruges,' said Fergus, bracing a hand on either side of the doorway. 'If you knew my father you would be aware of that.'

'Make no mistake, I know Kerr,' the man said as he easily pushed past Fergus. Striding into the hall, he bellowed Malcolm's name.

Fergus slammed the door. 'Who do you think you are, barging in here like this?'

The man had a foot on the steps to the solar. 'He has been seen on the river.' Crossing to the alcove that opened on to the kitchen yard, he glanced round, then returned to Fergus. 'He's keeping the silver to himself, isn't he? Or he's handed it over to Longshanks. He'll be doubly sorry if he has done so. You tell him that Gilbert Ruthven means to retrieve what is his. I'll return tomorrow – with others he owes.'

A Ruthven, landed and lordly. 'I'm his factor

but I know nothing of silver owed you or anyone else. Nor of any dealings with the English king.'

As Ruthven looked Fergus in the eyes, his expression softened. 'Then he is cheating you as well. Look to yourself, young sir, and trust not your greedy master.' He bowed and departed.

Fergus leaned against the door and began to go over the encounter. He examined it again and again, fanning a fire in his gut. The man had insulted the family honour. Yet, as Fergus calmed a little, he wondered whether there had been some truth in the man's accusations. It would be no wonder his father was in hiding if he had cheated a Ruthven and who knew how many others. Damn him for leaving Fergus to face his victims. Silver . . . that might have been what John Smyth was after. Fergus's anger shifted to his father. He wondered what else his da was hoarding, or trading to Longshanks. By St Columba, if his father proved to be in league with the English invaders Fergus would never speak to him again. To so humiliate his own son. Damn him. He would not see Fergus's face again, not on this earth. Aberdeen would be his new home.

And where was the stolen silver? Not in the house, that was almost certain. Fergus hid the casket of coins and jewellery in a chest beneath the solar stairs and headed for the warehouse.

The cool mist of early morning had lifted and the day had warmed, though the sun had not yet broken through the low clouds. Fergus's clothes clung to him damply and he slowed his stride in an effort to cool himself. But his mind could not let go of Ruthven's sympathetic tone, his father's deceit, and his own humiliation, and the anger heated his blood to a simmer. At the warehouse he jammed the key in the lock at an angle while he swatted at midges and then spent an eternity straightening it. Once within, he cursed to discover the body gone. He'd wanted to search it again, look at the hands.

Resigned to the loss, Fergus set about scouring for clues in the area in which the man had fallen.

After meeting with the prioress, Christiana had walked for a long while in the water meadow under the wary eyes of Dame Agnes's kinsman, seeking a tale that would send the English running to Perth for protection. But she was a receiver rather than a creator of visions and her mind kept wandering away from what might sufficiently disturb a soldier. The abrupt cliffs of Kinnoull Hill across the river held her attention. When she had first visited Elcho, the cliffs looming above the opposite bank had filled her with dread. Now, as on the night of the intruders, she thought how vulnerable the water meadow was, how all the low-lying fields, the river, and Friarton Island might be watched from that cliff. The cliffs' vantage point might make the English uneasy.

Back in the prioress's parlour she watched

understanding dawn on the faces of Agnes and her kinsman.

'They would feel far too exposed down here,' Thomas said, nodding thoughtfully. 'I am grateful to you, Dame Christiana.'

The prioress smiled benignly and commended Christiana for her clever scheme.

As Margaret made her way home from St John's Kirk she pondered what it would take to know her own heart, and it seemed to her that she must decide whether or not she trusted Roger. There was Aylmer as well – she no longer considered him insolent, but rather unaware that there was more to playing a servant than being called one. He was not the actor that James was. If he was so unprepared for the role she might learn much from his belongings. She would search them.

Celia was sitting in the doorway to the yard, using the daylight to mend a tear in one of Margaret's worn gowns. 'You'll be thirsty,' she said, moving to set aside her work.

Margaret shook her head. 'I'm going to search Aylmer's chamber. If anyone appears, come for me.'

Celia bowed her head. 'Have a care, Mistress.'

Margaret nodded and went within, hurrying up to her chamber for her tools. Back down in the hall she lit a piece of kindling from the hearth fire, and then crossed to the small chamber in the rear in which Jack and Fergus had worked on accounts and letters. Lifting the hide that covered the doorway, she lit the lamp on the shelf just within and looked around. She found Aylmer's travelling casket and pack beneath the small work-table. Lifting the casket to the table, she set to work picking the lock. Her trembling hands slowed her but the simple lock was soon opened.

Within were daggers, a small cache of coins, a jewelled belt, and a wallet like the one she had found in Roger's casket, filled with rolled documents. She sat back on her heels and examined the rolls in the wallet. All but one were sealed; the opened one bore Roger's name as well as what she thought might be a form of the name Bruce. She stared at the casket, willing it to reveal more. And in a little while it did, for she realised that the casket was not as deep within as it was from without. But there were no legs, nor was there a bottom compartment. She set to prodding and poking what must be a false bottom. With persistence she shifted it enough to insert a finger and pop it out. Beneath were more coins and several documents with broken seals – English royal seals. Setting those aside, she replaced the false bottom with care and then repacked the casket.

She would take these and the two from Roger's casket to Ada, who read as well as any priest. In fact she would do it now. She gathered the documents and went out into the town with them hidden beneath a cloth in her market basket.

At the Northgate crossing, she spied Fergus talking to an acquaintance a few doors from Matilda's. She nodded to him as he noticed her and was surprised when he quit the man and hurried towards her. His face was livid.

'We were close to starving and all the while he was hoarding coin!' he blurted.

Margaret glanced about uneasily. 'Who?' she asked softly. 'What coin?' She listened with increasing perplexity as he told her of his visitors. 'Does it not mean that Ruthven wants to recover a debt, rather than that Da is hoarding?' she asked. 'Has he paper to prove it?'

'Two men, Maggie, two days in a row, and Ruthven said others would accompany him tomorrow.' Fergus shook his head. 'Da is up to no good, you can be sure.'

Thinking of the royal seals on the documents she carried in her market basket, and her father's name in the text, she said, 'I'm on an errand that might prove enlightening. Be patient, I pray you. And I have found a travelling companion for you.'

He had resumed his complaints but her last comment caught his attention. 'How soon does he leave?'

'In a few days.'

Fergus cursed. 'More waiting. Who is this companion?'

'We really should not talk of such things out here in the street.'

'The body's gone from the warehouse. Did Roger take it?'

Margaret hushed him. 'Come to the house first thing in the morning, after Roger departs. I hope to have much to tell you.'

'I mean to be gone by the time Ruthven returns.'

'Lock up Da's house and bide with us.'

Fergus hunched his shoulders. 'You tell me nothing.'

'I'll tell you all I know. I pray you, be patient.'

He wagged his head, a gesture that could mean many things. 'I'm expected at Matilda's.'

'Will you come to me in the morning?' Margaret asked, uneasy about his mood.

'If you have much to tell me I'd be a fool not to, eh?' He forced a smile, but his eyes were sullen as he left her.

Puzzling over how she might have better handled her brother, Margaret continued on to Ada's. But she was met with frustration. Ada had gone out with her niece and the child to visit an ailing friend. Margaret told the servant that she would return in the morning.

In the end, Fergus did not dine with Matilda. He had not the constitution to accept two humiliations in one day. On his arrival he discovered one of

Matilda's old sweethearts seated in the hall, regaling her with tales of his adventures in Edward Longshanks's ranks. Her blue eyes were fixed on his suntanned face, sounds from her lovely throat expressing awe at every pause. She was enraptured by a traitor. Fergus was doubly shamed, by his lack of experience and his stupidity in falling in love with such a witless woman. He could not bear another night in Perth, no matter what Maggie had to tell him. In late afternoon he collected his travelling pack from Maggie's stable and was off north.

❧ 16 ❧

KINNOULL HILL

After Roger left for the warehouses in the morning Margaret lingered in the hall waiting for Fergus. She hoped his tardiness was a sign that he had stayed late with Matilda. To while away the time she engaged Celia in helping her hang the largest of Christiana's tapestries.

Quiet at first, her dark eyes pensive, Celia eventually broke her silence to ask whether Margaret dreaded the return of the English soldiers. Margaret was about to answer when Celia continued.

'Will they take an interest in Smyth's death? Do we have anything to fear?'

'They must control the townsfolk for the safety of their men, so they'll mark anything unusual. I'm certain they'll hear the rumour and come to question Fergus,' Margaret said. She explained

Roger's reasoning about the surreptitious burial. She understood Celia's sceptical expression, for it seemed less useful each time she recounted it. It was plain that she had not managed to reassure Celia. Margaret was sorry to leave her with such concerns, but she was anxious to take the documents to Ada and learn their contents for she must know the nature of her father's business with Longshanks. 'If Fergus comes, tell him I'll not be long away,' she said.

Ada answered her knock, elegant in her silk gown but too impatient to wait for a servant to open the door. Seeing something in Margaret's demeanour, she guided her in by the arm and closed the door. 'What has happened?' She lifted Margaret's chin so that she could clearly see her face. 'You look as if you're about to have a spell.' She touched one of Margaret's hands. 'And you're cold despite the day.'

'I'm in no danger of fainting.' Margaret was sorry to have caused Ada concern, but she did not wish to spend the visit reassuring her. 'I hoped you might read some papers to me. I've learned to read a little, but only enough to confuse myself.' She glanced at Ada's niece, who was rocking the baby's cradle with one foot as she spun wool. 'Might we talk where we would not be heard?'

Ada glanced with interest at Margaret's basket. 'The kitchen is deserted at present.' She led the way to a small building at the edge of the backland. Directing Margaret to sit at the table beneath the window, Ada tossed some herbs in a small pot, added water, and set it over the fire. Their relationship was that of friends, but Ada also enjoyed mothering Margaret, and her efforts were appreciated. Once she was seated she asked about the documents. 'Are they personal letters?'

'No.' Margaret's face burned as she drew from the basket one of the letters she'd taken from Aylmer's casket, suddenly shy about having taken what didn't belong to her. 'They may concern dangerous matters. You've only to say and I'll find someone else to help me.'

'Someone you would not mind endangering?' Ada asked with a wry chuckle. But her strong face tensed as she noticed the broken seal. 'It looks like rather official correspondence. Where did you find this?'

'In the possession of Roger's servant.'

'Servant,' Ada repeated in a thoughtful voice. For a long moment she held Margaret's gaze. It seemed neither of them breathed.

When at last Ada stirred, her eyes and mouth softened. 'I know you would not have searched had you not good cause.' She spread the document on the table before her. 'Let me see whether I can help.' She skimmed the document and nodded. 'The scribe has a good hand. That is to be expected, of course, in the household of King Edward of England.' She watched Margaret's reaction.

Sick at heart, Margaret crossed herself. 'So I was right in thinking the seal that of Edward Longshanks. Are you able to read the letter?'

'I can see that you are aware of the danger in reading such things, Maggie. Have a care.' Ada nodded to herself, as if satisfied that she had done her duty in warning her friend. 'The answer to your question is yes, by a good hand I mean that the writing is easy to read. You have learned some letters, you say?'

'A priest in Edinburgh was teaching me.'

'At your request?'

Margaret nodded.

'I'm glad you wish to learn. I'll take over for him if you like.'

By the rather inappropriate sparkle in Ada's eyes, Margaret saw that her friend welcomed the intrigue. Margaret had hoped that Ada's past with a noble lover might prove helpful, but she had expected some resistance.

Without waiting for Margaret's response, Ada lifted the document and began to read aloud. The letter acknowledged Malcolm Kerr's offer of the use of his ships for some of the king's business in Flanders. The king accepted the offer, with the arrangements to follow.

It was as Margaret had feared, her father had chosen the side of wealth and influence in this struggle. She turned away from Ada, shamed by her father's lack of honour.

Ada set down the document. 'Many in Perth would admire Malcolm for this,' she said in a thoughtful tone.

'I hate him,' Margaret said too loudly. 'I am ashamed to be his daughter, coward and traitor that he is.'

Ada shifted, her silks whispering richly. 'He might have done you a favour, Maggie.'

'How could this favour me?'

Ada smoothed out the curling document. 'If the English were in fact the executioners, they will never mention Smyth's death; if they had nothing to do with it but consider a thief in your father's warehouse a threat to either their supplies or their plans, again they won't mention it.' She gestured to Margaret to move closer. 'Come, I'll read the letter slowly, pointing to each word. Then we'll read the next.'

Following along as Ada read calmed Margaret's mind a little, but Aylmer's possession of her father's letter troubled her.

She next chose the document addressed to Roger that mentioned her own surname and bore part of a royal seal. She held her breath as Ada explained that it was dated shortly before Roger's departure for Dundee. It was not the royal seal, Ada said, after a quick look at the contents, but that of the constable of Carlisle Castle, a royal castle, and thus it incorporated some royal details in its design.

'The scribe wrote on behalf of Robert Bruce the constable of Carlisle,' Ada explained, 'father to the Bruce who some believe might lead us out from beneath Edward Longshanks's hammer.'

Margaret had not told Ada of Roger's connection to the Bruce. It was an unexpected complication, that Roger had been in contact with the father of the Robert Bruce whom Roger served. This Bruce was still publicly loyal to Edward Longshanks. Fearing the letter might concern Roger's rescue of Edwina of Carlisle, Margaret said, 'I don't know that I want to hear this one.'

Ada gave a silky shrug. 'It is a trifle, purely business. On behalf of your father, Roger was to receive some goods for the constable in Dundee and arrange for transport to Carlisle.' She looked up at Margaret. 'Would you care to go over the words?'

Margaret shook her head. 'Perhaps I can come again to learn more words.' She was relieved that Roger had genuinely intended to go to Dundee.

'Come as soon as you like,' said Ada as she handed back the document. 'Do you have another?'

Margaret produced the other document she'd taken from Roger, the one with the word 'Rex' in the text.

Smoothing it out, Ada glanced through it, her expression growing troubled. 'I believe this may be what you deemed dangerous. A letter from the younger Robert Bruce. Your husband should have destroyed this, once read.'

Her heart pounding, Margaret bent over the parchment. She recognised a few words but too little to understand the message. 'What does it say?'

Ada read slowly. It concerned Edwina of Carlisle, the wife of 'our good friend'. The wording was cautious, until mention of Edward's slaughter of the burghers of Berwick, a slip of passion in an otherwise harmless request for Roger to escort Edwina to Edinburgh and there await the funds to continue on to an unspecified safe haven. She would travel under the name Dame Grey.

So Roger had rescued Edwina at the request of Robert the Bruce.

'Does Roger think to survive by pleasing both sides?' Ada wondered.

'He had a change of heart as he travelled to Dundee on the elder Bruce's business,' Margaret said. 'I already knew of this.'

'Ah.' Ada rose and poured the contents of the small pot she'd heated into two cups. After handing one to Margaret she moved to the window with hers and stood quietly gazing out for a while.

The tisane was spiced with ginger, Margaret discovered as she held the steaming liquid to her lips, and it was still too hot to drink. She set down the cup, drew out another document. The rustle of silk made her look up. Ada had turned from the window. Her attention was on the basket.

'Are you also a supporter of the young Robert Bruce, Maggie?'

'No.' Margaret sipped the tisane, burning the tip of her tongue.

'Are you spying on Roger for someone else?'

Margaret shook her head. 'For myself. I need to know this man I married.'

Ada eased down beside her and took her hand, looking long into her eyes. 'My dear friend, I had guessed there was much you had kept from me. Your stories the other day were amusing, yet I sensed a great sadness behind them. I pray you confide in me.'

It took little more coaxing for Margaret to open up to her friend.

'Roger seems unable or unwilling to tell me the truth about how he came to disappear, what his bonds are with others.' She explained who Edwina of Carlisle was, and her lingering suspicion that she'd been Roger's mistress. 'Uncle Murdoch was so loath to tell me about her, I was ready to believe the worst. And then Roger reappears with a servant far too fine for his station.' Knowing she could trust Ada, Margaret also confided her own staunch support of John Balliol so that her dilemma was clear. 'You see, I've taken a scunner to my own husband.' She shook her head.

Ada listened to all of it attentively, asking no

questions though her eyes were alive with emotion, which Margaret found comforting.

'And yet I weaken at his touch,' Margaret added in a hushed voice, then blushed and looked away, thinking she had said too much. The last was not something to share with others, no matter how close. She closed her eyes and drank down the spicy tisane.

Ada was bent over the next document by the time Margaret was composed enough to open her eyes.

'I am glad to know all this,' said Ada. 'Now I know your mind.'

'I feared I'd said too much.'

Ada pressed Margaret's hand, then tapped the letter. 'As for this,' she said, 'it contains further arrangements for the king's use of your father's ships, acknowledging that Malcolm will be sailing on one of them.' She regarded Margaret. 'The first of these you found in the possession of Roger's servant, or whatever he is. This one, too?'

Margaret was only half listening. That Aylmer had one of Malcolm's letters was suspicious, but to have two was damning. She needed to know whether these letters had been in her father's casket at her uncle's tavern, whether Aylmer and Roger were the intruders who murdered Old Will.

'I know what you are thinking,' Ada said. 'It is strange that this man is collecting information about your father, indeed letters that belong to him.'

'I very much fear that Roger and his servant collected these documents in Edinburgh, and that Old Will, the boller I mentioned the other day, caught them in my uncle's undercroft.'

'And one of them murdered him to keep him silent.' Ada took a deep breath. 'This is a terrible business. What will you do now?'

'Put these back before they are missed,' Margaret said, rolling up the letter and returning it to the basket. 'There was another, but I think I know what I need to know.'

'Don't be so certain. Let's read them all.'

'I have what I need.' Margaret rose.

Ada caught her by the arm. 'How do you know, Maggie? You're frightened, and with good cause. But the more you know the better prepared you will be.'

She was right. Margaret could hardly run away. Settling back down, she drew out the third document she'd found in the false bottom of Aylmer's casket.

Ada unrolled it, and as she glanced through it she nodded. 'So. Aylmer is no servant but kin to the younger Robert Bruce. The Bruce places his trust in him.' She paused as she read further. 'He is to assist Roger in making his way to Perth, introducing him to those who can help him in such travel.' She paused again, frowning as she read, then set down the document and looked at Margaret. 'He says that Malcolm Kerr is someone with ties to both Edward and John Balliol and therefore would be a prized spy, unless he cannot be persuaded to be constant.'

'And then what?'

'It is left to Aylmer's imagination.'

Margaret's hands had grown cold. Her heart felt fluttery, as if she were ill. She prayed that her father was well away. Yet she also wished she might ask him where he had kept the two letters.

Ada sighed and shook her head as she returned the document. 'When you wed Roger I rejoiced for your good fortune. I imagined pretty children tucked to your breast and an attentive husband sitting beside you. Clearly I have not your mother's gift of prescience.'

'Much good hers did me. She kept her misgivings to herself.' Margaret hugged her friend. 'Bless you for coaxing me to hear the last letter. And for not telling me to stay out of trouble.'

'It is far too late for such advice. Our king is fortunate in having your support. But go with care, Maggie. Do not let Roger and the Bruce's kinsman see your fear.'

Fergus had made little progress. As he'd left the relative safety of the town he had begun to doubt the wisdom of travelling alone armed with the sketchiest of instructions as to the route, merely a drawing his father had once made to illustrate a tale and the names of a few landmarks and towns along the way. It was little to guide him, and provided no checks to judge whether he strayed. He spent the night in an outbuilding on his father's property in the countryside, out of the way of the cousin who farmed the land. He was too agitated to sleep, anxiously debating whether to return to Perth or to seek out the Wallace near Kinclaven, a destination he knew. He guessed it must be someone in Wallace's camp with whom Maggie communicated, and perhaps it was someone from that camp with whom he might journey to Aberdeen. He also missed his dog. He should have brought Mungo, for no one would care for him, not properly. Perhaps he should return to town and confer with Maggie. But to return to Perth was to risk seeing Matilda and that would be a reminder of his mistaken ardour. She had made him feel the greatest fool in all the land. Mungo was worth a hundred Matildas. And therefore Fergus should go back for him. What to do? He had never faced a more difficult decision. The birds were greeting the dawn when at last he felt himself being pulled down into sleep.

By the time he woke and went out to relieve his bladder he found the foreshortened shadows of noon. Back inside he chewed on the bread and cheese he'd left too long in the pack and resumed his debate.

*

On leaving Ada's house Margaret turned away from the river, needing time to compose herself before facing Roger, who might be home for the midday meal. She felt ragged, as if her stuffing were being nibbled by mice and birds and parts of her were already cut off from her heart and head. And she was giddy with fear, unable to still her mind. To the few who greeted her she responded absently. Those who pretended not to notice her were far more intrusive, their eyes boring holes into her back. When she found herself on Southgate, she sought a moment's quiet in her father's house. Fergus's dog Mungo greeted her with an anxious bark and led her to the door. He preceded her into the hall but stopped abruptly and growled upon discovering Aylmer.

The Bruce's kinsman rose from her father's favourite chair, cup in hand. His moon face was expressionless.

He'd made himself right at home. 'What is your business here?' Margaret demanded, interrupting his greeting. Intruders deserved no courtesy. She trembled with anger and feared that he'd already missed the papers, although she thought it unlikely.

Aylmer pressed his free hand to his ear. 'Can you quiet the dog?'

'He recognises an intruder,' Margaret said, but

she crouched down and tried to calm Mungo. He stopped barking but kept his eyes on Aylmer. Mungo was a good guard dog.

'Thank you, Dame Margaret.' Aylmer stepped away from the chair and offered it to her, then resettled on a bench nearby. Mungo moved to lie across Margaret's feet. 'I was sent to fetch your brother Fergus,' said Aylmer, 'but Jonet says he did not come home last night or this morning, and that dog has barked all the while.'

Margaret reached down to pet the dog. 'Mungo seldom barks for nothing.'

Aylmer dismissed the comment with a sniff.

'Did Jonet mention anyone coming to the house?'

'No. But I was visited earlier by some angry men claiming your father is in Perth and demanding to see him.' He regarded her intently.

'What men?' Margaret said as off-handedly as she could manage.

It must have been convincing, for he looked disappointed. 'You are not surprised by the claim that your father is here?'

'I'd already heard that rumour. What men, I ask you?'

'Only one gave his name – Gilbert Ruthven. As their spokesman he demanded the sterlings owed to all of them by Malcolm Kerr.'

'Everyone's eager to call in their debts,' Margaret said, amazed by her calm voice.

Aylmer shook his head slowly. 'Sterlings – they were clear about it, Dame Margaret.'

She found it unsettling, both of them aware that her father's ships had carried Edward Longshanks's men and that Malcolm had no doubt been paid well, probably in sterlings, the coin of the realm, and yet neither mentioning it.

'Sterlings, coins, what does it matter?' she asked, an honest question for she had no idea why Aylmer found it significant.

'Might I ask what you know of your father's trading?'

About to rebuff him, she changed her mind, thinking she might quite naturally put him off. 'Less than I know of my husband's, which is little. The household is my responsibility.'

Aylmer said nothing.

'What did you tell these men?' Margaret asked.

'That my master understood Malcolm Kerr to be in Bruges. I could not help them. It was but a small lie.'

'You know something of the sterlings?'

'No, but I believe your father has been in the town.'

Margaret wondered whether Jonet had told him. She should have admitted it when Roger first asked her. He would not have harmed her father. And yet there were the letters. 'In faith, little surprises me of late.' She rose. 'I must be going.' Mungo rose and stretched, obviously intending to stick by her.

To her dismay, Aylmer insisted on escorting her home. 'The men were quite agitated, Dame Margaret. I would not have you harmed.'

'No one accosted me earlier, and now I have Mungo to protect me.'

'You were fortunate to pass safely. But your husband would not wish you to risk walking alone again.' He nodded to the dog. 'As for him, he hid when the men arrived.'

Aylmer's determination silenced further argument.

They found Celia in the yard airing clothing. She greeted Margaret and bent to scratch Mungo behind the ears. Margaret was bemused to find fussy Celia fond of dogs. She told Celia briefly why he was there, and the maid offered to watch him while working out in the yard. 'You have been missed,' she said. She did not so much as look at Aylmer.

Roger was pacing in the hall when Margaret and Aylmer entered. He glanced from one to the other. 'What has happened? Did you find Fergus?'

'No.' Aylmer informed him of Ruthven and company's visit. When Roger exhausted his questions, Aylmer excused himself and withdrew to his room.

Margaret's heart sank. She could only hope that Aylmer was so confident the papers were well hidden that he did not obsessively check for them on return.

'Have you no idea what it is the men are demanding of Malcolm?' Roger asked.

Margaret stood beside the table at which Roger had apparently been going over the accounts. She set the basket out of sight on the bench pulled up to the table and fussed with a mound of tally sticks. 'I have never witnessed anyone descending upon my father's house in the mood that Aylmer described. Is there enough light for you to work in here?'

'Yes. And leave the tallies as I had them.'

Margaret shrugged and sank down on to the bench beside the basket and sighed as if weary.

'It is strange they do not think to come here about your father's debts when they find no satisfaction at his house,' Roger said. 'As if they know only Malcolm can satisfy their demands.'

'Sometimes I think Andrew is the only member of my family I understand.'

'I have seldom heard you praise him. You thought him lacking joy.'

'I have learned to value his steadfastness. And at present even Fergus lacks joy.'

'That reminds me . . .' said Roger. 'I sent Aylmer for Fergus. Where is he?'

'I don't know,' Margaret said. 'What did you want of him?'

'We need to make certain that the English hear

the same story about John Smyth from all of us.'

'I don't understand your secretiveness about his death. Everyone knows of it. We don't know what happened, but he shouldn't have been in the warehouse. He was trespassing. Isn't the truth our best defence?'

'Maggie, I know what I'm doing. Do not interfere.'

Margaret refused to back away. 'Then explain how you imagine it working.' She paused as she thought of a possible explanation for the scene at her father's house. 'I wonder. Smyth's death is no secret. Perhaps Da's creditors are worried that the English will seize him when he returns, and they fear their money will be claimed by the English.'

Roger cast his eyes down for a few breaths, then met her gaze with interest. 'That is quite possible. With whom have you discussed this?'

'Only with Aylmer. He spoke with the men. Why?'

He shook his head. 'I maintain that it's best the English find no proof of anything amiss.'

Margaret was about to appropriate Ada's reasoning and suggest that the English might have been the executioners, or would approve of Smyth's murder, but remembered in time that she should not know of Malcolm's cooperation with the English for she'd learned of it in the stolen letters.

'What of Smyth's kin?' she asked instead.

'What proof do they have? And I don't think the English will care enough to talk to them. They've bigger problems, with Wallace and Murray gathering troops near Kinclaven, and the Bruce they know not where.' He began to leave the room.

Margaret relaxed a little. She might at least return Roger's documents. But he suddenly turned in the doorway.

'Where is Malcolm?'

'I've wondered that myself. All but his family seem to have seen him. Aylmer believes he has been in Perth.'

'We've found signs of someone shifting goods as if preparing to move them. Whoever it is, he has not succeeded in hiding the preparations. But you've not spoken with your father?'

For the second time this day she regretted her promise to her father. His carelessness made her feel a fool. But she did not have time to consider the consequences of confessing to Roger. 'How could I have spoken to him without your knowledge?'

'Where were you this morning?'

'At Ada's. I'm worried about Fergus,' she said, changing the subject. 'It's not like Mungo to bark in the night, even when Fergus is from home. Do you think Ruthven and the others are watching the house? Do you think they might have taken Fergus?'

'If they had him, why would they storm the

house when Aylmer was there? More likely they would demand ransom. I'm still wondering why they don't come here.'

'Give them time,' said Margaret, 'they'll think of it soon enough.' She picked up the basket and rose, struggling to keep her mind from the damning documents she carried lest Roger somehow read her thoughts. 'Perhaps we should close up Da's house and let Fergus and Jonet bide here.'

'We'll discuss it.'

'I thought that's what we were doing.'

'I must think about it.'

'Oh. Then I'll be about my work.' Margaret brushed past Roger and climbed to the solar to return his letters to the casket.

Halfway back to Perth, Fergus halted. Fear of what he might face on the road was propelling him back into the trap of his family. But it occurred to him that because of his father's activities Perth might be the most dangerous place for him at present. Or was he using that as an excuse not to see Matilda? He could not think clearly.

The afternoon grew hot as Margaret, Jonet, and Celia shifted the airing bed linens. Celia kept up a patter about spreading linens on lavender shrubs, which Dame Katherine had recalled from her mother's youth in Suffolk in the south. That led her to perfumed oils and unguents. Margaret relaxed with the chatter, imagining an idle life in a richly furnished home with a glorious garden that bloomed even in winter. Mungo had been sleeping in the sun, but suddenly he stood up and growled.

Aylmer approached, giving the dog a wide berth. 'May I speak with you, Dame Margaret?' he asked.

She dropped her arms, stepped away from the line of bedding. 'What is it?'

He turned his head so that Celia could not see his face. 'Might we talk alone?'

Judging his expression as one of irritation, Margaret did not fuss but led Aylmer directly to the stable. 'Is this acceptable?' she asked, matching his impatience.

He surprised her by pulling off his cap and giving her a little bow. 'Forgive me for interrupting your work, but I am missing some letters from my travel chest.'

She forced herself to breathe. 'What has that to do with me?'

'With your servants, Dame Margaret. Have they been in my room?'

'As you see, we are airing the linens, so yes, one of them has been in there. But neither of them is a thief.'

'Are you so sure of them?'

Indignation came easily. 'Jonet and Celia have

been in the service of our family for a long while. Neither would suddenly turn dishonest merely because of your tempting belongings. Nor can they read.'

He was sceptical, and with good reason. With every word Margaret felt herself sinking into a trap that would catch her the moment she let down her guard.

'If not your servants,' Aylmer said, looking uncomfortable, 'perhaps – I would not have thought such a thing but – your father's sterlings, owed to someone, my papers – might your brother have helped himself to that which isn't his, and then fled?'

Margaret's cry of outrage escaped her before she had time to think. Suddenly Roger was beside her. He had appeared so quickly she wondered whether he was spying on her. Or on Aylmer.

'What is the matter?' he demanded.

'A misunderstanding,' said Aylmer. With a curt bow, he left the stable.

Not meeting Roger's eyes, Margaret said, 'The Bruce did you no favour in Aylmer.'

'He did not attack you?'

'What? Oh, no, it was nothing so—' She looked up, blushing. 'Nothing so terrible, Roger. I find him irritating, that is all. Nothing is to his liking.' She kissed Roger's cheek and he walked off, looking uneasy.

Returning to her work, she nervously waited for

Roger and Aylmer to leave together and then went within, Celia with her. In a short while she had returned the documents to Aylmer's casket. Exhausted by the day's events, she agreed to Celia's suggestion that she lie down in her chamber with a cool, lavender-scented cloth over her eyes. She woke much later, worrying about Fergus.

Dreams of Kilmartin Glen had filled Christiana's sleep the previous night, and she spent the day quietly, gathering what she could recall of the dreams and piecing them together. Whether or not she reconstructed them accurately, she sensed that it was the effort that would teach her what she must glean from them. It felt a validation of her new resolve to have such guiding dreams.

Marion helped her dress in one of her finest gowns, a blue that flattered her, and a white silk veil. She was resting when a novice came with Prioress Agnes's request for her presence in the hall of the guest house. The English had returned. As Christiana rose, Marion smoothed out her skirt and adjusted the veil, then smiled in admiration. She was better than a mirror.

The moment Christiana stepped into the guest-house garden she was drawn to look up at Kinnoull Hill. The novice was staring at her uncertainly.

'Let us hasten,' said Christiana.

The young woman bowed her head and led the way down the yard.

Prioress Agnes and her kinsman Thomas greeted Christiana with pinched faces. Her hands were cold, his odour sour with fear.

'You have nothing to worry about,' Christiana assured them. 'The soldiers will seek the safety of Perth.'

Prioress Agnes crossed herself. 'We must pray God to make that so.' She cast her eyes up and down Christiana's attire. 'Do you mean to dazzle the soldiers?'

'The English respect splendour,' Christiana said.

All three turned towards the sound of horses in the yard.

'I hope you're prepared,' Thomas said.

The captain was travel-worn, dusty and stinking of horse, yet he was clean-shaven, indeed still bled from a nick, and his clothes were well-tailored. He bowed courteously and greeted her with particular respect, saying that he had heard of her great gift. But once he sat he gave his full attention to the prioress as he asked permission to leave some of his men at the priory to watch the river.

'So it is not your men atop Kinnoull Hill?' Christiana asked. She meant to say more, but the prioress motioned to her to wait.

Thomas explained the strategic value of the hill, how it would be better to station men there to signal those on the Perth waterfront if anyone approached from downriver.

Agnes nodded. 'If your men are known to be here, we might be attacked. We ask you to leave us in peace.'

But the captain turned to Christiana. 'Why do you ask if our men are on the hill, Dame Christiana?'

Her surroundings began to fade and the hill filled her vision. 'Behind the two on watch there are a handful with weapons drawn.'

'I have only four men up there,' said the captain. 'Have you seen a vision of this?'

'I have them before me, Captain. They watch your men approach Perth.'

'What happened to my guards?'

Christiana shook her head. 'I see only these. Oh no.' She caught her breath, seeing the flies. 'Why did they not bury them?' she moaned.

From far away Thomas's voice said something to the captain. Christiana was sinking down, down.

The light was fading and the shadows had grown so long that Fergus slowed to be sure of his footing. He could not risk falling and being injured, for someone followed him. Ever since he had turned away from Perth in late afternoon he'd felt eyes on his back, heard sounds behind him as he walked, silenced when he paused to listen. At his easy pace anyone might overcome him, but they stayed behind him. They must want to see where he headed. He shivered with fear and did not know what to do. His present path would return him to the hut on his father's land at dark. He could not walk into the night. Yet perhaps that is what he should do – he would not sleep anyway, not with eyes watching the hut. He wondered what would happen if he turned back towards Perth. He hesitated, but could not turn himself around. Fear filled his bladder. It was miraculous, for he'd no water left and had not the courage to kneel at a burn and drink, imagining a sword coming down on his neck. He told himself beheading was not the method of stealth, but the image held.

Suddenly a heavy hand clutched his shoulder.

'Fergus Kerr. On business for your da, are ye?'

Piss ran down Fergus's leg.

Christiana returned to consciousness to find the prioress watching her with concern. Thomas stood a little away from them, a cup in hand.

'I should like some wine,' Christiana said. 'Is the captain gone?'

The prioress sighed and rose to call for a servant.

Thomas turned to Christiana. 'He has sent more men to the hill. If what you told him proves true, he will follow our advice and leave here.' He threw his head back and drained his cup. 'God help us when he finds his men safe and sound.'

'He will not,' said Christiana.

❧ 17 ❧

MORE CHILD THAN MAN

As Celia assisted Margaret in undressing for the night, she mentioned that Aylmer had not taken his evening meal with her and Jonet, who had moved into the kitchen. 'I don't like his disappearing without a word to anyone,' Celia said. 'He's too scheming.'

Margaret liked it no better than Celia. 'He might perchance be on an errand for Roger. I'll find out.' She pressed her temples. Mungo had resumed his barking on being closed in the stable for the night. 'We'll none of us sleep if we leave the dog out there.'

'Shall I bring him in?' Celia suggested.

'Oh yes. He might be quiet in the hall,' Margaret said. 'I pray Fergus returns soon.'

After Celia withdrew from the bedchamber, Margaret knelt to pray that God would watch over

Fergus if he had departed on his own for Aberdeen.

'Are you that worried about your brother?' Roger asked upon finding her on her knees. He tossed his belt on the bed and sat down on a bench to remove his boots. Margaret crossed herself and rose to help him.

'Fergus is more child than man,' she said, 'though he looks a man and will be treated as such by strangers.'

'Hm.' Roger put his boots aside and poured himself a cup of wine, turning half towards her. 'Is he so much a child?' he asked the air. 'Can it be mere chance that Aylmer's papers have disappeared at the same time as your brother?'

She did not yet know how to deal with Aylmer's having missed the papers she had since returned. 'Where is Aylmer this evening?'

Roger faced her. 'At your father's house. We thought it prudent to set a watch.'

'For Ruthven?'

'Or Fergus. Is it possible he has hidden the sterlings that are causing such a fuss?'

'Roger, you've known Fergus for years. Can you really imagine he'd do such a thing?'

Roger seemed absorbed in running a finger around the rim of his cup. 'A young man keen to strike out on his own might find it tempting,' he said in a thoughtful tone. 'And with the English in the town . . .'

'They have returned?'

'Late today.' He looked her in the eye. 'Can you be so sure of Fergus?'

His doubts increased Margaret's anxiety. If Aylmer did not find the papers or the sterlings in Malcolm's house, Roger might send someone after Fergus, someone who would not be gentle with him. She could not allow her brother to pay for her actions.

'I know that he is innocent of removing documents from Aylmer's room,' Margaret said. 'And as for the sterlings, if they exist he knows nothing of them. He came to me about Gilbert Ruthven's first visit and was disappointed when I could tell him nothing.'

Roger had settled back on the bench. 'How do you know he took nothing from Aylmer?'

Margaret took a deep breath. 'Because I did it – and returned the documents, but too late.'

Roger's gaunt cheeks remained slack for a moment, his eyes dull with confusion. 'You?' He set the cup aside. 'You?' he repeated, the word now loud and angry. He rose and grabbed Margaret's shoulders too quickly for her to have anticipated the attack. 'Why would you do such a thing?' he demanded, his face so close she felt his beard on her forehead as he shook her.

She tried to back away from him, but he dug his fingers into her shoulders.

'Why does Aylmer have letters to my father in

his possession?' she gasped. 'What right has he?'

'So, my sly wife has learned to read?' Roger shook her hard and shoved her away.

Margaret steadied herself against a bedpost, pressing her hands around her neck which ached from the shaking. Roger's tenderness towards her was easily shed. 'I've learned some words. But I certainly recognise Da's name – I have seen it many times.'

'You think to distract me from the point – why did you search Aylmer's belongings?'

'He's no servant, Roger, I've been certain of that from the moment he spoke to me at my uncle's inn.' She shifted back to sit at the foot of the bed, her shoulders and neck tender and her breath unsteady. 'So I set out to find out who he was.'

Roger raked his hands through his hair. 'What has come over you, Maggie? To search a guest's room – I never expected such behaviour.'

There was much he had not expected, Margaret thought. 'So now he's a guest? Your neglect has taught me to see to myself, Roger, and I mean to do just that.'

'So it's my fault. You insult a guest and blame me.'

'You did not introduce him as a guest, but as a servant in this household. I am the keeper of the keys and I have a right to know whether he can be trusted.'

'And so you took away some letters.'

'Letters to which he has no right. Why is he carrying Father's documents, Roger? Was it Aylmer who broke into Uncle Murdoch's undercroft and murdered Old Will? Did Aylmer do that to steal Da's letters?'

'Oh, Maggie, Maggie.' Shaking his head and smiling a little, Roger joined her on the bed and took her left hand in his. 'So *that* is what you fear. I understand now, but you've drawn the wrong conclusions. Aylmer was carrying the papers for *me*. They concern some of my business deals with Malcolm.'

There should be a sheen of sweat on his upper lip, or he should drop his eyes from hers, but he went on and on in that soothing voice, his eyes locked on hers, reassuring her. How smoothly he lied, she thought, with how little hesitation. It might be the most frightening discovery in this year of discoveries, that Roger had such a gift for deception. James's use of disguise was overt – he did not expect those who knew him to be fooled up close; but Roger expected her, his wife, his bedmate, to believe his act. She had lost the thread of his monologue and did not wish to pick it up.

'I care nothing for Aylmer or his fate, whoever he is,' she said. 'I'm worried about Fergus, I'm tired, and I'm going to sleep.'

She climbed into bed and pulled the covers over her head. Her heart was pounding, her cheeks hot.

*

After helping Jonet fix a bed for herself in the kitchen, Celia had brought Mungo into the hall and settled down near the fire to comb him. He fussed at first, whining and spooking at every sound, but eventually he relaxed beneath Celia's long, soothing strokes and her low voice telling him tales of her childhood animals. Despite the hairs collecting on her sleeves where no apron protected her gown she was glad of his company; at night the hall was a place of shadows. Neither did she like being in a room with many entrances after dark. Her imagination conjured all the beasts of legend creeping up behind her. But Mungo kept them at bay, and when he licked her face or shook his head so hard she could hear his ears slapping his neck she laughed and laughed. It had been a long while since she had laughed so much.

When at last Mungo had not stirred for a long while, Celia eased herself up, wondering at the lingering stiffness from riding. Her joints were cold, she decided, noticing how low the fire had burned. She headed up the stairs, but Mungo began to whine just as she reached the landing. Perhaps he, too, feared the shadows. She did not want him to climb the stairs. But if she took him out to the kitchen now she might frighten Jonet. His whining grew louder as he came to stand at the bottom of the steps.

Vowing to speak with Roger and Margaret in the

morning about some better arrangement, Celia hurried to the small room in which she slept and gathered her blankets and pillows into a heavy bundle, and awkwardly climbed back down to the hall to bed down with the dog. Stoking the fire in the hope that it would push back the shadows long enough for her to fall asleep, Celia settled down with Mungo, well out of the way of anyone's path should someone move about in the night.

'Damned dog,' Roger muttered.

Margaret, unable to sleep, had heard Celia in the next room. 'Celia's gone down to quiet him.'

Rolling on to his back, Roger sighed. 'What's the use of a dog like that?'

'He was a good hunter, but he's old now. He's seldom far from Fergus – that's part of my worry, that Fergus left Mungo at Da's house with only Jonet there.'

Roger propped his head up on an elbow. 'I'm sorry you're so worried about Fergus.'

She did not believe him.

As if he read that in her silence, he asked, 'Did you search my things, too?'

'I did,' she said.

He groaned.

'I cannot help but wonder what has kept you from me and your responsibilities here all this time,' she said.

'But I've told you.'

She rose up to face him. 'Yes. And if we were merely friends, perhaps even brother and sister, it would be enough. But you share my bed, Roger, and my body, and I can't go on without knowing your heart. I thought it was enough for me to love and serve you, but all the while you were away I felt so betrayed. I can't go back.'

He was losing his temper, she could tell it by his breathing.

She rolled over and refused to respond to his angry questions.

Some time in the night Mungo woke Celia with a low growl. A lamp burned dimly by the front door. She tried to calm the dog, stroking him between the ears while she peered into the darkness, staying low. A person was sitting on a bench beside the lamp, pulling off their boots she guessed by the movement and the sound of something dropping. Mungo's behaviour suggested it was Aylmer. And as he rose and stiffly bent to pick up the boots, then lifted the lamp, Celia saw that it was indeed Aylmer who now moved towards his chamber. He paused as he neared Mungo. The dog growled.

'Damned dog,' Aylmer said, 'you belong in the stable.'

Celia thought she saw a bruise on his face and stains on his shirt, as well as a torn sleeve, although the shadows from the lamp might be tricking her eyes. She must have moved or made some noise to call attention to herself, for now Aylmer saw her.

'What are you doing in the hall?' he demanded.

'I'm trying to keep the dog quiet so my mistress can sleep the night.'

Mungo growled and barked once.

'Now look what you've done.' Celia held Mungo back. 'Go off to bed and leave us.'

With a curse, Aylmer stumbled off to his chamber.

Celia's heart pounded. It was a long while before she slept again.

The crackle of fire and a murmur of men's voices entered Fergus's awareness and for a moment he forgot the gripping pain in his belly and tried to open his eyes, but his eyelids stuck together and the effort made him cough. He sank back and waited for the spasm in his throat to stop. When the pain had eased a little he tried again to open his eyes and succeeded, only to be blinded by the light of a campfire. But he fought tears long enough to see that a man sat near him, facing the fire.

'Where am I?' Fergus asked.

'In the camp of friends,' the man said, his deep voice matching Fergus's fleeting impression of a large man. 'Are you thirsty?'

Fergus moved his tongue around his mouth, identifying the salty, metallic taste of blood. There was little moisture.

'I am.'

He struggled to sit up, blinking furiously. His nose began to run. The man assisted him, then held a cup to Fergus's mouth. Cool water washed over his teeth and tongue, but as it trickled down his throat he began to cough again, and worse, for his stomach joined in the spasms. The man helped him bend over to retch. It felt as if he'd been knifed in the gut. He straightened slowly.

The man still sat beside him. 'I don't doubt you're in pain,' he said. 'But you've no mortal wounds that I can see.'

'I remember someone grabbing me by the shoulder and then nothing but pain,' Fergus said, his stomach cramping as he recalled that the man beside him was a stranger. But he had been too kind to be the one who had beaten him.

'One of my men came upon a pair of Englishmen hurrying away from a clearing, looking over their shoulders as if they might be followed. He retraced their steps and found you in a faint and your goodbrother's companion bent over you. Both of you looked beaten up, and he guessed the man was gauging how badly you were hurt. But then he rose, gave you a kick that might have killed an older, weaker man, and departed. What did he seek?'

'Aylmer?' Fergus whispered.

'That's the name,' said a new voice. 'He's one of the Bruce's men.'

'He attacked me?' Fergus asked. Beside the first man knelt a second, a travel-worn friar with an untidy tonsure. A deep cleft in his chin teased Fergus's memory.

The friar nodded.

They helped him ease back against a rock, and he found his voice again. 'He had no cause to search me,' Fergus said.

The one who had helped him drink was taller than Fergus and broad-shouldered, with large, calloused hands. A warrior, no doubt of it, though by his speech Fergus had first guessed him to be if not English, a well-travelled merchant. But he wore his red hair longer than a merchant, and his beard was rough.

'Who are you?' Fergus asked. 'I must know who to thank for delivering me.'

The friar chuckled. 'You must be the only young man in these parts who does not recognise William Wallace.'

'God have mercy,' Fergus breathed. He wiped his nose on his sleeve, though nothing could make him look presentable or erase his humiliation.

'I am glad not all know my face,' said Wallace.

Tongue-tied, Fergus looked away, noticing perhaps a dozen men sitting a little away from the fire, heads together. A few horses neighed. 'Are we at Kinclaven?' he asked.

'Is that where you were headed?' the friar asked.

Fergus closed his eyes. 'I had not come nearly so far.'

'Where were you headed?' the friar repeated.

'I couldn't decide. Aberdeen, Kinclaven, back to Perth . . .' He shrugged.

'Aberdeen,' Wallace said softly.

'You see?' the friar said to Wallace.

Wallace nodded. 'But not at once.' He turned back to Fergus. 'Friar James will escort you home. We've none to care for your wounds here.' Strong brows shadowed his face in the darkness.

Some time after Mungo's bark in the night sleep claimed Margaret. When she woke, Roger was sitting by the window in his shirt, the shutters opened to a sunny dawn. Rumpled from sleep, his bare legs sticking out of the bottom of his shirt, he looked his age, and weary, yet he sat straight. Both of them had changed in the past year, in many ways for the better. If only there were a way to erase all that had come between them.

Roger noticed her movement and returned to bed, sitting down beside her with his legs bent, outstretched arms propped on his knees. He steepled his hands and seemed to address them.

'Are we to war with one another from now on?'

Margaret's heart fluttered at the question so like that in her own mind. 'I don't know,' she said.

They said nothing for a while. Margaret searched for something honest she might say to patch the rift.

But it was Roger who spoke first. 'I regret laying hands on you last night,' he said.

'You did not injure me.'

Another silence ensued.

'Mungo barked in the night,' Margaret finally said. 'I wonder whether it was Aylmer returning from his watch at Da's house.'

'I didn't hear the dog after Celia went down,' Roger said.

'Why would Aylmer leave his watch in the middle of the night?'

'We don't know that he did.' Roger sighed. 'Aylmer is not your enemy, Maggie.'

'He thinks, as you did, that Fergus took the letters. And worse, he believes Fergus has stolen the money that Ruthven and the others are demanding.'

'That does not make him your enemy.'

Margaret turned to Roger. 'I fear for my brother with that man searching for him.'

'Aylmer would not hurt him.'

'Why not, if he believes him guilty? What is to prevent him? There's no law now, what would stop him?'

Roger began to speak, but looked away.

'You lied to me about the letters Aylmer carries,' Margaret said. 'My father's letters. I know what they say, Roger, and I'll ask you again – what is Aylmer doing with them?'

'So you *can* read?'

She shook her head. 'I took them to someone who can. I had to know, Roger. Though it has made it all worse, for now I fear you murdered Old Will.'

'Why do you go on about that old drunk? I didn't touch him, Maggie.'

'Did Aylmer?'

'Why would he?'

'Why does he have Da's papers?'

Roger pressed his hands to his face and grew quiet.

It had all gone so horribly wrong, Margaret thought, and yet she did care for Roger.

Dropping his hands, Roger said, 'I needed information about Malcolm's dealings with the English, something I could threaten to reveal unless he shifted his allegiance from Edward to Robert Bruce. We don't want his ships helping the enemy.'

'How did you know to look for the letters?'

'Something Malcolm said before he left alerted me that when he'd pledged his fealty to England in Berwick he'd made a business deal much to his liking. But I needed more – something to prove he was serving both sides.'

'You think so little of my father?'

'He's not so different from his brother Murdoch,' said Roger. 'Surely you've seen that?'

She had, and she could not fault Roger's suspicion. 'So where did Aylmer find the letters?'

'In Murdoch's undercroft – they are the originals. I knew your father would carry only copies of such documents when travelling unless the original was required.' Roger ran a hand through his hair. 'Oh, Maggie, why did you insist on prying?' His face compressed in anguish, chilling Margaret to the heart. 'How am I to explain?' He swung his legs over the bed and reached for his leggings.

'Explain to the Bruce's kinsman, you mean?' she asked.

He came around to her side of the bed. 'What are you talking about?'

'I know who Aylmer is.' She told him about the other letter Aylmer carried.

Roger turned away.

'You had not known that the Bruce sent Aylmer to lure Da,' she said.

'No. But I understand. I'm sure he was also concerned about my steadfastness once I was among my family. Anyone can swear allegiance.'

'The Bruce will be pleased when Aylmer reassures him that your family has no influence over you. I'm gey glad Da isn't really here.'

'We are in a war against a powerful force, Maggie.'

'Does it not give you pause that Robert Bruce set Aylmer to spy on you and my father?'

'You little fool, meddling in what you don't understand.'

The chill in his voice numbed Margaret. They dressed in silence and went their separate ways.

Celia saw the anger on both faces as the couple descended, first Roger, then Margaret not far behind. As Roger began to cross the hall to the street door Celia had offered him food but he shook his head and departed. Margaret stood in the middle of the room, hands hanging at her sides, as if she awaited some grim news.

'Come out to the kitchen, Mistress, I beg you,' Celia said, stepping into Margaret's field of vision. Aylmer had not yet risen, and she did not want him to come upon them as she recounted his return in the night.

❧ 18 ❧

A STRONG THREAD

'Were you up long with Mungo?' Margaret asked as the dog bounded across the yard to greet her and Celia.

'I slept with him in the hall,' Celia said.

'I'm sorry you had such a night.'

'You should not be.' Celia told her of Aylmer's state when he returned in the middle of the night. 'Had I not been there, we wouldn't know. He'll have himself cleaned up before he presents himself today, I'll warrant.'

'God watch over my brother,' Margaret whispered, crossing herself, certain that Aylmer had followed Fergus. Now that she knew Aylmer's true identity she saw that he was a strong thread in the complex knot of conflicting loyalties in which she was bound up, and she could not guess whose side Roger would take if the Bruce's kinsman harmed her brother.

It was mere chance that Wallace had been in the small camp across the river from Scone when Fergus was brought there the previous evening. Having observed the English garrison in Kinclaven moving about as if expecting reinforcements, Wallace had worked out a plan for the gradual dispersal of his troops and had come south to discuss it with his men there, including James, who had been biding in the smaller camp for quick access to Perth and Scone. Though Longshanks had robbed Scone of anything of worth and sent it south to England, it was yet a sacred place to the Scots.

'I'm sending some parties on to Dundee,' Wallace told James shortly after dawn. 'They'll travel in small groups. I'll wait at the Kinclaven camp for the last to arrive. I hope my party includes you and those you've coaxed from Perth.'

'Perth is for the English,' James said. He'd been brooding about the burden of Margaret's presently useless brother. 'Someone else could take the lad back to town.'

'No, James. Not all of the people there support Edward Longshanks.' Wallace listed the families on whom he was depending. 'It's important to me that you go to Perth. You're a Comyn, the king's kinsman. The people need to know that his kinsmen still fight for him, and that not all have been bound and taken to England.'

James knew from experience that the Comyn name was not always a welcome one. Power breeds resentment. 'They would rally even more to your call,' James said.

The face framed in rusty hair looked haggard. 'I am but one desperate supporter of King John Balliol, never meant for greatness, James. Think how strong we would be were the great lords of this land to stand by us.'

'Edward has taken too many of them to England,' said James.

Wallace nodded. 'It was clever of him.'

In the end James promised to talk to the families Wallace had named in Perth, and any other households they might suggest.

Going in search of Fergus, James found him curled up on his side napping under the watchful eyes of one of his rescuers.

'What do you think, can he travel?' James asked.

'He'll be slow.'

Fergus stirred. 'Are we off home, then?' he asked, rubbing his eyes and cautiously stretching out his legs along the uneven ground. Dew glistened on his straight, chestnut-coloured hair. He coughed after sucking in a lungful of the damp morning air and clutched his sides with a grimace of pain.

'I don't know that you've the strength,' said James.

'I'm sore but able to walk.'

'What's your hurry?' asked Fergus's protector.

'The English have returned to Perth,' said James. 'They're distracted by a skirmish on the far side of the river, but I want to be inside the walls before they've time to organise a watch on them.'

'They hadn't left one in place?'

James shook his head. 'They are too confident of the townsfolk.'

'With good cause, the cowards,' Fergus muttered. He had managed to sit up and was studying James. 'I know you,' he said. 'You came to the house the day Maggie returned to Perth. But you were dressed as a friar then. So it was you she's been meeting at the kirk.'

James had not expected Fergus to know him in his usual clothes. 'How did you recognise me?'

'By the cleft in your chin,' said Fergus. 'I remember thinking that the amorous cleft was wasted on you – unless the tales of lecherous friars are true.'

'I bow to your keen eye,' said James. 'At your age I would not have marked it.'

Unfortunately there was nothing James could do to hide his cleft short of growing a beard, which would be inappropriate for a friar. Perhaps it was time to change his disguise.

Fergus rose with some effort and the muscles in his neck were taut as if he were struggling to stay upright.

'You're in pain,' said James. 'You should rest today.'

'I'm stiff from sleep and sore, but I'll be so whether I walk or sit in camp.' Fergus shook out his legs and hurried away to relieve himself.

He was as stubborn as his sister, James thought. And as proud. But he moved more naturally the further he walked, and with reaching Perth before the English watch a concern, James decided to take the young man at his word.

'How did you meet my sister?' Fergus asked as they started out.

'Too much talk and we'll not only attract attention, but we'll not hear the noise of a pursuit,' James said quietly. 'Your attack last night should make you cautious.'

Fergus peered over his shoulder and said nothing more. They were following a burn south. Where the bank sank almost to water level the path skirted round marshy areas. They had been walking a while when James recognised an occasional wet, sucking sound behind them as that of shoes pulling up out of the marshy spots.

He tapped Fergus and whispered to him to follow as he struck off the path seeking a place to hide. Behind a tree on a wild, brushy hummock they crouched to watch the path. Fergus's breathing was ragged. Three men eventually appeared, alert and watchful. Two strode on past the point at which James and Fergus had left the path, but the third stopped, studying the path and then the marshy ground between him and the brush in which the two hid. His companions turned back to him.

Fergus caught his breath a little too noisily for James's comfort. He held his own, praying that no one had heard and that the young fool would now be quiet.

The men discussed something. One of the pair who had continued on lifted a foot and pointed to it. James could not make out their words. With a shrug, the tracker nodded and moved on with the others, casting one glance back before he disappeared into the trees.

James remained immobile for a while, and Fergus, though straightening up, said nothing and stayed in place.

'You almost gave us away,' James growled softly when he finally rose.

Fergus raked back his damp hair. 'I caught myself, didn't I?'

'I was grateful for that.' Remembering the young man's condition, James asked, 'Are you in much pain?'

'That wasn't why I almost spoke. I know two of them,' Fergus said. 'They're friends of our maid Jonet.'

'Friends, eh?' said James. 'Then she's befriended Longshanks's soldiers, for all three are known to me as his men. They've been to your house?'

'Many times over the summer. That bitch. She's why Mungo didn't bark.'

'Mungo?'

'My dog. It must have been Jonet who stuffed him into a feed bin the afternoon they searched the house. He could have died.'

James almost laughed. The young man had odd priorities – he'd not lost his temper over his beating the previous evening, but now he was livid over his dog's having been stuffed in a box. 'God has not blessed you with trustworthy servants – Aylmer, Jonet.'

'Aylmer is Roger Sinclair's servant, not mine— What are you doing?' Fergus hissed as James shoved him back down in the brush.

'They've headed back.' He'd heard a bird startle in the direction the three men had taken. The tracker must have convinced the others to search. James wondered whether the three were after Fergus or himself. He would soon know – a figure approached on the path, bent almost double and moving hesitantly. Fergus groaned softly beside him. James fingered the dagger on his belt.

But when the man came clearly into sight James realised it wasn't one of the three at all.

'Da,' Fergus whispered. 'It's my da.'

'Here?'

Malcolm Kerr straightened up at the point on the path nearest them and trained his eyes almost precisely on their brushy hideout.

'Don't be hasty,' James said, noting a dagger in the man's hand.

But Fergus took no heed. He rose and softly hailed his father.

Putting the dagger between his teeth, Malcolm lifted his arms in peace and walked slowly towards them. James thought it extraordinary, the pot-bellied elderly man picking his way silently and efficiently through the brush along the marshy ground. He was more adventurer than merchant.

'What are you doing here, Da?' Fergus hissed.

'Saving the two of you. You've three irritated men waiting for you further on. God was watching over you today, my son, for I'd almost given up my search for you and gone on. I know a way round them. Come!'

James had a new respect for Malcolm Kerr.

Angry with Aylmer and worried about Fergus, Margaret took out her frustrations on the kitchen garden. Despite being neglected since the previous autumn, the patch of earth had managed to bring forth some herbs but the soil was so packed and dry that the weeds snapped off just above ground, and digging for their roots disturbed the plants she wanted to save. It was just the sort of work she needed, and she fell to it with energy. Mungo kept her company, demanding an attentive pat now and then.

Roger returned from the warehouse and nodded

curtly as he passed her on his way into the house. She had expected him to say something to her about the arrival of the English troops. But Roger said not a word. She was annoyed by her disappointment – she could not both hate and love him. But hate was too strong a word. She was hurt by his lies and neglect, more sad than angry. She would have preferred anger.

Mungo interrupted her thoughts, barking loudly and spinning several times before dashing away towards Watergate. Margaret set her tools aside and chased after him, stumbling to an abrupt stop as her father and her brother appeared, the latter leaning down awkwardly to pet his excited dog.

'I thought you'd gone,' she said to her father, glancing back at the house. 'Roger's within.'

'The lad's injured, I could not let him limp through the town unaided, and your Comyn thinks he has even more cause than I do to hide from Sinclair.'

Margaret shooed the dog away and took Fergus's shoulders, searching his eyes. The left one was blackening. She noted that he remained stooped even now that Mungo had moved away.

'My God, what happened?'

'Beaten by some English soldiers, then kicked by your husband's man Aylmer,' said Malcolm.

'I'm not dying, Maggie, just sore.' Fergus flashed her a wan smile.

'Dying or not, come within,' said Margaret. 'Celia and I will attend you.'

Her father accompanied them to the door and appeared ready to enter the house.

'Have you decided to come along in?' Margaret asked, wondering at the change in her father's behaviour.

'I will, yes, Maggie. I mean to have my say with Sinclair and Jonet.'

'Jonet?' Margaret said.

'Fergus will tell you,' said Malcolm. 'Take him up to the solar while I deal with Sinclair.'

'Why have you chosen to confront Roger now?' Margaret persisted. 'With the English in town you are in more danger than before.'

'I'll do it and be gone, Maggie. I meant to see my son safe home and have my say with both Sinclair and that false maid, and then I can leave with a clear conscience.'

'You've a slow wit, Da, to fret over Fergus now. You might have spared him this had you agreed to his going to Uncle Thomas in Aberdeen months ago.'

Her father grunted and led the way into the house.

Roger was in the hall sitting at the table that was still littered with documents and tally sticks. He rose as they approached, his eyes moving from Malcolm to Fergus to Margaret, where they lingered accusingly. Margaret noticed ink stains on the fingertips of his right hand. That was more like the Roger she had married.

'I rescued my youngest from the hands of English soldiers,' said Malcolm. 'God's hand is clear in this, my having just disembarked in Dundee.'

'I'm not blind, Malcolm. I've known for a while that you've been here gathering goods.' Roger turned his attention to Fergus. 'You're injured?'

Margaret left them to tell Celia to bring her healing herbs up to the solar, where she intended to give Fergus Celia's small room for the night. 'Until we see whether Da's home is safe now the English are here.'

Celia agreed. 'I'll sleep in the kitchen with Jonet.' She followed Margaret back towards the hall.

Margaret paused before they entered the house. 'I didn't see Jonet in the kitchen. Da and Fergus learned something about her that has made them angry.'

'She offered to go to the market for me,' said Celia. 'What has she done?'

'I don't know yet.' Margaret stepped into the hall.

Fergus sat slumped in a chair by the fire circle. Her husband and her father stood on either side of the table loudly spitting venom at each other.

'I'm not keen to hear this,' Margaret told Celia. 'Let's help my brother up to the solar.'

Up in the small chamber Fergus sank on to the bed and groaned with pain and exhaustion as he pulled his shirt up over his head.

'God save us,' Celia exclaimed as he exposed the bruises on his stomach, side, and one shoulder. 'Can you tell whether you've any broken bones?'

With Margaret supporting him beneath one elbow, he eased down on to his back.

'These ribs maybe,' he said, pointing to his left side. 'But it hurts only when I breathe.' He winced as he chuckled at his own humour and cupped his blackened eye with his hand.

Margaret guessed he was trying to hide his suffering, but as she and Celia examined his injuries he kept up an animated narrative despite his fading voice. He sounded like a boy recounting a wonderful adventure.

'—and there were Englishmen following us, and then Da appeared, all worried for me of a sudden.' He stopped to sip the herbed wine Celia had prepared. The pause must have given him time to realise how he felt. 'I'll save the rest for later,' he said, then lay back and closed his eyes. 'The Lord was watching over me last night,' he added softly. 'I might have died.'

'What did Da mean about Jonet?' Margaret asked, hoping to learn more before her brother dropped into sleep.

'It was her friends who were following us today, two men who were about all summer. I caught her serving Da's wine to them on more than one occasion.'

Margaret would never have guessed Jonet could be so brazen. 'More than once? Why didn't you tell me about this? Surely you might have found another maid?'

'Without you or Ma here to show her how the households are run?' Fergus pressed a hand to his eye again. 'I never guessed they were Longshanks's men. It must have been Jonet who let them in to search while you were gone, and closed Mungo up so he wouldn't alert me.'

'Marion thought a woman accompanied the searchers,' Margaret recalled. 'But you could hardly have foreseen that.' He was near sleep. 'I'm relieved you mentioned nothing to Roger of James Comyn's part in your return.'

'They didn't beat all the wits from me,' Fergus mumbled. 'I like him.'

Their father entered the room. 'Is he badly injured?'

Celia shook her head. 'Bruises, but no wounds.'

'Will you talk to Jonet, Da?' asked Fergus.

'She's not here,' said Margaret. 'But we'll find her.'

Malcolm took a seat on the edge of the bed and reached out for Fergus's hand. With the other he took Margaret's. 'While I have you two here I want to explain why I've been hiding.' He sounded resigned, as if he had lost a long struggle.

Fergus withdrew his hand and propped himself up on his elbows. 'Is it about the sterlings?'

Malcolm nodded solemnly. 'I thought I'd been clever, taking Edward Longshanks's money for my ships and then cheating him right under his nose to help the men of our country. But I discovered I'd been burning my candle at both ends instead, and there's naught left to show for all my planning.'

'He's using your ships?' Fergus cried hoarsely. 'Da, how could you?'

'They carried men and weapons across the North Sea – away from us. It seemed a good use of my ships. And on board I'd hidden silver from people in Perth to be minted in the Low Countries. Longshanks has forbidden that because he loses the revenue of his mined silver being turned to coin in his mints. The mint gets a percentage, you know. It finances the bastard's wars. So a group of us thought we'd get our coins more cheaply and cheat Longshanks out of his share – a pittance, for sure, but the gesture felt grand.'

'What went wrong?' Margaret asked. 'What happened to the sterlings? Why are you avoiding the men you owe?'

'On my return, my ship was boarded by the English. I parted with most of the sterlings to walk off a free man.' He shook his head. 'I thank the Lord that so many of Longshanks's soldiers arc felons with little loyalty to him. But I've made enemies in Perth.'

'My God,' whispered Fergus. 'Ruthven and the others – you used their coin for your ransom.'

Malcolm sighed. 'I told Maggie – I did not know the land was yet filled with Longshanks's troops. I thought they'd all gone east.' He put his hands on his thighs, gazed at the floor. 'It was John Smyth who saw me on the river and spread word I was here.'

'And so you murdered him?' Fergus guessed.

'I didn't touch him,' Malcolm said loudly to the floor, then glanced nervously at his children to see their reactions. 'Will no one believe me?'

Margaret found it difficult. 'What was he doing in the warehouse?'

Malcolm shrugged one shoulder. 'I know not. He was so surprised to see me there that he brought the barrels down atop himself. Sweet Heaven, the Lord is punishing me for something, I know not what.'

Margaret could suggest a number of trans-gressions, but she said nothing.

'John Smyth seduced Jonet and made her believe that I lacked all morals,' said Malcolm. 'He told her that is why Christiana left me. So she helped his new comrades search Christiana's chamber at Elcho, my house, your house.'

'And you didn't tell us?' Margaret whispered, though nothing should surprise her in these times.

'It slipped my mind,' Malcolm said.

'What?'

'I had more serious problems by then,' he said, waving a hand.

'And you thought nothing of your family and the danger they could be in,' she said. 'At least you might have considered the safety of your wife in Elcho.'

'There's a good watch on the nunnery,' Malcolm said. He looked pathetic, sitting there leaning on his hands, head bowed, a grown man admitting to his misbehaviour as if it were a matter of dented pots and a lost spoon.

'Those same men failed to protect Perth from Longshanks,' said Fergus. 'What makes you think they can stand against him now?'

'That situation was much different, lad,' Malcolm said with a shake of his head. 'I thought you two would understand.' He rose with a grunt. 'I see I've wasted my breath.' He left the room a little unsteadily.

Margaret helped Fergus lie back against the pillows.

'I can't believe Longshanks's men are sailing on our family's ships,' he said.

'You must rest now,' said Margaret. 'There's nothing to be done about the past.'

She considered sitting watch, but Celia assured her that Fergus would sleep quite soundly for some time. The herbs were strong.

*

'That scheming whore,' Celia muttered as they left the room. 'She's been gone a good long while.'

Out on the landing Margaret saw that her father had gone down below and picked a fight. 'Wait up here,' she said to Celia. 'I have a plan.' She hurried down the steps.

Roger stood behind her father, pinning his arms behind his back, and Aylmer stood to one side holding a cloth to his bloody chin and swearing under his breath.

'You're a liar,' Malcolm growled.

'I searched your son,' Aylmer said thickly, 'but I did not beat him. I fought off the English who had fallen on him.'

'Liar!' Malcolm shouted. 'Wallace's men said you kicked Fergus hard in the gut after finding nothing of use on him.' He struggled to free himself but Roger held tight.

Margaret moved to stand between her father and Aylmer, facing the latter, looking him in the eyes. 'You kicked him after he'd already been beaten?'

Aylmer began to turn away from her, but Margaret reached out for his chin. He lifted an arm to hit her.

'Aylmer!' Roger said sharply.

The Bruce's kinsman dropped his hand. 'I'd been injured chasing off the robbers. And then to find nothing of use on him . . .' Aylmer swore and pressed the cloth to his chin. 'Wallace's men. So that's where the brat was headed.'

'Go on, Da, you've played father long enough today,' said Margaret, disgusted with all three. 'Hurry before the English discover you here. Your son is sleeping comfortably, he'll mend.'

'We must talk, you, Roger and me.'

'I'm not talking to Roger. You talk to him – you were so eager to have me wed him, see what you make of him.' She headed for the steps.

'Where are you going?' Roger demanded.

Ignoring him, Margaret gathered her skirts and climbed up to the solar. Celia still stood on the landing.

'Come within,' said Margaret, leading the way to her chamber.

Once inside, Margaret locked the door and with Celia's help slid a clothing trunk in front of it. Then she knelt to the casket in which Roger had stored some rope.

'It won't reach all the way down to the kitchen garden,' said Margaret, 'but I've worked the ground so it's quite soft.'

'Why are we sneaking out of the house?'

'I thought we might find Jonet at Da's house,' said Margaret, 'searching for the sterlings. No one has taken care not to mention them in her hearing.'

Celia helped Margaret tie the rope to the sturdy bedstead.

James sat in a corner of St John's Kirk hoping to see Margaret. He'd had misgivings about sending Fergus on with only Malcolm, a man of quicksilver moods and loyalties. Neither was he confident that either of them could be trusted not to mention James's part in the rescue. But over and above those good reasons to seek reassurance from Margaret, he had news of her brother Andrew. Wallace had received it from a courier out of Edinburgh. James knew Margaret feared for her brother and would be grateful for word that he was well, or had been weeks ago when he'd sent the missive to Father Francis at St Giles naming some of the Scots who were spying for the English.

Old memories stirred as Margaret stepped into her father's house. The cupboard near the hall door had the marks where she and Fergus had nicked it with their wooden wagon. She found the scar on one of the beams where Andrew's attempt at a knife trick had gone astray. Beneath one of the windows was the bench on which she had been sitting when Roger first tried to win her favour. Yesterday she had been too absorbed by Mungo's needy affection and Aylmer's intrusive presence to feel the pull of the past, but this afternoon it was powerful.

'It is a pretty house,' said Celia, running a hand along a carved shelf.

Margaret thought it looked bare, austere, but that was only in comparison to what it had been. 'You've seen Ma's room at the nunnery. This house was as full of colour and almost as crowded as that when Ma lived here. We needed a cook and a servant at the least to keep things tidy, two servants when we were little, and a nurse.'

'Will such times ever come again?' Celia wondered. 'You might have valued a lady's maid in better times.'

'What will be left when the English are routed?' Margaret shivered, seeing the future as a vast void. 'I'd rather think about the present.'

They both looked up as a board creaked in the solar above.

'She might not be alone,' Celia suggested in a whisper as she held Margaret back. 'Perhaps a few knives from the kitchen?'

'I've something better.' Margaret led Celia to a trunk beneath the steps. Her father stored an assortment of weapons in it. But as she knelt to it she saw that it no longer bore a lock. Lifting the lid, she found the trunk empty but for a few old pairs of shoes. Edgy now, less confident in her plan, she sat back on her heels and listened to the cautious noises above. 'I hear only a woman's tread,' she said.

Celia nodded. 'What is still up there?'

'Da's clothes, things Ma left behind, Fergus's belongings.'

'She won't be there for ever,' said Celia. 'Might we just sit down here and wait for her to discover us? She can't escape.'

'Go out to the kitchen for the knives while I wait here.' Margaret settled on the trunk.

But she was soon on her feet at the sound of Celia's voice in the yard, loudly denying that anyone was in the house. Footsteps came to the landing above.

'Who is there?' the maid called timidly.

Margaret moved beneath the open steps and held her breath as Jonet began her descent, readying herself to catch the maid as she came down. As Jonet's shoes appeared Margaret considered grabbing an ankle through the steps. She might get some pleasure out of the woman's tumble. But two men suddenly rushed in from the yard door, sending Jonet fleeing back up to the solar.

Impatience sent James from the kirk and through the backlands to Margaret's house. He moved slowly, in the character of the elderly friar. He reasoned that there was nothing suspicious in an old friar giving Margaret news of her brother. He might do so in Roger's presence without compromising anyone.

It was Aylmer who opened the door. He had not the courtesy to invite the old friar to step within, but he did leave the door ajar as he withdrew to fetch Margaret. Roger and Malcolm were in the hall, tensely facing each other across a table spread with documents. James saw no sign of Fergus but his father's presence reassured him that the party had arrived.

Roger suddenly rose and approached the door. 'I'm Roger Sinclair. My man says you have news of my wife's elder brother?'

James had not seen Roger closely since he'd suffered the injury to his cheek. In fact he had not seen him since shortly after Christmas. He noted with interest the changes in the man, the loss of weight, the scarring and hardening.

He bowed to Roger. 'One of my brethren saw Father Andrew at the great hospital and found him passing well and eager for news of his family.' He was thinking how implausible the account sounded, a friar freely speaking to the confessor of the soldiers, when the sound of wood splintering came from the solar.

With a cry of alarm, Roger disappeared within.

James thought it best to depart.

The two men warned Margaret away from the steps and went after Jonet. Relieved to see Celia unhurt, Margaret asked what had happened.

'They came for Jonet, calling her a thief and a traitor,' Celia said. 'I fear—' She stopped, distracted by Jonet's cries and curses.

Margaret found it no pleasure to see the

hysterical maid slung over the shoulder of one of the men and borne down the steps like a haunch of venison.

As soon as she was set down in the hall, Jonet bolted for the door, but she fell with a cry as she tripped on her skirts.

❦ 19 ❧

CURSED

As Jonet crumpled to the floor she became once more the family maid rather than the enemy of the past hours, and Margaret impulsively hurried forward to help her to her feet, Celia right behind her, but the man who had followed the other stayed Margaret with a firm grasp on her arm.

'You'll find some of your family's goods in there, I'll warrant, Dame Margaret,' he said, placing in her free hand a cloth bundle. 'I'm sure Hugh has done his best not to injure your maid, and when you understand how she has harmed your family you'll be glad I held you back. She does not deserve your charity.'

Margaret recognised Gilbert Ruthven, the one of whom Fergus had spoken. 'Why are you after Jonet?' she asked.

'We're after our sterlings and we think she's taken them,' he said.

'That does not give you the right to trespass in my father's house,' Margaret said. 'Gilbert, isn't it?' Her stomach churned and her breath was shallow but she was not going to swallow her outrage. 'You need not have invaded my family's home to take her. You're behaving like the English you despise.'

Gilbert smoothed out his brow into a placating expression. 'Dame Margaret, you don't ken what I'm telling you about this woman.'

'I know she has betrayed my family, and I intend to return her to my father and husband, for it is them she has wronged.'

The other man, Hugh he'd been called, stood menacingly over Jonet's curled-up form. 'She's stolen our sterlings.'

'I've stolen no siller.' Jonet's voice was muffled, but stronger than Margaret would have expected. 'I've given our deliverers food and drink – you'd do well to do the same.'

'Traitor,' Hugh said.

'You are wrong about the sterlings,' said Margaret. 'My father's ship was boarded by the English and his freedom required a goodly bribe in sterlings. It's my father with whom you must take up your cause. But you'll not come to an agreement by invading his household.' She moved forward, reaching out to Jonet. 'Come, there's no need to lie on the floor.'

'Let her do as she will, Hugh,' Gilbert said as his companion moved towards Margaret. 'This is the home of Dame Margaret's parents, and this woman is their maidservant.'

Hoping Margaret was in the other place he knew to look, James made his way to Malcolm's house on Southgate.

Margaret opened the door, her veil askew and her gown dusty.

James wondered whether she'd simply been cleaning, but remembering the sound of a splintering door at her house, he asked, 'Are you all right? Why are you here?'

'I might ask the same of you, Friar James, but I'm glad you've come.' She stood back to let him enter.

When James could distinguish people in the dimmer light within, he discovered Celia seated on a bench with an arm around the maid Jonet, who sat woodenly and stared ahead at nothing.

Margaret joined two men who stood near the solar stair looking uneasy. James recognised them as members of the families Wallace was counting on.

'What is this?' he asked, half to himself, of the odd assembly.

'These men forced their way into the house and

treated Jonet so roughly she is unable to walk,' Margaret said.

'She tripped,' said one of the men. 'Who is this friar to you, Dame Margaret?'

'My good friend and confessor.'

James was glad that the men did not have Fergus's keen eyes. 'You were wrong to trespass, the two of you,' he said.

'We thought she'd stolen our siller,' said Gilbert. 'But we've learned from Dame Margaret that we were mistaken.'

'But she's kept company with Englishmen of late,' said Hugh. 'I ken a traitor when I see one. Still, we'd no cause to treat her so roughly.'

Gauging the mood of the small party to be not so much hostile as unresolved, James thought he would accomplish more by revealing his identity. Straightening, he said, 'Forgive Dame Margaret and me for our play-acting, but we must be cautious. I'm James Comyn, sent by the Wallace to make sure of your families' support.'

The men had first looked bewildered, but now they seemed more at ease.

Knowing that Gilbert's townhouse was near the north gate, James said, 'I believe Roger Sinclair will soon arrive. We'll have no peace here. But we've much to discuss. Gilbert, might we come together at your home?'

Gilbert nodded, and both Hugh and Margaret agreed to the plan.

The injured maid came alive and looked about her as if thinking to escape, but Celia took her firmly by the elbow and helped her rise. Hugh joined them and, with either elbow supported, Jonet was able to stand.

Ignoring Aylmer's looks of impatience, Malcolm tried to reason with Roger. 'Maggie's no child, and she has that flint-eyed maidservant with her. Let's bide here calmly.'

'What if she's gone after Jonet?'

Malcolm had told Roger of the maid's suspected deeds. He chuckled now, imagining Maggie descending upon the unsuspecting maid. 'The town will be gossiping about it for a long time to come.'

'And the English will hear of it,' Roger reminded him.

Indeed. Malcolm was growing too old for intrigue. In his amusement about Maggie's escape, he'd forgotten his own danger. 'She'll have gone to Ada for advice,' he suggested.

'Stay here until we return,' Roger said as he rose and motioned to Aylmer that they were off. 'If Maggie appears, keep her here. And check that Fergus still breathes.'

He said that last coldly, and Malcolm cursed him.

*

Christiana followed the novice to the prioress's parlour. The English captain had returned.

'*Benedicite*, Prioress Agnes,' she said.

'*Benedicite*, Dame Christiana,' Agnes said in a dulcet tone, though her smile was strained.

Christiana sensed that something had gone wrong.

'You have my deepest admiration and gratitude, Dame Christiana,' the English captain said with a bow.

'What?' she said in surprise.

'Your warning allowed the capture of five of William Wallace's men. In thanks you have my word that this priory will be left in peace.'

'Captured?' Christiana whispered. 'Holy Mary, Mother of God, pray for them.' As she began to understand what she had done by telling the English captain of the watchers she crossed herself and sank on to a chair that a maid set behind her.

'God blessed you with a profound gift,' said the prioress. 'I am newly amazed.'

'Do the men yet live?' Christiana asked.

'Four do,' said the captain. 'The fifth fell from the cliff rather than be captured. They'd murdered all four of my men.'

The maid bent to ask, 'Are you unwell, Dame Christiana?'

Christiana lifted her eyes to Thomas, on whose face she saw pain and blame.

'I must leave you now,' she said quietly. 'I am not well.'

'Wine!' cried the prioress.

A cup was placed in Christiana's cold hands. She stared down into it and saw in the blood-red liquid a symbol of what she had done. 'I cannot drink this.' She thrust it aside as she willed herself to rise. This is what came of collaboration. She had known it was wrong, to produce a vision for the prioress. She had known it. 'I pray you, send Dame Bethag to me,' she said, and pushing past the prioress's agitated concern she fled into the yard. She would be cursed for this, and all her family with her. She must pray, pray for the dead man's soul and the rescue of the others. She must pray.

Roger returned too quickly.

Malcolm rose from the table as Aylmer handed him something tied in one of Christiana's forgotten veils. 'You did not find Maggie?' He placed the heavy bundle on the table.

Roger looked haggard and shook with an energy that would explode in violence if it found no other outlet. 'She was not at Ada's. Her friend had not seen her. So we went to your house. Someone had been there. Stools grouped in a circle. And that –' he nodded at the bundle – 'was on the floor near the door.'

Malcolm looked down at it, then back to Roger. 'What do you fear?' he asked softly, doubting his son-in-law's ability to contain himself. 'Why would she go to my house?'

'That is booty from your house, if I'm not mistaken,' said Roger. 'Did Maggie surprise thieves?' He shook his head. 'I don't know. I don't know. Tell me about the sterlings men have been demanding of you.'

The sins of the father shall be visited upon the children. 'Why would she go to my house?' Malcolm cried. 'She must have known there might be trouble.'

'When I told Ada about Jonet's friends, she suggested that Maggie would go after her, and that your house might be tempting, empty, unguarded. Jonet might be collecting items of value, hiding them.'

Malcolm looked down at the cloth. 'So Maggie and Celia might have frightened Jonet.'

'And then what? Where are they?' Roger asked angrily, as if he suspected that Malcolm knew.

Pressing his hands to his temples, Malcolm tried to think but his heart was racing and visions of men desperate for their money falling upon his daughter struck him dumb. He dropped back on to the bench and buried his head in his hands.

'You and your brother are two of a kind,' Roger said, his voice hoarse with emotion. 'If she's suffering because of your scheming I'll kill you.'

It was small comfort to Malcolm to realise that Roger's desperation was that of a devoted husband.

*

Having reassembled in the Ruthven hall and convinced Gilbert's wife that they needed no refreshment, the meeting was called to order by James.

'Shall we begin with Jonet?' he suggested.

Margaret had taken a seat beside the maid, and James stole glances at her throughout Jonet's narration. Her colour high, her jaw set, he found Margaret lovely and formidable, far more so than he'd considered her in Edinburgh.

'Dame Christiana chose that spineless Marion over me to be lady's maid,' Jonet was saying, her face livid with recalled anger. 'After all I'd done for her, all the times I made excuses for her. She was one mistress who never put her hand to any task about the house. Never. But you won't believe it, then they had the gall to leave me to see to both their house and Dame Margaret's. But John Smyth showed me how ill-used I was. He knew, for he'd been used by the family as well. He said Master Malcolm had done nothing to deserve my loyalty.'

James watched Margaret register a range of emotions from sympathy to anger to amusement.

But Jonet had left out what was most important.

'What did they hope to find?' Margaret asked.

Hugh leaned forward, only now becoming interested.

Jonet's eyes flicked round the circle. 'I could be hanged for saying.'

'I'm sure Smyth told you that,' said James, 'but he's dead, and the other spies will see you limping and understand that we beat the truth out of you.'

'They're stronger than you are,' she said, but her face was flushed and for the first time she looked frightened.

James shook his head. 'They are intruders, they are on foreign soil, surrounded by us.' He smiled to show her his confidence. By Celia's movement, he could see that she understood his purpose and found it discomfiting, but Jonet seemed to find comfort in it.

'You think that Master Malcolm was on your side,' she said, 'but I know that King Edward of England is using Kerr ships.' Her smile was little more than a sneer.

'Then why were the English searching his things?' James asked.

'They searched Master Roger's house, too,' she reminded them.

'Yes,' said Margaret, 'we know how thoroughly you have betrayed our trust, Jonet. There is no need to tell us.'

But if Margaret had thought her words would cow the maid, they seemed to have the opposite effect.

Jonet turned to James. 'You're a Comyn. It's your family and the Bruces who are killing us, not the English. You're fighting over the crown and we'll never have peace while either of your families have it. That's what King Edward knows.'

James was momentarily speechless. Gilbert muttered something under his breath.

Margaret shook her head at the maid. 'Clever words from John Smyth,' she said. 'He was not so clever while working for my father. Still, what he apparently did not understand is that we have nothing to fear from a struggle between the two great houses of Comyn and Bruce, for they are interested in killing only one another. But King Edward is slaughtering our people. He murdered so many of the merchants of Berwick that the streets ran with their blood. No Comyn or Bruce would ever condone such a deed.'

Jonet dropped her eyes to her hands.

Everyone was looking at Margaret, but she did not notice, bent as she seemed on enlightening the maid.

'What else did he tell you?' she asked Jonet.

'That William Wallace fought beside King Edward in Wales.'

Margaret glanced up at James.

'Many of our countrymen did, to our shame,' he said, 'but not William Wallace.'

Hugh shifted on his seat. 'Some say it is for that deed God is punishing us.'

Jonet shrugged.

'So what did Smyth and the others hope to find?' James asked, wishing to end this interrogation soon.

'Proof that Master Malcolm was not as he

seemed. That he was cheating the English at the same time as they were sailing his ships.'

'And did they find anything?'

Jonet looked at Gilbert and Hugh. 'Ask them.'

But it was Margaret who explained the silver/sterling exchange in which the two men had invested.

Having had much experience with Malcolm's brother Murdoch, James asked in confusion, 'Why *had* you entrusted Malcolm with your funds?'

'He's one of the most trusted merchants in Perth,' said Gilbert with indignation. 'We'd no cause to doubt he would be fair with us.'

'I would have trusted him with my life,' said Hugh.

'I believe my father miscalculated his risks,' Margaret interposed. 'He thought Longshanks had taken all the soldiers from this area with him to Flanders. He was taken by surprise when his ship was boarded on the Tay by the English and he thought only of his freedom. It was not the honourable thing to do, I grant you, and I am not defending him.' She glanced at Jonet, perhaps expecting to see a sneer, but the maid's spleen seemed to have been spent.

There was much more James wished to know, particularly what Jonet knew of the spies, but that could wait until they reached Wallace, who would still be at the camp outside town. He took Margaret aside.

'Wallace will want to talk to her, and it's time you met him. Are you willing?'

She did not hesitate. 'What of Celia? If she remains behind her silence will anger Roger – you know how stubborn she can be, and I know the extent of my husband's temper.'

'Have you a friend with whom she might stay the night?'

Margaret looked aside. 'A night,' she said, as if to herself. 'The men will be without a cook. What of Fergus?' She shook her head impatiently. 'He'll sleep through the night.'

James watched with interest.

Margaret met his gaze again. 'Ada,' she said. 'Celia can go to my friend Ada.'

'So you'll come?'

'Roger will be furious,' Margaret said.

'I should think he'd be worried.'

'Of course.' Margaret took a deep breath and nodded. 'But how will we get past the English?'

'They are not yet organised, but they will be soon. Jonet shall be your maid, and you heading for the lying in of a friend in the country, with an old friar escorting you.'

She surprised him with a mischievous smile.

His conscience bothering him, he warned her, 'We might have difficulty returning.'

'I am tired of holding my breath,' she said.

'And what of Fergus?'

'His wounds are not severe. His father can attend him. Lead on, Friar James.'

He would have kissed her if the others had not been there.

Celia still regarded James Comyn with suspicion. In her opinion, a person who so enjoyed playing someone else was too unpredictable to trust. So even though she could see that Margaret and Comyn were decided, she protested her separation from her mistress, and when ordered to Ada's she departed with a heart full of apprehension. She took care to avoid Watergate, where Roger might see her, because Margaret had seemed so worried about his taking out his anger on her. She recalled the marks on Margaret's shoulders one morning, small bruises, like the impressions of fingertips. Celia was a tiny woman and knew she would not survive a beating as well as her tall, strong-boned mistress. Nor did she want the lying, scheming traitor to lay a hand on her. She could not understand how she had believed her former mistress's constant litany of her son's virtues and wondered whether Dame Katherine had actually been deceived by him. Perhaps she had offered Celia's services to Margaret because she knew she needed protection.

Celia thought of the look of devilish enjoyment on Margaret's face as she told her of her plan to go to the camp of the Wallace and decided that the machinations of Roger and the Kerr family had driven her wits from her. Now it would be up to Celia to protect her mistress's reputation. But she must avoid a confrontation with Roger because he was too devious for her.

She arrived at Ada's safely and was immediately engulfed in the rose-scented silks of her mistress's best friend, only gradually managing to disentangle herself from Ada's strong embrace.

'Where is Maggie?' Ada asked, adjusting Celia's cap and tidying her own veil. She was a beautiful older woman, and apparently vain. 'Sinclair was here searching for her, and there is a tragic tale spreading through the town about her mother. I've been so worried.' Vain she might be, but her expression and voice bespoke honest concern.

Celia dreaded hearing of more involving the family she served, but she must know the worst. 'We'd heard no word of Dame Christiana.'

'Where is Maggie?' Ada repeated.

Celia reminded herself as she took a seat as far from Ada's niece and baby as she could find that Margaret trusted her friend more than she did her parents, so it might be safe to trust Ada with the truth. 'My mistress has taken the traitorous maid Jonet to William Wallace somewhere outwith the town.'

'God watch over her,' Ada said, pressing her hands to her heart. 'Does she have a worthy escort?'

Celia nodded.

'Then that is good news indeed. It is best she is away until the gossips have tired of the tale. But the Wallace.' She shook her head, then tilted it and studied Celia. 'I'll brew something to calm you.'

'I am fine.'

'Your eyes disagree.'

While Ada disappeared into the kitchen, Celia exchanged pleasantries with the woman's niece and admired the healthy baby.

'I pray she grows up in a peaceful world,' said the young mother. 'It is difficult to hope, but sinful to despair, so says my mother.'

'And what does your aunt say?'

The niece smiled shyly. 'That I must teach her to be strong and able to fend for herself.'

'You have a most wise aunt,' said Celia. 'For I've seen no great outpouring of Christian charity of late.'

'Amen,' said Ada from the doorway. She preceded a maid who carried a tray of cups to a small table and set a pair of cushioned chairs on either side.

Celia eased into the chair with a sigh of pleasure. Two chairs – and cushions. Dame Ada's lover must have been a great lord.

'Come now,' said the hostess, 'sit and sip your mistress's favourite tisane while I tell you of Dame Christiana's most unfortunate vision. Knowing her as long as I have, I pray for her, for I know she meant no harm.'

When Ada had recounted the deed for which the English soldiers were grateful, Celia sat with her hands in her lap, her head hanging, and prayed for her mistress, that she would hear of this from a friend who might soften the blow, and that God would protect her from her family's diabolical selfishness.

Having guessed the identity of the friar at the door, Malcolm had no doubt that Maggie, wherever she had been, was headed for Wallace's camp north of the town, and he was not about to betray his daughter to his unsatisfactory son-in-law. Sinclair had left it late to worry about his wife's safety. Malcolm must think of a distraction, something to waste their time until Maggie returned. If she did so.

Roger stood at the street door staring out into the sunny afternoon.

Aylmer sat near Malcolm, drinking watered wine and in general behaving like no servant a man would tolerate. 'I heard a whispering on Northgate as I waited without Dame Ada's house,' he said. 'Your good wife, Dame Christiana, warned the English of Wallace's watchers on the cliffs above the Tay. Kinnoull Hill?' He shook his head, uncertain of the name.

Roger drew closer. 'Were our countrymen caught?'

Aylmer nodded. 'So they were saying.'

'Are you certain you heard aright?' Malcolm asked. 'There are other women with the name Christiana in the town.'

'Not with the Sight,' said Roger. 'That damned woman.'

Malcolm felt ill. He'd always felt so when hearing of Christiana's misspeaking, but this . . . 'I'll not have you cursing my wife,' he said, though his heart was not in the words. 'By the Rood, it is that prioress, Agnes de Arroch, who has ruined her, I'm sure of it. That bitch thinks only of the wealth and renown pilgrims will bring to Elcho.'

'Her own kinsmen guard the priory from the English,' Roger said. 'I do not think Prioress Agnes would encourage Christiana to support the invaders.'

'She would if she saw profit in it,' Malcolm growled. But Aylmer had given him an idea. 'No doubt Maggie's heard the rumour and has gone to learn the truth of it,' he said. 'Oh, Christ, my foolish wife may have bought our family's safety with those men's lives. But Maggie will never forgive her.' An idea was dawning even as he spoke. If Christiana had been coerced into something so cruel by her prioress, she might be ready to abandon her cloister. 'We must go to her. Maggie will be there, I'm certain of it.'

Roger looked incredulous. 'Walk through the English saying sweetly that we're kinsmen to their visionary?'

'We'll go in the dark,' Malcolm said. 'So I've done many a time.'

Christiana could not warm her hands though she curled them around a warm cup of mulled wine. And yet her face felt as if it were on fire. Marion assured her that her forehead was quite cool to the touch and wrapped her in a plaid. Still Christiana shivered and her face burned.

'You are so shrouded in plaid on this summer day?' Dame Bethag exclaimed upon seeing her. 'Are you unwell, Dame Christiana?'

'My soul is encased in ice, Dame Bethag. I must confess to you.'

The nun shook her head, her eyes sympathetic. 'My dear sister, I cannot shrive you. You know that we daughters of Eve have not the strength of spirit to hear confessions.'

'I pray you, listen,' said Christiana, trying to calm herself enough to have the breath to speak what she must. 'Hear my sin and advise me before I commit the even greater sin of despair.'

'God help you, what has happened?' Dame Bethag glanced over at Marion for an explanation.

Christiana motioned Marion to withdraw from them.

The maid backed away, though not far.

'Please hear me, Dame Bethag,' Christiana said.

'In urgent need I can hear your confession,'

Bethag said and, bowing her head, she rested her hands in her lap and began to listen.

As she told the holy woman of her crime, Christiana witnessed in her mind's eye the suffering of the men, the black despair of the one who had leaped to the valley below. The others were being treated as wild beasts, hunted, caught, and then dragged away to be slaughtered. Christiana cried out to them, begging them for forgiveness.

'Mistress, can you hear me?'

Christiana opened her eyes.

Marion pressed a cup to her lips.

Dame Bethag sat beside her, her hands moving along her paternoster beads.

'I pray you,' Christiana said, 'pronounce a penance for me.'

The nun paused in her prayers and slipped a soft hand over Christiana's. Her direct gaze was gentle, kind. 'Be comforted, my sister. You did as God wished. It was He who gave you the vision at the moment you spoke it. You need no penance for that.'

'I cannot believe that,' Christiana said, withdrawing her hand.

'You are weary, Dame Christiana,' Bethag said. 'Rest now and know that you will be in all the sisters' prayers from this day forward. You have won us the protection of the English. God go with you.'

Christiana turned away from the nun and wept.

BOLD RISKS

Celia's reluctance to go to Ada's had not surprised Margaret, but her own excitement about the trek to Wallace's camp did, and once out in the street she expected to have second thoughts – to depart the town so suddenly was not the behaviour of a merchant's wife. But she continued to feel steady in her resolve to further her commitment by meeting with William Wallace. Margaret's only regret was that Jonet accompanied them – she would far rather inflict the sullen maid's presence on her father and her husband. But she understood that the maid might have more to divulge.

James, walking slowly now as the elderly friar, surprised her with news of Andrew: alive, well, and managing to spirit information out from Soutra Hospital. She could think of nothing that might cheer her more and better confirm the rightness of her path.

But her mood was not to last. As they approached the guard at the west gate, Margaret recognised him as a man of Perth and warned James.

'He has seen us,' said James. 'We must continue as if we have nothing to fear.'

The guard straightened at their approach and, raising a hand in greeting, called out, 'Dame Margaret! Blessings on you and all your kin.'

It was hardly what she expected from a man gone over to the enemy. Her confusion must have been plain to him.

'You've not heard? Your mother, the blessed Dame Christiana, saved our fair town from the thief Wallace this day. She had a vision of Wallace's men attacking the English guards on Kinnoull Hill – a great slaughter they had begun. She rushed outwith the gates of Elcho and warned the English captain in time to save some of the men. God give them rest who died in defending us.' He crossed himself, though he still beamed at Margaret, and then bowed to her with respect. 'I wish you and your companions a safe journey.'

Margaret did not know where to rest her eyes as he spoke, unable to bear his smiling gratitude, fearful of what she would read on James's face. The guard clearly enjoyed what must have been an embellished account of her mother's pronouncement. She nodded to him and walked on through the gate, James and Jonet close behind.

Her joy in hearing word of Andrew was as dust. She was gasping as if she were suffocating. Her forearms felt as if insects were crawling on them. Once out of sight of the gate, she left the road and leaned against a tree trying to catch her breath. The leaves seemed to ripple as if floating on water, and the ground undulated beneath her.

'Margaret?' James called to her solicitously.

She shook her head and stumbled away, feeling a terrible heat building within. 'Damn her!' she cried, then dropped to her knees, doubling over to retch. It was but bile, for she had not eaten since early morning, and she felt weak when the spasms ceased. Sinking back on her heels, she pressed her cold, almost numb hands to her cheeks and whispered Hail Marys until her breathing calmed.

In the quiet aftermath a thought teased her consciousness. It seemed blasphemy to Margaret and she refused it, but its persistence won out.

Was it not God's betrayal rather than Christiana's? He had given her a vision in the presence of the English captain. Did that mean His blessing was on the English? She could not accept that. But neither could she accept her mother as betrayer of her people. There was no part of Christiana MacFarlane that was English in sympathy. She had not even spoken their language until her parents thought it might make her more marriageable.

Think, Margaret commanded herself. Wallace had set watchers on Kinnoull Hill, overlooking the river and Elcho on the other side. Might someone in the nunnery have noted the men and asked the English about them? Her mother might be no part of it. Perhaps the English had used her name to prevent a backlash from the townspeople. Surely some of them must support Wallace's defence of Balliol's crown.

'Come, Margaret,' James said gently. 'We must not linger on the road.' He crouched beside her, his eyes sympathetic, yet he still held firmly to Jonet's arm.

'How am I to hold my head up after this?' Margaret moaned. 'My father, my mother . . .' The presence of Jonet angered her and cut short her lament. 'Yes,' she said firmly, 'we must continue.'

As James rose, Jonet tried to slip from his grasp, but received a twist for her troubles.

'Your parents' transgressions cannot be laid at your feet,' James said to Margaret as he reached out his free hand to help her up. 'You are no longer of their households, you have no control over them.'

'So you and those close to me understand. But not all people will see it so. I cannot return to the town. And what of the Wallace? He will find it difficult to trust me, or convince others to do so. I am damned.'

'So must our king feel, Margaret. His former

subjects jeer him, calling him "Toom Tabard" – empty coat, a mere English poppet. Can you imagine his humiliation? For surely he hears them, perhaps some even say it to his face.'

Margaret was uncomfortable discussing such things in Jonet's hearing but the maid seemed unmoved. 'John Balliol does not deserve such rebuke.'

'Nor do you, Margaret. Now come,' James said, 'Wallace is not such a fool as to blame you, and in following through with your purpose to see him and to work for the return of our rightful king you will prove yourself a woman of honour.'

His words resonated in her heart, and she accepted them. They continued on, a solemn trio, and as if God acknowledged they'd had enough trials this afternoon, He blessed them with an uneventful journey.

A company of men melted out of the brush near the camp, daggers drawn, faces grim until they recognised Friar James. The sight of these fight-hardened men intensified Margaret's fear. She was certain they bent their black looks on her, knew her as Christiana's daughter. James handed Jonet on to the men and took Margaret's arm when she hesitated, urging her forward. She walked with her eyes on the men's muddy boots as they moved through brush and skirted a marshy lowland, then climbed a steep slope. Looking up to see how far she must climb, she was blinded by sunlight and stumbled. James was there with a firm hand beneath her elbow, coaxing her up to the top. When they reached it, he gently pressed her hand and smiled at her before he let go. His kindness and her exhaustion brought her to tears. Margaret wiped them away with impatience and was grateful that James had already looked away.

Jonet stared down at the camp in the glen. 'So many!'

'This is but a small camp,' said James. 'Parties gather here and are guided to Wallace's camp further north. Is that why you are certain of our failure, Jonet? You thought there were only a few of us?'

The maid shrugged but she seemed to shrink in on herself.

Margaret wondered at James's frankness with the maid. 'Should Jonet see this? Should we not have covered her eyes?'

'She will not be released to return to her friends in Perth, if that is your worry,' said James.

He had not mentioned that before. Margaret had thought Jonet would return with her and face her father and her husband. She hid her confusion by gazing out on the camp and saying, 'I had imagined tents.' There were none, merely men sitting, standing, pacing amidst scattered plaids and travelling packs.

'Tents would slow us down,' James said.

Although there were campfires, none were lit. A

few game carcasses hung upside down from a low branch by one of the fire circles, too little for so many men as spread out before her.

Their guides led them among the clusters of men. Margaret bowed her head, certain they could see some sign on her that branded her as the daughter of the woman who had betrayed their comrades.

She recognised William Wallace standing at the centre of a circle of men, the late-afternoon sunlight burnishing his coppery hair. He stood taller than the rest, but that was not what most set him apart. It was rather the respectful distance the men kept from him. Though they pressed together to hear what was said, no one crowded the Wallace, no one so much as touched him with their garments.

Someone must have commented on their approach, for Wallace turned towards them. He nodded at James and began to smile, then his eyes were drawn to Margaret and she thought the smile faded.

The men drew back to let the newcomers through.

'I hoped to see you before I returned to Kinclaven camp, James,' said Wallace. 'Is this the supporter of whom you have spoken so warmly?'

James gave a little bow. 'This is Margaret Kerr. Margaret, William Wallace.'

'I am honoured to meet you, sir,' Margaret said, bowing her head.

'Dame Margaret, you are most welcome. And is this your handmaid?'

'She was,' said Margaret, 'but no more. She has consorted with the English to spy on my family.'

'We have brought her in the hope that she may have information of use to you,' said James.

'And what of her mother,' Jonet demanded, looking at Margaret, 'who favours the English with her visionary warnings?'

A murmur rose among the men. Wallace silenced them with a gesture and then led the newcomers to a fire circle sheltered in a rocky outcropping. It faced the others but was a few yards removed. A young man made room for them, lit a small fire, and offered them water.

It was clear and cold. Margaret rinsed the bad taste from her mouth, then drank her fill and splashed some on her face.

All this while she had kept her eyes averted from those around her. Wallace and James were quietly talking to Jonet. It seemed that the sight of so many men willing to risk their lives for their king had convinced her to cooperate, and she was providing names and activities without hesitation. Margaret leaned back against a sun-warmed rock and closed her eyes. Her turn would come, and she hoped to be calm for it.

Waking from a doze, Fergus found his injured eye swollen shut.

'It hurts me to look at you, son,' said Malcolm from a chair beside the bed. He leaned close. 'But your good eye is clear?'

'I can see you,' said Fergus. 'Where's Maggie?'

Malcolm shrugged. 'Heaven knows. Gone out the window, with that devoted maid of hers.' He handed Fergus a cup. 'This is the physick they left for you.'

The liquid was bitter, and though Fergus did not drink much he guessed he would not be awake long, for he'd not had much earlier. But it numbed his bruised side and shoulder nicely and he saw no reason to deny himself that comfort. 'I'm to return to the Wallace and carry a message to Murray near Aberdeen. I'll have a guide. You won't stop me.'

Malcolm grunted. 'You don't know what you're saying. Abandon our business now and you'll have no inheritance. You wouldn't be so foolish.'

'There's no trade.'

'There will be. I trow we'll chase those bastards back to the border and our ships will sail once more, with Dundee and Perth making up for our loss of Berwick.'

'I want Maggie.'

'I told you, she left by her chamber window and Sinclair cannot find her. We're off to Elcho at dark to seek her.'

'What of me?'

'Dame Ada came asking about you. She is

sending one of her servants to bide with you the night.'

'Why would Maggie be at Elcho?'

'You don't need to hear of that now, lad. Rest. I'll sit by you a while longer.'

I'll go to Aberdeen with or without your blessing, Fergus swore silently, his mouth unable to form the words. Not that it mattered. He knew his father would not listen. The bitter herbs pulled him back down into sleep.

The soft cadence and courtesy of Wallace's speech and the warmth of the rock had lulled Margaret into a doze. She awoke with a start, her mouth dry. Jonet was nowhere in sight, and another cup of water sat by Margaret. James and Wallace were talking quietly. Loath to call attention to herself, she lifted the cup and drank, thankful again for the soothing coolness. She wondered why James still wore the habit.

He glanced over his shoulder. 'You're awake.'

'Where's Jonet?' Margaret asked.

'She's no longer your concern,' said Wallace. He motioned to her to come closer.

They made a small circle of three.

'I see by your ease that you understand you are among friends, Dame Margaret,' said Wallace. 'I am glad of that, for I count on you to confide in me.' He smiled kindly when she blushed at the allusion to her nap.

He was perhaps her brother Andrew's age, but as so many of her countrymen did now, he had the eyes of an older man who had put aside the conceits and games of youth. Strange that he should so trust James, the devoted play-actor.

'I'll tell you anything that might be of help to our king, sir,' she said.

'Be assured that I do not hold you responsible for the activities of your parents,' he said. 'James says you have heard about Kinnoull Hill.'

Margaret glanced at James, who gave her an encouraging nod. 'I have,' she said.

'Two more of our men have died from their wounds,' said Wallace. 'It is best you hear it from me. Death is expected on such a mission. Our men brought death to theirs. They returned the violence. At the end of every mission I thank God for sparing me *this* time.'

Margaret bowed her head, seeing no need for words.

'James has told you of your brother Andrew's courageous help. Now I want your brother Fergus to carry a message to Murray near Aberdeen. He has a letter of invitation from his uncle the ship-builder, so he has a good chance of being released if he is caught. His youthfulness will also help – he seems younger than his years.' Wallace smiled when he said that. 'Is this acceptable to you?'

'I shall be proud of my brother if he accepts the mission,' said Margaret, 'but it is for Fergus to decide.'

Wallace nodded. 'Your father and your husband are of interest to me. I doubt that surprises you. Would you tell me what you know of their activities regarding our English troubles?'

Margaret turned to James. 'You have not told him what you know?'

'Not what I learned today,' said James. 'I thought you would wish to.'

'And Roger?'

'He knows what I do of Roger, but if you know anything more . . .'

She had not yet told James of the letters, and she felt unsure about what to say. So she began with her father.

Wallace listened so unresponsively that Margaret wondered at times whether she had lost his interest. But he interrupted her once to ask if she could describe one of the sterlings, which she could not, and when she had exhausted what she knew he asked a few questions that made it plain he had listened closely.

He sat back against the rocks, nodding thoughtfully, and gradually a bemused smile spread across his sun-browned face.

'Your father takes bold risks,' he said.

'Over-bold this time,' said Margaret.

'He was poorly informed,' said Wallace.

James chuckled. 'You think he might be of use, William?'

Wallace shifted forward, leaning an elbow on a

bent knee, his eyes alight. 'We need such men. Too many consider the risk and lose heart.'

Margaret thought him mad, but kept her own counsel. She let them talk a while as she thought about the letters. Aylmer was nothing to her, but Roger – she felt a lingering, perverse loyalty to him. She turned instead to the news that her mother was guilty of two additional deaths. Throughout her childhood Margaret had feared her mother's visions would come to some horrible disaster, and they finally had.

'God help them,' she prayed.

'What?' asked James.

Margaret realised she must have voiced the thought. 'I was praying for the men caught on the cliffs.' She crossed herself. 'I must go to my mother. She must hear and understand what she has done.'

'The deed is done,' said James.

'I see your point, Dame Margaret,' Wallace said.

She was glad of the great man's support, and puzzled by the angry look James gave him.

Shortly it was agreed that James would escort her downriver at deep dusk. Wallace's goal was not Christiana's contrition, but rather he hoped that to regain her daughter's respect she would be willing to explain the visions concerning the true king's identity.

Margaret tried not to be disappointed in Wallace's self interest, for it provided her the opportunity to confront her mother. Perhaps they would both be satisfied, she thought, and that was a doubly good result.

Malcolm did not think to use his wife's new favour with the English to depart the town openly. At the far end of dusk he led Aylmer and Roger through the backlands, slipping through the shadows. He was buoyant with hope, his senses alert, his step confident. He would recover his wife, heedlessly set aside when his head was too full of intrigue to realise how he needed her beside him. He thanked God for this chance to win back his Christiana, the light of his life. He did not let his thoughts rest overlong on the capture of Wallace's men. Christiana could not have foreseen the damage she would do by recounting her vision. Poor, foolish woman. He would cherish her all the more for her innocence. For that is what it must be, that she was unaware of the evil in men's hearts.

Once in the boat they kept close to the weedy bank, and only Aylmer, manning the oars, sat upright.

'Do you really think we'll get past the de Arroch guards?' Roger muttered.

'She's my wife. They have no right to deny me, and I'm bringing you to speak for me.'

'The English will be watching. Thomas de Arroch and his companions will not want to alarm them.'

'It is dark.'

'They'll have torches.'

'Quiet,' Aylmer muttered.

Both withdrew into silence.

Leaving Jonet at the camp, Margaret and James made their way to the river under escort as dusk lingered into the summer night. Margaret moved too eagerly in James's opinion. She did not sufficiently understand the danger of this mission.

'You can still change your mind,' he said, as the men removed a screen of branches and brush from a small boat.

'I must do this,' Margaret said. 'The English will hardly report to Ma that two more men died, and she must ken the mortal cost of her loose tongue.'

'You do understand that we might die on the water? The English will be watching the river.'

'Two in a small boat will not alarm them,' said Margaret, 'is that not what Wallace said?'

'He said perhaps.' And he had not wished to dissuade her, damn him.

Margaret looked out over the river. 'It's too dark. They'll not see us well enough to aim their arrows. But you can still allow me to go alone as I requested.'

'No.' James could not let her face death alone, or whatever lesser danger might befall her. He felt responsible for her involvement in this cause despite her argument that she had chosen it. He had heard the hesitation in her voice as she told Wallace of the documents she had taken to Ada. That Aylmer was the Bruce's kinsman had made her deed more dangerous than she seemed to realise. She was but a woman, with no training in defending herself.

By necessity, there would be little conversation once they were on the river. James would use the time to consider how he might teach her what she needed to know, for it was clear she was determined to carry out her mother's prophecy of mingling with soldiers.

The three men set down on a stretch of river bank near Elcho with enough brush and small trees to screen them from the guards. While Roger and Aylmer crouched beneath the trees and planned an approach that would not alarm the de Arroch men, Malcolm left them and wandered down closer to the river bank. Though he believed the guards would recognise him soon enough, he would wait a little longer to see whether the two came up with a better plan. He wanted nothing to go wrong. All he wanted was to set sail for Bruges with Christiana and leave this troubled land, and whether it was for a time or for good he did not care.

He let his mind wander back to their last meeting. Christiana's words had sent him away, but there had been something in her gestures, her voice, her eyes that hinted at a passion that all her prayers had been unable to still. He might have pleasure of her yet, and he would be gentle with her, slow and patient, attentive to her desire. He grew hard planning the only strategy that interested him now.

'Down!' James said, pulling the oars out of the water and folding forward. He had guided the boat close to a ship docked just north of Perth, unusually far upstream from the shipyard but fortunate for their stealthy purpose as there were soldiers on the bank beyond.

Margaret hesitated, not knowing what was more terrifying, looking up at the hulking mass of the ship or crouching blindly in its shadow. She had never been on the river at night, much less with a ship towering above. What by day was a fascinating beehive of activity was now a thing out of her most frightening dreams.

James reached out and pulled her down.

He used the paddle just to steer the skiff safely downstream now, so they had slowed to the summer current. Margaret's heartbeat slowed, too, and she was beginning to believe they would make it to Elcho without incident when she heard the soft singing of an arrow and then James's groan. She sat up and saw that they had just passed Greyfriars'. James pressed her back down and bent low over her.

'Where is your wound?' she managed to whisper.

'Left shoulder. I don't think it's deep.'

They huddled so for what seemed an eternity, their shallow breaths mingling. Margaret could hear James's heart racing.

Finally James straightened. 'Cursed luck. One arrow and I caught it. You'll have to steer, Maggie.'

She straightened up and, taking the paddle, turned the boat so that she was facing downriver.

James lifted his habit and used a knife to cut a strip from the shirt he wore beneath. 'It's but a flesh wound, I think. I was some idle bastard's sport, a bored guard shooting at anything moving on the river.'

But it was bleeding freely, and the cloth he held to it was soon dark. Margaret read in his movements that James was shaken, and she understood. It might have been much worse, so close to his heart.

She leaned towards him once they were past Friarton Island. 'We've but to show Thomas de Arroch that you are wounded and they'll let us through.'

'And if they don't, it's not my right arm, I can bloody them all. Begin guiding us to shore,' he said.

A splash distracted Malcolm. Whatever caused it was still upriver and faint, but it was the first sound he'd noticed on the water. Which in itself was strange. He wondered whether it was a night creature or a vessel on the river. He leaned forward, cocking his best ear towards the Tay, and held his breath.

Another splash, and yet another. Oars dipping into the water, Malcolm thought. And the irregular rhythm suggested it was drifting towards shore.

He crept back to his companions and alerted them. Aylmer sprang to his feet, dagger drawn, a conditioned fighter. Though his eyes had adjusted to the darkness, Malcolm did not see as well at night as he once had, and he sensed rather than saw Roger's grim mood. Both men seemed certain they were about to engage in battle.

'It might be but a deer crossing the river,' Malcolm whispered. He prayed it was so. The men guarding Elcho were trouble enough for one evening, and a confrontation would only delay his reunion with Christiana.

'Draw your weapon and prepare to defend yourself,' Roger said.

'They're close now,' Aylmer murmured.

⋙ 21 ⋘

MAYHEM

Resisting the urge to swat at a cluster of midges, Malcolm looked a little to the side and his peripheral vision showed him a dark shape floating towards the bank. Someone was speaking softly – age had not dulled his sharp hearing. As he strained to make out the figures in the boat – for he guessed the one speaking addressed a companion – he heard a branch break behind him and drew his dagger. They were caught between two unknowns.

'Devil take them,' muttered Roger. 'They've attracted company.'

'Or their companions are coming to meet them,' said Aylmer, backing away from the water towards the sheltering brush.

The marshy bank received the boat with a sucking sigh. The paddle thudded on the bottom of the boat, which rocked, the ground complaining wetly, as a man rose and stepped out on to the slippery bank. As the second passenger arose, Malcolm heard the rustle of skirts.

'A woman?' he murmured.

Both figures at the boat froze.

'Who goes there?' came a voice from behind the three watchers. Before anyone could respond, the speaker became aware of the trio in the bush and shouted, 'Over here!'

'It is Margaret Kerr,' came the response from the bank. 'My companion is injured.'

'Sweet Jesus,' Malcolm cried, 'what madness is this? Roger, it is your wife.' Hearing grunts, he turned and found Roger and Aylmer engaged with two of the Elcho guards. 'Stop!' Malcolm cried. 'We are—'

Roger gave a choked cry.

Malcolm was grabbed from behind and held in a vice-like grip.

'Roger? Oh, dear God,' Margaret moaned in the darkness.

When a torch was shone on the scene Roger was down, bleeding from the chest and the back of one leg, and Aylmer was held firmly like Malcolm, though his captor allowed him to cradle an injured hand. Margaret knelt to Roger, and the friar held a bloody rag to his shoulder as he explained his presence to the torch-bearer. There were six guards in all, more than on the earlier nights.

Malcolm swore under his breath and was rewarded with sharp pain in his chest as the vice closed even tighter. 'You've broken my ribs, you bastard. I'm Malcolm Kerr, come to see my wife,' he gasped.

Had he not heard the agony in Margaret's cry James might have laughed at the absurdity of the scene despite his useless, bleeding arm. A family gathering of the Kerr clan turned mayhem. From what he'd seen of the family it was fitting.

But it was far from amusing, the guards talking anxiously about the English on the cliffs across the river. Roger Sinclair was carried to the nunnery on a makeshift litter, Margaret hurrying beside him, her gown stained with his blood.

They had been taken to the priory guest house, and after much arguing about her own state, Margaret had convinced the sisters that she was able and determined to assist Dame Eleanor with Roger. As she helped the nun cut Roger's clothes away from the wounds, he stared up at her. She thanked God his eyes were so focused. With the grace of God and the sister's skill he should recover. When she had heard his groan she had feared the worst, and finding him on the ground, his life's blood pooling . . . She choked back a sob and prayed silently.

'Why did you come here, Maggie?' Roger asked,

his words slurred from the physick the nun had given him.

'Lie quietly and rest,' she said, smoothing his damp hair from his forehead.

'What are you doing with a friar?'

'We'll talk later,' Margaret said. 'You've lost much blood.' Her own gown had been so heavy with his blood and damp from the marshy ground on which she'd knelt that the sister had insisted she step out of it before she was permitted to assist.

'Bring the hot water,' the sister said, 'and the clean cloths.'

Roger closed his eyes. By the time his wound was dressed he was asleep.

Weak with fatigue, Margaret did not join James and the others down below, but crawled on to the pallet the sisters had provided her in Roger's room and let sleep carry her away.

A cough roused Malcolm from sleep. Gripping his side in agony, he struggled to sit up and reached in the dark for the watered wine the sisters had left for him. He needed something far stronger, but this would have to do. Draining the cup, he held his breath hoping to keep his rib still while he rose. By the time he stood he was gasping and dizzy. The hearth circle glowed invitingly but his bladder needed emptying before he could enjoy the heat. Outside, the sky and the river were silvered with the coming dawn and the world yet slept. He turned away from the river and considered the guest house. He could see well enough in the odd light and although he had never been permitted to visit Christiana in her chamber, he had watched her come and go there on more than one occasion and he knew the room she now called home was towards the rear. He brushed off his clothes, wincing at the touch of his own hand on his side, and headed back through the quiet yard. On his earlier visits he had not noticed the flowers that carpeted the ground beside the guest-house stairs. The blossoms were closed now, awaiting the sun, but they'd been artfully planted. And there were small trees. It saddened him to see such evidence of comfort. He'd thought of the priory as a drab place, and Christiana's time here as a waiting, an in-between state, a limbo that she would be eager to escape, loving colour and beauty as she did.

He climbed the steps slowly so that he need not expand his lungs to breathe. At Christiana's door, he hesitated. She and Marion would yet sleep, and he would frighten them with a knock. But to wait when so near would be agony. He might sneak in and slip into Christiana's bed. From long memory her body would welcome him. And by the time she woke . . . Malcolm groaned at the thought of such pleasure, but rejected the idea. Such a dishonourable act was not the way to win her back.

Taking a seat on the bench without, he listened for sounds of awakening.

A sweet-faced sister woke Margaret, who found that the exertions of the previous day had brought stiffness throughout her body. She sat up more slowly than usual and glanced over to see that Roger still slept.

'You have had a difficult time,' said the sister.

She handed Margaret a mazer of honeyed almond milk. It did little to fill the emptiness of her stomach, but Margaret savoured it.

The nun settled on a stool beside Margaret, her hands already moving along her paternoster beads.

'You are not the sister who dressed my husband's wounds last night, I think,' said Margaret.

'No, I have no such gift. That would have been Dame Eleanor. I am Dame Bethag, and I've come to ask a favour. I hope you will break your fast with your mother this morning.'

'I thought to eat here, with the others. I would see how James fares this morning.'

'The one disguised as a friar?' asked Bethag.

'Yes.'

'He is yet asleep. Only your father is awake. And gone to your mother, which will anger the prioress.'

Margaret was not surprised. She had guessed he had come to beg Christiana one more time to leave with him. Yet it did not explain the presence of

Roger and Aylmer. 'Do you wish me to fetch my father away?'

Bethag shook her head. 'I would not be so bold. My concern is your mother's grief over the man killed on Kinnoull Hill, and the ones taken. She blames herself overmuch and has neither eaten nor slept since she learned of it. She will not be comforted, not even by our chaplain. But the vision came to her as she stood before the English captain. It was not quite the vision she had composed at Dame Agnes's request. Surely God inspired her.'

'The prioress requested a vision?'

Dame Bethag explained the purpose.

Margaret was incensed. 'What right had Dame Agnes to so use my mother?' she cried then, remembering where she was, she checked that Roger still slept.

'The scheme was ill-advised,' said Bethag, 'but the Lord used it for His own mysterious purpose.'

Margaret did not know what to think. 'I came here to speak to Mother of the tragedy her words caused, not to comfort her, but . . . You say she is neither eating nor sleeping?'

'She is inconsolable.' Bethag regarded Margaret. 'You blame her for delivering God's message to the English captain.'

'Do you believe this vision came from God?'

'If not, whence comes such knowledge?'

'I don't know,' Margaret confessed. 'I've feared

that her visions were from the devil. Or that pagan spirits possess her.'

Dame Bethag leaned over and patted Margaret's hand, smiling kindly. 'You need not worry, I have seen the light of God's grace in Dame Christiana's eyes.' She sat back. 'But you must do as your conscience tells you, as well as your daughterly intuition of your mother's needs.'

Margaret did not know whether the nun's assurances were comforting or disturbing.

Roger stirred.

'I'll break my fast here,' said Margaret, 'then go to Ma.'

Bethag took the mazer from Margaret and, with a whispered blessing, departed.

'Don't listen to her,' Roger said weakly from his pallet across the way.

Margaret went to him. He looked exceedingly pale and the veins in his forehead pulsed angrily.

'I would help you drink, but I am afraid to put my arm beneath your chest to help you sit.'

'Slip another pillow beneath this one,' he suggested.

She did so, and though he gasped at the pain he thanked her. She held a cup of watered wine to his lips. His breath was foul with suffering.

'Why were you by the river?' she asked.

'I ask you the same. Did you come from Murray or Wallace?'

'James Comyn brought me here, and for his pains he was injured.' She thought it sufficient information.

'Him?' Roger coughed. 'He would be with them for certain.'

She sat carefully on the pallet. 'He is a good friend from Edinburgh.'

'No doubt. He followed you here?'

'I have questions for you, Roger.'

He closed his eyes and took a few breaths.

'I don't like the sound in your chest,' she said. The questions must wait. 'Will you try another pillow?'

'Why are you attending me? You brought Comyn here to have his wound tended.'

'His was not so . . .'

'Mortal?'

'Disabling. You will live, Roger. The sister who dressed your wounds seemed skilled.'

'What would she know of battle wounds?'

'She was confident in her ministrations. No one is truly cloistered while Edward Longshanks's army is on our land.'

Margaret slipped another pillow beneath the others.

'Holy Mother!' Roger groaned, a hand hovering over his dressing.

'I'll fetch Dame Eleanor.'

Roger caught Margaret's hand. 'Not yet. I mean to tell you all in case . . .' He paused for breath. 'I do not share your confidence in a cloistered nun's skill with sword wounds.'

'Roger, I pray you—'

'That night in Murdoch's undercroft,' he said, 'Old Will discovered us. I saw his state of drunkenness and guessed he merely sought a place to lie down out of the cold. But Aylmer would not hear of it. Before I could reach the old man, the deed was done. Once he was mortally wounded, there was nothing I could do for him.'

'Aylmer,' Margaret whispered. She had no difficulty accepting his guilt. 'Did he take Old Will back to his rooms?'

'I insisted.'

'How kind.'

'Maggie.'

'You might have spoken out against Aylmer.'

'You know who he is, Maggie.'

'I do. Did his violence not cause you to question your allegiance to his kinsman? Is your conscience no longer your own?'

'Maggie, Aylmer was right. The old man had seen us, and we could not risk his recalling what he'd seen, revealing our presence before we chose to appear. I can't expect you to understand, Maggie, but it is the way in war.'

In her mind's eye she saw again the two caskets, her father's with a broken lock, Roger's merely left unfastened, the lid closed sloppily on some documents. How easily she'd been misled. And how smoothly he'd continued to lie to her. Here was what she had feared, a chasm too wide to be bridged. 'I doubt anyone would have believed Old Will over you. And he was innocent.'

'No, Maggie. He was spying for the English. They'd paid him well.'

'Old Will?' So that was the source of the money for the shoes and the ale – and why the English took action upon his death when they had not after all the others. 'That is why the English searched his lodgings,' she said. 'They wanted the siller for another spy.'

'But Mary Brewster was there first, and they'll never retrieve the siller from her clutches.' Roger smiled wanly. 'That is the only satisfaction in the story.'

Satisfaction. God help him in his blindness. 'Can even Mary Brewster be safe from the English garrison?'

'Her daughter Belle ensures that, Maggie. The men would not wish to lose her.' Roger was quiet a moment, breathing shallowly.

Margaret leaned down and kissed him on the forehead, then smoothed his hair from his fevered brow. 'I'll leave you to rest,' she said.

'To go to James Comyn?' Roger's eyes shone unhealthily. 'How is it he had not discovered the truth about Old Will's spying?'

'Perhaps you are more clever than he is.' Margaret attempted a smile though she did not like the direction their conversation was taking.

412

'And yet you love him.'

Jealous. She would have cried with joy had he exhibited jealousy a year ago. 'I did not say that, Roger. I loved you. I still do.' She said it with far more certainty than she felt. Worry softened her feelings for him, but he'd lied to her from the moment he reappeared in Edinburgh.

'You have doubts, Maggie. I see it in your eyes.'

His insistence frightened her a little. She prayed James did not read her confusion in the same way. 'You've chosen the worst time to pay heed to my feelings.' She felt tears coming and busied herself soaking a cloth in a bowl of water as she said, 'We are so far apart.' For it worked both ways – she had kept much from him.

'Are we so divided? We both hate Edward Longshanks.'

'Do we? I've seen no proof that Robert Bruce hates him.'

'What can he do to convince you?'

'I don't know, Roger.' She placed the cool cloth on his forehead, then kissed him on the cheek. 'You are in good hands here.'

Roger caught the neck of her gown and prevented her from rising. 'You'd leave before I'm recovered?'

He was too weak to hold her, but she did not move away.

'There is no trust between us. I must fight for every morsel of truth I wring from you.'

'So you leave me now, when I am helpless to stop you?'

Someone knocked.

Margaret took Roger's hand from her gown, resting it gently on his chest. 'I am leaving. If the Bruce rewards you richly for your service, you might spend some of the siller to free yourself from me, to buy an annulment.'

'Never. Maggie!'

She walked to the door on trembling legs.

Roger struggled to sit up.

'Be still!' Margaret cried, but resisted the urge to return to his side.

'If you can forgive your mother for her betrayal, you must forgive me.'

'I do, Roger, I do. But it's not enough.' She opened the door to Dame Eleanor. 'I'll leave you with my husband. He fusses too much when I'm here.' She stepped out and shut the door behind her.

The morning was cruelly beautiful with drops of dew glistening like gems of many colours on the gallery posts and the air sweet with late summer flowers. Margaret sank down on her haunches, wrapped her arms around her legs, and pressed her forehead into her knees. She shivered with the terrors of the previous night that she had pushed aside in order to nurse Roger. James might have been killed by the arrow loosed so casually, the arrow that had been shot from the riverfront of

414

Perth, her home. And Roger's wounds – the de Arrochs were vicious in their guardianship of the nuns; he, too, might have died, and might still. The world had become a terrible place without sanctuary.

The thought of leaving Roger, of opening wide the rift and pulling free to drift alone in this bleeding land terrified her. She was nothing without him, an unmarried woman dependent on her family once more, and yet she could hardly depend on her parents, both of them adrift in nightmares of their own making. Celia, her staunchest friend, was a servant with nothing. She did have Ada, and James was her ally, but only in regard to her work for his kinsman. And she must tread carefully with him; he must not misconstrue her motivation. A long while Margaret crouched there shivering, letting go her pent up-tears, sobbing for all that she'd lost.

But as the waves of emotion subsided she discovered a flicker of confidence. Over the past months she had proven herself significant in her own right. She had remade her life in Edinburgh, worked for the return of her rightful king, and discovered the truth of Old Will's murder as well as the intrusions in Perth and here at the priory. These were no small accomplishments. She was not without resources. She pushed herself up, wiped her eyes, and took great gulps of the cool morning air. When she felt steadier, she descended to the hall.

James stood near the hearth circle, his left arm bound to keep the shoulder immobile. He looked up at Margaret's approach. She was suddenly aware of her borrowed gown's short sleeves and skirt and she irritated herself by fussing with it.

'You've been weeping,' James said, stepping closer. 'Is Sinclair . . .' He hesitated. 'How goes your husband?'

'He has wearied himself with talk, but it is a good sign. Dame Eleanor has some skill, I think.'

James glanced down at his shoulder. 'She does, to have made me as comfortable as she has.'

'He lost much blood from the chest wound, but it is the slash behind his knee that he will remember. You are not in pain?'

She had never seen James so unkempt and hollow-eyed.

'None of this need have happened,' he said. 'There must have been a way to prevent this.'

Margaret shook her head. 'What good are such thoughts? We cannot return to the past and undo it.' She sank down in a chair and accepted a cup of ale from a servant. 'But I know, I know.'

James sat down beside her. 'How far back would you go if you could?'

'Would I undo my marriage? Is that what you ask?'

'Would you?'

'It would have spared me much suffering. But there have been moments—' She stopped. This was not something she meant to share with James. 'I wish I had seen Jonet's dissatisfaction. I wish Ma had gone to Bruges where she might have done no harm. But things are as they are and I must live with them.'

She stopped, noticing that Aylmer had awakened and was listening from his pallet.

'You,' she said, rising and moving towards his pallet, her anger growing with every step. 'You're naught but a coward, murdering an old man when he was too drunk to defend himself, then leaving him on the floor of his chamber to die.'

With a curse, Aylmer began to rise. 'I listen to no woman's babble,' he growled.

Margaret shoved him back down with her foot.

'Margaret!' James pulled her back just as Aylmer grabbed for her foot with his uninjured hand. 'This serves no one.'

'My mother can neither eat nor sleep for sorrow about the deaths she caused and you – I saw how dead your eyes were after you killed the soldiers at the bridge below Stirling. You have no soul.' *Woman's babble*. She would not be so dismissed. She shook James off and withdrew, but not before hearing Aylmer grunt from a blow. Cursed man, cursed master.

Malcolm woke to sunrise and Marion crouching in front of him with a cup of ale. By St Rule, he was an old man to fall asleep at such an important juncture in his marriage. He drank down the ale and rose.

'You cannot see Dame Christiana,' said the handmaid.

'Stop me,' he said, pushing her aside and entering the chamber.

Marion fluttered behind, making anxious noises. Malcolm was accustomed to her and paid her no heed. But the room confused him. Pieces of his married life littered the place – chairs, tables, tapestries, chests, lamps – crowding it so that he wondered how the two women fitted within. This room belonged in a market place, not a priory.

'Does she move all this out on to the gallery to entertain?' he asked.

'My mistress leads a quiet life here,' said Marion.

Malcolm walked up to Christiana's favourite carved screen and beyond it discovered her still abed, buried beneath cushions and bedding in disarray as was her custom. He was increasingly disappointed. He had imagined an ascetic life, with Christiana rising before dawn to kneel on the bare earth in prayer.

Marion dutifully set a cushioned chair beside her mistress's bed. 'I'll bring more ale, sir,' she said. 'But you mustn't wake her. It's the first time she's slept since . . .' She crossed herself and withdrew.

Malcolm leaned closer and called out his wife's

418

name. The bedclothes shifted a little. He tried again.

Christiana's head emerged from the blankets, her hair wild, her eyes wilder, with huge black pupils.

Malcolm's heart sank. He knew this look, and he knew it was true she had not slept, and that she still could not.

'Women in cages,' she keened in the other-worldly voice of her most terrible visions, 'hanging over castle yards, open to the leering crowds.' The covers slipped further and she sat up, scooting back against the cushions, an arm thrown up to protect her. 'The bridge beneath the castle is slippery with blood, the marsh grass is red with it.'

'God help us,' Margaret whispered behind him.

He turned and took his daughter in his arms despite the pain. 'Oh, Maggie, Maggie. Was ever a family so cursed?'

Prioress Agnes kindly gave Margaret another gown that fitted her passably.

'Dame Bethag is devoted to your mother,' she assured Margaret. 'She will sit with her as much as possible until she recovers.'

Margaret was not as optimistic as the prioress regarding her mother's recovery. She had never seen her so ravaged. But as long as the prioress had hope she would see to Christiana's care. 'Dame Bethag seems a patient woman,' said Margaret.

'I'll remember her in all my prayers. And Dame Eleanor as well.'

'Your husband is strong. He will recover completely, God willing, and then you shall have him home again.'

Margaret could not form the words to enlighten the prioress. 'We'll be leaving in a little while,' she said. James waited for her at the guest house.

'But you will come to see your mother from time to time?'

'If Edward Longshanks permits,' Margaret said.

The prioress gave her a puzzled look, then said, 'Ah. Yes, that is so. My kinsmen say he is not finished with us.'

She would spend a quiet day or two with Ada, Margaret had decided. She did not want to be alone. She was riddled with doubt, remorse, and she knew she would agonise over whether to go to Roger once more though she knew it would be pointless. Now he needed her, and he was jealous. But the moment he was well enough to continue his service for the Bruce he would be gone again, particularly if he discovered that Margaret actively supported King John. If she were in her own home Fergus would wish to speak of things she did not wish to think of for a few days.

She had told her father and James what she'd learned from Roger about Old Will's work for the English, his murder, Mary Brewster and Belle.

'Well, at least that crime is solved, God curse

him,' said Malcolm. 'We must annul your marriage. Searching for items to use against me – he's not for you, Maggie.'

'We have neither the influence nor the wealth to annul a marriage, Da,' said Margaret. 'Now give me some peace.'

James courteously lagged behind, but she guessed he'd heard and she did not want to know his reaction.

'Your mother will recover as she ever has done,' Malcolm went on, 'and then I'll return to take her to Bruges. But what will you do, Maggie?'

'I don't know, Pa, except that I mean to keep my pledge to work for the return of King John.'

'If he cares to return.' Malcolm had paused and looked Margaret in the eyes. 'The Bruce is here, fighting with his men. Balliol is far away.'

'He has been exiled, Pa.'

Although he did not look convinced, Malcolm had nodded. 'Perhaps he'd be here if he could, I'll grant you that possibility.' He'd put a small pouch in her hands. 'You're a brave woman, Maggie. And perhaps Roger is a fool to back a Bruce – that family has always played with the devil.'

James had overtaken them and disappeared inside.

Margaret opened the pouch now, as she walked towards the guest house. Sterlings. Enough perhaps to buy the annulment herself. Her stomach fluttered and she went cold. The prospect terrified her. With every step she moved further away from the rules by which she'd lived her life and into a future in which she depended on herself to survive. But there was no going back. The flint had been struck and the flame burned within her. She had a purpose, and what she did from now on would matter to her people though they would never know her part. There would come a time, she prayed that it would be in her lifetime, when the streets and the riverfront of Perth were bustling with commerce, and a trip down the Tay could be taken openly and without worry. A time when her brother Andrew was free. That would be more satisfying than making do with a heartbroken marriage.

James was glad when Celia took her mistress in hand at Ada's, preparing a hot bath, dosing her with some herbs to help her rest. Margaret had been so distracted on the journey back to the town he suspected that she had confronted Roger. Or perhaps she did not believe he would survive. In either case, she needed comforting. He'd been tempted to take her in his arms and assure her that all would be well, but he'd caught himself before making such an empty gesture. All would almost certainly not be well. It was not the way of things.

As he returned to Margaret's house to make plans with Fergus, James wondered what she would choose to do now, what use she would make of the sterlings he felt quite sure weighted that pouch. She had such fierce loyalties, and there was such anger in her that he did not imagine for a moment she would stop here. Wallace and Murray were crowding the English, and a great battle was brewing, he could feel it. In the meantime he did not lack for tasks for Margaret. He felt guilty for using her, and a little apprehensive. She was no one's but her own, and would therefore remain unpredictable unless he could find a way to understand her heart. If she had not been a married woman he might have wed her to keep her loyal to him. But that had not worked for Roger. He must befriend her, become necessary to her. He must think how.

EPILOGUE

A drizzle began as Margaret and Fergus left
Sunday Mass. Despite the weather they walked
slowly. He carried a small pack and kept Mungo
by him with a cord attached to a collar he'd
fashioned from a belt – the dog had worried it at
first, but once he'd understood that he was to walk
beside his master he seemed calm enough. He'd
slept at Fergus's feet in the kirk.

They were headed to the north gate, where
Fergus would meet his companion for the journey.
James was bringing him. Margaret worked to hide
her agitation from her brother. He was going so far
away that she feared she would not see him again.
Her only consolation was his joy in finally
embarking on an adventure.

'Ada is teaching me more words,' she said as
they drew near the gate. 'You might find someone

coming this way who could carry a letter. Would you write to me?'

'I'll be busy, Maggie,' said Fergus. 'I cannot promise.'

'I know,' she said.

They had reached the gate. Still treated with special courtesy by the English guard, Margaret was free to walk out through the gate with Fergus.

'I'll not come far,' she said. 'I would just like to see your companion, so I can imagine the three of you.' She leaned over to pet Mungo.

Fergus sighed, and when Margaret rose he caught her in a strong embrace.

'I'll write, Maggie, and you do, too.'

She felt how stiffly he held himself and understood that he, too, worked to hide his agitation.

'I will, Fergus. Be happy in your work with Uncle Thomas. I'll pray for you every day.'

And then James was there, in his own garb, greeting Mungo with a pat.

A compact, homely young man accompanied him. He eyed Fergus up and down and nodded. 'You look untried. Good. And the dog is good.' He bobbed his head at Fergus and Margaret. 'I am Duncan,' he said. 'We'll be journeying together.' He, too, crouched to greet Mungo, who sniffed him and seemed to approve.

Margaret stepped back and watched as Fergus introduced himself and fell into conversation with his travelling companion. James joined her.

'It's a good match, I think,' he said. 'Duncan knows the way, and he's silent and fast with a dagger.'

Margaret took a deep breath. 'We should go back. I only embarrass him.'

James took her hand and squeezed it once. 'And they must depart.'

She dared not reach down once more to Mungo. 'Godspeed, both of you,' she said with false cheer. She raised her hand in farewell and then turned back towards Perth.

'The guard is watching,' said James. He reached for Margaret's hand and tucked it in the crook of his arm.

She blushed and began to pull away.

'For his benefit, Margaret, we must look like old friends well met after a long separation. Smile up at me now.'

'Let us rather talk in earnest about the crops on your property,' Margaret said, keeping her eyes well away from his. She was grateful to him on Fergus's behalf and glad to have his company to distract her from this difficult parting, but she meant to be James's equal, and that meant creating her own comfortable disguise and guarding her heart.

AUTHOR'S NOTE

An ocean of ink has been spent justifying war, arguing its morality and necessity, and almost as much has been used in seeking financing for what is always an expensive endeavour.

In the 1290s King Edward I of England was stretched thin by war with Wales, France and Scotland. He built formidable castles in Wales, sailed the Channel to defend his ducal fiefdom of Gascony, crossed the northern borders into Scotland, and even sailed to the Low Countries to protect his welcome in their ports, necessary to moving troops into France from the north. This was expensive. 'The total amount of money in circulation [in England] . . . was probably about one million pounds.' [Prestwich 401] The 'total cost to Edward of the wars between 1294 and his return from Flanders in 1298 was in the region of

£750,000'. [Prestwich 400] By the summer of 1297 his money had run out and neither his creditors nor his subjects were inclined to replenish his coffers. He had taxed the laity and the clergy yearly and set high duties on wool exports. He had brought his Italian bankers to ruin.

As if the situation weren't gloomy enough, Edward's mints were losing business because merchants were taking their silver to continental, rather than to English mints [Mayhew 1992]. The pound of silver was stretched to make more coins in Europe. England historically prohibited the widespread use of foreign coins in the country. But with the government distracted by wars on so many fronts, foreign coins were in circulation. 'In the late 1290s crockards and pollards, silver coins very like those struck in England, were struck in huge quantities in the Low Countries where the activity of the mints was in stark contrast to the lack of work in England. The very debasement which made these coins so unpopular in England, permitted the mints of Flanders, Hainault and Brabant to offer the bullion holder a much higher bullion price than the English mints, attracting silver which might otherwise have been brought to London and Canterbury.' [Mayhew 1992, pp. 137–8] The wonder of it is that Edward resisted following the lead of France and the Low Countries in debasing the currency struck in his royal mints. The economy was the better for it at the end of the century.

But for now Edward had little to show for his expenditures. King Philip IV of France had duped Edward into an agreement in which he gave up what little he had won in France. The Welsh were still periodically rising up in rebellion. And then King John Balliol of Scotland made an alliance with King Philip IV – it was this alliance with France that spurred Edward I to invade Scotland and dethrone Balliol.

In 1297 some of Edward's most powerful barons refused his summons for yet another campaign in Gascony. The two most prominent members of the resistance were the earls of Norfolk and Hereford, the hereditary marshal of England and the constable of England respectively, who had been passed over for the plum positions of leadership in Edward's wars.

As if all this weren't enough to make Edward testy, trouble was brewing in the Low Countries, instigated by Philip of France. That is why Edward had entrusted Scotland to his administrators in the course of *The Fire in the Flint* and sailed to Flanders. Only he arrived too late, and meanwhile in Scotland . . . But that story forms the next chapter in Margaret's life.

Research into the coinage issue uncovered some interesting facts. For example, gold coins were not minted in England until the fourteenth century, when prices rose high enough that silver coins were impractical for some transactions. Also, coins were required to be a certain weight and certain

429

fineness (content), so frequently the total weight of coins rather than the number was specified in transactions. Clipping coins and normal wear with use led to their debasement, and eventually required recoinage, when the people who held the money were ordered to return certain coins to the government and were reissued new coins – with a percentage skimmed off the original value kept for the government. Edward proceeds to do this in the late 1290s.

But back to Scotland. If you have been to Perth lately, a lovely river town easily walkable in an afternoon, you might be surprised to know that it was far larger and more economically significant than Edinburgh in the late thirteenth century. The River Tay linked Perth to its trading partners across the North Sea. Indeed, Perth was quite a cosmopolitan city. Excavations have revealed wares from all over Europe. It was also just down-river from Scone, the ancient seat of the realm of Scotland, and surrounded by a fertile valley. Sudden thaws in the highlands have caused flooding in the area over the centuries, and this phenomenon has preserved layers of the past beneath the modern town. Fortunately for those curious about the history of this historic burgh, modern-day developers cooperate with the Scottish Urban Archaeological Trust allowing digs that have materially added to our knowledge of the town's past.